GOING LA LA

Alexandra Potter

HODDER

First published in Great Britain in 2012 by Hodder & Stoughton
An Hachette Livre UK company

A version of this book was first published in
paperback in 2001 by Fourth Estate

2

A CIP catalogue record for this title is available from the British Library

B format Paperback ISBN 978 0 340 91962 0
A format Paperback ISBN 978 0 340 99384 2

Typeset in Plantin Light by Hewer Text UK Ltd, Edinburgh
Printed and bound by Clays Ltd, St Ives plcP

Hodder & Stoughton policy is to use papers that are natural, renewable
and recyclable products and made from wood grown in sustainable
forests. The logging and manufacturing processes are expected to
conform to the environmental regulations of the country of origin.

Hodder & Stoughton Ltd
338 Euston Road
London NW1 3BH
www.hodder.co.uk

For Kelly, my beloved big sister,
who's been going la la for the last 25 years . . .

ACKNOWLEDGEMENTS

Thanks to Isobel Akenhead and everyone at Hodder for breathing new life into this book and giving it a fabulous new cover! Big thank you as always to my wonderful agent, Stephanie Cabot.

I also want to say a big thank you to my sister, Kelly, my amazing mum and dad, and all my brilliant friends on both sides of the Atlantic. Fact followed fiction, and a few years after writing this book I moved to Los Angeles and started going la la myself. Thanks to everyone for all the great times, let's hope there are many more.

LETTER FROM THE AUTHOR

I'm really excited at this new publication of *Going La La*. I wrote this book over ten years ago, and at the time I had no idea it would be a premonition of how my life would turn out. That a few years later I would follow in Frankie's footsteps and find myself with a broken heart and a suitcase, jumping on a plane to Los Angeles . . .

But let's rewind for a moment. Back to the early 90s where I first got my inspiration for this story. Aged twenty-one, I'd just left university, and not knowing what I wanted to do with my life I decided to visit my sister who lives in LA.

From the moment the plane touched down at LAX airport my life completely changed. I went from attending university lectures to star-studded parties in the Hollywood Hills where I met a whole crazy cast of characters that would later fuel my imagination. And then there was the weather! They don't call it 'sunny California' for nothing. Out went the grey skies and woolly jumpers, in came the bikinis and palm trees. During the week I worked various jobs and at weekends my sister and I would drive down to the beach in her 1966 Mustang and rollerblade on the path that runs alongside the ocean. It was some of the most fun I've ever had and I still have scrapbooks filled with memories.

But after a few months my desire to be a writer brought me back to the UK, and eventually London, where I went on to work for various women's glossy magazines before finally plucking up courage to write my first novel, *What's*

New Pussycat?. A book deal followed, and *Going La La* was my second novel. 'Write about what you know' is a piece of advice often given to writers, and so I drew on my experiences of the wonderful time spent in LA, the people I met, the adventures I had, never imagining at the time I was writing that fact was going to follow fiction . . .

And yet there I was, a few years after its publication, jetting off once more again to La La Land. Only this time it didn't turn out to be just a visit. Like Frankie I ended up falling in love and before I knew it I was swapping my life in London for life on Venice Beach.

There's so much written about LA in magazines and newspapers, yet there's so much more to this city of angels than mere celebrities. Yes, it's fun to spot A-list actors standing in line in Starbucks or the supermarket. And just for the record most of the men are tiny, and most of the women look *nothing* like their photographs. But living in LA also means waking up to a constant lavender blue sky. To 80 degree weather in January. To being able to swim in the ocean and hike in the canyons. To being encouraged to live out your dreams. *To be who you want to be.*

And yes of course, it can be crazy and whacky and it's true, there is far too much plastic surgery (please! stop with the trout pouts!), but one thing's for sure, life in LA is never boring!

I now split my life between LA and London and I think it's these two halves that make me the writer I am today. I was born and bred in Yorkshire and my classic down-to-earth British sense of humour runs through my books like the words in a stick of Blackpool Rock. But it's my time spent in Los Angeles, the land of make-believe, that adds that special touch of magic.

After all, like I say in *Going La La*,

'*Who says it only ever happens in the movies?*'

GOING LA LA

I

Have you ever drunk vodka at nine o'clock on a Sunday morning? Neither had Frankie, but she was about to. Bracing herself, she took a deep breath – one . . . two . . . three – and swigged back the contents of her glass, wincing as the clear liquid burned an acidic path to her empty stomach. It tasted disgusting. Wiping the bitter residue from her lips with the damp paper coaster, she beckoned the barman, who was lolling against the optics reading the celebrity exposé on the front page of the *News of the World*.

'Another one please. This time can you make it a double?'

Grumbling, Terry – whose name-tag was safety-pinned upside down to the grimy pocket of his thin nylon shirt – put down his newspaper and sullenly measured out the vodka from the large bottle fixed on the wall.

Frankie watched him, feeling decidedly queasy. She wasn't used to any sort of alcohol first thing in the morning, except of course on Christmas Day, when traditional family celebrations meant lying on the sofa with a hangover and a glass of Bristol Cream Sherry, watching telly and humming along with Julie Andrews, who was skipping yet again up and down an Austrian hillside with a guitar and seven brats dressed head to toe in a pair of old curtains warbling Doh, Ray, Me. But today wasn't 25 December and Frankie certainly wasn't celebrating.

On the contrary. It was the middle of October and she was propping up the bar at Heathrow's Terminal 4, trying hard to drown her sorrows in Smirnoff. A week ago she'd been deliriously happy, looking forward to a promotion at work, a proposal of marriage and a party for her twenty-ninth birthday. Fast-forward seven days and she had no job, no boyfriend and certainly no party. Which is why a normally sensible and sober Frankie was now gloomily knocking back double vodkas and feeling sorry for herself. In less than a week she'd gone from having everything to having absolutely sod all.

'Last call for Miss Francesca Pickles on flight BA 279 to Los Angeles.'

The clipped nasal voice reverberated over the Tannoy system, crackling out of speakers inside the duty-free shops flogging perfume and giant-size bars of Toblerone, over-priced cafés offering lousy coffee euphemistically described as cappuccinos and souvenir stalls selling dodgy tartan head-scarves and Houses of Parliament fridge magnets. Frankie wrinkled her forehead. Was she imagining things or had she just heard her name? She strained to catch the rest of the announcement but it was impossible. All she could hear was Cliff Richard on continuous play through the reproduction Wurlitzer jukebox. Shrugging her shoulders, she took a sip from her glass. She must have been mistaken. Absent-mindedly she glanced at her watch – 9.20. For a split second the time didn't register. She glanced again. This time it did.

Oh my God. Despite the neat vodka, her mouth suddenly went very dry. *Twenty past nine!* Where on earth had the time gone? In less than ten minutes her flight was supposed to be taking off and if she didn't get her arse to gate 14 pretty damn quick, the only thing taking off would be her luggage – *from* the aeroplane.

Hastily putting down her drink on the mock-Tudor bar, she slid off her barstool, laddering her tights in the process. Shit, she cursed silently, watching the hole in her new pair of opaques weave its way down to her ankle, and realised she was actually feeling a bit tipsy. In fact, to be honest, she was more than tipsy – she was pissed. Frankie groaned. Why was it that she always seemed to miss out on the giddy, tiddly stage and go straight to the drunken staggering about stage?

Frankie tried to sober herself up by taking a few deep breaths. The vodka was meant to help blot out last week's disastrous chain of events, it wasn't supposed to blot out the rest of this week as well. Inhaling deeply, she fell to her knees and began scrabbling around on the garishly patterned beer-sodden carpet, gathering together her sprawling mountain of hand luggage, which had somehow taken on Everest-like proportions. What was it about hand luggage that made it multiply so alarmingly? She'd started out with one piece – as instructed at check-in – but despite all good intentions, after a couple of hours spent trawling around Terminal 4, her carefully packed compact rucksack had doubled in size and given birth to two bulging carrier bags straining dangerously under the weight of glossy magazines, a tube of Pringles, two packets of Jaffa Cakes, a Walkman, an inflatable pillow and fifty quid's worth of duty-free perfume she'd whacked on her credit card in a desperate attempt to cheer herself up. It hadn't. It just meant that now she could be depressed in Eternity.

Grimacing as the handles of the plastic bags cut sharply into her fingers, she stood up and began staggering towards the departure gate, struggling to keep hold of everything. But it was no good. Before she'd managed more than a few hundred yards a thinly stretched handle snapped, spilling the contents of one of the plastic bags all over the floor and sending the tube of Pringles catapulting like a missile across the departure lounge to wedge itself under one of the rows of plastic chairs. Frankie groaned in frustration. This was ridiculous. At this rate she was never going to make it to the gate in time to catch her flight.

Then suddenly out of the corner of her eye she saw it – the answer to her prayers – a shiny silver trolley, and it had been left unattended outside Knickerbox. Feeling a wave of excitement, she made a dive for it and, with a technique worthy of Magic Johnson, triumphantly threw her rucksack into the basket area. At last, something was going right. Taking a deep breath, she was about to enjoy a huge sigh of relief when she was interrupted by a voice behind her.

'Excuse me, that's mine.'

'Pardon?'

She swivelled around. Standing in front of the '50% off G-string promotion' was a bloke wearing faded jeans and a checked flannel shirt. Frankie's eyes travelled upwards, noting the scuffed leather boots, fraying Levi's and rolled-up shirt sleeves revealing tanned forearms and a couple of those hippy-dippy woven wrist bracelets. A silver chain glinted against the nape of his neck and he wore a battered old cowboy hat that cast a shadow over his face. He looked like a scruffier version of the Marlboro Man. Frankie suddenly realised she was staring.

'That's my cart.' Marlboro Man spoke in a deep Texan drawl, lazily rubbing his chin, which was covered in what looked like a week's worth of beard growth.

Frankie looked at the trolley and then back at the American. She hated any kind of confrontation and seemed to spend her whole life apologising, regardless of whether or not it was she who was at fault. But the mixture of vodka, last week's triple whammy and airport nerves had had a peculiar effect. She might have lost everything else, but there was no way she was losing this trolley. 'I think you must be mistaken,' she replied politely but firmly. 'It's *my trolley*.' She spoke slowly, deliberately emphasising the words and shielding the trolley defensively with her body. With any luck Mr Cowboy here would bugger off and get his own.

He didn't. 'I don't think so.' He shook his head and started piling his luggage on to the trolley – large black tripods, scratched metal camera cases, an oversized holdall.

Frankie watched in utter disbelief. This guy had some cheek. Determined not to be outdone, she piled her stuff on top and grabbed the handle. So did he.

'Hey, I ain't got time for this. I've got a plane to catch.' He pushed a strand of hair away from his eyes and stared hard at Frankie.

She glowered. *He had a plane to catch!* What about her? What the bloody hell did he think she was doing in Departures? Enjoying a day out? She gritted her teeth in determination. 'Excuse me, but I've got a plane to catch too, you know.'

He shrugged his shoulders. 'Well, that makes two of us then.' And he began wheeling the trolley across the departure lounge, accompanied by Frankie, who adamantly refused to let go of the handle.

'Bloody hell, you're so rude,' she gasped in amazement as he pushed defiantly on to the moving concourse, the hint of a smirk playing at the corners of his mouth. '*This is my trolley.*' Chivalry was obviously a four-letter word in the United States.

Infuriatingly, he completely ignored her.

'Didn't you hear what I said?'

It would have been impossible not to, with Frankie's voice echoing loudly along the corridor, but he chose not to answer. Instead he continued striding down the moving walkway with both of his large, strong hands firmly on the trolley. They made a bizarre sight – him cool, calm and collected in his cowboy hat, her drunk and dishevelled with holes in her tights, both clinging grimly on to one trolley – but neither of them was laughing. Instead they were caught in a silent duel until, suddenly, they reached the end of the conveyor belt causing Frankie to trip as they lurched on to the carpet where they came to an abrupt halt.

Presuming he'd realised the error of his ways, Frankie felt a rush of victory. It was to be short-lived.

'Well, thanks for coming along for the ride,' he drawled sarcastically. 'This is where I get off.' He started unloading his bags – leaving hers to fall on the floor, scattering her duty-free products. 'It's all yours.' He smiled broadly and, tipping his hat in mock politeness, threw his bag over his broad shoulders and strode towards his gate and a cluster of stewardesses, who took one look at this burly passenger and rapidly changed their impatient scowls to flirtatious smiles.

Frankie was gobsmacked. She'd been taken for a ride – literally. Watching him disappear down the jetty to the plane, she suddenly noticed the gate number displayed in digital lights – 14. She was at gate 14. Her frustration was momentarily replaced by relief that she hadn't missed her flight – but it didn't last for long. As soon as she'd handed in her boarding card it dawned on her that the trolley rustler was obviously on the same aeroplane. And probably in the seat next to her. She swiftly dismissed the thought. Nobody – not even she – could be that unlucky.

Hurrying on to the plane, she was greeted by a stony-faced stewardess handing out boiled sweets and a 747 full of grumpy passengers who looked at their watches and eyed her accusingly. Frankie smiled apologetically and started bumping and banging her way down the gangway, struggling to keep a grip on her carrier bags – and their contents – while searching for her seat number. Out of the corner of her eye she could see a familiar-looking Stetson looming ominously ahead and as she edged closer she saw that slap bang across the aisle, next to the window, was an empty seat. Her heart sank. She didn't even have to double-check her boarding card. She knew it was hers.

Resignedly stuffing her bags in the overhead locker, she squeezed herself into the economy seat and fastened her seat belt. She stared resolutely ahead, determined not to look in his direction, but after a few minutes curiosity got the better of her. Barely moving her head, she sneaked a look at him out of the corner of her eye. Resting his chin in his hand, he had his eyes closed and was breathing slowly and heavily, as if he was in the first stages of falling asleep. Tufts of dark hair bleached almost blond by the sun had escaped from underneath the brim of his hat and faint lines flickered around his eyes – the result of squinting in the sun. Frankie noticed his eyelashes, thick and dark against his tanned and slightly freckled skin, and the small squiggle of a scar cut across his left eyebrow. At a guess he was in his early thirties and, although she hated to admit it, he was sort of handsome, in a rugged, unkempt kind of way.

Not that Frankie liked rugged and unkempt. She liked clean-shaven and smart. Starched collars, freshly pressed suits and the faintest whiff of aftershave. Just like Hugh. Closing her eyes, she could see him now in his Ralph Lauren shirt, his neatly knotted tie, his short fair hair neatly gelled into a little quiff. Gorgeous Hugh. Her Hugh. She bit her lip, trying to stop a tear she could feel prickling her eyelash from falling down her cheek.

The noise inside the cabin suddenly rose to a high-pitched whine as she felt the Jumbo begin its slow journey down the runway. Craning her neck, she stared out of the small porthole window, watching as Heathrow Airport began to whiz past, blending into a blur of grey concrete. Suddenly there was a surge as the engines roared beneath her and she felt the thrust of the g-force as the plane tilted sharply upwards, the wheels leaving the ground.

Taking a deep breath, she slunk down in her seat. Well, this was it. It was finally happening. She was waving goodbye to London and her life as she knew it. A mixture of relief, panic and second thoughts washed over her. Was she doing the right thing? Frankie didn't know. All she knew was that yesterday she'd been depressed, dumped and on the dole and today she was on a 747 bound for LA and the bright lights of Hollywood. It was too late to change her mind, but as daunting as it was, she knew she couldn't have stayed. It would have been just too painful. Closing her eyes, she wiped away the tear that had trickled down the side of her nose and for the first time in ages started to smile. Yep, the decision was made and, whether she liked it or not, there was to be no turning back. Frankie was going to Hollywood . . .

2

It had all started less than a week ago when she'd discovered the receipt from Tiffany's the jeweller's. Not that Frankie had been meaning to go through her boyfriend's pockets, but it was a Monday morning, she was late and she'd been looking for change for the tube. After taking apart the sofa – cushion by cushion – scouring the edges of the carpet along the skirting boards and emptying all those little candle-holders and ethnic bowls along the mantelpiece, she'd almost given up. Until in desperation she pulled out Hugh's grey woollen overcoat from the cupboard in the hallway.

Breast pocket – nothing; inside pocket – an empty Snickers wrapper and a lottery ticket; side pocket – a pound coin and a scrunched-up receipt. She was about to throw it away when something stopped her. A gut reaction, sixth sense, woman's intuition: whatever it was, something caused her to carefully unfurl the piece of paper, lay it on the kitchen work-surface and smooth out the creases with the palm of her hand. That's when she saw it came from Tiffany's and the words 'item of jewellery' printed underneath. Feeling a jolt of excitement, she tried to see the amount, but the ink had gone all blurry. Undeterred, she held it up to the sash window and squinted – it looked like a 2 and a few noughts. Her mind raced from nought to 2,000 in less than a second. *Two thousand pounds!*

Her heart accelerated into fifth gear to keep pace with her imagination. Hugh had bought jewellery at Tiffany's for two thousand pounds. Nothing cost that much, unless of course . . .

She couldn't bring herself to even think the words, let alone say them. But it was her birthday in a couple of days and he had been acting very oddly recently. Still, surely he wouldn't have, he couldn't have . . . could he? She looked at the receipt. He had! *He'd bought an engagement ring.* There, she'd said it. He'd bought a Tiffany's engagement ring and was going to propose – and on her birthday!

Feeling her legs tremble as if they were going to buckle and give way beneath her, she plonked herself down on top of the stainless-steel pedal bin, still clutching the receipt. Her stomach was doing gymnastics and she felt as if she was going to laugh and cry at the same time. It was such a surprise. Such a fantastic surprise. Looking down at her left hand, she wiggled her ring finger in anticipation. Mrs Hamilton, Mrs Hugh Hamilton. Grinning ecstatically, she thought about Hugh. She'd had other boyfriends, but she'd never felt like this before. Never had a man made her regress from being a twenty-eight-year-old career girl with a private pension, gym membership and a Boots club card, to a dippy, daft, dumb-struck teenager every time he even looked at her. Never before had she spent her precious weekends getting grass stains out of golf trousers or shivering under an umbrella in the pouring rain, watching him playing rugby, when she could be snugly tucked up on the sofa with a cup of tea and an old black and white movie. But now she did. *And* she enjoyed it. Frankie was in love.

They'd met nearly two years ago. It had been the week before Christmas and she and her flatmate Rita had just been bluntly informed by their scrooge of a landlord, Mr Figgins, that the lease was up on their cramped flat above Toni's Tanning Salon on Westbourne Grove and he wanted them out before the new year. His timing was lousy. Rita – receptionist/shop assistant/part-time hairdressers' model and now budding actress – was in panto in Southend-on-Sea ('You may laugh, but playing the back end of Daisy the Cow is just the beginning,' she'd sulked at Frankie, who, on hearing the news, had collapsed in a fit of hysterics and nearly choked on a veggie sausage. 'Every actress has to start somewhere. Just look at Anna Friel – she was a lesbian!') and it was therefore left up to Frankie to sort out their housing crisis.

Which is why she'd sneaked out of the office at four thirty one afternoon and fought her way through hordes of half-crazed Christmas shoppers spewing out of the tube station hungry for tinsel, Christmas compilation CDs and glittery boob tubes for the office party. With only six shopping days to go, Kensington High Street had become a no-go area – one false move and you could be poked in the eye with 'three for the price of two' rolls of metallic wrapping paper – and shops that were normally perfectly safe were now potentially hazardous. In Marks & Spencer, empty shelves in the food hall were causing a threatening furore among present-buyers desperate to snap up boxes of chocolate truffles and gift-wrapped wooden cases of vintage port and matured Stilton, while in WH Smith an ugly fight had broken out over the last pack of charity Christmas cards.

Making little progress with polite 'excuse me's, Frankie had adopted a rugby stance – head tucked in, elbows out – and, breaking out of the scrum, headed blindly for the blue and white striped awning of Binkworths Estate Agents. On making it, she'd wearily pushed open the heavy glass door and had been hit by the warmth of central heating. Loosening her fluffy mohair scarf, she'd stumbled gratefully inside and, with flushed cheeks and watering eyes, slumped herself and her quilted puffa jacket into one of the shiny leatherette chairs in the sales and lettings department.

'Do you need any help?'

Frankie looked up from the glossy property magazine she was idly flicking through and into the velvety green eyes of a very good-looking man who'd sat down behind the desk opposite. Raising his eyebrows, he smiled at her as he leaned back against his chair and ran his fingers briskly through his blond hair. Frankie was slightly taken aback. She'd been expecting to meet one of the usual run-of-the-mill estate agents: early thirties ex-public schoolboy, pigeon-toed and portly, wearing a nasty pinstriped suit and pinky ring, with a permanently red face from a shirt collar that was too tight and dug into his burgeoning double chin. But the man behind the desk was none of the above. Slim, self-confident and sexy, this particular estate agent was a very handsome member of the male species.

Feeling suddenly self-conscious, she promptly removed her mangy old sheepskin hat. It was one of those that had flaps you could pull down over your ears – the type that always makes models in *Vogue* look seductive in a lip-glossed Russian-spy kind of way but makes anybody without Kate Moss cheekbones look like a chubby five-year-old in a furry bonnet. Frankie fell into the second category.

'Er, yes, I'm looking to rent a two-bedroomed flat,' she answered, fiddling with her hair, which had been squashed against her forehead in a highly unattractive side parting.

Mr Good-looking straightened up in his chair, nonchalantly loosened his tie and undid the top button on his collar. 'So is there anything you're particularly interested in?'

Yes, *you*, thought Frankie, watching his Adam's apple bobbing seductively up and down against the pale clean-shaven skin of his throat and wishing she was one of those confident, mouthy types like Rita who wouldn't think twice about chatting a guy up. 'Erm, not really,' she mumbled awkwardly. Stick her with a bunch of girlie mates and she could talk the hind leg off a donkey – hell, she'd even been a member of the debating society at university (albeit she'd only gone once after discovering it consisted of blokes in corduroy jackets with elbow patches spouting a load of old twaddle) – but unexpectedly coming face to face with the best-looking bloke she'd seen all year had turned her into someone with the vocabulary of David Beckham.

Mr Good-looking continued staring at her, waiting expectantly.

She tried again. 'But I'm willing to consider anything. You see, I've got less than two weeks to find a new flat.'

'Why, what happens in two weeks?' His brow furrowed with concern. It made him look even more handsome.

Frankie bit her lip. It was becoming increasingly difficult to concentrate on her housing problem and not on the estate agent. 'Our landlord kicks us out.'

'Us?' He picked up a Mont Blanc pen from his desk and began twirling it between his fingers like a propeller.

'My flatmate Rita and I. Luckily she's OK for a couple of months because she's away in a panto.'

'She's an actress?'

'You could say that . . .' A smile played on Frankie's lips as she tried not to laugh at the thought of Rita trotting around on stage in her black and white Friesian costume.

Sharing her smile, he rested his chin on his elbows and leaned across the desk towards her. 'You do realise that with it being nearly Christmas, it could take a little longer than two weeks to find you a rental property—'

Frankie interrupted. 'It can't. I've got to find somewhere.' She thought about Figgins the landlord, with his nicotine-stained fingers and revolting habit of wiping his constantly running nose on the back of his cardigan sleeve while he spoke to her chest. She wasn't going to ask him for any favours.

'There's nobody who could put you up for a couple of weeks?'

She shook her head.

'A boyfriend perhaps?' He lowered his voice against the steady hum of the office.

'Nope.' She smiled, feeling surprised and slightly embarrassed. Anybody would think he was chatting her up.

He was. Breaking into a broad grin, he gave the bezel on the face of his very expensive-looking Rolex a satisfied twirl. 'Well, I'm sure we'll be able to come up with something . . .' He nodded, swinging his legs from behind his desk. Easing himself up from his black leather chair, he strode past one of his portly pinstriped colleagues and over to the filing cabinet. 'But first I'll need to take a few details.' Yanking open the top drawer, he grabbed a photocopied piece of paper, slammed the drawer shut, strode back across the room and handed it to her. 'By the way, I didn't introduce myself. I'm Hugh. Hugh Hamilton.' He held out his hand.

Standing up, Frankie hurriedly pulled off her pink woolly mitten. 'I'm Frankie. Pleased to meet you.' She shook his hand, trying not to blush as his fingers wrapped warmly around hers. Was she imagining it or was he holding on to her hand for just a little too long? Nope, this was definitely longer than normal. A gust of excitement fluttered in her stomach, and she couldn't help hoping there might be more on the market than she'd bargained for after all.

Over the next week Frankie met Hugh many more times. Unfortunately, it was only on a strictly professional basis, and after looking round a dozen dodgy flats with second bedrooms that could have been mistaken for closets, hideous 1970s avocado bathroom suites with shag-pile toilet seat covers and enough mould in the kitchen cupboards to make a year's worth of penicillin, any hopes she'd harboured of finding a flat, or getting a date with Hugh, were fading fast.

Which is why she was taken by surprise in flat number

thirteen on the twenty-seventh floor of a council high-rise in Acton. Fully fitted with rising damp and an infestation of cockroaches, she was ready to admit defeat and give up when Hugh cornered her by the fridge freezer and confessed his undying love. Well, not exactly – but he did admit to giving her a guided tour of the worst flats in west London, just so he could carry on seeing her. Flattered – and somewhat relieved that she wasn't going to have to live in a squat after all – she agreed to a date. Seventy-two hours later and she was celebrating New Year's Eve drinking champagne and singing 'Auld Lang Syne' in her lovely new flat with her lovely new boyfriend. *Correction*: by half past ten she'd finished off the Moët and, unable to remember any of the words to 'Auld Lang Syne', was being drunk and disorderly with Hugh under the duvet. It was the perfect ending to the year.

Now it was two years later and they were living together. Not that they'd planned to or anything, but three months before Rita had legged it to Los Angeles, leaving Frankie with the problem of trying to find someone new to share the rent with. It hadn't been easy, and after meeting several would-be flatmates images from *Single White Female* began to spring to mind. Just as she'd resigned herself to sharing her Earl Grey teabags with a potential murderer, Hugh had said she could move in to his bachelor pad in Fulham. It was the result she'd been hoping for.

Not that their cohabiting hadn't led to a few teething problems. Hugh's suggestion that she move in hadn't allowed for the sheer tonnage of Frankie's belongings. Minimalist Hugh, with his Habitat two-seater and concealed cupboards, was less than impressed with Frankie's collection of clutter. Never one to travel light, she'd crammed his VW Golf GTI with five binliners of clothes, her cheese plant which she'd had since university and was now a straggling six-footer held together by pieces of Sellotape and string, her collection of old movies, a cardboard box full of hair-straightening products, a roof rack full of her grandad's old gardening books, and then, of course, Fred and Ginger.

Found abandoned round the back of Tesco, Fred was a twelve-year-old tabby and Ginger was his much younger red-haired feline friend. Frankie adored them both. Unfortunately Hugh didn't. Not being an animal lover, cats were only acceptable in an Andrew Lloyd Webber way. Matters weren't helped by Fred and Ginger immediately sensing Hugh's dislike and behaving accordingly – sharpening their claws on his brand-new sisal matting and pissing all over his golf clubs. It hadn't exactly been the kind of house-warming Hugh had had in mind . . .

Frankie was suddenly brought back to her Monday morning by the sound of the breakfast-TV theme music. Glancing across the open-plan living room, she realised it was the closing titles. Christ, she was late. If she didn't hurry up and get a move on, she'd have her boss breathing down her neck. Which, considering that the woman had chronic halitosis, was hardly a pleasant·thought. Frankie sighed and prised herself off the pedal bin. If she ran to Earls Court tube station, she could probably make the office by ten. Grabbing Hugh's coat, she took one last lingering look at the receipt, before scrunching it up for authenticity and replacing it in his pocket. Her birthday was on Friday, so all she had to do was sit tight until then. After all, she could hardly spoil his surprise, could she?

Pulling on her jacket, she glanced at her reflection in the large gilt-edged mirror which hung in the hall. She looked the same as she always did first thing in the morning: no make-up, hair all over the place, another spot on her chin. But today she had something different. There was a warm

Ready Brek glow around her, and it had nothing to do with the central heating. It was the thought that in four days she'd be engaged. *Engaged!* God it sounded so grown up. She felt as if she was that chubby four-year-old again playing at being a bride in her mum's grubby old veil and winkle-picker shoes. Except she wasn't. She was nearly twenty-nine and this time it wasn't a game.

Closing the front door behind her, she clattered down the steps and turned right into the street. It was a dull, grey wintry morning and she hurried towards the station, weaving her way through the last straggles of commuters. Everybody looked so grumpy, dowdy and fed up, but she couldn't help the huge grin plastered on her face. She must look deranged, like one of those people you see wearing newspaper shoes and talking to themselves. But she didn't care. She'd found the fella she wanted to spend the rest of her life with, and he wanted to spend it with her. It was like scooping the lottery jackpot. The odds were a million to one, but she had the winning ticket – and it was crumpled up inside the pocket of Hugh's overcoat.

3

'And where the bloody hell have you been?'

With a moustache of cappuccino froth, Audrey, her editor, collared Frankie as soon as the lift doors slid open and she entered the lobby of *Lifestyle*, a magazine for thirty-something, scented-candle-buying, career-climbing women who wanted to read about how to have the perfect orgasm/dinner party/relationship/thighs – all for just £2.60 a month.

'Sorry. I was running late . . .' gasped Frankie, out of breath from doing the four-hundred-metre sprint from the tube station. 'I'm really sorry . . . I had to go to the cashpoint, and then the Central Line was playing up and we got stuck in a tunnel, and then—'

'Stop!' Audrey held up her huge meaty palm as if she was a lollipop lady. 'I'm not interested in excuses.' With an air of managerial superiority, she fixed Frankie with a beady Cyclops eye, magnified several times due to her inch-thick glasses. 'You've been with us for six weeks and I thought you'd have realised by now that at *Lifestyle* we're interested in results . . .' Struggling to fold her arms over her ample bosom, she paused, determined to milk this moment as much as she could for dramatic effect. 'And members of staff who can manage to get their backsides out of bed and in the office. *On time.*'

Frankie nodded dutifully, trying to look repentant. 'Look, I'm really sorry. It won't happen again, promise.'

'Hmm.' Audrey raised her eyebrows disbelievingly. 'By the way, I need you to write a feature before lunch . . .'

'OK.' Squeezing herself between the fire extinguisher and Audrey's fuchsia bottom – despite fashion tips that dark shades and vertical stripes were slimming, Audrey had plumped for an entire wardrobe of primary colours and patterns – Frankie legged it down the corridor and pushed open the fire doors.

'Ten Easy Steps to Feng Shui Your Relationship . . .'

Audrey's bark was drowned out as she let the doors swing loudly behind her.

You have one new message.

Frankie's mailbox flashed up on her computer screen. She double-clicked on her intray and saw that it was Rita. Frankie smiled. Because of the eight-hour time difference between London and Los Angeles, she often e-mailed Frankie in the middle of the night.

Happy birthday! I know it's not until Friday, but I thought I'd get the congratulations in early. Hope everything's OK – still loved-up with Hugh and the new job. Guess what? I think I've fallen in love with my acting coach. Before you say it, I know what you're thinking. What happened to Kurt, the valet parker? Turns out he was married. What is it with me and married men? Anyway, Randy's much nicer. And he definitely lives up to his name!!!!! As for my name, it's still not in lights, but I've got an audition next week. Fingers crossed. Meanwhile I'm 'resting' – actress speak for only working on my tan. Would you believe it's October and it's 80 degrees! You don't know what you're missing. Randy's taking me to the opening of some new bar on Sunset tonight. I can't wait, you know how much I love star-spotting! Oh, blimey, that's him at the door now. Better go. Haven't finished putting the slap on yet. Love yer lots and lots and lots and wish you were here . . .

Frankie grinned to herself. Despite being complete opposites – Frankie had a steady job, a steady boyfriend and a wardrobe full of Next suits and Jigsaw jumpers; Rita juggled temping with acting auditions, had flings with married men and an overflowing wardrobe of multicoloured Lycra and Top Shop accessories – for six fun-filled, vodka and cranberry-drinking, *EastEnders*-watching years they'd been best mates and flatmates. But when a number 27 bus smashed into Rita's Mini, causing a broken wrist, whiplash and a 'disfiguring' i.e. barely noticeable gash on her forehead, she received a substantial insurance payout from Westminster Council – and everything changed.

Giving it a lot of careful consideration – an evening spent chatting to Frankie over a bottle of white wine and a packet of Benson & Hedges at the Prince Bonaparte – Rita made the decision about what to do with her unexpected windfall. At thirty-one she realised a career at Manpower, a few panto roles, a sanitary towel commercial and a walk-on part in *The Bill* were never going to make her rich or famous. So, ignoring the advice of Frankie, who did the sensible-friend bit and suggested a savings account with the high-street building society, she packed in her day job, packed up her belongings and, with a dream in her heart and fifteen grand in her wallet, bought a ticket to LA and moved, lock, stock and two bursting suitcases, to Hollywood. Rita had never been one to do things by halves.

Frankie clicked on reply.

Have I got news for you . . . She typed hurriedly, keeping an eye out for the reappearance of Audrey, who had a habit of sneaking up behind her. *I think Hugh's going to* . . .

Her computer screen suddenly went blank. Frankie wrinkled up her forehead. What was going on? She pushed on/ off several times, but nothing. Just a black, empty screen. Deliberating whether or not to ring one of the nice, nerdy blokes from IT, she swivelled round in her chair, only to see everybody else in the office fiddling impatiently with their computers.

'What's going on?' grumbled Audrey, her mouth full of almond croissant. 'What's wrong with these bloody machines?' She gave her monitor a few hearty thumps with her fist.

'The photocopier isn't working either,' whimpered Lorraine, the teenage work experience girl, who, suddenly realising she'd spoken out loud for the first time, looked mortified and went the colour of Audrey's trousersuit.

'There must be something wrong with the central system,' know-it-all Becka, the stick-thin fashion stylist, said, putting down her fruit salad. 'Where's Simon?'

Simon Barnet was the managing editor and owner of *Lifestyle*. An ex-hairdresser from Essex, he'd cut his publishing teeth on several popular hair magazines before venturing into the glossy women's market, and he seemed to spend most of the time in his office, fiddling with his feather cut and rubbing aromatherapy oils into his pulse points. Nobody ever saw him, unless he was going out on appointments, when he'd shimmy through the office in his pastel-coloured jackets and pleated trousers, leaving behind a whiff of vanilla essence.

'I'm here.' Simon made an unexpected appearance from his office. He looked serious. Gone was the pistachio Miami Vice suit; instead he was wearing navy-blue pinstripes. And he hadn't even pushed the sleeves up round his elbows. Something was wrong.

'I'm afraid I've got some bad news.' He fiddled nervously with his gold identity bracelet.

'Is it the computer system? The bloody thing's just died on us,' interrupted Audrey, tutting loudly and shoving her glasses up her nose with a podgy finger.

'I'm afraid it's more than just the computers . . .' Simon cleared his throat and looked nervously at the floor. 'I've just had a meeting with my bank manager and . . . Well, there's no easy way to say this, but they've called in my loan.'

'What does that mean?' asked Frankie quietly, feeling a knot beginning to grow in her stomach.

He paused for a moment and swallowed slowly. 'It means that I've just lost my business. And you've just lost your jobs.'

Silence. Deadly silence. It seemed to go on for ever, until the work experience girl dropped a pile of envelopes, sending them scattering on to the floor.

It brought Audrey back to her senses. 'What do you mean? We're in the middle of an issue.' She picked up one of the wire trays on her desk that was overflowing with unfinished feature pages and began waving it defiantly around in the air. 'We can't just stop.'

A few members of staff murmured their agreement.

Simon shrugged his shoulders. 'We don't have any choice. I've run out of money. Everything's rented . . . I can't pay the bills, so they want it all back.'

As he stopped speaking, Frankie suddenly noticed a bald-headed bloke in an orange boilersuit emblazoned with the words JESSOPS REMOVALS appear from Simon's office. He was carrying the central computer.

The scene that followed would have been funny if it hadn't been so awful. Audrey ran around like a headless chicken, protesting frantically and playing tug-of-war with the removal men over bits of furniture, while Simon sat cross-legged on the floor – his leather chair having been taken from underneath him – puffing furiously on Menthol cigarettes and doing some kind of meditational chant.

Frankie didn't do anything. She just stood and stared, unable to take on board what was happening. She'd just lost her job. Gone. Disappeared. Taken away, along with the office furniture. *She'd been made redundant!* She flinched at the words. They sounded so alien to her. Being made redundant was something that happened to other people – coal miners and car manufacturers, middle-aged men who lived up north. Not twenty-something, university-educated women who worked in publishing and lived in west London. For years she'd paid no attention to newsreaders going on about unemployment figures. She should have done. She'd just become one of them.

In a daze she started emptying the drawers of her desk, throwing away out-of-date Cuppa Soups, a pair of unflattering flesh-coloured tights, a mouldy old packet of Lockets. She'd been trying for a job like this for ages and now she'd got it it was being taken away from her. What now? Temping? The dole? She'd been used to mornings writing features, lunchtimes shopping on Oxford Street, afternoons sharing office gossip and using the phone to make long-distance calls to her family and friends. Now what did she have to look forward to? Mornings with terrible TV talkshows, lunchtimes holed up in the flat with only a plate of beans on toast for company, afternoons scouring the job ads, trying to convince herself that insurance telesales might be rather fun. Picking up a couple of A4 files, she put them with the rest of her stuff. There wasn't much. It was depressing to realise she could fit her career into one cardboard box.

She said a few lame goodbyes. Nobody knew what to say, not even Audrey, who for the first time in her life opened her mouth to find no words came out. Picking up her things, she went into the corridor to wait for the lift. It arrived carrying two permed secretaries from the solicitor's firm on the seventh floor, who, as soon as they saw Frankie and her cardboard box, stopped gossiping about the rumoured redundancies at

Lifestyle magazine and fell into an embarrassed silence. The atmosphere was a killer. Trying to avoid their pitying stares, Frankie stared fixedly at the stained nylon carpet, wishing the lift would get a bloody move on. It didn't. Instead it took it upon itself to stop at every floor and wait for a few minutes, opening and closing its doors for no apparent reason.

It was at the third floor when, out of the corner of her eye, she noticed the edge of a photograph poking out from underneath the files in her box. Pulling it out, she saw it was a photo of her and Hugh, who was looking sexy in a dinner jacket, his bow tie hanging loosely around his neck. It had been taken last year at his work's Christmas party and they had their arms around each other, smiling drunkenly into the lens. God, what on earth was she wearing? It was a ruffled, purple satin *Gone With the Wind* number from Laura Ashley – a desperate I've-got-nothing-to-wear panic buy that she'd regretted before the ink had even dried on the three-hundred-quid cheque. In her frenzied delirium, the shop assistant had managed to persuade her she looked like a seductive Scarlett O'Hara, but in the full-length mirror at home she'd discovered the awful truth: she looked like someone's bridesmaid. Luckily Hugh had come to the rescue by saying he'd always had a thing about bridesmaids and kissed her reassuringly.

Smiling as she remembered, Frankie suddenly felt a wave of relief. Thank God she had Hugh. Losing her job was a shock, but Hugh would soften the blow. He was someone she could rely on, someone whose shoulder she could cry on, someone who would put his arms around her and tell her how much he loved her – P45 or not.

The lift finally reached the ground floor and, with a ping, the sliding doors opened. Without a backwards glance, Frankie strode across the carpeted lobby, past the uniformed porters and out through the revolving doors. She suddenly found herself outside in the cold, not sure which direction to take. She paused, and it was only then that she realised that the knot she'd had in her stomach had unravelled and disappeared. A sharp gust of wind tugged impatiently at her coat and, wrapping it tightly around her, she set off through the crowded streets of Soho. She didn't have a job, but she had Hugh and everything would be OK.

4

Frankie turned on the hot tap and emptied into the bath a mixture of all the fiddly trial-size Body Shop bottles of raspberry jam gel, white musk lotion and spearmint goo she'd amassed over the last ten years and kept in a dusty wicker basket on top of the bathroom cabinet. She'd once read that hot baths were a beauty no-no, something about how they gave you cellulite, broken veins and sluggish circulation – but what didn't? Coffee was enemy number one, alcohol was just as bad, and as for sunbathing and smoking . . . they were beauty suicide. Easing herself into the bathtub, she watched her legs turning a steamy scarlet and took a sip from her glass of ice-cold Chardonnay. Following all that health and beauty advice meant drinking gallons of water, slapping on SPF50 and being wrapped in cold, slimy seaweed twice a week. She knew which she preferred. Taking another mouthful of wine, Frankie lay her head back on a pillow of wet froth and poached herself in a medley of scented bubbles.

She'd been unemployed for four days, one of which she'd spent in the Benefits office filling in dozens of colour-coded forms and waiting in a maze of queues, before being told by Brenda in Claims that it would take at least six weeks before she received her 'jobseekers' allowance' which would just about cover a Friday night out. Depressed, she'd gone home and spent the rest of the week outrageously embellishing her CV, floundering nervously through typing speed tests at intimidatingly trendy media temping agencies, and buying lots of beaded things on her credit card at Accessorize to try and cheer herself up and convince herself this was just a hiccup in an otherwise flourishing journalistic career.

Hugh's reaction to her redundancy hadn't exactly buoyed up her sunken spirits either. Instead of putting his arms around her and telling her not to worry, he'd gone all pale and twitchy and started talking about bills, the rent and the price of Whiskas cat food. It wasn't what she'd wanted to hear. After trying to put on a brave face all day, she'd been hoping for love and affection. Not a financial lecture on how she was going to have to tighten her belt, beaded or otherwise.

But today was her birthday, and she didn't have to think about tightening belts, or saving money, or any of the other depressing stuff that came with not having a job. It was her twenty-ninth birthday and, unemployed or not, she was going to enjoy herself. She'd slept in decadently late. Hugh had already left by the time she'd woken up, but there was a card and a note telling her to be ready for seven. She didn't know where he was taking her, but last year it had been a wonderfully expensive French restaurant in the West End. She'd forgiven him for being such a grumpy sod the last couple of days. After all, he was probably worried about their financial situation, what with a wedding to pay for.

She felt a guilty pang about the new Karen Millen outfit she'd bought that morning, but it was just that, a pang, and it was swiftly replaced by an overwhelming feeling of excitement. Tonight was the night. *The proposal.* She closed her eyes and surrendered to her imagination. Would he get down on one knee? Hugh was a sucker for tradition, but surely he wouldn't go that far. Would he? Her stomach fluttered excitedly as she tried to imagine how she'd react. Would she pretend to be surprised, or would she come clean and confess to finding the receipt for the ring? And talking of rings, what would it be like? An in-yer-face diamond, a sophisticated cluster of rubies, a traditional solitaire? Would the band be 24-carat gold, white gold or platinum? A million thoughts whirled endlessly around in her head like confetti and, relishing every one, she poured herself a top-up, sank deliciously back into the bubbles and hummed happily along to the sounds of Abba wafting from the stereo in the living room.

Her daydreams were interrupted by the sound of a key in the latch. It was Hugh, home from work. She heard the door open and slam shut behind him, the heavy thud of his briefcase on the floor, the jangle of keys thrown on to the table. He turned off her CD and switched on the radio.

'Frankie?' He sounded grumpy.

She hesitated. 'I'm in the bathroom.' She hid her wine glass under the bubbles. She didn't want him thinking she was drinking already.

Footsteps. The door opened. 'I hope you're not going to be in there for ages. The cab's booked for seven.' He walked over to the mirror, wiped away the steam and ran his fingers impatiently through his hair.

'Don't I even get a kiss?' She puckered her lips in a petulant, playful pout, ignoring his bad mood.

'Sorry, I've just got a few things on my mind.' Avoiding her lips, he brushed the side of her face with his mouth, barely touching the perspiration on her skin. 'Did you like my card?' he asked, changing the subject. Loosening his tie, he took it off and threw it over the towel rail.

'Yep, it was lovely.'

Frankie loved receiving cards from Hugh, though she couldn't help wishing he'd written something a bit more romantic this time than his usual 'Lots of love Hugh' and a smiley heart face. He drew one whenever he gave her a card.

At first she'd thought it was a cute, couply gesture, but then she noticed he did it on everyone else's birthday cards too.

She leaned forward, resting her head on her soapy knees, a damp curl falling across her forehead. 'Hugh, where are we going tonight?'

Opening his mouth, Hugh started flossing his teeth, tipping his head backwards and forwards as he moved between each molar, flicking out bits of leftover tuna sandwich from lunchtime. Frankie watched him. Hugh was obsessive about his appearance. Always plucking, shaving, tweezing, brushing, he spent longer in the bathroom than anyone she'd ever met.

'Hugh . . . did you hear me?'

Gargling with mouthwash, he sloshed it from side to side, and spat the blue liquid out into the sink. 'Yes, I heard you. And no, I'm not telling you. It's a surprise. Wait and see.' Wiping his mouth on a towel, he flashed a smile at himself in the mirror and, pleased with his reflection, marched out of the bathroom.

Wait and see. Frankie grinned to herself and, wiping the froth off the rim of her wine glass, drained its contents in one go.

'You can't look yet. Two more minutes and we'll be there.'

Hugh sat in the back of the cab barking directions to the taxi driver and covering Frankie's eyes with the palm of his hand. Frankie leaned back against the PVC seats, the floor heaters warming her bare legs, and wondered where they were going. At first she'd tried to work out if they were heading towards Soho, Chelsea or Notting Hill, but orienteering had never been her strong point and after a couple of minutes of turning left and then right she'd become totally confused and given up.

Suddenly the cab swerved and, braking hard, screeched to a standstill.

'We're here. I'll go first. Keep your eyes closed.'

Hugh opened the door and she could hear him paying the driver. Frankie pulled a face. Hugh could be so bossy sometimes, she thought, grasping his hand and stepping tentatively out of the cab. The air felt cold and damp and she shivered in her high heels. Stumbling slightly, she leaned on Hugh, who led her briskly up the concrete path. Then she heard the sound of a door being opened. Suddenly she experienced a jumble of warmth, light and noise.

'OK, you can look now.' He took his hand away from her face.

There was a chorus of voices: '*Surprise!*'

Opening her eyes, Frankie was greeted by the sight of Hugh's old school chum, a ponytailed advertising executive called Adam, and his much younger girlfriend, Jessica. They were grinning like clowns and wielding two huge black shiny balls. Frankie's mouth went dry as she took in her surroundings, her excitement escaping like steam from a kettle. It was replaced by pure, 100 per cent proof horror. This wasn't a candlelit, white-linen-tableclothed, champagne-serving restaurant. It wasn't even a restaurant. *It was a ten-pin bowling alley.* Her face plummeted like a bungee-jumper. She was in the middle of a bowling alley on her twenty-ninth birthday wearing a dry-clean-only Karen Millen outfit and a pair of hideously expensive Pied à Terre slingbacks. Suddenly aware that everyone was staring at her, her face bounced back like elastic and into a glassy grin.

'Jessica, Adam, what a surprise!' Struggling to sound enthusiastic, Frankie gave them a kiss on each cheek.

Jessica started giggling. She sounded like a flat battery. 'Isn't this totally groovy? I knew you'd love it when Adam suggested it.' Standing on tiptoes, she kissed Adam on his nose and grinned like a lovesick teenager. 'Isn't he clever?'

Frankie tried hard to swallow the lump, the size of a bowling bowl, which stuck in her throat. 'Adam's idea?' Not having a clue what was going on, she looked desperately at Hugh for an explanation.

Oblivious of her crushing disappointment, he nodded in amusement and began one of his anecdotes. 'Well, I'd booked a restaurant and was going to take you out for dinner – as I always do.' He puffed out his chest slightly, as if proud of this fact. 'But then Adam had this rather fabulous idea of coming to a bowling alley. He arranged it for Jessica's twenty-first birthday last year and she loved it.'

'It was brilliant,' piped up Jessica, putting her arm around Adam's spare tyre, which he'd tried, and failed, to conceal underneath a vintage Hawaiian shirt. 'A totally wicked idea.'

Frankie tried hard to silence the scream within. Wicked wasn't the word she would have chosen. Dreadful. Awful. Hideous. They were more like it. She gave Adam, the pleased-as-punch instigator of this heinous crime, a withering look. This couldn't be happening. Surely it was some kind of practical joke. Wasn't it?

It wasn't.

'Keeping secrets can be difficult, but Hugh must be pretty good at it.' Adam chuckled loudly and looked at her high heels. 'You didn't have any idea, did you?'

Forcing a ventriloquist's smile, Frankie muttered through gritted teeth, 'No, I guess not.'

5

It was the bitterest pill she'd ever had to swallow. Standing in her red, white and blue lace-ups, Frankie felt she was doing a bad impersonation of Paul Weller in his Jam days. She looked at Jessica, flicking her curtain of glossy blonde hair around as she skipped to and fro in her cut-off logo T-shirt, hipster jeans and pierced bellybutton. Tiny, Kylie-esque Jessica could make even Union Jack shoes look cute. Next to her, Frankie felt like an old frump. Three-inch snakeskin stilettos had given her designer outfit a sexy edge, but a pair of scuffed, rented laceups made her feel as if she were a Volvo-driving mum on the school run.

Things couldn't get any worse. Or so she thought, until she saw Jessica in action. Not only did she look the part, but she'd obviously been a champion bowler in a former life. Wiggling her hips, she strutted daintily to the line and, with a flick of her wrist and a toss of her hair, scored a perfect ten each time. Every male in the bowling alley was mesmerised by her technique: cardigan-wearing OAPs out on their weekly bowling night drooled over her ball control; young lager-drinking trendies salivated at the power in her fingertips. Yep, there was no doubt about it, Jessica had them well and truly by the balls.

If only the same could be said for Frankie. Like a loose cannon, she flung her ball half-heartedly down the alley, trying not to fling herself with it, and cringed as it veered off to one side, missing every single skittle.

'Better luck next time,' giggled Jessica, who giggled at everything. When she wasn't giggling she was, well, giggling.

Fighting back tears of disappointment and frustration, Frankie glanced across at Hugh for support, but he was being the absent boyfriend. Drinking beer with Adam, he was thoroughly enjoying himself, halfway through a witty anecdote of how he'd just gazumped an offer on a four-bedroom semi. Frankie sighed. Boyfriends were always the same, always leaving you to chat to their friends' girlfriends while they discussed business/golf/rugby scores. Not that there was anything wrong with Jessica, unless you counted the fact that all she talked about were clubs, DJs and her collection of underground garage and hip-hop CDs. Frankie tried to look as if she knew what Jessica was going on about, but her clubbing days had finished when her pension contributions had started and her CD collection was made up from the easy-listening section: Elvis, Frank Sinatra and Abba. Two dead crooners and a retired Swedish import. Hardly cutting edge.

After sixty minutes had ticked painfully slowly by, Frankie could no longer pretend she was enjoying herself. She was bored, knackered, completely fed up, and to make matters worse she was lucky to be in even fourth place. Every skittle was standing, every fingernail was broken. And while Hugh had hardly spoken to her, preferring to discuss endowment mortgages and interest rates with Adam, Jessica hadn't stopped. Thankfully she'd finally come up for air, complained she was 'totally starving' and dragged Adam to the neon-lit refreshments booth.

It was time to leave. Frankie collared Hugh, who was standing with his hands in his pockets by the Coke dispenser. 'I want to go home,' she muttered, miserably sitting on one of the fold-down plastic chairs and rubbing the bruise on her shin that was working its way through all the colours of the rainbow.

'Why?' He looked surprised.

It was the final straw. 'Why do you think?' she snapped. 'It's my birthday and I'm in a bowling alley. I'm bruised, bored, my fingers hurt, my feet hurt, and on top of all that you've hardly spoken to me all night.'

Silence. Hugh ran his fingers through his gelled quiff and looked at the floor.

Frankie softened. She always did when he played with his hair. 'Look, if you've got something on your mind, just say it.' He hadn't given her a present yet, so no doubt he was waiting for the right time to bring out the ring. Obviously he wanted to do one of those wacky kinds of proposal – the hot-air-ballooning, scuba-diving, in a bowling-alley type that people have to show they're not boring traditionalists. But, to be honest, although she appreciated his ingenuity, she'd rather have had the boring old-fashioned candlelit-dinner proposal any day.

There was an awkward pause. 'Well, actually there is something I've been meaning to say for a while, but this probably isn't the right time or the right place . . .' Hugh sat down. Not in the chair next to her.

It was like somebody playing a piano chord in a minor key. It jarred ominously. But Frankie didn't hear it. All she could hear was the sound of wedding bells. Mistakenly thinking he was nervous, she tried to help him along.

'Look, if this makes it any easier for you, I know what it is you want to say.'

'You do?' He wrinkled his forehead, his thick blond eyebrows blocking the light from his eyes.

'Yep.'

'Oh.' He looked taken aback. 'And you're not upset?'

Frankie gasped and, slipping off her seat, crouched down by his knees on the dusty floor. She rested her hand reassuringly on his. 'Hugh, what are you talking about? Why would I be upset? I love you. Of course I want to marry you.'

Silence.

'What did you just say?'

Frankie rushed over the words. 'I'm sorry, I know I'm jumping the gun a bit. You see, I didn't mean to snoop, but I found the receipt for the engagement ring in your pocket.' Her words came out in a jumbled gabble.

Hugh went ashen. Moving his hand away from hers, he stood up and paced around in a circle. Frankie watched him, feeling bewildered. She wasn't exactly a seasoned pro when it came to marriage proposals, but even she knew this wasn't how it was supposed to happen.

'I think there's been a bit of a misunderstanding.' His voice was clipped and flat. As if he was talking to a client, not his girlfriend, not someone he was supposed to love. He looked at her. His face was drained of blood and emotion. Hard and colourless. It was a look she would never forget.

'What?' Her voice was almost a whisper.

There was a commotion behind them. With disastrous timing, Adam and Jessica burst upon them.

'Hey, guess what, guys!' trilled Jessica breathlessly. 'Look what Adam just hid in my hotdog!' Waving her hand under Frankie's nose, she flashed a beautiful Tiffany's engagement ring. 'Isn't it wicked? We're going to get married!' She jumped up and down like Zebedee, the diamond sparkling under the harsh glare of the illuminous strip-lighting.

Frankie didn't say anything. Neither did Hugh, apart from a half-hearted 'Congratulations' to Adam, who was standing to one side, grinning modestly.

Turning to Hugh, Adam fell serious for a moment. 'Before I forget, I think I've left the receipt in the pocket of that overcoat of yours – the one I borrowed one lunchtime last

week when it was raining. Better have that, just in case . . .
Insurance and all that. Good job I remembered. It could have
got you in all kinds of trouble with the missus.' Winking at
Frankie, he nudged Hugh in the ribs before putting his arm
around his over-excited fiancée. 'This calls for a drink. Better
see if they sell champers in this place!'

Whooping like a chimpanzee, Jessica snogged the side of
Adam's face, leaving behind a trail of berry lip gloss. And
nuzzling Jessica, who was clinging to him like a life raft,
Adam led her back into the crowd.

Frankie's eyes began to well up with tears. She was suddenly
aware of the sound of her heart beating really fast. In the
background she could faintly hear Hugh – the steady hum of
his voice. She caught snatches of words, phrases, strings of
vowels, but nothing registered. It was like listening to a voice-
over in a foreign language . . .

'. . . things aren't working out between us. Not for me,
anyway . . . I don't want to settle down yet . . . I'm not ready
for this level of commitment . . . I feel claustrophobic . . . I
need space.'

The last word registered. Space. He wanted space. Looking
up at him, she saw his face through a bleary film of tears.

'What are you saying? Are you saying you want me to
move out?' Her voice broke as she struggled to bear a sudden
overwhelming pain.

It was the longest pause. Finally he spoke. 'I'm saying it's
over.'

For a split second time paused. Until someone pressed
play and the impact of his words hit with the force of a bowling ball. And, like a dozen skittles, her life came crashing
down around her.

6

The journey home passed in a blur. Frankie lay huddled in the back of the car, shock seeping through her body like an anaesthetic, dulling the pain, fuzzing the edges. She vaguely remembered running out of the bowling alley, the bewildered look on Adam and Jessica's faces as she bolted past them, knocking the bottle of cheap plonk flying out of their hands, mumbling apologies as she stumbled into the drizzly car park and fell into the back of a minicab.

Looking out into the rain, she numbly watched as the lights of the bowling alley disappeared, before turning her face away from the window. Shivering, she stared miserably down at the floor, and it was only then that she noticed she'd forgotten to change her shoes. It was like rubbing salt into her wounds. Staring right back at her were those bloody red, white and blue lace-ups.

Letting herself in through the front door, she could almost fool herself that nothing had changed. Everything looked the same, everything was still as they'd left it: Hugh's coffee cup by the phone, her make-up bag on the hallway table. It reminded her of a party game she used to play as a child. Where you had to close your eyes and somebody removed something from the room and then you had to say what was missing. But it wasn't a game and she knew what was missing. Love. It sounded corny, worthy of a toe-curling line from a slushy Mills & Boon, but it was true. Hugh didn't love her any more and it made everything around her look different.

As if she'd been watching life on a colour television and now, suddenly, everything had switched to black and white.

Dropping her keys in the silver ashtray on the coffee table, she slumped down on the sofa. Fred opened a lazy eye and, without changing his Sphinx-like position, extended a furry paw on to her lap. Always the more demonstrative, Ginger uncurled her body, arched her back and yawned, before tiptoeing delicately on to Frankie's bare knees. Nuzzling her small damp sandpapery nose into her neck, she began to purr. Normally Frankie would stroke both cats lovingly, tickling them under their Velcro chins and fondling their soft, velvety paws. But this time she didn't. Unable to move, she lay limply against the cushions, staring vacantly into space.

An involuntary sob rose in her throat and her bloodshot eyes began brimming again with tears. Never in a million years had she expected this to happen. They didn't argue – well, not really, only over stupid stuff like whose turn it was to wash up or who'd used the last of the loo roll, and they had a good sex life, at least she thought so. She felt her stomach tighten. Oh God, don't say it was that, anything but that. OK, so she wasn't swinging from the chandeliers – not that they had a chandelier, it was one of those white paper Chinese lanterns you get from Habitat for a fiver – but he seemed to enjoy it.

Frankie cringed, as one awful thought after another fired at her like poison darts. It was probably all just an act, all that kissing her neck and nibbling her ear lobes – Hugh was big on ear lobes; his hard-on was probably a fake too. After all, if women could fake orgasms, surely men could fake erections. Even worse, maybe he'd been imagining she was someone else – Suzy 'with the nice pair' in accounts, or that new temp with the French accent who kept buying him croissants. Jesus, don't say he was having an affair with her. Don't say he was giving her a pain au chocolat behind the filing cabinets. The more she thought about it, the more she remembered how he had been odd these past few weeks. Distant, less attentive, as if he had something on his mind. Bloody hell, what an idiot she'd been. There was she thinking he was contemplating marriage, and all the time he was thinking about splitting up.

And as if things weren't bleak enough, she now had to find somewhere else to live. But how? If she had a job she could start looking, but somehow she didn't think the dole would stretch to two-hundred-quid-a-week flats in W2. There was always the option of calling up a few friends and asking to kip on the sofa, but she dismissed the idea. Nobody wanted a weeping, wailing wreck camping out in their living room, however sympathetic they might be to her plight. That only left her parents, but she didn't want to worry them. She was twenty-nine years old, she should be able to sort out her own problems and not have to run home crying as if she was a kid again and she'd come last in the egg-and-spoon race, or dropped Tiny Tears head first into next-door's ornamental pond.

They were both getting on a bit now – her dad would be seventy-two next May and her mum wasn't far off – but they were still happily married, even after fifty years. Her mum always loved telling her the story of how they'd first met ballroom-dancing in Blackpool, and how, when they'd married six months later, they'd waltzed down the aisle and foxtrotted to the reception. But her mum's all-time best, oft-repeated tale was the one about when she'd turned forty and started feeling unwell. And how, terrified, she was fearing the C word. But – and this was the bit she loved telling the most – it had turned out to be the P word instead. She wasn't dying, far from it. She was four and a half months pregnant with Frankie – she'd discovered the right kind of lump.

* * *

Covering her face with her hands, Frankie started to cry again and her sniffling tears gave way to loud, choking, convulsive sobs. Fred and Ginger looked at her, confusion reflected in their amber-flecked eyes. On and on, until their fur was soaked with her unhappy tears, and her face was blotchy and bloated. And then she couldn't cry any more.

Taking rapid, desperate breaths, she wiped the end of her runny nose with the sleeve of her new jacket, streaking it with salty tears and saliva, and, easing herself up gingerly from the sofa, walked across the living room to the large sash window. Pressing her hot, clammy cheek against the soothing coolness of the glass, she stared into the street below, half-heartedly hoping to see Hugh turning the corner, climbing the flight of steps two at a time up to the front door. But there was nobody outside, nothing apart from rows of parked cars and ugly piles of rotting autumn leaves.

She didn't know how long she'd stood there before she noticed the answering machine, lying on the table beside her flashing. For a few moments Frankie watched it, not registering at first that there was a message, before leaning across and pressing Play. There was a click, and then the sound of Rita's voice, her thick Lancashire accent, loud and familiar, filling the room.

'Hi, Frankie, it's me,' she was shouting – it sounded as if she was on a mobile. 'I've bought a car . . . a convertible . . . and I'm driving along Sunset, so I don't know if you can hear a word I'm saying, but I was just ringing to wish you happy birthday. I sent you an e-mail but I don't think you got it, 'cos you never replied. I don't know where you are . . . probably out having a brilliant time with Hugh at some swanky restaurant, you lucky sod!' The sound of a horn blowing and Rita swearing. 'Bloody hell, some of these drivers don't look where they're going.' Another sound of the horn. 'Get out of the fucking way!' God, sorry about that. Some stupid bastard in a Roller . . . Hang on, I think it's Rod Stewart.' Rita's high-pitched cackle. 'Anyway, changing the subject. When are you going to come and see me? It's been three months and you did promise. Can't you leave loverboy for a couple of weeks? You know what they say about absence making the heart grow fonder and all that . . .' The screeching of brakes. 'Oh, shit, what now?' A pause. 'Christ, I think it's the cops. Better go. Love yer!' The sound of kisses and then the phone went dead.

Mad-for-it, foul-mouthed, kind-hearted Rita. She'd been dumped more often than she cared to remember but always seemed to bounce back. But Frankie had no best mate to help her bounce back. Rita was on the other side of the Atlantic. Miles away. Which is exactly where she wanted to be. Miles away from the whole sorry mess that her life had turned into . . .

And that's when the embryo of the idea was conceived and, as it grew bigger, and bigger, it triggered off an unexpected endorphinal rush of defiance. Sod Hugh. Sod *Lifestyle* magazine. And sod the fact that she was nearly thirty. She wasn't going to lie back and take everything that was thrown at her. She was going to do something. She was going to take control of her life for a change.

Wiping her eyes she picked up the phone and dialled Rita's number. There was no one in, but Frankie left a garbled message on the voicemail. Rita was always inviting her out to Los Angeles. Well, now she was going to take her up on the offer. Her mind was made up. If Hugh wanted space he could have it. Six thousand bloody miles of it.

7

With a muffled thud, the wheels of the 747 touched down on the tarmac and, decelerating sharply, the plane jolted noisily along the runway. The sudden impact woke Frankie from a deep, dream-riddled sleep. Opening her eyes, she squinted as the bright sunshine glared in through the rows of oval-shaped windows, throwing spotlight beams across her face. Groggy from nearly ten hours of uninterrupted uncon-sciousness, she blinked a few times, trying to focus on her surroundings. For a brief moment she didn't know where she was, couldn't work out what was happening, then suddenly she heard the plummy voice of the British Airways captain over the loudspeaker.

'The time is twelve-thirty p.m. and the temperature outside is 87 Fahrenheit. Welcome to a hot and sunny Los Angeles, ladies and gentlemen.'

Los Angeles! Thrusting herself forward in her seat, Frankie peered out of the window. Above her the sky was hazy with sunshine and smog, while ahead LAX shimmered in the heat like a mirage. But it wasn't. This was for real. *This was Los Angeles*.

It was hard to take in. Only last night she'd been in London, sorting through drawers full of sentimental junk – old cinema tickets, champagne corks, dried rose petals from last year's Valentine's bouquet – and trying not to get weepy as she'd turned the pages of photo albums. Only hours since she'd called British Airways' twenty-four-hour reservation line, maxed-out her credit cards and bought a ticket to LA, then yanked her battered suitcases out from underneath the bed and hastily stuffed them with an assortment of clothes, shoes and God knows what else.

Dawn had broken with the sound of the minicab honking his horn outside in the street below and she'd locked the front door, put her keys through the letter box and clambered into the back seat. Arriving at Heathrow as the check-in desk was opening, she'd been greeted by the uniformed ground staff, bleary-eyed beneath their carefully applied masks of blusher and lipstick, and, without hesitation, signed the credit card slip and collected her ticket. Only then had the adrenalin stopped pumping, allowing her to stop and think about what she was doing. It was all very well packing her bags and flouncing off to LA – it was strong, it was decisive, it showed she had balls, initiative, an I-don't-give-a-shit attitude. It was her way of singing Gloria Gaynor's 'I Will Survive' without having to do karaoke. But if she was so bloody strong, why did it feel as if her heart was breaking?

'Will everyone please remain seated until the seat-belt sign is switched off,' a red-faced steward pleaded frantically over the intercom, but his desperate attempts at crowd control fell on two hundred and fifty pairs of deaf ears. Like caged animals, irritable and impatient passengers began scrambling out of their seats, grabbing their hand luggage and pushing and shoving each other in the aisles, desperate to reach the exits and disembark a few vital minutes early.

Watching from the safety of her seat, Frankie glimpsed a Stetson bobbing about at the front of the plane. It was that arrogant American. Trust him to push forward.

Turning away, she stared out of the window. Unlike everybody else, she wasn't so eager to get off the plane. Last night, shocked and upset, running away to LA had seemed like a good idea. Now, feeling homesick and hungover, she wasn't so sure.

She'd only ever seen LA in the movies and on TV, when they showed the lifestyles of the rich and famous. From what she'd gathered, it was glamorous and glossy and inhabited by exercise-mad, health-obsessed, surgically altered people who drove around all day long in stretch limos with tinted windows. A city where women needed to have one of two things: a skinny body with giant-sized silicone breasts or a very old boyfriend with a very fat wallet. She had neither. She was now a very single 34B, who wore jeans and woolly jumpers, had a rapidly wilting bottom – in LA you were meant to have buns instead of bottoms – and enough cellulite to believe G-strings should carry a mental health warning. OK, so she had gym membership, but her workout consisted of twenty minutes in the jacuzzi, three times a month, and on top of all that she ate chocolate, got drunk, travelled by public transport, and the only surgery she'd had was to remove her tonsils when she was nine. Frankie closed her eyes again: this could all be one very big mistake.

LAX was a rabbit warren of corridors and moving walkways. Like a rat in a laboratory experiment, Frankie turned corner after corner before finally spotting the escalators that led down to baggage reclaim. Feeling relieved, she leaned wearily against the handrail. Below her, the tops of people's heads became visible and, gliding downwards, she watched as their bodies gradually came into view. Only then did she realise that these masses of people were part of a queue – a roller coaster of a queue, an-August-Bank-Holiday-at-Alton-Towers of a queue – that zigzagged backwards and forwards around carefully erected barriers. This was Immigration.

Joining the end of the line, Frankie eyed the butch,

uniformed guards with pudding-bowl haircuts and fingered her green form nervously. Would they be able to tell she was a desperate, dumped girlfriend, on the run from the dole, singledom and an ex-lover who went by the name of Hugh? She studied the other people around her – backpackers with well-thumbed guidebooks and Converse All-stars, families of four with fold-up pushchairs and pockets full of wet-wipes, businessmen with shiny leather briefcases and take-me-seriously laptops – before looking down at her laddered opaques and motley assortment of plastic-bag hand luggage. It didn't look good.

Despite the number of people, the hall was eerily quiet as, one by one, jet-lagged tourists edged closer to the front of the line, trying to look all blasé and in holiday mode, while turning their immigration and customs forms into blotting paper in their sweaty palms. This wasn't passport control, it was Russian Roulette. Impossible to tell who was going to be let in and who was going to be kept out. The seemingly random selection meant that while a tattooed, dope-smoking Hell's Angel sauntered through without a hitch, an old dear with a blue rinse was gripped under her polyester, flowery-print armpits by two armed guards and frogmarched off into an interrogation room.

Frankie stood and awaited her fate, still reeling from the shock of Hugh's bombshell. What the hell was she doing here? Everything had happened so quickly. One minute she had a job, then she didn't – a boyfriend, then she didn't – a home, then she didn't. One minute she was in a London bowling alley, the next, Los Angeles Immigration. From the sublime to the ridiculous, and she didn't know what the bloody hell to think. Did she want to be waved through, free to start a new life in LA? Or, bypassing the bravado, if she was honest with herself, would she rather be escorted on to the next plane bound for the UK and flown back to her old one?

*   *   *

'Next in line.'

This was the moment of reckoning. Frankie was beckoned forward by an official wearing a tight beige uniform and a pair of Ray-Ban aviators. He looked like Poncherello from *CHIPS*.

'And what is your reason for coming to the United States?'

Sitting behind his counter, Poncherello flicked suspiciously through her passport, pausing to stare at the unflattering mugshot she'd had taken in one of those crappy photo booths at Waterloo Station. Frankie peered over his shoulder, regretting her choice of the sickly blue curtain. She should have gone for the warmer orange.

'A holiday,' she lied, trying to pretend she was a jovial holidaymaker and not a jilted this-close-to-being-a-fiancée. Her acting was lousy, but it didn't matter. At least it proved she wasn't a wannabe actress, arriving in Los Angeles with dreams of becoming a film star. In other words, she wasn't Rita, or a heroine from a Jackie Collins novel.

'And how long do you plan to stay?'

Never once looking up, Poncherello began typing into his computer. Probably some central, worldwide Big Brotheresque computer that contained every detail about her life, from how much she'd spent at Tesco last week to her smear test results. In fact it was probably programmed to flash up any kind of criminal record or misdemeanour she'd committed. Frankie suddenly remembered the overdue video wedged down the back of the Habitat two-seater. Surely Blockbusters wouldn't have access to this computer – would they? She crossed her fingers.

'Erm, two weeks.'

Well, now was hardly the right time to blurt 'For ever', was it? She'd be strapped back into her BA economy seat before she'd even adjusted her bodyclock. And the more she thought about it, she had to stay. Going home just wasn't an option – after all, there was nothing to go home for.

Lots more frenzied movements over the keyboard. Poncherello would have no difficulty passing one of those typing speed tests, mused Frankie who was still bristling from being informed by one of the trendy Soho temping agencies that they didn't accept people who could only type with two fingers. Luckily it had been over the phone, otherwise she'd have been tempted to show them what else she could do with two fingers.

Finally Poncherello stopped typing and, stamping her passport, stapled something inside before scribbling lots of incoherent graffiti across the pages with his biro.

'Enjoy your stay.'

His face never moved as he solemnly handed back the passport. Frankie smiled with relief. She wasn't on the next plane home after all.

Waiting by the luggage carousels, she pulled out her compact mirror from the bottom of her make-up bag and, angling it towards the light, peered at herself. My God. She looked about *eighty*. The pressurised cabin and a week's worth of alcohol units had left her with dry, dehydrated skin and two piggy little eyes. Frankie felt even more depressed. How was it that celebrities could spend their life circumnavigating the globe and still manage to waft through international airports looking all chichi in leopard-skin mules and dark glasses, with their skin fresh and dewy? She'd only taken one transatlantic flight and her face looked as if it had been freeze-dried.

Gloomily holding the mirror with one hand and prodding her face to see if she actually *had* any cheekbones, she suddenly caught sight of that horrible American bloke again, staring at her from over the opposite side of the carousel. Embarrassed, she snapped the compact shut, wishing she too had a pair of dark glasses to hand. In fact any kind of disguise would do, just as long as she was unrecognisable. Now she'd reverted to her usual, sensible, sober self, just thinking about how she'd been wheeled, kicking and screaming, through Heathrow made her cringe with humiliation. No wonder the guy was gawping at her. He must have thought she was *off* her trolley, not on it.

Ignoring his gaze, Frankie defensively grabbed hold of her cart – well, she was in the States now – and moved closer to where the suitcases were about to begin spewing from the chute. The sooner she got out of there, the better. There was a heavy thud and the first suitcase made its entrance, its black vinyl chest puffed out with pride. Jesus, it was hers! Frankie was gobsmacked. In all her years of air travel, she'd always been one of the last remaining straggle of forlorn passengers, forced to watch a pair of skis and a bashed-up 'handle with care' box trundle round and round on the carousel, as she waited with mounting desperation for her holdall. Never, ever had she been in the hallowed position of seeing her luggage cross the finishing line first.

Feeling that her luck had changed, she grabbed her suitcases, breezed through Customs and pushed onwards and upwards towards the exit. Excitement stirred as the automatic doors slid open and she was suddenly greeted by crowds of people hanging over the railings, holding up cards with names or bunches of flowers for loved ones. For a brief moment she wished Hugh was there to meet her, but she caught herself. It was over, she had to forget about him.

Standing on tiptoes, Frankie looked over heads, scanning the arrivals hall. There was no sign of Rita. Maybe she was late, maybe she'd never got the message, maybe . . .

Frankie pushed through groups of people wearing T-shirts'n'shorts, Santa Monica suntans and Persol sunglasses, jangling their car keys, talking on cellphones, drinking from giant-size cups of Coca-Cola. Everything was big, bright and noisy. The collective buzz of a hundred conversations echoed loudly around her. It felt weird hearing so many American accents, as if she'd suddenly found herself on a film set.

Walking over to the smoked-glass windows, she leaned against the wall, feeling the currents of air from outside waft past her, hot and humid against the coolness of the air-conditioning. She stifled a yawn. Her jet lag had kicked in full-time and she wished Rita would hurry up. She knew it was a vain hope. Rita's timekeeping was a law unto itself. She probably wouldn't be there for hours . . .

This depressing thought was just sinking in when she heard a familiar noise. Normally it irritated the hell out of her, now it was music to her ears.

'Yoohoo.'

It echoed around the arrivals hall, bouncing off the walls like a demented cuckoo clock.

'Yoohoo.'

It grew louder until, like the biblical parting of the waves, the crowds split and through the middle cantered a five-foot-nothing redhead in velvet hotpants and three-inch platforms.

8

'Blimey, sorry I'm late. The traffic was a ruddy nightmare!'

Flustering and out of breath, Rita impatiently pushed behind her ear a chunk of scarlet hair that had escaped from her ponytail and began tugging at the sides of her shorts, which were fast disappearing up the cheeks of her bum.

'Still, better late than never.'

Breaking into a grin, she stopped yanking down her hotpants and, as if suddenly remembering where she was and why she was there, threw her arms around Frankie's waist and began shrieking like a Catherine wheel, 'I can't believe it. I can't believe you're here!'

Frankie smiled weakly, pinned to the polished floor of Arrivals by Rita's enthusiastic welcome. Neither could she.

They finished wedging Frankie's luggage into the boot of Rita's car – a baby-blue 1950s Thunderbird convertible that stretched out its fabulous fin-tailed limbs along the side of the kerb. Frankie had never seen anything quite like it. It was lean and about twenty feet long. A far cry from the beaten-up Mini that Rita used to bomb around in at home.

Noticing her look of wide-eyed amazement, Rita grinned. 'So what do you think of the new motor? I figured if I was going to be a Hollywood actress, I better start looking like one.' Throwing herself across the bonnet, she struck a classic Rita Hayworth pose – leg up, chest out. 'Suits me, don't you think?'

Frankie nodded. She had to agree. It had Rita written all over it.

'So, is that the lot then?' Rita slammed the boot shut and slid into the driver's seat.

'Nearly,' sighed Frankie, 'I've just got to pop back inside and get one more piece of luggage. Won't be a minute.' She disappeared through the airport's sliding doors.

Waiting in the car, Rita carefully reapplied her brick-red lipstick in the rear-view mirror and, slipping on her sunglasses, began trying out different acting poses for an audition she had later that week: a vulnerable shy-Di head dip, a sultry over-the-shoulder Marilyn pout; a bags-of-confidence, straight-at-the-camera Madonna smile. She was just about to attempt a tearful Oscar-winning Gwyneth Paltrow lip tremble when she caught sight of a gorgeous bloke walking up behind, laden with luggage. Angling the mirror to get a better look, she watched as he strode by the car. Doing a shy-Di head dip, she smiled. He smiled back and carried on walking. Rita's tongue was practically hanging out. *Fucking hell, who was he?* Talk about sex on legs. She stared lustfully as he began loading his bags into a taxi, eyeing up his bum, his broad shoulders, the tufts of hair escaping from underneath his beaten-up old Stetson. 'Easy, cowboy,' she muttered, giving free rein to her wild imagination and picturing herself doing a spot of bareback riding.

Watching the cab pull out, she followed its progress through the traffic. It was just disappearing out of the airport when Frankie re-emerged carrying something large and bulky, partially concealed by a vinyl cover.

'Bloody hell, what've you got in there? The kitchen sink?' Tearing herself away from her X-rated daydreams, Rita balanced her sunglasses on the end of her upturned nose and peered at Frankie. 'How much stuff do you need for a two-week holiday?'

Frankie hesitated, looking more than a little anxious. 'Actually, I was going to tell you earlier . . .'

'Tell me what?' Seemingly oblivious of Frankie's unease, Rita started fiddling with dials of the original 1950s radio, trying to tune in to a station.

'I was thinking of staying a bit longer.'

As if on cue, there came sounds from underneath the vinyl cover and the object Frankie was holding shook violently.

Rita's glasses slid off her nose and on to the dashboard. 'What the hell is that?'

She couldn't put it off any longer. Frankie nervously removed the cover to reveal a white plastic cage. Two pairs of disgruntled eyes blinked in the bright sunlight. 'It's Fred and Ginger.'

Driving along the 405 Freeway, Frankie told Rita everything. Discovering the Tiffany's receipt, losing her job, being dumped at the bowling alley on her birthday . . . everything . . . even the bit about Fred and Ginger and how, when she'd made her sudden decision to come to LA, she'd been determined they were going to come with her. At first it had seemed impossible. Even though they'd already had all the necessary vaccinations – Frankie was like a protective mother when it came to her beloved cats – the brusque official she'd spoken to on the phone had insisted that the airline needed twenty-four hours' notice to complete the paperwork. Full stop. End of story. But Frankie hadn't been going to give up that easily and so, using both her own powers of persuasion – in other words, bursting into hysterical tears – and that of her Visa card – she'd managed to melt the red-tape wrapped around the BA official's heart and get Fred and Ginger on her flight.

'I couldn't leave them with Hugh. He'd probably swing them by their tails and use them as golf clubs . . . He's always hated cats . . .'

Rita listened, puffing on a cigarette and hooting her horn at various cars, as Frankie wrung out every last detail, lurching from tears, to anger and back to tears. It took over an hour, and when she'd finished she slumped down in her leather seat, knackered after her emotional spring clean.

'Look, I know you're not going to want to hear this, but if you ask me – and I know you're not but I'm going to tell you anyway – you're better off without the bastard.' Never one to mince words, Rita went straight for the jugular. 'Hugh might be good-looking, but he's an arrogant son of a bitch, and he's so flaming bossy. He has you running around in circles after him.' She flicked her ash into the ashtray, not seeming to notice that it was instantly whipped away by the wind and scattered around them. 'To be honest, I always thought there was something dodgy about him.' She turned to Frankie, who, propelled out of her self-pity by Rita's rally-driving techniques, was gripping the edges of her seat as they raced hell for leather along the freeway. 'I mean, how can you ever trust a bloke who tweezes his eyebrows, for God's sake?'

Shaking her head in exasperation, she was about to continue with her snipe-by-snipe destruction of Hugh when she saw Frankie's expression. She was close to tears again.

'Not that there's anything wrong with a man plucking his eyebrows, of course . . .' Rita changed tack, suddenly remembering the sacred rule: never slag off your mate's boyfriend, however much of a bastard he's been, they'll only end up hating you, not him. 'I mean, you don't want him to end up looking like Noel Gallagher or anything, do you?' She smiled brightly, but it was no good, her attempts at salvaging the situation were just digging her a deeper and deeper hole.

Frankie wiped away a tear. 'But I love him. I thought we were going to spend the rest of our lives together. He's my soulmate.' Sniffing, she wiped her nose on a tissue that had seen better days. 'What am I going to do without him?' Her face screwed up as she started crying all over again.

Rita took her eyes off the freeway and looked across at her. 'Oh, c'mon, cheer up, Frankie . . . please,' she begged, reminding herself never to offer her services to the Samaritans. 'I know it's going to be hard, but you've got to try and forget about him now and get on with your own life.' She leaned across and squeezed Frankie's fingers. 'You're going to love LA, and don't worry, you can stay with me as long as you like. It'll be just like old times – you and me . . .' She glanced in her rear-view mirror at Fred and Ginger's cage trembling on the back seat . . . 'and the two scaredy cats.' She grinned and, without indicating, careered across three lanes of traffic, before slamming on the brakes and ducking behind a cop-car. 'Now just chill out.'

As they raced along the freeway the classic track 'Hotel California' came on the radio and, turning up the volume, Rita lit another fag from the dying embers of hers and offered it to Frankie. She hesitated. The last time she'd cadged a fag to satisfy a drunken nicotine craving, Hugh had gone berserk and made her put it out. He absolutely hated her smoking. The memory made up her mind. Well, tough shit. Rita was right. She had to try and forget about Hugh and get on with her own life, a new life that didn't involve him. Relishing the feeling of empowerment and the blasts of humid wind whipping through her hair, she accepted the cigarette, defiantly pressed it to her lips, and took a long, indulgent drag. It was hedonistically satisfying.

Rita gave her a go-for-it-girl grin and began singing along to the Eagles at the top of her voice. Slamming her foot down on the accelerator, she began overtaking an articulated lorry that was belching out noise and fumes. The driver honked his horn and swerved, but Rita merely waved a freckled arm in the air, the bright orange sparks from her cigarette trailing behind them as they pulled away. Frankie closed her eyes and, feeling the nicotine rush into her bloodstream, put her stockinged feet up against the dashboard and relinquished herself to the head rush.

9

Half a packet of cigarettes later they were negotiating their way round the zigzag bends in the road leading up into Laurel Canyon. Rita's decision to give Frankie a guided tour of LA on the way back from the airport meant it was getting late as they finally headed back to her apartment. Darkness had descended and high in the Hollywood Hills there was no light apart from the two beams projecting from the Thunderbird's headlights. Tired and disorientated, Frankie was almost falling asleep when Rita turned into Pacific View Drive, pulled into a driveway and turned off the engine. The headlights died, as did the stereo. Silence. After the roar of the freeway and the constant rumble of the engine, it was unexpectedly still, the only noise being the rhythmic chirping of a lonesome cricket.

'Well, this is it.' Cranking on the handbrake, Rita climbed out of the car and clattered down the small concrete path that ran alongside the garage and led to her apartment. Following closely behind with Fred and Ginger, Frankie heard her rummaging furiously around in the bottom of her handbag. 'Shit, I've forgotten my key,' she muttered, before tutting loudly. 'Oh, well, don't worry. My neighbour will be in.'

She was about to knock on the right-hand door when it suddenly flew open and a torch was shone in their faces. 'Hold it right there, I've got a gun.'

'What?' Frankie stumbled backwards, blinded by the sudden brightness of the light in her eyes.

'I'm armed and I'm ready.' The voice was deep and gruff.

'Christ Almighty, what are you doing?' Rita gasped impatiently. Frankie was stunned to hear that she sounded ratty, rather than scared for her life.

There was lots of scuffling and the sound of a dog yapping as the torch was switched off and the hallway light came on. Frankie's pupils took a second to adjust, but as they came into focus she saw a very strange sight. Standing before them, clad in a full-length leopard-print bathrobe was a tall, slightly receding, thirty-something male. In one hand he was holding what looked like a gun; a shih-tzu dog was tucked under his other arm. It was shaking violently – as was its owner.

'Jesus Christ, I nearly had a fucking heart attack. How was I supposed to know it was you? I thought I had intruders or something . . .' His voice rose an octave, switching from a deep ghetto growl to a high squawk. Closing his eyes, he took several deep breaths.

Frankie stood and stared, not knowing what to do. Luckily Rita took control. 'Bloody hell, Dorian, you frightened the life out of me, you idiot.' She slapped his chest, as if she was swatting a mosquito. 'And you probably frightened Frankie to death as well. It's hardly the kind of welcome to give to my new flatmate, and your new neighbour.'

Dorian opened his eyes, seemingly aware for the first time of Frankie's presence. 'Fucking hell, why didn't you say so in the first place?' Promptly dropping the dog, which squeezed itself through Rita's legs and scampered outside, he put down the gun and grabbed Frankie's hand in his. 'I'm Dorian, it's wonderful to meet you.' With his sense of vanity returned, he turned on the charm, flashing a perfect set of even teeth. 'Rita's told me so much about you, but she never said how gorgeous you were . . . Did you, Rita?'

As Rita rolled her eyes and Frankie smiled self-consciously, Dorian finally let go of her hand and, tugging on his belt to

tighten his robe, stepped to one side. 'Well, come in, come in
. . . Don't stand on the doorstep all night, it's fucking freez-
ing.' And puffing out his chest, he waved them both inside.
'Get your gorgeous little bottoms inside, *immediately*!'

Dorian's apartment was a higgledy-piggledy assortment of
hi-fi equipment, televisions, shelves full of knick-knacks and
fairy lights running around the fireplace that switched off
and on automatically in differing rhythms. Pride of place was
held by a large 1980s leather sofa, chrome and black smoked-
glass coffee table littered with dollar bills and an overflowing
ashtray shaped like a pair of double-D breasts. Frankie was
taken aback. It was like being in an adult Santa's Grotto –
a fussy, kitsch, eclectic den that was a far cry from Hugh's
minimalist beige and cream – cushions on their ends, DVDs
arranged in alphabetical order – flat, and she loved it.

But all this was overshadowed by the spectacular view.
Perched on stilts above the valley, the apartment had one wall
entirely constructed from glass, with sliding patio doors that
led on to a small deck hung with a hammock and littered with
bongo drums, Indian embroidered cushions, plants, snow-
boards and a didgeridoo. Overawed by the scene before her,
Frankie was incapable of taking it all in. Standing on the deck,
the inky valley receded, giving way to a carpet of flickering
golden fairy lights that was downtown LA. For the first time
in days, her mind completely cleared as she looked across to
the horizon. The City of Angels in all its magical, inviting,
anything-can-happen-out-there glory. It blew her away.

While Frankie was admiring the view, Rita lugged her stuff
from the car into her apartment and released Fred and
Ginger from their mobile home. Relieved to stretch their
paws, they padded inquisitively around her bedroom carpet,
checking out piles of dirty laundry, cupboard doors left

ajar, waste-paper baskets brimming with empty chocolate-bar wrappers, before gobbling up the remains of a smoked salmon bagel.

Dorian was meanwhile flitting around his apartment, pacing up and down the open-plan living room's wooden floor, sipping liquorice tea and answering one mobile after another. He appeared to have several dozen in fact, and they rang, vibrated, beeped and played 'The Charge of the Light Brigade' at various intervals, creating an orchestral symphony of ringing tones. One after another, he snatched brief conversations, like a well-practised telephone operator, and proceeded to make frantic notes in a pad. Finally, after a rush of callers, he collapsed into the wicker chair that hung from the ceiling.

Rita came back inside from next door and flopped on the sofa. 'So you like the view, then?' Her voice broke Frankie away from her thoughts.

'It's amazing.' Frankie smiled as she came back inside. 'Do you get the same one from your apartment?'

'Not quite. Dorian's got the more expensive view. We'll go next door in a minute and you can have a look.'

'Yeah, I'd love to. Better get Fred and Ginger as well, the poor things must be starving.'

'Don't worry. I've just fed them. They're already asleep on my duvet.'

'God, thanks.' Frankie smiled appreciatively. 'They must be as knackered as I am.'

'Knackered. *Knackered!*' Dorian mimicked her like a mynah bird. 'You can't be knackered, you've only just arrived.'

'I know, but I think I've got jet lag,' Frankie tried feebly to protest. She didn't want to come across as a boring old fart in front of someone she'd just met, but quite frankly she felt like putting on her pyjamas, having a cup of tea and going to bed. Even if it was only early.

Dorian was having none of it. Beaming brightly, he rubbed his hands together as if he was trying to light a fire. 'In that case I've got just the thing to perk you up.'

'Not that bloody awful liquorice tea,' interrupted Rita, fanning herself with a copy of the *National Enquirer*.

Dorian tutted. 'Have you no faith, woman?' Standing up, he put his hands on his hips, legs akimbo, and declared dramatically, 'What I have is a party.'

A party? Frankie widened her eyes in horror and mouthed the words to Rita. It was the last thing she felt like. Unfortunately, Rita didn't appear to share her misgivings.

'A party, whose?' She gripped the edge of the sofa excitedly.

'Aha.' Dorian smiled smugly, satisfied with the response. 'I'm not telling, but I do know there's going to be dozens of celebrities, fountains of champagne and –' he paused and winked mischievously – 'even though I know you won't want to look at another man with me by your side, I've heard rumours that there's going to be lots of prime rump for ladies such as yourselves.'

He beamed at Frankie, who smiled weakly. First he'd waved a gun in her face, now he was offering her *prime rump*.

'Great!' enthused Rita. 'Randy's away on business, so I'm footloose and fancy free.' She caught Frankie's forlorn expression. 'Come on, Frankie, it'll do you good. A party's just what you need.' Sitting on the edge of the sofa, she squeezed Frankie's hand comfortingly.

'Yep, I know.' Frankie nodded, trying to look enthusiastic but fooling no one.

Dorian wasn't about to take no for an answer. Pouring out three tequila shots, he passed them round. 'This will help get you in the mood.'

He knocked his back eagerly, as did Rita. Frankie was less enthusiastic, screwing up her face as the liquid scorched the back of her throat. Refilling his glass, Dorian picked up one of his remote controls and flicked on his stereo. Suddenly Flamenco music was beating down from the overhead speakers.

'Come on, you'd think we were going to a funeral,' he hollered, slamming his shot and picking up a pair of castanets. He rattled them at Frankie, who was still coughing from the tequila fumes. 'I guarantee you'll have a fabulous time.' He gripped her around the waist and, before she had time to stop him, began twirling her around the sofa, his leopard-print bathrobe flapping around his ankles. 'You're with me –' suddenly tipping her backwards, he pressed his mouth to her ear and growled – '*and I'm a party animal.*'

10

Sunset Strip was chock-a-block with traffic and they sat bumper to bumper with white stretch limos, watching the overhead traffic lights change from red to green to amber and back to red. Frankie pressed her nose against the tinted windows of Dorian's silver Mercedes convertible, staring at the adverts that loomed above her on colossal billboards.

Why, oh why, had she agreed to go to the party? Why hadn't she gone next door to Rita's apartment and curled up in her pyjamas next to Fred and Ginger? Instead of sitting here, all dolled up in her trusty black dress and heels, her blotchy, tear-stained complexion hidden under a generous helping of Body Shop bronzer and Rita's thousand-calorie mascara. She looked at Rita and Dorian in the front seats – Rita was smoking a cigarette, while Dorian was chatting into his hands-free mobile and putting gel in what was left of his hair. It was eight o'clock on a Sunday night. Back in London it would be four the next morning and Hugh would be asleep in bed. However hard she tried, she couldn't help wishing she was snuggled up next to him . . .

'Thank fuck, we're finally moving.'

Dorian put his foot down and, taking advantage of the lights, switched lanes. Ahead, the road was a mass of white headlights and red tail-lights, a sharp contrast to the ghost-like emptiness of the pavements. Frankie scanned them for signs of life, but she couldn't see a single pedestrian. Probably because there weren't any. The entire population of Los Angeles was on wheels. Everyone was going somewhere – either literally or metaphorically, up or down – everyone was on the move.

Instead she saw a couple of neon-lit bars, three liquor stores, the derailed carriage of a train that was now a diner and a huge cutout of the Marlboro Man. Frankie glowered at this abrupt reminder of the arrogant arsehole at the airport, and was about to start stewing over the whole thing again when she was distracted by the sight of an impressive-looking hotel, lit up by swirling violet-blue strobes. It loomed ahead and, as they got closer, Dorian took a sharp right and they swept up a glittering driveway lined with colossal palm trees, swaying gently in the evening breeze.

A gaggle of uniformed valet parkers dived on the doors, ushering them out, and deftly whisked the car away, ready for the next arrival. Being unexpectedly thrust into the glare of the strobe lights, Frankie froze like a frightened rabbit, her mind going into overload at the lavish surroundings. A continuous stream of Rolls-Royces, Ferraris and stretch limos glided past, and as she watched them she noticed that the driveway really did sparkle. Made of tarmac mixed with glitter, like millions of miniature stars, it twinkled and shone in the bright spotlights. Only in LA could she have the stars at her feet.

At the entrance a crowd was gathering. Willowy girls in hipsters, big-haired femmes fatales in Gucci, square-jawed men with terracotta tans, all trying to get into the party. A bouncer the size of a portakabin was doing his all-action-hero impersonation, barring them with his arm and shouting into his microphone headset. He bore a remarkable resemblance to Mike Tyson. Perhaps it was Mike Tyson, mused Frankie.

Assuming they were going to have to wait with everybody else, Frankie tried to figure out where to stand. She didn't want to look as if she was pushing in. 'Excuse me, is this the back of the queue?' she asked a blonde twenty-something next to her.

'The queue?' The blonde twenty-something, who looked exactly how a blonde twenty-something in Los Angeles should look, wrinkled her forehead as if she didn't understand.

'Yeah, the queue, to get in.'

The blonde looked puzzled. The pensioner on her arm helped her along. 'She means line, sugar.' It was like watching the lights being switched on. Giggling brightly, she turned back to Frankie. 'Oh, sure, honey, this is the queue.'

She looked thrilled to bits with herself. As did the pensioner, who squeezed her eighteen-inch waist tightly. Grinning like a proud grandparent and not the lecherous cradle-snatching boyfriend that he was, he showed off fifteen thousand dollars' worth of fluorescent veneered teeth. Frankie nodded dumbly, blinded by his dental work.

'Yoohoo!'

It was that sound again. Frankie swivelled round and, standing on tiptoes, scanned the crowd. At the front of the queue she spotted Rita beckoning her madly, arms rotating wildly, like those of a parent trying to dance. Oh God, she cringed. Rita always did this. She always pushed to the front of any queue – be it in the post office, at the bus stop or at the bar – and Frankie would follow behind, dying with embarrassment and trying to duck the dirty looks being slung at them.

Feeling as if she was on the catwalk, she nervously tottered past the line of people, who looked her up and down, trying to work out which film they'd seen her in. Was it a Quentin Tarantino, or maybe a Spike Lee, or, surely not, a Spielberg?

Unable to place her, they whispered among themselves. Naahhh, with those tits and teeth she was obviously British. Probably a Merchant Ivory or, even more likely, a Ken Russell. After all, she must have been in *something* – how else would she be on the guest list?

'Come on, you silly sod. We're with Dorian.' As if she was rescuing her from drowning, Rita grabbed hold of Frankie and pulled her in through the entrance.

Frankie was nonplussed. 'So?'

'*So?*' Rita pulled one of her faces. 'So, we walk straight in.'

'Why?' She still didn't get it.

'Bloody hell, I don't know,' spluttered Rita, exasperated by Frankie's inane questions. 'Who the bloody hell cares? We're in, aren't we?' She made it sound as if they were bank robbers who'd cracked the sophisticated alarm system installed at great expense to keep out Joe Public. 'C'mon,' she hissed and, without waiting for any further questions, clattered through the marbled lobby in her gold spangly boob tube and matching miniskirt. Frankie, meanwhile, was in funereal black: black dress, black tights, black shoes. Despite Rita's earlier pep talk, she was still in mourning for Hugh.

They rushed past security on the lookout for Dorian, but he was nowhere to be seen, having disappeared through the lobby carrying a silver attaché case, his full-length fur coat sweeping the floor behind like ermine robes. Following in his wake, they hurried through the swathes of white muslin suspended from the ceiling and billowing out like the sails of a boat, on towards the sounds of chattering, music, laughter and the chinking of glasses.

And then suddenly they'd arrived.

Frankie faltered at the entrance. She'd never seen a party like it. It was being held in the hotel's bar, the famous Cloudsbar, but it wasn't like any bar she'd seen in a British hotel. There were no mock Victorian fireplaces, vases of dried flowers, chintzy armchairs and curtains with tasselled tiebacks. There wasn't even a bar, oak-panelled, brass-plated or otherwise. Instead it was alfresco and there was an Olympic-size swimming pool that was being lit by dozens of real-flame torches held by Roman statues on marble columns. Around its sides was a mosaic-tiled floor strewn with hundreds of cushions – and not the kind found in primary colours from IKEA, but great big stonking cushions the size of futons, covered in a soft white pearlescent velvet and plumped full of goose feathers – on which lots of people were lounging around, elegantly sipping champagne.

It was like stepping into another world. Flames from the torches cast a flickering light across people's faces, giving them a golden glow she'd only ever seen in Dutch old master paintings. It was a world of Kens and Barbies. Perfect, plastic people. But while the men looked vaguely recognisable, give or take an all-over tan and gym-honed pecs, the women were something else. Frankie felt as if she'd discovered another species: the LA Child Woman – females who went through puberty only from the waist upwards. While the bottom half had no sign of a bum, tum or – God forbid – hips, the top half sported a pair of Pamela Anderson specials. They were twelve-year-olds with double-D silicone chests and, to cap it all, legs as long as skyscrapers. Frankie stared up at them. Despite being five foot eight, she suddenly felt like the little guy in *Fantasy Island* who used to keep shouting, 'The planes are coming, the planes are coming.'

Trying not to look intimidated – and it was difficult – she followed Rita, who appeared to have no such worries and was marching confidently across the floor to a vacant pair of cushions.

Flopping down on one, Rita readjusted her boob tube and began stretching her Lycra miniskirt over her thighs, like clingfilm over a pair of chicken drumsticks. 'Blimey,

I'm thirsty, aren't you?' Without waiting for an answer from Frankie, she beckoned one of the überbabe waitresses floating around in Buddhist-orange sarongs and bare feet, holding trays of champagne. Rita grabbed four glasses with her fingers and thumbs. 'Well, you hardly get anything in these fiddly, little things,' she tutted, sucking the Moët from her gold nail varnish and passing two to Frankie. 'Bottoms up.' She chinked glasses. 'I bet you could do with a drink.'

Frankie sighed gloomily. 'Since Hugh dumped me, I've done nothing *but* drink.' She looked sadly into her glass.

Rita misunderstood. 'That's my girl.' She grinned encouragingly, finishing off one glass and making an immediate start on the second. For a pint-sized person, she could outdrink almost anyone. She drained the dregs. 'Won't be a mo – just off to the loo.' She hoisted herself off the cushion, displaying rather more flesh than she'd intended, and tottered off in search of the Ladies.

Alone on her giant cushion, Frankie felt like Thumbelina on her lily pad. Lost and insignificant. She toyed with the idea of going to find Dorian, but changed her mind when she caught sight of him in a far corner. Despite his flamboyance, which was often verging on camp, he was a raving heterosexual. Reclining on a cushion, he was surrounded by gorgeous, glossy women feeding him sushi and champagne, like a Roman emperor with his slaves. Frankie checked her watch. God, Rita had been gone for ages. For the second time that day she wished she'd hurry up.

Frankie finished off yet another glass of champagne. She felt self-conscious. She wasn't used to being by herself at a party. Normally she had Hugh to talk to, or at least Hugh to watch, as he discussed house prices and interest rates in a corner with some random bloke. She was used to being part of a couple, and even if she wasn't actually with him, it gave her a feeling of safety. Like having an airbag – you know it's there if you need it. But she was single now, and that meant small talk, flirting and making an effort, despite having completely forgotten how to. And even if she hadn't, she didn't have the balls to launch herself into this terrifying scene. When Hugh told her it was over, he'd robbed her of her confidence, leaving plenty of room for a whole load of neuroses. Now, all she could think about was what was wrong with her. The size of her bum? Her boobs? The dreaded cellulite? Or was it because she was too boring? Or crap in bed? Or the fact she got pissed and sang Frank Sinatra songs? The list could go on and on. One minute she'd been part of a couple: happy, settled, confident. The next minute – wham, bam – she'd entered the Bridget Jones zone: a neurotic, nicotine-addicted singleton.

Plunged even further into gloom at this depressing thought, she caught sight of a crumpled sky-blue packet of American Spirit peeking out of the gold sequined handbag that Rita had left behind. She didn't blame her, she wouldn't be seen dead with the bloody thing either. She pulled out the packet and, trying to convince herself that no, she didn't need the nicotine crutch, and she was really a non-smoker, she surreptitiously looked inside. There was one cigarette left. Oh, well, one teensy-weensy cigarette wasn't going to do any harm, was it? She only wanted a drag. And Rita wouldn't mind. After all, it was an emergency. Putting it in her mouth, she grabbed a box of matches from one of the handcarved-in-Bali-type bowls that had been painstakingly scattered around. She was just about to strike one when she heard, 'I'm sorry, it's no smoking.' She looked up. Like a genie, a waitress had appeared.

Frankie was nonplussed. What did she mean, no smoking? She was in a bar. 'Excuse me?'

The waitress repeated the sentence robotically. 'I'm sorry, it's no smoking.'

Frankie started to feel impatient. It wasn't her hearing that was at fault. 'You mean I can't smoke anywhere?' She looked in confusion at the abundance of matches around her, all emblazoned with the bar's logo. What did people in LA do with them all if they didn't smoke? Make matchstick models? Somehow she couldn't imagine the likes of Madonna putting the finishing touches to a model of the *Mary Rose*.

The waitress shook her head. 'Not in a public bar. It's California state law.' She sounded as if she was reading from an autocue. 'You can always go outside.'

'But I am outside,' retorted Frankie, looking incredulously up at the dark, open sky above her.

Ignoring her, the waitress put her hands on her non-existent hips, her earlier smile now set in a grim line. 'If you intend to smoke, I'm going to have to ask you to leave the bar area *and go outside*.' She motioned to the patio doors at the far end of the swimming pool.

'OK.' Realising that there was no point trying to reason with Ms Personality, Frankie stood up. It was then she saw that she had an audience. Everybody was staring at her. *And nobody was smoking.* Feeling like a criminal, she took the fag out of her mouth and, as there was still no sign of Rita, bolted the full length of the pool and out through the doors.

Outside it was dark and felt cool after the warmth of the bar. Her head whirled – too much champagne. Taking a lung-ful of air, she looked around her. It was deserted. There was no noise but the faint hum of the party and the distant roar of the traffic. So this was the smoking section, she thought, thinking how different it was from London, where banished smokers always huddled together in jovial camaraderie, happily working their way through packets of B&H, drink in one hand, fag in the other.

Feeling a bit unsteady, she leaned against the stone balus-trade that ran around the far side of the patio, lit her cigarette and, inhaling deeply, looked out at the streets below that made up a gridwork of lights. Her mind drifted back to thoughts of Hugh. He was miles away on a different continent, in a different time zone. Miles away from her. Maybe Rita was right, maybe he was arrogant, maybe she did run around after him in circles, but she still loved him. She missed him.

Her eyes filled up and she knew she was going to cry again. Suddenly she heard footsteps behind her and she sniffed vigorously instead. She turned round. After the lights of the traffic, it was difficult to see in the darkness, but she could make out the shape of a man – tall, broadish. She couldn't see his face.

'S'cuse me, have you got a light?' His voice seemed loud against the faint hum of the background noise.

Nodding, she held out the matches and watched as he looked for a place to put his drink.

'Here, I'll do it.'

Ripping a match from its cardboard roots, she scraped it against the emery strip. The phosphorus flared and, moving forward, she held the match close to the end of his cigarette. Putting down his glass, he cupped his hands around hers as he sucked hard on the orange filter, the flame illuminating his face, exposing tanned skin, heavy stubble, a roughness around the mouth. He seemed familiar, as if she knew him from somewhere . . . For a brief moment she glanced into his eyes, before the dying flame burned her fingers and she snatched her hand away. The penny dropped at the same time as the match. *Jesus Christ, it was him.*

11

Jesus Christ, it was her. The girl from the airport. He'd come outside for a smoke and at first he thought he was alone, until he'd heard a sniffle and seen someone leaning against the balcony. It was difficult to see in the darkness, but he could make out the shape of a woman. Slim, tall, great butt. She looked cute, from the back anyway. At first he was going to go back inside, she sounded as if she was crying, but then he'd thought, What the hell, damsel in distress. Maybe she needed his shoulder to cry on. So he'd asked her for a light – the old ones were always the best – and he thought his luck was in when she'd leaned closer and lit his cigarette. She smelled gorgeous and he was right, she was very cute. The odd thing was, she was also *very* familiar. Had he met her before? He'd flicked mentally through his little black book – was she someone he'd worked with, a girl he'd chatted up in a bar somewhere, a one-night stand? Then he'd realised. And he couldn't believe it. She was the girl who'd tried to steal his cart at Heathrow. The crazy English chick. The woman he'd last seen disappearing out of LAX.

'It's you.' Frankie jumped back as if she'd been bitten. Sucking her singed finger, she scowled at him through the darkness, her initial surprise swiftly turning to annoyance. 'You're that bloke.' She hadn't recognised him at first without that stupid bloody cowboy hat. But it was definitely him. The lying, cheating, stealing Yank from the airport.

He sighed. 'Look, about before . . .'

But Frankie wouldn't let him get a word in. 'You're the bloke who nicked my trolley at Heathrow.' She couldn't believe it. It was definitely him. Christ, he'd got a nerve. Swaggering over as if nothing had happened, asking for a light.

He rubbed his stubble lazily. 'Hey, I promise you it was my cart.' He started smiling. The last thing he wanted was another fight. In fact, he wouldn't mind calling a truce and getting her number. 'It doesn't matter anyway, does it? It was a mix-up.'

'A mix-up?' Frankie could feel her hackles rising. Was he being deliberately patronising?

'Well, c'mon, you'd had a few drinks.' He laughed, trying to make a joke of it, hoping she'd laugh along. He was wrong.

She fumed. The cheeky bastard was still saying it was her fault, and to make matters even worse he was laughing at her – *again*. 'What are you trying to say? That I was *drunk*?'

Christ, he'd really hit a raw nerve. 'I didn't say that.' He tried to back-pedal, but it was useless. He could feel the situation freewheeling out of control towards another blazing row.

Frankie pounced. 'You don't have to. But, for your information, I wasn't *drunk*. I'd had a few drinks to calm my nerves, that's all. That doesn't make me *drunk*.' Were all American men so bloody arrogant?

'Hey, OK, I take it back. There's no need to be so touchy.' Hell, what was wrong with her? Were all British women this fucking uptight?

'Well, what the hell do you expect, with people creeping up on me?' she snapped.

'Woaah.' Putting his hands up in surrender, he stepped back. 'I was only asking for a light.' Jesus, she really *was* crazy.

Frankie didn't say anything. Instead she took a drag of her cigarette and began self-consciously fiddling with the catch on Rita's gold handbag.

He watched her, his temper dying as quickly as it had ignited. She looked so lost and vulnerable. 'I heard you crying . . . I thought maybe I could help.'

Frankie snapped the bag shut and looked at him suspiciously. What was he playing at? Was this genuine concern or was he making fun of her? She decided on the latter. 'I don't need help from someone like you.'

Now it was his turn to get annoyed. '*Someone like me?*' The muscles in his clenched jaw started twitching rapidly with agitation. 'What the hell do you mean by that?'

Frankie sighed irritably. 'Look, just leave me alone, OK?' She glared at him.

'My pleasure.' He glared back.

Silence.

The clatter of stilettos and a flash of spangly gold outfit through the foliage heralded Rita's arrival. Appearing from around the corner, she caught sight of Frankie. 'Bloody hell, is that where you are? I've been looking for you all over . . .' Her voice trailed off when she saw Frankie was talking to a bloke. And not just any bloke. Her eyes locked on full beam as she realised it was the man from the airport. The Gift from God. The sexy cowboy. *Phwooarr.* Feeling her juices rising, like sap in a tree, she hurriedly began fluffing her hair and pulling down her boob tube – for maximum cleavage effect – as she glanced from him to Frankie, then back to him. Nobody was speaking. Tension hung thickly in the air like stale cigarette smoke. Not that Rita noticed, any scrap of sensitivity she possessed being elbowed to one side by her raging hormones.

She turned back to Frankie. 'So aren't you going to introduce me?' Flashing her mega-watt smile, normally reserved exclusively for casting directors, she peered at the incredibly handsome stranger and giggled coyly.

Frankie gritted her teeth. Introductions were the last thing on her mind. Instead she scowled at her unwanted guest, wishing he'd go away. He got the message. 'Actually, I was just leaving.' He looked straight at Frankie, who refused to meet his eye and turned away, before nodding to Rita. 'Nice meeting you.'

'Yeah, you too,' squeaked Rita, who always sounded like Minnie Mouse when she was on heat.

Frankie didn't say anything. Instead she kept her back turned until she heard the scrape of his boots on the concrete as he walked away.

Unable to wait until he was out of earshot, Rita nudged Frankie in the ribs. 'Bloody hell, you're a dark horse. Where did you meet *that*?'

Turning around, Frankie watched as his figure disappeared into the darkness and felt a tinge of guilt. Maybe she did fly off the handle a bit there. Maybe he was only trying to help . . . She dismissed the thought as quickly as it had appeared. What was she thinking of? Of course he wasn't trying to help, he'd been gloating. He probably thought it was amusing that she was upset. He was that type. One of those clever, arrogant jerks. It was obvious he'd recognised her from the airport and thought he'd try winding her up. Cheeky sod, going on about how she'd been drunk. Well, OK, so she had been a bit, but what had it got to do with him?

'Well?' chivvied Rita impatiently, interrupting Frankie's thoughts.

'Oh, it's a long story,' she sighed wearily, and looked at her empty glass. 'Can we go home? I'm tired. Too much champagne.' Her head felt heavy and fuzzy.

'Oh . . . yeah, of course we can. We'll get a cab. Dorian never leaves a party before lunchtime.'

Trying to hide her disappointment at the distinct lack of juicy details, Rita linked arms with Frankie and steered her back through the party, towards the entrance and the line of waiting taxis. There was no point trying to get anything out of Frankie when she was in one of her moods, she thought, beckoning a cabbie, but on the other hand when had that ever stopped her.

'So what's his name?' Trying to sound blasé, she opened the door of the cab, gave the driver the address and clambered inside.

'Who?' asked Frankie, squeezing in next to her and slamming the door.

Fidgeting with her skirt, which had risen up to her waist, Rita huffed exasperatedly. Wasn't it obvious? What was wrong with Frankie? Had being dumped made her blind to mankind – and she was talking grade A mankind. 'That sexy bastard back there.' She motioned behind them as the taxi pulled out of the driveway.

'*Him?*' Frankie thought for a brief moment as they pulled on to Sunset and realised that, although she'd now had two rows with the guy, on both sides of the Atlantic, she didn't have a clue what his name was. 'I don't know,' she replied lamely.

Rita groaned with frustration. 'Well, whoever he is, he's bloody gorgeous.'

Closing her eyes, Frankie leaned her throbbing head against the back of the seat and didn't say anything. Bloody gorgeous? More like bloody-minded.

Back at the apartment, Frankie lay under the duvet. She couldn't sleep. Spread-eagled next to her was Rita, wearing black satin eyepatches and industrial-strength earplugs, her face smeared with wrinkle-removing, skin-tightening, pore-reducing, look-eighteen-again-for-only-eighty-dollars night cream. She was snoring faintly. Frankie listened to the rhythmic drone. She was used to sharing a bed with quiet-as-a-mouse Hugh, who would lie in the foetal position all night without stirring. Unlike Rita, who alternated farmyard animal impressions with bursts of kick-boxing.

Nursing a bruised shin, Frankie stared miserably up at the ceiling. It had started to rotate like the drum of a washing machine. She closed her eyes, thinking this might help. It didn't. It only made her more aware of the half-dozen glasses of champagne fizzing like battery acid in the pit of her stomach. Why the hell did she drink so much? At this rate her newly acquired status, single unemployed smoker, was fast turning into single unemployed *alcoholic* smoker. On second thoughts, single unemployed *depressed* alcoholic smoker was more like it. It was a sobering thought. But not as sobering as the parched, dry-as-a-bone thought that interrupted her self-pity by waving its arms in the air and gasping 'Water'.

Seized by her boozy thirst, she wriggled out of the futon, trying not to dislodge Fred and Ginger, who were curled up in two tight balls of fluff at the bottom of the duvet, and stumbled blindly across the bedroom, tripping up over Rita's discarded stilettos. Fuck, she cursed silently. Staggering upstairs to the kitchen, her arms outstretched in the darkness like a divining rod, she yanked open the door of the fridge.

It threw out bright light across the darkness of the open-plan kitchen and into the living room. Blinking as her eyes adjusted, she peered gingerly inside – Rita was not renowned for hygiene – but there was no sign of water, and she'd been told not to drink it from the tap (which ruled out clinging on to the sink, head upside down, hair trailing in the washing up as she clamped her mouth around the mixer tap). In fact the fridge was pretty much empty, apart from a mouldy old half-eaten Domino's pizza cowering on the top shelf and a bottle of some kind of thick green revolting-looking protein and vegetable shake called Defense Up. Frankie's stomach waved a white flag in horror, but dehydration and the threat of one hell of a hangover won the day. She took a tentative swig. It tasted like liquidised sprouts. Yeeuchh. She put it back. Defense Up was going to be thrown up if she drank any more.

Defeated, she retreated from the fridge and wandered across the living room to the sofa. Absent-mindedly she looked at her watch: midnight. Back in London it would be eight on a Monday morning. Hugh would still be asleep in bed. She closed her eyes, thinking about him. Any minute now his radio alarm would click on to Capital FM, and he'd lazily roll across the mattress, eyes still closed, and prop his head up against a pillow. And he'd lie there, not moving, until the news had finished, before opening his eyes, turning off the radio, climbing out of bed, stretching in front of the window, yawning twice, running his fingers through his flattened hair and sleepily rubbing his smooth chest. Then, clad only in a pair of Calvin Klein boxer shorts, he'd pad across the landing to the bathroom, check out his stomach in the mirror – full on, side view (relaxed and breathing in) – inspect for any nasal, ear or rogue eyebrow hair (removing any culprits quickly with his tweezers), before disappearing into the shower with the Aveda range for a good half an hour.

She sighed wistfully. His lengthy bathroom routine used to drive her mad, but now she missed it, as only a heartbroken ex-girlfriend could do. If she could just have him back, she swore she'd never get annoyed again. She'd never stand in her dressing gown, tugging at the shower curtain and moaning at him to get a move on, she'd never complain at all the little bits of dental floss she kept finding like wiggly white worms around the flat, she'd never tell him off for using the last of the moisturising conditioner – again. She missed him and she wanted him back.

Suffering both inside and out, she hugged her sofa-cushion boyfriend and stared vacantly at the debris on the coffee table. And that's when, amidst the jumble of magazines, tissues and clutter that followed Rita wherever she went, her eye fell on something. The telephone.

The temptation was too much. Reaching over, she picked up the handset. It was like holding a loaded gun. For a moment she hesitated . . . Should she pull the trigger?

Of course the answer was no, no, no, no. Don't Drink and Dial. But it was too late. There was silence on the other end of the line. Then a ringing tone. Her mouth went dry and she tried to swallow. She waited.

Suddenly there was a click and the sound of a voice. 'Hello?' It was Hugh.

Her heart raced. Her mouth seemed to seize up. The phone felt like a grenade in the palm of her hand.

'Hello?' His voice again. This time more impatient.

She had to speak. She wanted to speak . . . 'Hugh, it's me, Frankie,' she blurted out, the desperation in her voice scotching any hopes she might have had of playing it cool.

'Frankie?' One word. Two syllables. From that she had to try and work out if he was pleased, pissed off, excited, concerned, sad, *missing her*. He didn't wait for her to answer. 'Where are you?'

'Los Angeles.'

'*What?*'

She could hear him scrabbling about, and the radio providing the background music was switched off. 'What did you say?'

'I said I'm in LA.' She tried to steady her quivering voice.

'*LA?*' His voice rose an octave. 'What the hell are you doing there?' (Was that concern, annoyance or jealousy? She wasn't sure.)

'I'm staying with Rita.' Damn. Why hadn't she said something witty, clever, funny? Why hadn't she breezed, '*I'm having the time of my life.*' Her eyes started to well up with tears. Probably because she was having the shittiest time of her life. 'I miss you.' Shit, shit, shit. *What was she doing?* She had to be strong – cool – collected. 'I miss you so much.' The words tumbled out as she started to cave in. And now she was crying. She could almost hear any points she might have gained by flouncing off to LA being scrubbed off, one by one, with each sniffle.

Hugh didn't say anything. There was an awkward pause. She heard more fumbling in the background, the sound of a door closing. 'Look, this isn't a good time to talk. I'm getting ready for work and I'm running late.'

Frankie looked at her watch. Five past eight UK time. Normally he'd be doing the stomach thing in the bathroom mirror.

'I'll call you back.' He sounded so official. As if he was arranging a business meeting.

'When?' she stabbed, the alarm ringing loudly in her voice. By this point she was past trying to remain cool and aloof. She white-knuckled the handset.

'Soon.'

She wanted to shriek, '*What day? What time?*' so she could stay in the apartment glued to the phone. But of course she didn't. Instead she gave him her number. Twice.

Then he said goodbye and put the phone down. Just like that.

Puffy-eyed, she stared dismally at the receiver. She knew Hugh was never going to ring back. Deep down she'd known that even when she was giving him her number, but she'd so desperately wanted to believe him. As desperately as she'd wanted him to say that he'd made a terrible mistake, that he loved her, wanted to marry her and spend the rest of his life with her. But Hugh hadn't said any of those things. And she knew he wasn't going to. This wasn't one of those movies she used to watch with her mum, with their soft-focus, saccharine-sweet, girl-gets-boy happy endings. This was real life. Her life. No life.

Clutching the phone tightly to her chest, she curled into a ball, burrowed her head into the sofa and sobbed her bloody heart out.

12

'Who was that?'

'Oh, just a friend.'

Walking back into the bedroom, Hugh put the phone down and leaned across the crumpled duvet, brushing his hand across the pair of 34A breasts belonging to the young skinny blonde he'd met last night at Adam and Jessica's engagement party. She was lying naked in his bed, her St Tropez tan smeared over his pillowcases and the twin peaks of her Wonderbra lying, like two black lacy yoghurt pots, on the carpet.

'Why are they ringing so early?' The blonde opened one smudged-mascara eye and peered at Hugh, who was engrossed with playing with her nipples, twiddling them backwards and forwards between finger and thumb as if he was trying to tune in a radio. Why did men always think that turned women on? She stifled a yawn. She had such a stinker of a hangover. All she wanted to do was go back to sleep.

'Ummm, who knows?' replied Hugh, putting one of her nipples in his mouth and sucking determinedly as if it was a boiled sweet.

Talk about bad timing. He'd woken up feeling horny and had just been in the middle of groping the blonde when the phone rang. At first he wasn't going to answer it, but he'd had second thoughts. It could be work-related. It wasn't. It was Frankie, crying down the phone and telling him how much she missed him. Which was the last thing he wanted to hear when he was trying to shag some girl he'd picked up at a party.

Not that the phone call had come as a surprise. He'd been expecting it ever since he'd come home to the flat and discovered she'd packed her bags and disappeared with those bloody cats. To be honest, that had been a surprise. He'd assumed she'd be waiting for him when he got home, wanting to talk for hours, trying to persuade him to change his mind. He never thought she'd just move out without saying a word. And not only that, but move to Los Angeles. He'd thought she'd stay at her parents', or on somebody's sofa, but never *Los Angeles*.

He couldn't believe it. Frankie was normally so sensible. She never made a rash decision, was always so cautious about everything. This was totally so unlike her – and LA of all places, it just wasn't her style, she'd hate it. In fact she'd probably be home in no time. She was obviously really upset, but what could he do? Like Adam said, he shouldn't feel guilty about what had happened. OK, the timing could have been better, what with her losing her job and all that, but what else could he have done? They'd been going out for nearly two years and they'd had some really good times, but at the end of the day he was only thirty-two. He wasn't ready to settle down and get married, and that's what Frankie wanted. Apart from Adam, most of his mates were single and always going out on the piss, having a laugh, pulling women. He'd been missing out.

He squeezed the blonde's breasts, as if they were a couple of ripe plums. Here he was, about to get his end away, and he was thinking about Frankie. What the hell was he doing? He shoved all thoughts of her and the phone call to the back of his mind. He'd think about it some other time. Right now he had more important matters to hand.

With the resurrection of his hard-on, his boxer shorts began to strain uncomfortably. He tried to casually wriggle out of them. It wasn't easy. He managed to get them past his hips but then the elastic waistband wedged around his knees.

'Are you sure it wasn't your girlfriend?'

The blonde was suspicious. The flat was very tidy for a bachelor, and she had found a pair of eyebrow tweezers on the shelf in the bathroom.

Hugh was starting to feel frustrated. He'd now been single for over forty-eight hours and he was desperate to celebrate his new-found freedom. Last night the blonde had seemed up for it, flirting with him at the bar, letting him have a bit of a grope in the taxi, agreeing to come in for coffee. And then of course, when they'd got off with each other, he'd thought it was in the bag, right up until just before the grand finale, when she'd suddenly played the modesty card, saying they hardly knew each other, and he'd had to make do with a hand job. Now she wanted to lie in his bed and talk about Frankie. He hadn't invited her back to *talk*, for God's sake.

'No, it was a friend, OK?' he snapped impatiently.

Disgruntled, the blonde tutted sulkily and pulled the duvet tightly around her.

Realising that he wasn't going to be celebrating anything if he wasn't careful, Hugh quickly changed tack and kissed the end of her nose. 'Come on, Carol. Don't you like me?' he whispered in his best baby-talk whine, kissing the side of her face, her neck, along her collarbone, nibbling at her ear lobe.

'It's Cheryl,' pouted the blonde moodily, hanging resolutely on to the duvet.

'I meant Cheryl,' cooed Hugh between gritted teeth, edging himself further on top of her.

The blonde lay stiffly beneath him. Christ, this was hard work, thought Hugh, remembering the warm, easy, comfortable sex he'd enjoyed with Frankie. He stepped up his efforts. 'Mmm, you're just so gorgeous,' he continued, kissing her neck, throwing in a few moans for good measure. 'Mmmm ... mmmm.'

Tireless in his pursuit of a shag, he was determined to hang on in there – he glanced at his watch – well, at least for another five minutes. After all, he didn't want to be late for the office.

Luckily it didn't take that long. Like a doctor trying to find signs of life, he suddenly felt her move ever so slightly beneath him, as if she was starting to respond to his valiant attempts at resuscitation. Feeling success at his fingertips, he increased the moans.

'Aren't you getting a little hot under there?' he whispered, tugging at the duvet. She loosened her grip and, with a quick jerk as if he was a magician pulling away the tablecloth, he finally freed both the duvet and his boxer shorts and squashed his naked body triumphantly against hers.

'I really like you, Cheryl,' he murmured, moving in for the kill. 'You're just so different from other girls.'

'I bet you say that to all the girls,' she protested, but it was somewhat half-hearted.

'No, it's true, honestly. I think you're amazing. And I'm not just saying that because I want to make love to you –' that sounded so much better than shag – 'because if you don't want to make love, that's OK.' Just as long as you tell me now, so I can cut the crap and get ready for work.

'Hmm, that's what all blokes say,' gasped the blonde as Hugh stealthily edged his fingers up her inner thighs. She was beginning to sound doubtful.

'No, seriously, I've never felt like this before. It's not as if I sleep around, you know. I'm the kind of guy that wants to be in a relationship.'

Christ, if Frankie could hear him now. There was a pause. The blonde was definitely weakening. It must have been the relationship bit that did it.

'And I'd really like it if you and me could get to know each other better . . . a lot better.' Lay it on with a trowel – thickly – quickly.

'You do?'

He could almost hear the key in the lock turning. He was getting closer ... and closer ... Her legs were being eased apart.

'In fact I think you're the kind of girl I could fall in love with.' It was his final, last-ditch effort. It worked.

'Ooohhh.'

Like a champagne cork popping out of a bottle, the blonde let out an explosive shriek and grabbed firmly hold of his buttocks ...

Bull's-eye.

Hugh grinned triumphantly. She'd fallen for it. He'd cracked it. He was in.

13

'I don't know how to tell you this, but I'm three months pregnant,' blurted Rita. She looked at Frankie, her bottom lip quivering.

'*Pregnant?*'

Rita nodded tearfully. 'And it's twins.'

'My God,' whispered Frankie.

'But there's something else.' Rita paused to wipe a tear that had rolled down her cheek. 'The doctors have told me I've only six months to live.'

Silence. 'Well, what do you think?' asked Rita, flinging the script for *Malibu Motel* on top of the restaurant's menu.

'I think the part's yours.' Frankie smiled. 'After tomorrow's audition it's going to be Goodbye, unemployed actress and Hello, soap star. You were great, honestly.'

'I was?' Rita grinned happily, feeling very pleased with herself. 'So you think I was believable?'

'No,' smirked Frankie, 'but isn't that the whole point? You're auditioning for an American daytime soap. And, from the ones I've seen back home on Channel 5, they're not exactly what you'd call realistic, are they?' Picking up the script, she flicked through the first few pages, running her eyes across the blurb at the top of each page. 'I mean, your character, Kimberley Kartier, is supposed to be pregnant with twins and dying of a mystery illness, yet she's still got time to murder her husband, have an affair with her best friend's fiancé and run a successful fashion empire. Talk about busy. What's she going to do next? Run for president?'

'I dunno,' shrugged Rita, topping up the water in their glasses. 'Probably wake up in the shower and realise it was all a dream.'

There was a moment's pause before they both burst out laughing, sending mouthfuls of water spraying all over the table.

They were sitting outside Hankerings Restaurant on Sunset Plaza, a pocket of desirable restaurants, trendy cafés and chic boutiques full of shoppers, diners and – unusual for LA – pedestrians that provided a bustling oasis in the middle of the traffic-laden, deserted-pavement, concrete wilderness of Sunset Boulevard. By sheer luck – and without knowing anyone in 'the industry' – they'd managed to bag one of the more desirable tables outside, where you could see and be seen.

And there was plenty to see. Hankerings was heaving with LA's glamorama: directors and producers were talking big-budget movies across colossal Caesar salads; Beverly Hills wives, who'd been sliced more times than a Tesco's loaf, were swapping surgeons' cards over glasses of Pellegrino and peering into their gold Chanel compacts to check on last month's facelift scars; young, gym-honed execs were sitting by themselves eating bowls of penne arrabbiata and cutting deals into their cellphone earpiece; while, in the far corner, trying to hide under a giant parasol and a baseball cap, one of Hollywood's most famous actresses was picking at a plate of no-oil, no-salt, no-flavour fish and steamed vegetables. Desperate to shift that last seven pounds for her next million-dollar movie role, she was on the third week of her protein zone diet, which explained why she was staring jealously at the overflowing bowl of fries, glowing in all its unhealthy greasiness, which wafted past her to one of the other tables. The other table being, of course, Rita and Frankie's. After all, who else would order fried food in LA?

Frankie had been in LA for a week, but instead of playing the tourist and exploring the city's attractions, she'd stayed in the apartment, crying over Hugh. He'd never called back, even though she hadn't left the apartment, holding the phone hostage, waiting and waiting for it to ring. She knew it was pathetic, and she knew she should try and get over him, but she couldn't, it was impossible. She'd never thought she could miss someone so much. All she wanted to do was lie in bed and sob her heart out. Except finally Rita wouldn't let her. She had other ideas about how to deal with heartbreak. Like French fries.

Leaning back in her chair, Frankie shielded her eyes from the bright Californian sunshine and looked around her. It was difficult to take it all in. Today was a Monday lunchtime, in the middle of October. Usually she'd be pushing through harassed shoppers on a rainy Oxford Street, trying to grab a quick coffee and a sandwich at Pret à Manger, before rushing back to the office. Instead she was in Los Angeles, sitting at some trendy, film-starry restaurant with her best mate, getting a suntan and playing 'spot the celebrity' and 'I-Spy the surgery'. It was unreal.

She smiled to herself. Rita was right, she did feel better, but it was LA, not food, that was responsible for her change in mood. With so much going on around her, it was difficult to wallow in thoughts about Hugh, even though she wanted to. Squinting in the sunshine, she watched the people around her in fascination – and learned LA Rule Number One: *Sunglasses must be worn at all times.*

Whether they were tortoiseshell Persols, blacked-out Ray-Bans, gilt-edged Chanels or fashionistas Prada, Frankie noticed, everybody was wearing a pair. Everybody, that was, except her. She'd left hers in a drawer somewhere in Hugh's flat. God knows where. She hadn't worn them since their holiday in Spain, when Hugh had left her by the pool every day and gone off to play golf. In London it was umbrellas, not sunglasses, that were the order of the day. But here in LA, the only umbrellas she could see were blue and white striped ones, fixed to each and every table to provide shade from the glorious weather.

Lost in a sea of designer shades and feeling like the English tourist that she was, she closed her eyes and tilted her face to the sun. This was another world. As if she'd stepped through the wardrobe into Narnia, only to discover Hollywood was doing a sequel and had renamed it La La Land. Feeling the warmth on her face, she smiled contentedly. Maybe she could get used to this. Beginning to feel better, she made a mental note to buy some sunglasses.

'Mmm, they look delicious,' sighed Rita, salivating as the waiter plonked a huge portion of curly fries in the middle of the table. 'Can I nick one?'

'Help yourself,' said Frankie, breaking from her daydreams and opening her eyes. 'Didn't you order any?'

'No, I'm still on a diet,' groaned Rita, dipping a corkscrew fry in a gloop of ketchup. 'But just one won't hurt, will it?' It was a rhetorical question, she didn't want to know the answer. She wolfed it down and licked her fingers. 'Not as good as the chippy, but still delicious,' she said, a look of divine rapture on her face. 'They'd be even better with gravy.'

Frankie shook her head. Ever since she'd known her, Rita had been dieting, vowing each and every time that this was it, that in four weeks she was going to be able to get her bum into that pair of size 10 jeans she'd worn on her twenty-first birthday. Ten years, and hundreds of broken diets later, she still couldn't get the aforementioned Levi's past her knees. Nor did it help that she was allergic to any form of exercise unless, of course, it involved a bloke and took place in the bedroom . . . over the kitchen table . . . in the back of the car . . .

'What did you order?' Frankie nibbled a fry. Normally she tried to stick to a healthy low-fat diet – she was on first-name terms with the Marks & Spencer Count On Us range – but what the hell. A few fries wouldn't kill her. And even if they did, so what? After last night's phone call, death by calories might be a welcome escape from the alternative: life without Hugh.

'Salad.' Rita wrinkled up her nose as if there was a nasty smell. As if on cue, a giant-size bowl of lettuce appeared in front of her.

'Is that it?' Frankie peered at the bowl. There wasn't a tomato, cucumber or stick of celery in sight. Just an unappetising mountain of iceberg lettuce.

'Yep.' Rita speared bravely with her fork. 'It was supposed to be a Chinese chicken and noodle salad, but I asked for no chicken, no noodles and dressing on the side.'

'Why?' Frankie was still a newcomer to the LA school of thought.

'Look around you.' Rita waved a forkful of lettuce in the air. 'Every woman in this town's stick thin. And do you want to know why?' Her voice started getting louder as she clambered on to her soap box. 'Because they're all actresses, models, singers. If they're not, they want to be . . . and the camera adds ten pounds. Believe me, you've got to look like a bloody lollipop to get anywhere.' She looked down at her skintight T-shirt and prodded her spare tyre. 'I'm going to have to lose some weight.' She shook her head decisively, jangling her dangly earrings. Munching like a rabbit, she eyed Frankie's chips like a starving child. 'Still, you don't have to worry, do you? You're tall and skinny. Lucky sod.'

Frankie pulled a face. 'Big deal. It's hardly a guarantee for success, is it? Look at me. My boyfriend's dumped me, I've been sacked—'

'Made redundant,' corrected Rita.

'OK, redundant, I'm living out of a suitcase—'

'You're living with me.'

Frankie ignored her. 'Anyway, I'm hardly a walking advert for fortune and happiness, am I?'

Rita refused to be convinced. 'You're still 126 pounds. God, I'd give anything to be 126 pounds.' She looked dreamily into the distance.

'Being 126 pounds didn't do me much good, did it? It didn't make Hugh love me.' Shit, there she went again. Thinking about Hugh. It was so difficult not to.

'What? And being 140 pounds would?'

Frankie had to smile. It was impossible not to with Rita around. 'Oh, well, never mind. At least there's some consolation in making a complete fool of myself when I made that drunken phone call. It's made me realise it really is over between us . . . for him anyway.'

Dipping a fry in ketchup, she drew a loveheart on her plate. 'You're right. I'm going to have to just get on with my life and try to forget about him.'

'Exactly.' Rita nodded. 'You need to start dating.'

'Oh, I don't know about that.'

But Rita wasn't going to be put off at the first hurdle. 'What about that gorgeous bloke from the party?' Raising her eyebrows, she gave Frankie one of her looks.

'You must be joking. That scruffy American. He's definitely not my type.' Frankie suddenly realised she could protest too much. 'And anyway, it's miles too soon,' she added hastily.

Trying to imagine life without Hugh was hard enough, imagining life with someone else was bloody impossible.

'Hmm, well, don't leave it too long. Trying to find a decent bloke's like trying to find a bargain in the sales. If you don't get a move on, you'll get left with all the crap that no one else wants.' Ignoring her salad, Rita polished off a few more fries. She comforted herself with the thought that she was surrogate comfort-eating for Frankie. 'LA's full of fellas, but you've got to be careful. Believe me, there's some funny types out there.'

'*Beepbebebeepbeep.*' The hooting of a car horn interrupted their conversation, heralding the arrival of Dorian's Mercedes convertible, which swept along the pavement in front of the restaurant and pulled up behind a bright red Ferrari. '*Beepbeep.*'

Looking at Frankie, Rita raised her eyebrows. 'See what I mean?'

14

'Good afternoon, girls.'

Waving jovially, Dorian turned off the ignition, pulled down the sun visor and began rearranging his windswept hair, trying to cover his thinning patch. Cuddling up next to him in the passenger seat was a scantily clad bronzed brunette who was giggling loudly and trying to hold on to Elvis, Dorian's shih-tzu, who was yapping impatiently and trying to wriggle free.

Frankie glanced at Rita. 'Who's that?' she mouthed, motioning with her eyes towards the girl who was tickling Dorian's neck as he fussed with his fringe.

'God knows,' Rita shrugged. She could never keep track of Dorian's ever-changing assortment of women, none of whom appeared to have been chosen for their personality.

Intrigued, they watched as Dorian gathered together his collection of mobiles, sunglasses, silver attaché case and the aforementioned brunette. Clambering out of the car, he released Elvis's extendable leash, letting him scamper across the pavement towards Rita and Frankie, wagging his tail. Dorian followed closely behind in his fur coat, his arm wrapped tightly around the leggy brunette's exposed midriff. Even in LA, their unconventional appearance caused a ripple of glances.

'Mind if we join you?'

Without waiting for an answer, Dorian pulled up a chair and, only when he was satisfied that enough people were looking at him, did he oh so casually press his car's remote control. Frankie watched in fascination as the compartment at the back of the Mercedes electronically opened and out popped the black leather hood. It started to unfold like a bat's wing and, pointing skywards, stretched across the roof of the car before silently clicking into place. It was posey, but impressive. And it sure as hell beat Hugh's VW Golf GTI.

Dorian, meanwhile, pretended not to notice. Instead he hungrily grabbed a bread roll, ripped off a piece and scooped up a large dollop of the complimentary olive pâté. 'Oh, by the way, this is Jamie. Jamie, meet Rita and Frankie, my neighbours.'

'Hi,' twanged Jamie, manically chewing gum and looking not the least bit interested.

Rita smiled thinly, while Frankie tried not to stare at her dishevelled hair, creased outfit and smudged make-up. She looked as if she'd been up all night. She had.

'Jamie and I have just come straight from a party at the Playboy mansion,' boasted Dorian, looking very pleased with himself. King of the social circuit, he reigned supreme. 'What happened to you two lightweights? You were invited . . .' Licking his lips, he wolfed down the rest of the herb and garlic focaccia.

'I was tired,' explained Frankie sheepishly, wishing she could sound all hip and trendy, and not like a twenty-nine-going on ninety-nine-year-old.

'So, was it any good?' quizzed Rita, eyeing the brunette with suspicion. She noted that her midriff was nut brown and ironing-board flat. Not a freckle or bulge in sight. It was sickening. She stopped stealing fries and had another attempt at tackling the lettuce mountain.

'Well, if you call partying until dawn, playing strip poker and ending up in the jacuzzi with some of Hollywood's most beautiful women good, then yes it was. Very good indeed.

It's a shame you weren't there. The more the merrier.' He squeezed Jamie's thigh. 'We had a fucking fabulous time time, didn't we, Jamie?'

Jamie giggled jitteringly, pulling the gum from between her teeth with her long manicured talons and letting it snap back.

'I think we had a lucky escape,' mumbled Rita drily.

'Believe me, you don't know what you were missing.' He winked suggestively.

Dorian had been trying to get Rita into bed for the last three months, but so far she'd resisted his charms. God knows how. It must be something about that English stiff upper lip. Not that he dwelled upon it. Dorian's attention span rivalled that of a goldfish. He quickly glanced from Rita to the menu.

'Now, what shall I eat? I'm ravenous.' Rolling his r's, he shook out a white linen napkin with a flourish, tucked it tightly into his collar and clicked his fingers for service.

Frankie stared. She'd never met anyone like him. He reminded her of one of those characters she'd seen on documentaries about Hollywood who are so OTT they don't seem real. She'd always been convinced they were actors hired by the producer to make the viewers back in the UK shake their heads and say how wacky and wild everyone was in California. But Dorian wasn't playing a part. He was for real. She looked at him, dressed like a polar bear and soaking up the sun like a solar panel, in amazement. Wasn't he hot?

'Don't you want to take off your jacket?' she suggested. It was 80 degrees *and he was wearing a fur coat.*

'No, I'm fine,' he lied. He was sweltering, but this was Los Angeles. Appearances were more important than comfort.

'Hi, my name is Julie and I am your waitress.' A strawberry blonde appeared by the table in white bobby socks, trainers and orthodontic braces. 'Would you like to order anything from the menu, sir?' She rattled off her spiel, smiling brightly, notepad at the ready.

Snapping upright like a spring, Dorian grinned at her. 'I'd like a double helping of you, please, with no dressing.' He flirted outrageously, regardless of the brunette, who'd slung herself around his shoulders. Not that she noticed. Coked up and spaced out, she was there in body, not in mind.

Julie the waitress was taken aback. 'I'm afraid that's not available, sir . . . but perhaps you would like to order something from the menu?'

As an out-of-work actress she'd learned her waitress lines off by heart, but nobody had warned her about the possibility of improvisation. By deviating from the usual 'I'll have . . .' Dorian had thrown her well-rehearsed dialogue into disarray.

Frankie watched her grinning and blinking. She was like a robot malfunctioning.

'Oh . . .' Dorian pretended to look disappointed. 'Well, in that case I'll have to make do with my regular. Yvonne the maître d' knows just how I like it.' It was his best attempt at a *double entendre*, but it seemed lost on Julie, who beamed blankly. 'And I'd like a plate of smoked salmon for Elvis.' Bending down he tickled the dog, who was sweltering in the heat and trying to find shade under the table.

'And for you, madam?' Julie the waitress finished jotting her order down on her notepad and, not to be put off by the earlier misunderstanding, beamed eagerly at Jamie. She looked so happy to be serving customers, she was almost bursting with enthusiasm. As if nothing could satisfy her more than ordering coffee, bringing extra cutlery or filling up their glasses with iced water. Jamie shook her head. Despite her suntan, she'd suddenly gone as white as the tablecloth. What she wanted wasn't on the menu either. Excusing herself, she set off unsteadily towards the loos, followed closely by Rita, who was determined to quiz her for diet tips – she had a sneaky feeling that midriff hadn't been achieved by lettuce alone.

Julie the waitress wasn't about to be deterred. 'Anything else, sir?'

Dorian narrowed his eyes (he would have twiddled the ends of his moustache if he'd had one). 'Don't tempt me.'

The waitress scuttled away, ponytail swinging, bobby socks bobbing, leaving Dorian and Frankie by themselves. He flicked his attention to Frankie, who was staring into space, daydreaming about Hugh.

'So tell me, why the long face?'

Frankie jumped, realising she'd been rumbled. 'How much time do you have?' Feeling awkward at being put on the spot, she looked down at her plate. It was empty. She decided not to eat for the rest of the day. The LA thin-bug was catching.

'It can't be that bad. You're here in Los Angeles, what more do you want?'

His cheery dismissal of a situation about which he knew nothing annoyed her.

'My ex-boyfriend, a job and some money,' she snapped. She couldn't help it. He reminded her of one of those builders who always shout, 'Cheer up, love, it might never happen' when it already has.

Dorian didn't take offence. 'Well, I can't do much about your love life, but if money's a problem ...' Pulling out a huge wad of hundred-dollar bills from his wallet, he fanned through it like a pack of cards. 'How much do you need?'

'Oh, God, no.' Frankie put her hand on his. 'Thanks, but I didn't mean that.' She felt embarrassed for being so grumpy when he was only trying to be nice. 'No, I meant that I needed to earn some money. Get a job.' It was the first time she'd really thought about it, but considering she only had forty quid – the grand total of what was in her bank account when she'd paid a visit to the NatWest cash machine at Heathrow – and Hugh wasn't begging her to come home, she was going to be staying in LA for longer than she thought, in which case she needed a job.

'Have you got a green card?'

Frankie shook her head. Not unless he counted the Andie MacDowell DVD that was still probably wedged down the back of the sofa in London.

'Hmm, tricky . . .' He watched her face fall before adding, 'But not impossible.' Never one to say no to a female, Dorian flicked open his phone and tapped away in earnest concentration – with his extensive range of electronic gizmos, he rather fancied himself as a Bond kind of figure – and made a call. 'Good afternoon, it's Dorian,' he chirped into his silver cellphone. 'Do you still need someone for tomorrow . . . You do? Excellent, I've got the perfect person. A wonderful girl. Beautiful, talented, intelligent . . .'

Frankie cringed. Was he being serious?

'No, this isn't one of my jokes. Do you want her or not?' Silence then he chortled knowingly. 'And she's cheap.'

What the hell was he saying? She began to feel worried.

'Fabulous . . .' Wedging the phone in the crook of his neck, he scribbled something down on his notepad. 'Perfect . . . Do you want to speak to her . . . Oh, OK.' He snapped the handset shut and slapped it down on the table triumphantly.

'Who was that?' Rita reappeared from the loos, catching the end of the conversation. She sat down and stared inquisitively at Dorian. Years of being the office gossip had taken their toll. She hated to think something was going on that she didn't know about.

'A friend of a friend.' Dorian was being deliberately vague, milking the intrigue.

'*And?*' She spoke for Frankie, who'd been struck dumb by the speed of the *fait accompli*.

'He couldn't talk, he was in the middle of a shoot.' Dabbing remnants of olive pâté from his lips with the napkin, Dorian calmly tore the page from his pad and, deliberately bypassing an agitated Rita, rested it on top of Frankie's empty plate. 'The details are on there.'

Frankie stared blankly at the page. She was taken aback. Talking about getting a job was one thing, but suddenly having one presented to her, quite literally on a plate, was another matter. It made being in Los Angeles suddenly more real. More definite. It meant she wasn't a tourist any more. 'What's the job?' she mumbled, suddenly finding her voice.

'Photographer's assistant. His regular one is sick, tonsillitis I think.' Dorian pulled a face. 'So how good are you at putting up a tripod?'

Before she had time to answer, Julie the waitress reappeared, brandishing Dorian's pasta carbonara as if it was a trophy. Looking very pleased with herself, she was just about to bring the plate into land when Dorian waved his arms in the air like air-traffic control and cooed apologetically, 'I'm sorry, sweetie, I'm running late. I'll have it to go.'

Julie the waitress looked gutted. Her moment of glory had been stolen, her hopes of grinding the black pepper and sprinkling the Parmesan dashed.

As she slunk back to the kitchen, Dorian glanced at his state-of-the-art digital watch. He never spent more than half an hour in one place and his time was up. He was ready to leave. Flashing a smile, he stood up, dropping a hundred bill on the table, as if it was nothing more than a bus ticket. 'Please excuse me, girls, business calls.' Gathering up his ensemble, he tucked Elvis under his arm and scanned the table as if he'd forgotten something.

'Jamie,' prompted Rita.

As if on cue, she reappeared, sashaying and sniffling through the middle of the restaurant with a new lease of life, and planted a kiss on Dorian's cheek. He puffed out his chest proudly and, linking arms, they swept out of the restaurant, wafting past Julie the waitress, who stood on the sidelines holding his take-out like one of those devoted groupies who offer drinks to marathon runners. They slid into his car and sped off in the direction of Melrose Avenue.

'Well, at least something good's happened. It looks like you've just got yourself a job.'

Watching them disappear, Rita pushed the pile of lettuce to one side. Sod salad. After a trip to the loo, it appeared Jamie's size 4 figure was a result of what she shoved up her nose, not in her mouth. Frankie nodded, looking worried. She didn't know if she should be happy or not. Her, a photographer's assistant? Her knowledge of photography consisted of two things: point the camera and push the button. She looked at the ripped-off piece of paper and read it out loud.

'Enterprise Studios. Eight a.m. Reilly.'

'*Reilly*,' repeated Rita. 'Unusual name. That must be the photographer, your new boss. I wonder what he's like.'

Frankie bit her lip as her stomach released a cage of butterflies. 'God knows.'

15

Driving down Laurel Canyon at six thirty the next morning, Frankie was having a serious attack of second thoughts. In fact she was way past second and through third, fourth and fifth. What the hell was she thinking of, agreeing to be some photographer's assistant? She hadn't spent three years at university studying for an English degree, and eight years struggling to climb up the publishing ladder, to carry tripods and lug cameras around. She was a features writer. A professional person with a frizz-eased bob who wore smart trousersuits or, ever since she'd got her new job at *Lifestyle*, skirts and a lovely pair of Russell & Bromley knee-length boots. *Correction*: she used to be a features writer. Now she was an illegal alien, forced to work cash in hand, scrape her hair into an unflattering ponytail and wear scruffy jeans, a sweatshirt and a pair of mouldy old trainers.

The tune of Sting's 'English Man in New York' came on the radio and, changing the words to 'She's an English girl in LA' she sang them through gritted teeth as she anxiously gripped the steering wheel of the Thunderbird, on loan from Rita, and concentrated on weaving her way around bend after heart in the mouth bend, her foot glued to the brake pedal. *Bloodyhellbloodyhellbloodyhell*. She was in her best friend's most prized possession – two tons of baby-blue and white fin-tailed metal which felt about thirty feet long and ten feet wide. It was not – repeat not – like driving Rita's Mini.

A set of traffic lights loomed ominously ahead. They were green. Silently she prayed they wouldn't change so she could blindly follow the stream of traffic turning right. Her prayers went unanswered. *Ssshhhiiittt*. Stamping on the brakes, she skidded out on a limb to the front of the queue, feeling as if the whole world was staring at her. With her heart playing the bongos, she gingerly looked around her. Although it was early in the morning it was like being in the rush hour: two lanes of traffic to the right, four in front, two to the left. There was no way out, but forwards.

'*Stay on the right, stay on the right* . . .' She repeated Rita's highway code advice like a mantra. Behind her a big four-wheel-drive with fuck-off tyres honked his horn menacingly. Oh, shit, Rita mentioned something about being able to turn right on a red light – *didn't she?* She couldn't remember. She hesitated. There was a fanfare of horns. Oh, sod it. Taking her life in her very sweaty hands, she put her foot down and lurched forwards. 'Uninsured British driving coming through,' she hissed under her breath, veering right and accelerating down Sunset. Phew, she'd made it. One false move and she could find herself up someone's exhaust, causing whiplash, being sued for millions . . . By the time she was pulling into the studios, her imagination had got carried away and she was being sentenced to ten years in prison for reckless driving.

The car park was jammed. Huge silver lorries carrying lighting equipment, trailers full of props, a dozen different types of four-wheel-drive vehicles and lots of other American cars that she didn't know the name of had taken every available space apart from a tiny one in the corner marked COMPACT. Well, that ruled her out. She was driving a bloody cruiseliner. She circled the car park for five minutes on the lookout for somewhere to park, getting more and more desperate – and more and more dizzy. It was nearly eight o'clock and the last thing she wanted was to be late.

Beginning to panic, she scanned the car park one last time for signs of life. *Wait a minute* ... In her rear-view mirror she suddenly caught sight of a cream-coloured Honda Civic pulling out of a space at the far end. Hurrah! With a whoosh of relief, she grabbed the automatic gear stick, rammed the car into reverse and stamped on the accelerator. The engine whined as she shot backwards. Nearly there ... nearly there ...

The sudden jolt, jerking her forward in her seat belt, was simultaneous with the sound of crunching metal and break-ing glass. 'What the ...?' She looked in her rear-view mirror. And couldn't believe it. Rammed into the back of her was some bloody great big Bronco truck thingy. *Fuck.* Like knocking over the first domino, her emotions began toppling forward. Anger taking over first. What a stupid idiot! The driver had obviously been trying to nick her space and had crashed right into her. Hadn't he seen her reversing? Hadn't he been looking? It was obviously a man. She knew she was being sexist, but right now she didn't give a monkey's about being politically correct. Her car was a wreck. *She was a nerv-ous wreck.* Her anger fell into horror – she'd crashed Rita's pride and joy, Rita was going to kill her; and then panic – she wasn't insured, what was she going to do?; and ended with fear – how the hell was she going to pay for the repairs?

Putting her head in her hands, she leaned against the steering wheel, feeling the tears welling up – again. Just when she'd thought things couldn't get any worse, this had to happen. She took a few deep breaths to try and calm her nerves, and heard the door of the Bronco slam shut. With a sense of impending doom, she listened to the footsteps stomping across the tarmac, growing closer ...

'You crazy fucking idiot,' she heard a man's voice shouting.
She wanted to hide. She couldn't.

Knuckles rapped against her car window, making her jump. 'What the hell were you doing? Didn't you see me?'

Filled with trepidation, Frankie lifted her head and looked sideways at the irate motorist. Even though she knew it wasn't her fault, she felt as if she should apologise. But as their eyes locked through the glass she changed her mind. '*You*.' Their voices were in stereo. Frankie stared in disbelief. It couldn't be . . . It wasn't . . . Yep, it was. Him again.

Frankie was stunned. Of all the people in Los Angeles, she'd had to bump into that bloody American from the airport again, and literally. After a moment's silence, she found her voice. 'I should have known it was you. Do you make a habit of nicking things off other people?' She'd definitely decided against apologising.

'What?' He couldn't hear through the glass.

She wound down the window. 'My space.' She motioned to the space that was now the scene of the accident. 'You were trying to steal my space, weren't you?' She wasn't going to let him say it was her fault, not after the last two times.

'What the hell are you talking about? It's not your space. And anyway, you should look where you're going. If you can't drive, you shouldn't be at the wheel of that museum piece.' He looked in disgust at Rita's Thunderbird, which was now less fin-tailed and more hammer-tailed. Pieces of the car were lying on the ground. Flakes of paint were falling on to the tarmac like confetti.

'This wasn't my fault, you know. It was yours, you weren't looking where you were going.' She glared at him, trying to stand her ground when her legs were shaking. He was wearing that stupid hat again. No wonder he couldn't see.

He sneered. 'Hey, I wasn't the one who reversed into you.'

'No, you were the one who drove into me.'

They dead-eyed each other. They were having another row. Sighing in exasperation, he took off his hat and ran his fingers through his flattened hair. This was becoming a habit. A bad habit.

'Look, I can't stand around arguing, I've got a job to do.'

'Me too,' retorted Frankie. Shit. The job. She'd forgotten all about it.

'So I guess we should swap names and numbers. *For insurance purposes.*' He emphasised the words.

Frankie felt her stomach flip. With her British accent, he obviously suspected that she wasn't insured. She watched as he felt around in the back pocket of his faded Levi's that hung on his hips, two sizes too big, and inside his battered leather jacket that was ripped down one arm, and decided to bluff it. Well, she wasn't going to tell him the truth, was she? They were hardly on the best of terms. He'd probably take great delight in calling the cops and having her slung in jail. Her insides turned to ice. Perhaps her imagination hadn't got carried away, perhaps it had been a premonition.

Eventually he produced an old leaking biro that was chewed at the end. She stared at it. Trust him to have a pen like that. An image of Hugh's Mont Blanc, which he kept clipped on his inside breast pocket, flashed through her mind.

'OK, what's your name?'

'Frankie . . . Frankie Pickles.' She reeled off Rita's telephone number, feeling her cheeks burning with guilty fear.

He scribbled it down on the inside of a packet of matches and then, tearing off the edge, wrote his. He poked it through the window. 'Here's mine.'

Snatching the piece of cardboard from him with a shaky hand, she glanced at it. And that's when she realised. In between the blobs of ink, in surprisingly neat handwriting, was his telephone number and underneath his name: *Reilly*. Her heart took a nosedive. She'd just met her new boss.

*   *   *

Inside the studios there was a hive of activity. Beer-bellied 'grips' in heavy-metal T-shirts were clambering up twenty-foot-high scaffolding, while 'sparkies' with paisley bandannas and skull'n'crossbones tattoos rigged up hundreds of thousands of dollars' worth of lights. Skeletal stylists in head-to-toe black were gliding around with rails of clothes, the art department was running about unloading props and panicking that they'd forgotten something, and in the far corner Make-up was fussing over sponges and foundation.

Away from the mayhem sat the director, producer and clients. Perched like royalty on high canvas chairs, they surveyed the scene before them and discussed 'concepts' and 'brand images' over coffee, muffins and Krispy Kreme Donuts, provided specially by Shirlene, the busty Texan in charge of Craft Services, the catering department. Having worked before with this particular heavyweight East Coast director, Shirlene knew they were his favourite and had been up at dawn, loading her catering truck with fresh supplies from the Krispy Kreme Donut shop in Van Nuys.

Today Pacific Productions were shooting a commercial for a new, 'totally wild' breakfast cereal which, for some reason, required a jungle set, a couple of real lions (who paced around their cages hungrily eyeing everybody up while the animal trainer, a balding man of about fifty, gingerly fed them white mice through the bars) and a bloke dressed up as Tarzan. Being new to all this, Frankie couldn't understand the connection, but then she hadn't been given a five-hundred-thousand-dollar budget to think of one. Instead she was being paid a hundred and fifty dollars to be laden down like a packhorse with two tripods, three reflectors, a camera bag, and a suitcase full of lights. In the world of photography, she'd discovered that assistant, translated, meant dogsbody.

*   *   *

Feeling like the new girl in class, she hovered nervously at the edge of the studios, which stretched out before her like a giant aircraft hangar. Everything and everybody was so unfamiliar. Anxiously, she glanced around her at busy people. Confident people. Intimidating people.

'Hi there!' An LA Child Woman wearing Gap khakis (size 0, long) and a knotted at her can't-really-be-that-tiny waist white shirt motored towards her. She had the entire production uniform: clipboard, pager, walkie-talkie. And she only looked about nineteen. Frankie glanced briefly at her and immediately regretted her choice of walking-the-dog-on-a-Sunday outfit. Trust her to get the dressing-down idea all wrong. Instead of looking casual yet trendy and attractive like Ms Gap Khakis, she looked like an unfashionable, unattractive, shapeless frump.

'I'm Tina from production.' Tina's job was to meet and greet. She blazed fake friendliness. A skill she'd learned as a Gap shop assistant. Which explained the khakis. 'Are you Reilly's assistant?'

'Er, yeah,' answered Frankie's begrudgingly.

Reilly's assistant. The words left a bright-red slap mark on her ego. She was still smarting from having to confess to him – of all the photographers in Los Angeles – that she was his new assistant. It had nearly killed her. Especially when she'd had to stand there in the car park, not saying a word, as he'd piled her up like a sherpa. She knew he was doing it on purpose to get his own back, but what could she do? She'd wanted to tell him to stick his job where the sun didn't shine, but she'd had to swallow her pride and just get on with it. She needed the money. Now, more than ever.

Tina ran her square-cut fingernail down the list of names on her clipboard, reminding Frankie of the attractive girls who stand next to the doormen at hyped-up bars in Soho, smugly telling shivering punters desperate to hobnob with the likes of Take That, 'If you're not on the list, you're not coming in.' But Tina wasn't British and bitchy. She was American and enthusiastic. 'Ggggrrreeaattt,' she cheered, using her highlighter pen to draw a wiggly line across her clipboard. 'You've been allocated a location near the jungle stage, so—' She was interrupted by her pager, which began vibrating and omitting a shrill beep. 'Oh, man,' she gasped, clutching her forehead and switching from joy to tragedy like the wannabe actress she was. 'I'm needed in Wardrobe. Set up over there.' She waved her clipboard dismissively towards the lion's cage before dashing off across the studio, delegating loudly into her walkie-talkie and trying to strike the right balance of stressed-out-but-in-control.

The lion's cage? Frankie hesitated. This was the moment of truth. This was when she had to look as if she knew what she was doing. Although she didn't have a clue. Nervously, she eyed the king of the jungle, who licked his lips and watched her hungrily. What was that saying about being thrown to the lions?

16

After ten minutes crouching down in the corner on her hands and knees, unzipping the bags, unloading the suitcase and trying to put up the tripods, Frankie's worst fears were confirmed. This was bloody impossible. If only she'd listened to her second, third, fourth and fifth thoughts, done a U-turn at Sunset and gone back to bed. She grappled with a tripod. Surely you didn't have to have a brain like Carol Vorderman to work this out, she thought, fighting with legs that kept shooting out at varying lengths and kicking her. How could something with only three legs be so complicated? She took that back. Look at men. They only had two and nobody could ever work them out.

From the corner of her eye she could see Reilly, who'd just walked in and was giving high-fives to the rest of the crew. Laughing and chatting, he took off his jacket, threw it over the back of a chair and, sauntering across to Catering, poured himself a coffee. Frankie was jealous. She could murder a coffee. Having had to get up at such an unearthly hour, she'd slept through the alarm and hadn't had time to make one. She watched as he shared a joke with Shirlene, who was plying him with doughnuts. Her stomach rumbled. She hadn't had time for breakfast either.

Leaning up against a wall, Reilly dunked the edge of his doughnut into the polystyrene cup full of blisteringly hot coffee and bit into it, enjoying the rush of sugar and caffeine.

Boy, did he need that. He looked across at Frankie. Would you believe it? Of all the women in LA, his new assistant had to be her, that stuck-up, pain-in-the-ass Brit. He was gonna kill Dorian. When he'd called yesterday and said a girlfriend of his needed a job, he'd assumed he was talking about one of those sexy airhead babes he hung around with. He should have said no, in fact he was going to, but then his dick had overruled his head. What man could refuse the opportunity to spend the day with a good-looking female? He'd probably have some fun, a little flirt. The coffee burned his tongue. *Flirt?* What a joke.

Frankie saw Reilly looking over and toyed with the idea of waving the white flag and asking for his help. But something made her decide against it. That something being Tina, Shirlene and one of the stylists, who, one by one, were edging closer towards him until they were circling round like a hungry pack. Laughing and joking, they hung on his every word. Tina was tossing her hair like a salon advert; the stony-faced French stylist, who looked as if she was in the Resistance and who 'took 'erself and 'er work very zerious', was giggling like a drunkard, cheeks flushed, eyes racoon-wide; while Shirlene had put the diamanté collars up on her stonewashed denim jacket and was flirting like a trooper.

Christ, no wonder he had such a big ego. Frankie felt peeved. There he was, being a babe magnet, and she was stuck by herself in the corner as if she didn't exist. Clenching her teeth, she ignored him and carried on unpacking. Well, someone had to do it, didn't they?

'Hey, do you need any help?'

Frankie looked up, about to fire a curt 'No, I'm fine thanks' to Reilly. Except it wasn't him. It was the fake-tanned Tarzan in his loincloth. 'Oh.'

'Hey, it's cool. I don't bite.' He held out his honey-brown hand. 'I'm Matt.'

Matt was a blond brawny surfer dude from Malibu who was trying to break in to acting. 'This is my first gig, so I'm kinda nervous,' he explained, fiddling with his shoulder-length hair, striped with chunky yellow-white highlights from the sea'n'surf. He didn't seem to mind that he was practically naked apart from a scrap of leopard-print material sewn on to a jockstrap, courtesy of the French stylist, and a pair of fraying Converse. Frankie didn't mind either. Who would with a body like that? It looked like something from *Baywatch*, and she wasn't talking David Hasslehoff.

She smiled. 'I'm Frankie.'

'Are you Australian?'

'No, English.'

'Way out, man!' He grinned, clutching fistfuls of hair distractedly. 'I've got a friend in England. You might know him, his name's Stephen.' Matt spoke slowly, like a vinyl seven-inch on 33 rpm.

She shook her head. ' 'Fraid not.'

Not to be deterred, he continued, 'He's got dark hair, about my height.'

Frankie smiled apologetically. How big did he think England was? The size of a postage stamp? 'No, sorry.' She felt guilty. He was so earnest, so eager that she should know his friend. Maybe she should have lied.

'Oh, well . . .' Like a large Labrador puppy, he bounced back. 'I was just hanging around . . . Hey, hanging around . . .' he laughed at his joke. 'Me, Tarzan, you know, on the vines . . .'

'Yeah, I know.' She nodded to show she'd got the joke – the first time.

'. . . and I thought, Hey, man, that chick looks like she could do with a hand.'

'Thanks.' She smiled gratefully. After her solitary confinement in the corner, it was a relief to talk to someone. Even if it was like speaking to Bill and Ted's younger brother. 'This is my first gig too,' she confessed, lowering her voice and adopting his lingo.

Matt jumped back, wide-eyed at this amazing coincidence. 'Hey, man, that's totally weird!' He grinned, bending down, grabbing a tripod and wedging it under his arm like a surfboard. His muscles rippled down his flanks like a keyboard. 'But pretty cool.'

Unfortunately Matt's dazzling conversation and handyman skills were cut short by Cedric from Make-up, who dashed across the set in a flurry, wielding a plastic spray bottle. Panting like a prank caller, he began spritzing Matt with baby oil and rubbing in more fake tan. 'Quickly, quickly, you're needed on set,' he chastised, lustfully slapping Matt's bare buttocks.

Matt looked apologetic. 'Well, this is it.' He shrugged, grinning sleepily. 'Stay cool, Frankie.' And giving the peace sign, he loped off, practising his Tarzan strut, while Cedric chased behind, spraying him as if he were a cheese plant.

Reilly watched the muscular guy playing Tarzan speaking to Frankie. What were they talking about for so long? What was he doing helping her with the camera gear? Why was she smiling so much? Feeling a bit put out that she only ever seemed to scowl when he was around, he made his excuses to the people he was talking to – female friends he'd worked with on past shoots – and, grabbing another cup of coffee, walked over to her. He found her on her hands and knees surrounded by a spaghetti junction of sync leads, wires, battery packs, tripods.

'Finished?' he asked, unable to resist winding her up.

Frankie scowled and didn't look up. She continued battling with the tripod.

'Maybe you should try screwing that bolt, it keeps the legs in place.'

Maybe you should do it your bloody self, thought Frankie, bristling at how he was standing above her, giving instructions. Biting her tongue, she did as she was told and stood the tripod upright. It stayed upright. She was both peeved and relieved.

'Easy when you know how,' he drawled, slurping his coffee.

God, that noise. Slurp. Slurp. It set her teeth on edge. He sounded like a dog drinking out of a bowl. Clambering off the floor, she brushed the dirt from her knees and wiped her hands on her sweatshirt. Curly clumps of hair had escaped from her ponytail. Pulling out her scrunchie, she shook her hair, which had begun to ping out all over the place, and tried to retie it.

Reilly watched her, trying to stuff her curls back into her ponytail. She had nice hair. Dark chestnut brown.

'Here, I brought you some coffee. Thought you could do with some.'

Frankie eyed him suspiciously, but her pride gave way to her caffeine craving. She took it from him, resentfully.

Sighing, Reilly rubbed his stubble. He always found it difficult to stay pissed off – it was too much effort – and anyhow, he could feel his annoyance beginning to wane. Instead, he was starting to feel guilty. OK, so even if she was the stubborn, awkward, bad-tempered bitch who'd stolen his cart, told him to get lost at the party and now smashed up his car, he was fed up of fighting with her.

'Look, I know things got off to a bad start, but we've got to work together today. The job's not that difficult. I've just got to take some stills for the ad agency and a few publicity shots . . . but it'll be a damn sight easier if we're not arguing the whole day. Can we call a truce?' He held out his hand, his freckled fingers still sugary from the doughnut. 'I'm not such a bastard, you know.'

Frankie wasn't sure about that, but for once she had to agree with him. She was sick of fighting too. She held out her hand. 'Truce.'

They shook hands. His palm felt like sandpaper, strong and coarse and sticky with icing. A long lazy grin spread across his face, crinkling up the corners of his eyes like sweet wrappers. It was like a yawn. Frankie couldn't help smiling back.

Finally they'd called a ceasefire. For now, anyway.

The commercial took for ever. All day long the jungle beat on the stereo was accompanied by the sound of the clapper-board slow-clapping its way through the endless takes and retakes: loincloths had to be changed, a blow-up banana had to be located and one very grumpy lion had to be persuaded to roar for the camera. Thankfully, Shirlene solved the problem by giving him a rack of spare ribs and he roared with approval. As did the animal trainer, who was standing on the sidelines armed with tranquillisers – for both himself and the lion. It was all an eye-opener to Frankie, who'd never realised how much time and effort went into advertising breakfast cereal. Never again would she nip out and make a cup of tea when the commercials were on.

Reilly was on set as the stills photographer, but in the breaks between filming he set up various publicity pictures with Tarzan and the lions. Hunching his broad frame over his camera, the frayed sleeves of his T-shirt rolled up, hair flopping over his forehead, he peered down the lens, screwing up his eyes as he focused. Click, click, click. The shutter rattled off, one frame after another. Frankie watched him, surprised at how different he was behind the camera. Before he'd seemed cocky and arrogant, the kind of bloke

'OK, take nineteen, aaaannnnddddd . . . Action.'

Tarzan flew across the stage, beating his chest, giving an Academy Award-winning performance of OoooOooOoo OoooOooo.

The director loved it. It was in the can.

'OK, it's a wrap,' yelled Tina, who'd been waiting to say that all day.

There was a lot of clapping and whooping. The shoot was finished. It was over.

Feeling a huge sense of relief, Frankie crawled over to Reilly. It was gone nine and they'd been so busy they'd hardly spoken since the morning.

'So, you managed to survive?' He looked up from dismantling his camera equipment.

'Just,' she groaned, flopping on to one of the fold-up chairs.

She waited for him to tell her to get up and give him a hand. But he didn't. Instead he lit up a cigarette and, taking a long drag, passed it to her. 'Don't let anyone see you smoking. The fire officers will freak out.' Sitting down on the floor opposite her, he leaned his head against the wall.

'Thanks.' Frankie took it and, closing her eyes, inhaled.

He watched her, sprawled like a spider in that God awful sweatshirt, her long limbs hanging over the edge of the chair, trying to figure her out. 'So, what are you doing in LA?'

Frankie shrugged her shoulders, passing him the cigarette. 'I don't know, I'm still asking myself that question . . .' She hesitated. Who was she trying to kid? She knew exactly why she was in LA. 'I had to leave London.'

'Why?' He looked directly at her.

She glanced away, feeling uncomfortable. His questions were too close for comfort.

'Some guy?'

'No . . .' she answered quickly. Too quickly. She wasn't going to talk about what had happened with Hugh. Not to him of all people.

Reilly regretted what he'd said. He shouldn't have pushed it. She had been beginning to open up and now she'd snapped shut like a Venus Flycatcher. 'Hey, look, I'm sorry. I didn't mean to pry . . .'

Frankie looked up. He did seem genuinely concerned. Maybe she was wrong about him. 'Well, OK, yeah, if you must know, there was a guy . . . my boyfriend, Hugh . . . and a job. I lost them both in the same week.' There, she'd said it.

'Unlucky.' Reilly shrugged, grinding the Marlboro out under his boot.

Unlucky? Frankie bit her lip. Losing a fiver was unlucky. Being caught in the rain without an umbrella was unlucky. But what had happened to her? How could he trivialise that in the same way? He obviously didn't have a clue how it felt, or what she was talking about. How stupid of her to think that he might. Annoyed and upset, she stood up, her hands on her hips. 'Have you ever had someone who you really love, a job that you really love, a home that you really love? And then had them all taken away from you? Have you any idea how that feels?'

Her reaction took him by surprise. Jeez, he'd touched a nerve. 'Hey, look, I was only saying . . .'

'Well, don't. You obviously haven't a clue.' Turning around, she began walking off across the studio.

'Hey, where are you going?'

'Home.' A part of her just wanted to get the hell out of there. But a part of her wanted him to call her back again. Ask her to stay. She turned. 'Why?'

'What about all this gear, it needs packing up.' Wrong answer.

Frankie looked at him square in the face. 'I've lost one job, what's another?' She glared at him before flouncing back round and marching off.

Leaning back against the wall, he watched her. 'Frankie,' he muttered under his breath, but it was no good. She was gone.

Taking a lighter out of his jeans pocket, he lit up another cigarette. But after only one drag he stubbed it out. And sighed. That girl was doing his head in.

17

Rita took the news of the car accident surprisingly well. 'Oh, well, it's only metal,' she'd said, shrugging, standing in the driveway in her sheepskin slippers and Fred Flintstone nightie, shining the torch on the back wings of the Thunderbird, which had been clipped and had crumpled up like a concertina. 'It's not the end of the world.'

But after three days of being marooned in the apartment while the car was being repaired, it began to feel like it. Three whole days of reading back copies of the *National Enquirer* and *US* magazine, listening to next-door-but-one's gardener, who – instead of using an old-fashioned sweeping brush – seemed to spend all day blowing leaves around the path with an irritatingly loud whirring machine, eating take-outs from anywhere that did home delivery and watching *E*, 'America's number one entertainment show', on a continuous back-to-back reel every night on the telly. It was groundhog day, with less excitement. But they had no alternative. This was the only kind of life available to poor souls living in Los Angeles without a car. Not that anybody would be foolish enough to live in LA without a car. Except Frankie and Rita.

By Saturday morning Rita had had enough. 'That's it, I can't take any more *Hollywood True Stories*.' She flicked the remote control on the TV and stared at Frankie, who was sat next to her on the sofa with Fred and Ginger, tickling their ears and reading the adverts for cosmetic surgery in the *LA Weekly*, a free listings newspaper. This week there seemed to be a sale, with two-for-the-price-of-one offers: 'Have your breasts enlarged and get your thighs liposuctioned free' or 'Treat yourself to a facelift and enjoy a complimentary $2,000 rhinoplasty'. She was particularly intrigued by the special promotion on 'penis enlargements' and 'vaginal rejuvenation', whatever the hell that was. Obviously there was a lot more nipping and tucking in this town than met the eye.

'I need to go out,' wailed Rita, not getting the attention that she wanted. Stubbing out her cigarette, she hoisted herself up from the sofa and stared frustratedly out of the window, watching as one of her environmentally aware neighbours diligently emptied her rubbish into the recycling bins at the end of her driveway, before jumping into her gas-guzzling, energy-inefficient, air-polluting four-wheel-drive and roaring off down the street. Turning away, Rita took a sip from her cup of cold instant Nescafé, pulled a face and shoved it on the side with disgust. 'And I need a decent cup of coffee.'

Frankie looked up. She was coping with the cabin fever better than Rita, having practically slept through the last few days, getting over stubborn jet lag and recovering from the day at the studios. 'Why don't we go out for a walk?' she suggested brightly.

'*A walk?*' Rita flung the words back at her like a soggy dishcloth. 'I'm bored, not barmy. Nobody walks in LA. Even the homeless have shopping trolleys . . .' Wandering over to the kitchen, she leaned against the cupboards, grabbed an Oreo – her third within the hour – and bit into it sulkily. 'Which might not seem much, but at least it's a set of wheels. And that's a lot more than we've got right now.'

Frankie was going to remind her of the diet, but thought better of it. 'What about Dorian? Have you tried asking him if he'd lend us a car? After all, he's got four in his driveway.'

Dorian bought cars like some people bought shoes: the four-wheel-drive Toyota Landcruiser was like a pair of boots, perfect for when it rained (which in LA was for a week, around about February); the open-topped Jeep a pair of open-toed sandals, cool and easy to slip into for summer; for going out he had something special – the silver Mercedes convertible with tinted windows – a pair of designer heels; and for around town he had the navy-blue BMW with leather seats and air-conditioning, as comfy and reliable as a pair of Nikes.

Rita shook her head. 'I've already thought of that, but he hasn't been home for days and he's not answering any of his mobiles. Knowing Dorian he's probably on a bender at a week-long party, or at some female's apartment.' Splitting the Oreo in half, she began scraping off the fondant filling with her teeth.

'What about Randy?' Frankie was still to meet the infamous Randy, who'd gone to New York on business the day before she'd arrived. 'When's he back?'

'Not until Monday.'

They looked at each other. Both thinking the unthinkable. Another forty-eight hours.

The phone rang. 'Saved by the bell,' whooped Rita, diving on it. 'With any luck it's somebody who can come and rescue us.' Picking up the handset she flicked the on/off button. 'Hello?'

Frankie listened. Fingers crossed.

There was a moment's pause as her face fell. 'Yeah . . . Who's calling?' Grumpy with disappointment, she held the phone out towards Frankie. 'Some bloke selling insurance, wants to speak to you.'

'Me?' Baffled, Frankie took the handset. 'Hello?'

'Hi, would you be interested in car insurance?'

Frankie panicked. Was this something to do with the car accident? 'Erm.' She hesitated, not knowing what to say.

'Because we have a special policy that covers reversing into Broncos . . .'

The penny dropped. Reilly. 'Oh, it's you.' She tried to sound annoyed but she couldn't help smiling.

'Who is it?' hissed Rita loudly, her ears pricking up with interest.

Reilly, mouthed Frankie.

Rita went wide-eyed, her thousand-calorie mascara making her look spookily like Malcolm McDowell in *A Clockwork Orange*. 'What's he want?' she stage-whispered. Not that it was very whispery. You could have heard her in the Valley.

Frankie shrugged and, feeling suddenly self-conscious, stuck her finger in her ear so she could concentrate on what he was saying, and not on Rita. Peeved, Rita sulkily turned her attention back to the fast-disappearing packet of Oreos.

'I was going to call earlier . . .'

Frankie interrupted. 'Look, if it's about your car, I can pay for the damage . . .'

'No, no, the car's fine,' he butted in quickly. 'Well, nothing a hammer couldn't sort out.' He paused, and she could hear him lighting a cigarette. 'No, I was calling about the money I owe you. A hundred and fifty bucks. You walked off before I could pay you . . .'

'Oh . . .' She felt guilty for jumping down his throat. Again.

'So I was wondering if you were free to meet up . . . Sometime today maybe . . .'

'Erm . . .' His question threw her. It was totally out of the blue. Meet up with him? Where? What were they going to talk about? It wasn't as if they were friends, was it? She hardly knew him. She could get to know him. Did she want to? Her mind was racing at a hundred miles an hour. She applied the brakes. 'I'm sorry I can't, I don't have a car.'

'I can pick you up . . .'

'No, that's OK. I . . .' She caught Rita's eye. Mouthing *Yes Yes Yes*, she had her hands clasped together in prayer, begging for mercy and a set of car keys.

Frankie took the hint. 'I mean, yeah, if it's no bother.' Not sure that she was doing the right thing, she gave him her address while looking across at Rita, who obviously didn't share her reservations. Instead she was lit up like a light bulb. With her red curls and beaming grin, she looked like Orphan Annie about to break into 'Tomorrow'.

'Well?'

Frankie put the phone down. 'Twenty minutes.'

Reilly was expecting to see Frankie, so he was rather taken aback when he knocked on her door and came face to face with a curvy redhead dolled up in a pair of hipsters and a cropped top from Rampage, LA's equivalent of New Look. But not as taken aback as Rita. 'You never told me it was *him*,' she hissed to Frankie as they both squeezed themselves on to the front seat of his truck. Not expecting a third person, Reilly hadn't refitted the back seat he'd removed a couple of weeks before. Frankie pretended she hadn't heard Rita and concentrated instead on balancing between the edge of the seat and the door, while nearly suffocating in Rita's liberal appliance of Bodyshop White Musk. Which wasn't a bad thing, seeing as Reilly's Bronco stank like an old ashtray.

'Are you OK?' Trying to make more room, Reilly grabbed an armful of junk, intending to stuff it into the glove compartment, but that was already crammed full of rubbish. Unfazed, he chucked it in the back. 'Don't mind the mess.' He smiled, turned on the ignition and reversed back down the drive.

Obviously he didn't. An overflowing ashtray spilled on to a carpet of scrunched-up fag packets, sandwich wrappers and Coke cans, while pens and pencils, the remains of a tool kit, oily rags and back issues of *Vanity Fair* all fought for space on the dashboard. Frankie cringed. She was used to being in Hugh's Golf, with its 'No Smoking' sticker and Christmas tree dangly air-freshener. A vehicle that Hugh had kept so immaculate it still had the plastic covers on the seats – and it was a P registration. Gingerly she put her feet on the floor. And felt them stick to something.

Five minutes later they pulled into a strip mall in Studio City to grab a much-needed coffee. Frankie looked out of the window. She still couldn't get used to these concrete rows of single-storey shops which always seemed to include a Trisha's Nails, a sushi restaurant, a Blockbusters and a Rite Aid drugstore. But LA seemed to love them. They were dotted around all over the place, like mini versions of British high streets but with plenty of space for parking. Except of course people in LA didn't saunter up and down, indulging in the European pastime of window-shopping. Instead they parked, jumped out of their car, made a quick purchase in a store and jumped back in. Looking at the depressing 1970s-style prefab buildings, tired neon signs and ghost-town like desertedness, Frankie didn't blame them.

But Coffee Bean and Tea Leaf was a different story. It was bustling with people breezing in and out, lounging around on the comfy wicker seats reading the free newspapers or making a mess near the sugar and milk section. There were even customers sitting outside at the few tables thrust bravely on to the empty pavements next to four lanes of traffic in an attempt to recreate a continental feel.

Pushing open the door, Rita put her nose in the air like the Bisto Kid, filling her lungs. 'Just smell that coffee,' she gasped, clattering over to the glass-fronted counter in her platforms and eyeing up the coffee crumble cakes and cheesecake slices that glistened temptingly under the lights.

The assistant behind the counter took one look at her outfit and eyed her back. And who could blame him? Rita looked more Friday night disco than Saturday morning cappuccino.

Frankie followed behind with Reilly. Standing in line, she watched as he pulled out a dog-eared wallet from his back pocket and flicked it open. As he did, she couldn't help noticing a photo of a pretty blonde tucked inside the clear plastic pocket. Was that his girlfriend? The thought took her by surprise, although she didn't know why. Why shouldn't he have a girlfriend? She looked away before he caught her.

'Before I forget . . .' Pulling out some dollars, he gave them to her.

'Oh, thanks.' Glancing at the cash, she realised he'd given her fifty dollars more than agreed.

'It was a long day. Call it overtime,' he explained, before she'd even said anything. 'And a bribe,' he added, looking down at his boots self-consciously. 'I wondered if you'd do any more shoots, though after Tuesday you probably won't. My assistant's still sick.'

She hesitated. The money would come in handy, but it meant seeing Reilly again. Did she want to? Looking at him waiting for her answer, she noticed his face bore the creases of his pillow and that his hair was still damp from the shower. He must have just woken up. She smiled. Obviously he didn't set his alarm and have a forty-minute bathroom routine like Hugh. And, thinking about it, she realised she was glad he didn't. 'Yeah, OK.' She nodded.

'Great.' He smiled back, visibly relaxing. 'Coffee's on me. What are you having?'

'Erm . . .' She looked at the board listing the mind-boggling number of different types of coffee. It was like one of those boards she'd seen at airports, but instead of saying Ibiza, Malaga and Corfu it had far more exotic countries: Cuba, Morocco, Mexico, India. Any minute now she expected the letters to twiddle round with an update. She studied it, not knowing what the hell to choose.

At the front of the queue a forty-something bloke in J Crew and loafers was placing his order: 'I'll have a non-fat, double choca, mocha, grande roomy, two-thirds decaf, one-third caffeinated American roast without the froth. Thanks.'

Blimey. Frankie hadn't realised coffee could be so complicated. Normally at Pret she ordered a cappuccino, but seeing as the choice was limited to either that, a latte or a hot chocolate, it wasn't that difficult. Still, she was a modern inner-city woman. She'd lived in London, for God's sake, a metropolis crawling with any number of Seattle Coffee Companys, Starbuckses and Caffé Neros. She was hardly a coffee virgin. She looked at the board again. To be honest, she actually felt like a cup of Earl Grey.

'Till open, no line waiting.' A cheery soul with a peaked cap and a bad case of acne waved them over. It was time to order.

'Well?' Reilly looked at her expectantly.

She took the easy way out. 'I'll have whatever you're having.'

Sipping their coffees, they went outside to get some fresh air. Not that the air was anything faintly resembling fresh. Dusty, smoggy, humid, yes; fresh, no. It was another sweltering day in LA, pushing 90 degrees, and in the Valley that meant 80 per cent humidity and 100 per cent smog. Still, it was either that or the icy air-conditioning inside, which was fast turning their cappuccinos into iced coffees before the froth had settled.

So, opting for smog, they sat down at one of the tables on the pavement. For a few moments nobody spoke as they drank their giant-size cups of caffeine and inhaled a mixture of cigarette smoke and exhaust fumes. Feeling that she should start a conversation, Frankie tried to think of something to say. But she couldn't. Thank God Rita was here. At least she'd break the ice.

Except Rita didn't break it. She crushed it.

'Are you married?' Rita looked up from trying to stir in her sweetener, which was fizzing ominously and coagulating into aspartame lumps.

Frankie gulped her cappuccino, burning the roof of her mouth.

Taking a drag of his cigarette, Reilly started smiling. 'Why?' He seemed amused.

'I just thought I'd ask. Every bloke I meet these days always turns out to be married and so I thought I'd start asking marital status along with name, age, job. At least then you know where you stand.'

'Well, no, I'm not married.' Flicking his ash on the pavement, he took a sip of his coffee as if he was weighing up how much to reveal. 'I'm divorced.'

Frankie didn't say anything, instead she struggled to appear uninterested. *Divorced?* Reilly had been married? It was strange to think of him being someone's husband. He seemed too . . . Too what? She couldn't put her finger on it. He just didn't seem the marrying kind. She thought about the picture in his wallet. Maybe she was his ex-wife.

'Why, are you married?' He looked at Rita, who was now attacking a fat-free blueberry muffin with gusto.

'Not yet.' Speaking with her mouth full, she wiggled her empty wedding finger. 'But I'm seeing someone. He's in New York until Monday.'

Listening in silence, Frankie began to feel uncomfortable. Marriage was the last thing she wanted to talk about. Taking the cigarette that Rita had left burning in the ashtray, she took a drag.

Rita noticed and was surprised. Frankie was like a vampire when it came to smoking – the fags only ever came out after dark or when she was upset. And then she realised. 'Oops, sorry, I didn't think.' She clamped her hand over her mouth, but it still didn't stop her. 'Trust me and my big mouth,' she tutted, before turning to Reilly and hissing, 'Frankie's single.'

Frankie cringed. You'd think she had some terrible life-threatening disease.

Taking the last puff of his cigarette, Reilly threw it on the floor. 'I'm sure she won't be for long.'

Feeling him staring at her, Frankie began to feel very self-conscious. And she still couldn't think of anything to say.

Luckily she didn't have to. Instead, Rita came to the rescue by suddenly sitting up like a meerkat and declaring, 'I don't fucking believe it,' in an X-rated Victor Meldrew kind of way.

'What?' Frankie seized the bait, relieved that the subject had been changed and further embarrassment averted.

'Over there . . .'

'Where?'

'There . . .'

Frankie looked over to where she was pointing and saw a man – dark, six foot, about thirty-five – walking across the road to an open-topped Isuzu Trooper. Climbing inside, he leaned over to a woman – fair, skinny, about twenty-five – who was in the passenger seat. He began kissing her. And it wasn't on the cheek.

'Who's that?' she asked, turning to Rita. And then wished she hadn't. One look at her ashen face and she knew his name before Rita could gasp it.

'*Randy.*'

18

'Bastard. Bastard. Bastard.'

Chanting the word under her breath, Rita balanced precariously on one leg in the middle of a power yoga class in Beverly Hills. She was supposed to be doing a Salutation to the Sun, but while the rest of her classmates were ohmming and ahhing and praising distant planets, she was cursing not so distant sons-of-bitches called Randy who weren't in New York on business but at home with *their wife of four and a half years*.

Changing position, she balanced on the other leg. It was one thing him cheating on her, *but cheating on her with his own wife*. It was the stuff Jerry Springer shows are made of. Closing her eyes, she breathed deeply in and out, repeating, 'Wanker. Wanker. Wanker.' After a few minutes she began to feel much better. So this is what they meant by power yoga.

With a trembling leg sticking out behind her, Frankie struggled to hold herself in a position. It was seven on a Saturday night and she'd been dragged along to the Beverly Hills Life Center by Rita, who'd enrolled on a six-week yoga course as part of her voyage of self-discovery. A voyage that had begun as a result of the discovery of Randy with his wife outside the Coffee Bean and Tea Leaf.

Only a week ago Frankie had watched through her fingers as Rita had jaywalked over to the Isuzu Trooper, waited patiently until Randy had come up for air from his passionate clinch and then given him a different kind of smacker. Coming from a family of featherweights – her dad, Seamus, had been the County Cork champion five years in a row back in the 1950s – Rita was always rather proud of her left hook. Needless to say, it then all got rather ugly. The woman packed a different punch by announcing she was Randy's wife and quickly followed it with a few jabs of her own by calling Rita a whore and threatening to sue for damages, while Randy cowered like a mute next to her, nursing his bruised chin and checking for chipped teeth. It wasn't until Frankie had intervened and bundled the by then sobbing Rita into Reilly's getaway truck that the nightmare had ended.

Except it hadn't. Over the next couple of days Rita, who normally sedated the pain of a cheating boyfriend with cheap white wine and Marlboro Lights, found that this time it still hurt, no matter how many bottles of Trader Joe's $3.99 Chardonnay and cartons of American Spirit she got through. To make matters worse, the next day she'd had her audition for *Malibu Motel*, which she'd thought was going OK until the casting director, a forbidding forty-something female in Donna Karan, had cut her off mid-sentence with a 'Don't call us, we'll call you, honey'. Suffice to say they hadn't.

Rita was totally pissed off. This time she didn't feel like saying 'Fuck it', slapping on some make-up and going out on the pull. This was LA, not London. Staggering around in her heels with a Bacardi and Coke in one hand and a fag in the other wasn't so much fun when it meant being fined for smoking and probably carted off to AA by concerned bar staff.

So she decided to take a different approach. In LA that meant two choices. The first was going to see a therapist, but the thought of paying a complete stranger a hundred bucks an hour to listen to her moaning about her problems made her feel even more depressed, especially when she could moan to Frankie for free. So she plumped for the second choice, a much cheaper and far more popular option: self-help books.

After three days of lying in bed, Rita had worked her way through the whole range of Ben and Jerry's and *Surviving Change, Wave Goodbye to Rejection* and *Women are Normal, Men are from Another Planet.* And she'd re-emerged full of hope and self-help. It all seemed pretty straightforward. Being calm, fulfilled, happy and successful was easy, all she needed to do was to follow ten easy steps (which when added together from every chapter made about three hundred not-so-easy-to-remember ones). According to the learned authors of such literature – bespectacled men and women who'd survived rejection, divorce, life-threatening illnesses and traumatic birthing experiences with their toothpaste-ad smiles intact – she also needed a few props. After all, these self-help books were a multi-million-dollar-spinning enter-prise. They weren't going to help her for free, were they?

So, biting her cynical tongue, Rita decided to pay another visit to the Flowering Tree bookshop, filled with incense and windchimes and feathery bits of leather that were supposed to catch your dreams, and under the guidance of Melissa, the chilled-out shop assistant who lived in Topanga Canyon and had henna tattoos, wore charm bracelets, silver rings from India on every finger and jingle-jangled wherever she walked, she bought life-giving crystals, stress-relieving aromatherapy oils, a mini-ature Zen garden and book on Feng Shui. Delighted with her purchases, she then drove to Beverly Hills, enrolled on a yoga course and popped into the local organic supermarket and celebrity hang-out, to buy lots of fruit, seeds and sprouting things. By the time she'd got home she'd spent over a thousand dollars. Helping yourself was a bloody expensive business.

* * *

'Breathe in, and ... do the Dolphin.' The gym-honed instructor fired out commands over his earpiece like a sergeant-major to a bunch of squaddies, except these squaddies were beautiful, eternally young types with limbs so tanned and muscle-ridged they looked like human pretzels. 'Change position, hold, faster, squeeze, push, stretch, sweat.' His punishing drill was relentless. On and on and on. There was no let-up in the rigour of power yoga. Just the smell of burning calories, a whopping fifteen hundred an hour, if the strapline across the flyers advertising the class was to be believed.

Frankie believed it. She could barely keep up, let alone contort herself into the kind of positions she'd only ever seen in the *Kamasutra*. This wasn't the kind of yoga she'd imagined when she'd been roped into it by Rita. Where was the hippy teacher in a pair of Birkenstock sandals? Where were the incense and relaxation tapes? Where were the rosy-cheeked middle-aged women with pepper-flecked hair and black leotards always pictured on the back of those soothing yoga videos? Probably at home with their feet up, eating chocolate and watching telly, she thought, trying to wrap her legs round the back of her elbows. Which is exactly where she wanted to be.

'I feel so much better. Don't you?' As the class finished, a glowing Rita skipped towards her, towel draped across her shoulders, looking very pleased with herself.

Frankie could barely speak, she was too busy trying to catch her breath. 'You've got to be joking. I'm knackered. And I'm sure I tore something in my calf when I tried to touch my toes.' Limping out of the mirrored studio, she pushed open the swing doors into the communal changing rooms.

'Serves you right for having such long legs,' Rita replied unsympathetically.

Frankie ignored her and, wiping the droplets of sweat off her forehead, slumped against the lockers.

Rita sat next to her. 'It's certainly got Randy out of my system.' Grabbing one of the fluffy complimentary towels, she wrapped it round her waist and began peeling off her gym kit underneath. For somebody who loved revealing flesh in figure-hugging clothes, Rita was surprisingly coy when it came to getting undressed in a room full of strangers.

'I wish I could say the same about Hugh,' sighed Frankie. 'But I think it's going to take more than a few Sun Salutations, Trees and Dolphins.'

'You're still really cut up about him, aren't you?'

Frankie nodded. 'I can't help it. Nobody comes close to Hugh.' She began peeling off her leggings, which felt as if they were vacuumed-packed to her calves. 'It sounds corny, but if there is such a thing as a soulmate, mine's Hugh.' Standing back up, she twisted her body sideways, checking out her bum in the full-length mirrors. She pulled a face. 'I know you think I should be going on dates with other blokes, and I know you're right, but when it comes down to it I can't. Just thinking about being with someone else, and not Hugh, makes me feel even worse.'

Rita untied her hair. 'I don't blame you. After what's happened with me and Randy, I've come round to your way of thinking. You're absolutely right about fellas. I think we both need a break from them.'

'You?' Frankie couldn't hide her disbelief. A celibate Rita. It was a bizarre concept.

'Yep. It's girl power from now on. I can't be bothered to waste any more energy on men.' Leaning close to the mirror, she checked out her complexion and began squeezing a few blackheads on her chin. 'All that chasing, flirting, playing hard to get . . . and I don't even play that hard to get. When I think about how much time I've spent worrying about men, thinking about men, wondering if they're going to call, wondering why they haven't called, working out exactly what they meant when they did call ... Christ, it's a full-time job. If I'd put as much effort into acting as I have into boyfriends I'd be up for the Oscars by now.' Tutting at the angry red mark that had appeared on her chin, Rita tore herself from the mirror. 'Anyway, it's not as if I've met anyone who's worth falling off the celibacy bandwagon for.' She spoke about it as if she'd been on it for years, not just a week. 'Though that Reilly was nice.' Rummaging around in the bottom of her bag, she pulled out a body scrub, a loofah and a new tube of Clarins anti-cellulite, skin-firming cream that promised dimple-free thighs in eight weeks. 'If I hadn't given up blokes, I'd go for him.'

Frankie felt herself stiffen. For some reason she felt self-conscious at the mention of Reilly's name.

'Though of course you get first refusal – if you're interested, that is.'

'Me? Don't be stupid. I'm not interested in him.' Slamming her locker door firmly shut, she turned the key.

'You don't have to be so touchy,' complained Rita. 'I know you haven't got over Hugh, but Reilly seems like a really nice guy. I thought he might start to grow on you. Especially now you two are going to be working together.'

Frankie looked apologetic. She hadn't meant to snap. 'I'm working *for* him, Rita. It's not the same as working with him. And anyway I'm doing it for the money. No other reason. If I never saw him again I wouldn't give it another thought.'

Grabbing her shampoo and conditioner, she pushed open the doors to the showers and pulled back the shower curtain. Turning the dial to hot, she stood underneath as the spray of water blasted on to her body and thought about what she'd just said. Actually, it wasn't strictly true. She had given Reilly another thought. Quite a few thoughts, if she was honest.

Pouring a pool of shampoo into the palm of her hand, she began lathering her hair. For the past few days she had found herself thinking about Reilly, but so what? It didn't mean anything. It wasn't as if she fancied him, for God's sake. She fancied Hugh, and Reilly was his complete opposite. Untidy, scruffy and unshaven, Reilly chain-smoked, drank beer from the bottle and, judging from the food wrappers in his Bronco, lived on a diet of burgers and fries. Even if she wasn't still in love with Hugh, which of course she was, she'd never be interested in Reilly. Not like that anyway. He wasn't her type. Closing her eyes, she bent her head under the shower and began rinsing out the shampoo. But she still couldn't help thinking about him.

Squeezing the water from her hair, she rubbed in conditioner. She put it down to the fact he'd been so patient and concerned when Rita had been bawling her eyes out over Randy. Hugh wouldn't have got involved. He hated any kind of public emotion, it always made him really embarrassed, as if for some reason he felt it reflected badly on him. The fact that it was Rita wouldn't have helped either. They'd never exactly been the best of friends. Knowing Hugh, he'd probably have just left her there on the pavement. But Reilly didn't. He came to the rescue. Not exactly the knight in shining armour on a white charger, more the bloke in a scruffy leather jacket in a beaten-up truck, but it was still nice of him. After all, he hardly knew either of them.

Washing out the conditioner, she waited until the water ran clear before turning off the shower. She didn't know much about him either. After he'd dropped them both off he'd said he'd give her a ring about work. But he hadn't. It had been a week and she'd heard nothing.

Wrapping the towel around her head like a turban, Frankie walked back into the changing room, relishing the cool air. Maybe his regular assistant was better now and he didn't need her any more. Which wasn't such a big deal. She'd find another job. Grabbing the hairdryer, she pulled off the towel, shook out her hair and, tipping her head upside down, blasted it for a few moments with hot air. Thinking about it like that, it didn't matter if he called or not. She didn't care either way. Turning off the hairdryer, she looked at herself in the mirror, frizzy-haired and flushed. So why did she feel she was trying to convince herself?

'I'll tell you what I am dying for,' announced Rita, appearing from the shower sporting a cleansing clay face mask, 'and I haven't had one for ages.'

'I thought you were off sex,' deadpanned Frankie, taking out her make-up bag and rubbing concealer on to the shadows under her eyes.

'Very funny,' she tutted. 'I'm not talking about sex.'

'What then?' Frankie dreaded the answer. She didn't think she could bear any more of Rita's self-help tactics. Yoga she could stretch to – bad puns aside – but she'd had to put up with wheatgrass and macrobiotic food and, after reading her Feng Shui book, Rita was forever going on at her about leaving the lid up on the loo.

Rita smiled. The kind of smile she always gave when she fancied getting drunk and disorderly. 'Margaritas. On the rocks. Salt around the rim.'

Frankie smiled back. 'Now that's the kind of self-help I like.'

19

'Who's the woman?'

'What woman?'

'The woman on your mind.' Dorian began snapping his fingers in the air like a Flamenco dancer, trying to grab the attention of the waitress.

'I don't know what you're talking about.' Reilly fiddled with his packet of Marlboros. He was dying for a cigarette.

They were sitting at a table in El Fiesta, a Mexican restaurant famous for its lethal margaritas, taking advantage of its happy hour. And they weren't the only ones. The place was buzzing with the hip Hollywood crowd, gathered around the wooden tables, knocking back rounds of tequilas and eating cheese quesadillas and plates of refried beans and rice. This was Hollywood's idea of Mexico. On the white-washed walls multicoloured striped Mexican blankets fought for space with mocked-up REWARD posters for moustached, sombrero-wearing bandits (all bearing an alarming resemblance to Chevy Chase), the Gypsy Kings belted out of the speakers and Latino beauties wearing brightly coloured frilly skirts and ruched tops served five-dollar jugs of margaritas. Only in LA could the waitresses look like Salma Hayek and Jennifer Lopez.

'Come on, you've hardly said a word for the last half an hour.' Dorian caught the eye of one of the waitresses at the far end of the room and flashed a smile. 'It's got to be a woman.'

'Nope.' Reilly shook his head. 'I'm not interested in women.'

'Are you out of your mind?' Dorian's eyes travelled up and down the waitress's uniform and rested firmly on her impressive cleavage. 'How can you not be interested in a pair of those?'

Reilly ran his fingers through his hair. It still had traces of oil from when he'd been working underneath the truck, trying to fix the leak that had sprung in the head gasket after being smashed by Frankie's Thunderbird. 'I thought you were talking about women, not their tits.'

'I am. I am.' Dorian fussed with the collars of his Gucci silk shirt and sat up as straight as possible, puffing out his chest. 'I got distracted.' He winked at the waitress as she sashayed her way through the maze of tables and chairs towards them. 'So there's definitely nobody on the scene?'

'Nope.' Reilly slouched across the table, resting his chin in one hand. He stirred the complimentary bowl of guacamole with a stale tortilla chip, deciding whether or not to brave it.

'Why not?' asked Dorian, hastily rubbing cherry-flavoured lipsalve across his lips. 'It's been over two years since you split with Kelly. You need a girlfriend.'

'I like being by myself. No hassle.'

'No fun.' Dorian smacked his lips together, ready for action.

'I don't see you having a girlfriend.'

'I have *girlfriends*. Plural is much more enjoyable.'

Reilly grinned lazily. Changing his mind about the guacamole, he abandoned the tortilla. It stuck up, like a shark's fin in its sea of lumpy avocado. 'So what's the count at the moment?'

'About twenty.' Dorian smiled flirtatiously at the waitress as she appeared to take their order. 'Twenty-one with any luck.'

*   *   *

Dorian ordered them two margaritas each, the extra-strong variety made with José Cuervo tequila, Cointreau, fresh lime juice and plenty of ice. Reilly knocked back the first one, enjoying the sting at the back of his throat, while Dorian chatted to somebody on one of his mobiles.

'So what happened with Frankie at the shoot?' Snapping his phone shut, Dorian licked the salt from the rim of his glass and tasted his drink. 'Mmm, fucking marvellous.' He looked very pleased with himself.

'Nothing.' Reilly started on his second drink before looking back up at Dorian, who was staring at him, eyebrows raised. 'What are you trying to say? Did I sleep with her?'

'I wasn't going to ask, but now you've mentioned it . . .' Dorian feigned a look of innocence, as if the thought had never crossed his mind. It didn't fool Reilly.

'Jeez, you're a dog on heat, man.' Lying back against the seat, he tried rubbing a splodge of brake fluid from his T-shirt. It didn't budge. 'Sorry to disappoint you, but no, I didn't.'

'And you're not going to see her again?'

'Maybe, but if I do it'll be at a shoot. I said I'd call her if I had any jobs in this week, but it was pretty quiet, so I didn't.' He stirred his drink with one of the plastic cactus-shaped stirrers. 'As far as Frankie and I are concerned, it's a work thing. My assistant was sick and she filled in. End of story. If I never saw her again it's no big deal.'

'And that's it?'

'Yeah.' Draining the dregs of his drink, Reilly crunched up the ice cubes. What he'd just said wasn't strictly true. He had thought about Frankie a few times that week. In fact Dorian was right, she had been on his mind tonight. But he wasn't sure why. He didn't want to date her. In fact he didn't want to date anybody. Over the past couple of years, since the divorce from Kelly, he hadn't wanted anything more than a casual fling, and somehow he couldn't see Frankie as the one-night-stand type. To be honest, he wouldn't want a one-night stand with her anyway. Not that he didn't think she was cute, because she was, but she wasn't his type. She was uptight, stubborn, had one helluva temper and, judging by what she ate for lunch at the breakfast cereal shoot, one of those pain-in-the-butt vegetarians. Catching the eye of the waitress, he ordered the same again. But if it was no big deal whether or not he saw Frankie again, why did he feel as if it was?

Taking the ticket from the waistcoated valet parker, Rita tucked it into the fake Chanel handbag that she'd just bought from a stall on Venice Beach and, linking arms with Frankie, steered her towards the entrance to the restaurant, a doorway strewn with multicoloured Christmas tree lights.

'This place does the best margaritas in town,' she announced as the doorman held open the door for them and they walked inside, the sound of the Gypsy Kings and the smell of refried beans floating towards them.

'What's it called?' asked Frankie, trying to keep up with Rita, who, desperate for a drink, was propelling her down the small terracotta-tiled lobby that led into the main restaurant.

She paused for a moment at the entrance to adjust her miniskirt. 'El Fiesta.'

Reilly saw Frankie before she saw him. There she was, standing in the doorway with her redheaded flatmate, towering above her in a T-shirt and a pair of jeans. He watched her chatting to her friend, before looking over and catching his eye. At first she looked surprised, but then she smiled. He smiled back, suddenly feeling nervous. What was the matter with him? He was thirty-four years old and he felt like a teenager.

'Oh, my God, Reilly's here,' hissed Frankie, her heart suddenly speeding up to keep time to the Flamenco beat of the Gypsy Kings. 'Don't look.'

It was the wrong thing to say to Rita.

'Where?' shouted Rita over the top of the music, standing on tiptoe. She spotted them in the corner. 'Oh, over there, with Dorian.' She waved brightly. 'Come on, we'll join them.' She set off, pushing through the crowds of people. Frankie had never needed a margarita more than she did right at that moment.

'Bloody hell, there's no escaping you, is there?' whooped Rita, throwing her arms around a delighted Dorian and giving him a kiss on each cheek.

Frankie hung back, looking embarrassed. So did Reilly, who finally said, 'Hi.'

'Hi.' She smiled awkwardly.

'Hey, look, I'm sorry I didn't call this week, but work's been pretty quiet.'

'Oh, it's fine.' She tried to look as if she didn't care, when really she was already dissecting the sentence in her head. *I didn't call this week, but work's been pretty quiet.* At least that meant he hadn't been deliberately avoiding her. But on the other hand, it also meant that as far as he was concerned, their relationship was strictly work-related. She didn't know why that should bother her. After all, that's how she'd described it to Rita. But she was bothered. 'I've been pretty busy anyway,' she added breezily. So what if that was a white lie. She had been busy, if you could call doing yoga, sunbathing on the balcony, having lunch and flicking through Rita's self-help books busy.

'Great.' He looked relieved. 'To be honest, I felt a bit guilty, not getting in touch. Especially when I asked you to work.'

'It's OK, honestly.' She fiddled self-consciously with her hair, wishing she'd done something with it and not just given it a quick blast from the hairdryer. She could feel it shrinking into curls as she stood there. A big curly halo around her head. Lovely.

Dorian interrupted. 'So what are you two gorgeous babes drinking?' He looked at Frankie and Rita.

'What do you think?' replied Rita, pushing him playfully. 'And I want two. I'm gagging.'

Letting out the dirtiest laugh, Dorian squeezed her round the waist. 'Me too,' he leered.

Empty stomachs and pint jugs of margaritas determined the kind of evening it was going to be. The party spirit was helped along by Dorian – who else? – who started flirting with a bunch of twenty-first-birthday-partygoers, a bevy of silicone blondes from the Valley, and invited them to join their table. Which meant everybody ended up squashing in next to each other as they shuffled along the benches. Not that anyone seemed to mind. Rita happily tucked herself next to Reilly and the bowl of guacamole and tortilla chips, while Dorian sat next to Cindy, the birthday girl, but kept swapping places so he could take turns in wedging himself up against each of her friends.

Frankie, however, found herself pushed into the corner away from Reilly, Rita and Dorian, and stuck next to one of the blondes, a six-foot stunning Gwyneth Paltrow kind of blonde with flawless honey-coloured skin Frankie had previously thought could only be achieved by airbrushing. Gwyneth turned out to be called Sandy, a girl who appeared to have been born without the modesty gene. Striking up a conversation, Frankie found herself hearing all about her 'totally cute' boyfriend, a basketball player called Ben (nick-named Big Ben), her 'totally divine' new Mustang and her 'totally amazing' modelling career.

An hour finding out all there was to know about Sandy's totally awesome life left Frankie totally sickened and, making her excuses, she escaped to the loo. Locking the door behind her, she leaned against the washbasin. For some reason she couldn't stop thinking about Reilly. All night she'd wanted to talk to him, but he'd been sat at the other end of the table. She'd watched him out of the corner of her eye, joking with Rita and talking to Cindy, the birthday blonde. A couple of times he'd caught her eye before she'd had the chance to turn away and smiled.

Despite the drinks inside her, she still felt jittery about seeing him. God knows why. Splashing some cold water on her face, she looked in the mirror. A piggy-eyed, ratty-haired person stared back. Christ, no wonder he'd been looking at her in such a funny way earlier. She looked bloody awful. Digging out her make-up bag, she daubed on a bit of eyeliner, plenty of concealer, a few coats of mascara. She even rubbed on some hot-pink lip gloss that had come free with some magazine or other and pulled her hair back into a ponytail. Staring at her reflection, a thought struck her. Why was she doing this? Who was she trying to impress? Don't be ridiculous. She wasn't trying to impress anybody. What was wrong with putting on a bit of make-up? She was doing it for herself, to make herself feel a bit more presentable, especially having to sit next to Sandy, Ms Totally Perfect. And it wasn't as if anybody was going to notice anyway.

'Whoooh, who's dolled herself up then?' foghorned Rita as Frankie sat back down at the table, luckily managing to avoid Sandy, who was now being chatted up by Dorian. She felt herself blush salsa red and threw her a desperate '*Shut up*' look. Rita didn't notice. Normally she could drink anyone under the table, but tonight she was nearly sliding underneath it. Completely bollocksed, she'd entered the stage of drinking called 'not knowing where the hell I am'. A stage she'd reeled into thanks to the two rounds of tequila slammers she'd downed while Frankie was in the loo.

Noticing Frankie's reaction, Reilly smiled at her encouragingly. 'You look great,' he said, then lowered his voice. 'But you should keep your hair down, it suits you when you wear it loose.' It was the first time he'd spoken to her all evening.

'I have to tie it up, otherwise I get too hot,' she lied, wishing she'd left it alone.

'Who fancies hitching a ride with these fabulous girls?' asked Dorian, breaking off from Sandy, having just discovered the existence of Big Ben, the basketball-playing boyfriend.

'Yeeeaaahhhhhh,' cheered Rita, polishing off the bowl of guacamole and stale tortillas. She burped unceremoniously. 'Ooops, sorry.' She giggled, putting her hand over her mouth. 'I'm feeling a bit pissed.'

'Where to?' asked Frankie.

'The Cowboy Palace,' piped up Sandy, shaking back her honey-blonde mane. 'Cindy wants to ride the bull.' She looked at Cindy, who flushed and started laughing, and then at Frankie, who stared at her nonplussed. 'Come along, guys. It's totally wild.'

'Yeeehhhhaaaa,' whooped Rita, stumbling to her feet and knocking over a few glasses. Swaying dangerously, she clung on to Dorian, who was leading the girls out of the restaurant like the Pied Piper.

The birthday blondes had hired a white stretch limo for the evening and, as they clustered outside the restaurant, it rose out of the car park. A big, fuck-off, flashy thing with a satellite aerial on the back, blacked-out windows and a strip of white lights down the side. It pulled up next to them.

Everyone piled in. Frankie hung back. Reilly was missing. Where was he? Had he gone without saying goodbye? She felt surprised. But more by how disappointed she felt than by his disappearance.

'Aren't you coming?' hollered Dorian, poking his head out of the door as the limo began creeping its way along the kerb.

Frankie hesitated. She didn't know what to do. Everybody was smashed and ready to have a good time. She was drunk, but not drunk enough for the Cowboy Palace to seem appealing. She thought about catching a cab home. Alone.

Reilly suddenly appeared by her elbow. 'Sorry, I just went for a smoke.' He smiled apologetically.

Frankie felt relieved. And taken aback by how pleased she was to see him.

Grinding the cigarette butt under his boot, he glanced across at the limo and grinned wryly. 'I'll go if you go.'

For a moment she looked at him, and then back at Dorian. It was an easy decision to make. She grinned, before yelling at the top of her voice, 'Wait.'

20

Frankie had never been in a stretch limo before. She'd seen a couple at Piccadilly Circus in the Friday night rush hour, squeezing their way through four lanes of black cabs and double-decker buses, but they hadn't looked as glamorous as when she'd seen them on TV gliding up to the Oscars. It probably had something to do with the fact they'd been in London, not LA, and the leather seats hadn't been brimming with film stars and their Academy Awards, but hen parties who kept popping their permed heads out of the sun roof, cigarettes in one hand, glasses of something boozy and bubbly in the other. Yet everybody rushing for the tube still stared, it was impossible not to. Love them or hate them, limos guzzled attention. Hugh said they were tacky and he'd never be seen dead in one, but she'd always secretly fancied a ride in one. The passengers always looked as if they were having such a laugh. Who cared if the nearest they were going to get to Hollywood was Planet Hollywood?

Sinking into the black leather seats, she ran her fingers over the burled wood that ran along the sides of the doors, smooth and lacquered like polished glass. It was just as she'd imagined. Big. Flashy. And very LA. Sitting opposite the drinks cabinet, complete with decanter and crystal cut glasses, she watched as Sandy began pouring out champagne that had been chilling in a bucket of ice, spilling most of it on her seven-hundred-dollar beige suede trousers from Fred Segals. Without batting a false eyelash, she passed them round.

'Here's to the totally gorgeous Cindy. A girlfriend who's kind, loyal, generous, loving . . . The best person you could ever hope to meet . . .' In true Gwyneth Paltrow Oscar-winning-speech style, she wiped a tear from her eye. 'Happy birthday, sweetie.'

Laughing, Cindy clashed glasses with everyone. 'Thanks, guys, this is so cool,' she gushed, giggling as Dorian squeezed her thigh and whispered something in her ear. It wasn't 'Happy Birthday'.

They drove along, drinking and fiddling with all the gadgets. There was a TV which was playing MTV with the sound turned down, a car phone which Dorian immediately pounced on, a remote-control glass screen that went up and down between them and the driver, a mini-disc player complete with a dodgy collection of CDs, lots of concealed ashtrays and drinks holders and, of course, an electric sun roof.

Spotting the sun roof, Rita lurched up from her seat. 'I've always wanted to do this,' she cried drunkenly. Wobbling dangerously on her six-inch snake-skin stilettos, she stood up, her head disappearing out of the roof, and could be heard yelling gustily 'Yeeeaaahhhhh, I love LA,' before reappearing moments later, windswept and watery-eyed. Bending down she grabbed Frankie. 'C'mon,' she urged, dragging her up from the heated leather seats. 'It's fucking brilliant.'

Frankie tried to resist. Nobody else was putting their heads out of the sun roof and shouting at passers-by. All the blondes were playing it cool, sipping champagne and redo-ing their make-up. Dorian was flirting with Cindy and show-ing off by using the car phone to get them on the guest list for an exclusive members-only club later on. Even Reilly was chilled out, lying back in the leather seats, smoking a cigarette and sharing a joke with the driver on the intercom. She couldn't suddenly stand up. She'd feel like an idiot. And anyway, she never did things like this, preferring instead to sit back and watch other people be outrageous and make fools of themselves. She hesitated . . . Oh, what the hell.

A blast of cool night air hit her, catching her hair and blowing it around like a mass of whirling chestnut ribbons. Bracing herself against the wind, she took a deep lungful of air and watched as the wide boulevards rushed past, streams of white headlights, gas stations, liquor stores, restaurants, strip malls. She didn't feel like an idiot, quite the opposite. She felt fantastic. It reminded her of that famous *Titanic* scene and she had a sudden urge to shout 'King of the World'. She grinned to herself. She wasn't going to, but even if she did it wouldn't matter. She was in Hollywood, wasn't she? And this was the nearest she was ever going to get to feeling as if she was in the movies.

Rita reappeared and passed her a cigarette. What would Hugh think if he saw her now, champagne in one hand, fag in the other? Probably have a fit, knowing him. She took a long, satisfying drag. Not that she cared. Rita was absolutely right. It was fucking brilliant.

It took less than fifteen blocks to drive from Mexico to Texas. LA's version of Texas being the Cowboy Palace, a huge wooden ranch decked out with strings of white light bulbs, wagon wheels and saddles. A hugely popular theme bar, it stood out on Sunset Boulevard like a gaudy Disneyland attraction plonked in the middle of exclusive hotels, showbiz bars and multi-million-dollar homes.

Pulling up outside, the uniformed chauffeur got out and held open the doors for them. They all stepped out, except for Rita, who was still so drunk she fell out. Luckily Dorian managed to catch her before her knees grazed the tarmac and, scooping her up under her armpits, half carried her towards the main entrance.

'You're so lovely ... thank you ... I think you're really lovely ... I really do ...' slurred Rita as he helped her up the stairs.

Dorian smiled. Tightly. All night he'd been working on chatting up Cindy, the birthday girl – with any luck she was going to mark her twenty-first birthday by becoming his twenty-first girlfriend – and now all the headway he'd made in the limo was lost. Running ahead with Frankie and Reilly and her friends, she'd left him trailing behind with Rita, who, despite being only five foot, was like a deadweight in his arms.

Pushing open the Western-style swing doors, Frankie realised why Cindy and her pals had been so keen to come to the Cowboy Palace. The place was wall-to-wall men. From gangs of fresh-faced high-school jocks with fake IDs to balding middle-aged husbands with roving eyes, the huge barn was less of a cowboy palace and more of a cattle market. You could almost smell the testosterone – which made a change from the usual cigarettes. The no-smoking policy meant that even the die-hard wannabe ranchers in Stetsons and cowboy boots weren't smoking. So many would-be Marlboro Men and not a Marlboro in sight.

Tonight was a special line-dancing night and there was a live band, the Silver Spurs, whose female lead singer was wearing a ra-ra skirt, shaggy perm and one of those suede jackets with fringing and silver buckles. She looked like Shania Twain's mum. Belting out Country and Western tracks, she jigged around on stage while everybody else jigged around on the dance floor. The couples dancing were a mixed bunch. Some didn't have a clue how to line-dance and were trying desperately to learn, others were just doing it for a laugh and kept bursting into hysterics, and a few in Stetsons, bootlace ties and spurs had been doing it for years and were taking it all very seriously, two-stepping with intense concentration.

Walking past the restaurant area – vegetarianism hadn't hit the Cowboy Palace and trestle tables were packed with customers tucking into huge racks of barbecued spare ribs and sixteen-ounce steaks – Cindy and Co. sashayed their way through the crowds to the bar that ran along one side of the wooden dance floor. As expected, the sight of four statuesque blondes caused quite a stir, and they were immediately swooped on by an eager crowd of men, who gathered round them, buying drinks and throwing compliments around with their dollar bills. Dorian didn't stand a chance. Pushed out of the picture by the time he'd arrived at the bar and ordered, no one was interested in him or his champagne.

'Oh, my God, look, there's the bull,' yelled Rita, clutching Frankie's arm in excitement.

Railed off in the corner was a large, padded ring and in the middle was a mechanical bull around which people were queuing up to take their turns to ride rodeo style. Arms flailing, backs arched, men were eagerly trying to show off their prowess in front of girls who clustered round in their tight tops and miniskirts chanting, 'Ride the bull. Ride the bull.'

'That looks great,' gasped Rita. 'I want to have a go.' Having been nearly unconscious five minutes earlier, Rita had miraculously risen from the dead and found her second wind.

'In that skirt?' said Frankie. 'Are you mad?'

'Yeah.' Rita grinned. She was drunk and determined. 'Coming?'

Frankie shook her head.

'Spoilsport,' Rita said, laughing, and set off, tottering unsteadily across the sawdust floor to join the back of the queue.

Leaving her to it, Frankie looked across at Reilly. He was standing next to Dorian, taking swigs from his Michelob beer and half-heartedly watching the dancing. Now was her chance. After not being able to talk to him all night, this was the perfect opportunity. She faltered, wondering what she was going to say, trying to plan how she was going to start the conversation. She caught herself. What was the big deal? Just be casual, she thought to herself, plucking up her courage to walk over there. Just be friendly.

'Hi, would you like to dance?' Catching her by surprise, a good-looking guy blocked her path. Stocky and clean-shaven, he was wearing a very tight white T-shirt that showed off the three hours a day he spent in the gym. He was smiling ardently at her.

'Erm . . .' she hesitated. For a split second she considered his proposition – after all, he was very good-looking and it wasn't every day she got asked to dance by a good-looking stranger – before deciding against it. 'No, thanks, I'm pretty useless at dancing.' For someone who had a ballroom-dancing champion as a mother, and had been taught how to dance by watching Fred Astaire and Ginger Rogers movies when she was six years old, this wasn't strictly true.

He wasn't to be put off. 'Hey, that's OK. I'm a pretty good teacher.' He smiled even wider, not making any motion to move away. He held out his hand, flexing the diamond-studded Rolex strapped to his wrist. 'I'm Jonathan.'

Surrendering to the inevitable introductions, Frankie said hi and shook his hand, knowing that now they were on first-name terms it was going to be impossible to escape. She was right, especially when he discovered she was from London, which, in terms of getting male attention in Los Angeles, came a close second to silicone boobs.

'You don't say?' Looking delighted he brushed back his thick blond hair, which fell neatly into a centre parting. 'One of my businesses is based there!'

She smiled lamely. It was obvious he wanted her to ask what kind of business he had, but she didn't want to. She'd met Jonathan's type before in bars. He was the sort of bloke who always appeared from nowhere when her mates had gone to the loo and she was by herself, the sort of bloke whose idea of chatting her up meant talking about himself until he ran out of breath. The sort of bloke she always ended up getting stuck with all night because she hadn't got the heart to tell him to sod off. Luckily, or rather unfortunately, depending on whether you were Frankie or Jonathan, she didn't have to ask him anything. Bashfulness wasn't one of Jonathan's character traits and, without any encouragement, he happily launched into a monologue about his wildly successful Internet shipping company.

Jonathan, it turned out, was a dot.com millionaire – young, self-assured and boastful – and it wasn't long before Frankie knew all about his house in Beverly Hills, the new three-storey apartment he'd just bought in Miami, how he was going to exchange his Mercedes Sports for the new Jaguar, and how much fun he had on board his speedboat that he moored at Marina Del Rey. But wealthy or not, she didn't want to listen to Jonathan's *This is Your Life*, she wanted to talk to Reilly. She waited for him to pause so she could butt in and make her excuses, but he didn't. Instead he went on, and on, and on. Frankie could feel the minutes ticking away. If only she had the balls to tell Jonathan to shutthefuckup.dot.com.

'So, perhaps you'd like to have dinner some time? I've got a wonderful table at the Mondrian.' Despite being thirty, handsome and obviously rolling in it, Jonathan was unsurprisingly single.

'Well, actually I'm a bit busy at the moment.' She was turning down a millionaire. And a good-looking one at that. Her parents would never forgive her.

'And I really can't tempt you with that dance?'

Did this guy never give up? 'I'm a terrible dancer, honestly.'

'Honestly?'

The conversation was like a game of tennis. Words passing backwards and forwards. If only she could serve an ace.

She felt an arm around her waist. 'Wanna dance?'

Reilly. Frankie felt her stomach hit the roof of her mouth. Looking up, she saw him studying her face intently, a smile playing in his eyes. She felt herself breaking into a grin and, oblivious of Jonathan, who stared, speechless for the first time in his life, heard a voice – her own voice: 'I'd love to.'

21

'I hope I didn't interrupt anything there.'

'Thank God you did, otherwise I'd have been stuck there all night.'

'Yeah, you did look as if you needed rescuing.'

'Just a bit.'

Holding hands, Reilly and Frankie stood side by side on the edge of the dance floor, stepping backwards and forwards. For someone who could waltz with her eyes closed, she kept getting her feet muddled up.

'Sorry, I'm crap at this.' She groaned with embarrassment as she stood on his toes.

'You're doing great.' He smiled down at her. 'A natural.'

She grinned awkwardly. God knows why she was so nervous. It was crazy, she felt like a teenager, not a twenty-nine-year-old. She stared at her feet, trying to concentrate on the beat of the music. It was very difficult when all she could hear was the beat of her heart.

'Oops, sorry.' Shit, she'd stood on his foot. Again.

'Stop apologising,' he said. 'Just relax.' Squeezing her hand, he pulled her towards him and twirled her around under his arm.

His sudden closeness took her by surprise and she felt her cheeks flush. She desperately tried to think of something to say so that she'd appear normal, cool, nonchalant. The exact opposite of how she was feeling right at that moment. 'Do you come here a lot?' She cringed. What the hell did she say that for? It sounded like a chat-up line, and a bad one at that. 'Sorry . . .' She realised she was apologising again. 'I mean . . .'

'You mean how come I'm such a great dancer?' He smiled sardonically.

She shared the joke, grateful he hadn't dwelt on her moronic one-liner. 'Yeah, that's what I meant.' Knowing that's what she hadn't meant at all.

'My dad taught me. He used to take me to the rodeos when I was a kid and afterwards there was always dancing.'

'You're from Texas?' So that explained the Stetson.

'Born there. We moved to New York when I was thirteen. My family still live on the East Coast.'

Absorbing this piece of information like a sponge, Frankie didn't say anything. Instead she let the music carry her along, feeling her confidence beginning to return. Dancing forwards and backwards, each step made her more and more relaxed, until this time he didn't need to lead, she did, and holding his hand she twirled herself around under his arm.

'Hey, you're getting the hang of this.'

She laughed. It reminded her of when she was a kid, standing on her mum's patent-leather shoes being waltzed around the living room. Excited. Carefree. Happy. She could feel thoughts of Hugh, her old job at *Lifestyle*, the flat in Fulham slowly fading into the background as Reilly tightly held her hand, guiding her around the dance floor. A rush of exhilaration overcame her and, not caring what anyone thought, she shook her hair free from her ponytail, feeling it fly out around her as she whirled backwards and forwards. She'd been miserable for such an awful long time, letting her hair down felt bloody wonderful.

'How was the bull?' Dorian stood by himself, nursing his bruised ego with his champagne.

'A load of bull,' wisecracked Rita grumpily. 'They wouldn't let me on it. Stupid height restrictions or something.' Hoisting herself up on a bar stool, she peered into the ice bucket. 'Mmmmm, is that champagne?'

'Help yourself.' Dorian had given up on Cindy. Surrounded by men, she hadn't surfaced for the last twenty minutes. 'There's a whole magnum to get through.'

Grabbing the heavy bottle, Rita poured herself a glass, overfilling it in drunken eagerness. A foam of bubbles fizzed over the side. 'So come on, what's up?' She lapped up the froth trickling on to her fingers.

'Nothing . . .'

Rita twigged what was causing the sullenness. 'Don't tell me you've actually got the brush-off.' She was amazed. She'd never known Dorian fail when it came to seducing a woman.

Ignoring her, he took a swig of champagne.

'Oh, come on, Dorian, it happens to the best of us. Look at me and Randy.' She took another mouthful, feeling the bubbles explode against the roof of her mouth. 'Drink some more of this, you'll soon get over it.' She tried to suppress a hiccup. Why wasn't 'Get legless on champagne' one of the ten easy steps in her self-help books? It was far more effective than all that yoga, meditation and deep-breathing exercises put together. In fact, she hadn't felt this happy in ages.

'I am over it,' said Dorian, still bristling from Cindy's cold shoulder. 'I just thought she and I were going to have a little fun together.'

'In other words you wanted to shag her.'

'Did I say that?'

'You didn't have to.' Rita smiled, shaking her head. 'You're bloody terrible, you are. When are you going to stop being a playboy and settle down?'

'When you'll have me.'

Laughing, she pushed him playfully. 'Can you imagine me and you together? We'd be a nightmare.'

'Would we?' The laughter died and he stared at her.

'You're drunk.'

'So?' He continued staring. 'Aren't you?'

The question packed a punch. Rita didn't answer. Instead she looked at Dorian, and for the first time saw someone other than just her next-door neighbour. A different bloke, not the outrageous, extravagant, mad-for-it ladies' man she knew. But someone with big, gorgeous green eyes flecked with amber. And broad shoulders underneath his black Gucci shirt. She'd never thought of him as being good-looking before. Even fanciable, if you went for Richard E. Grant types. Aware that nobody was speaking, she was about to say something when he suddenly leaned towards her, as if to kiss her, and Rita suddenly came to her senses. What was she doing? She was drunk and wearing beer goggles. She couldn't get it on with Dorian, for God's sake. 'Where are Frankie and Reilly?' Very obviously changing the subject, she grabbed her glass and, taking a large gulp, finished off her champagne.

Dorian didn't answer. He didn't have to read between the lines to realise he was getting the brush-off for the second time that night. Leaning back against the bar, he pointed his glass towards the dance floor.

Rita looked to where he was pointing. 'Bloody hell.' She stared at the couple in the middle of the floor, laughing, twirling, holding hands. It was Frankie and Reilly. 'They make a great couple, don't they?'

He nodded. 'Shame he's not interested in her.' Bitter at being rejected – twice – he was determined to pour scorn on anybody else's chances of romance.

'How do you know?' she snapped, feeling defensive for her friend.

'He told me tonight.'

'The cheeky bastard.' From thinking Reilly was a nice guy, she'd suddenly gone right off him. 'Well, it's lucky for him she's not interested either.'

'It doesn't look like that.'

'Well, it's true. She told me she wouldn't care if she never saw him again.'

Dorian finished off the last of his glass and reached to refill it. 'Funny. That's what he said.'

They looked at each other, neither of them saying anything, before staring back at the dance floor.

The song began to wind down and, as the pace slowed, Frankie glanced at Reilly. He looked such a mess. His hair was all over the place and he had to keep brushing away the strands that fell in his eyes. Her eyes travelled downwards, noticing the smears of oil on his once-white T-shirt, his Levi's, frayed and torn from scraping against the floor because he didn't wear a belt, boots that hadn't been polished in God knows how long and were now so scuffed and sun-bleached they'd lost all trace of colour.

'Are you OK? Do you want to sit down?' Reilly caught her looking at him.

'Me?' He'd taken her by surprise. 'No, unless you do.'

'No way.' He smiled wickedly. 'Why would I want to sit down when I've got the most gorgeous woman here in my arms?'

Frankie grinned. It was clichéd and she loved it.

The band finished the song and started to play a slow dance. A few couples disappeared, others moved closer, wrapping their arms around each other. For a few seconds she wasn't sure what to do, but before she'd had too much time to think about it Reilly pulled her towards him.

For a moment she stiffened. Feeling awkward, unsure, as his arm curled tightly around her waist. His body against her body. This was the first man she'd been this near to since Hugh, and it was strange. Strange to feel another man's arms around her, to feel him next to her with only their flimsy cotton T-shirts between them. To feel his face only inches away from hers. Tobethisclose.

Gingerly she put her arm around his neck. He was much broader than Hugh, but not in a pumped-up muscular way. Just bigger, taller, heavier. The inside of her arm rubbed across the side of his chin, rough and bristly due to his stubble. She was so used to Hugh's clean-shaven, moisturised skin it felt different, unfamiliar, but it was the way he smelled that she really noticed. There was no whiff of aftershave, hair gel, shower gel, mouthwash – Hugh's concoction of artificial scents. Instead Reilly smelled of beer, tobacco, oil, *himself*.

Barely moving around the dance floor, they looked at each other, but this time neither said a word. No polite questions. No small talk. No smiles. Feeling suddenly awkward, Frankie lowered her eyes, pretending to be concentrating on her feet, which were moving slowly, a complete contrast to her mind, which was racing. Reilly was the antithesis of Hugh. The way he looked, talked, smelled, dressed. He was so different. So alien. *So Not Hugh*. She was conscious of Reilly's hand gently, confidently, protectively resting in the small of her back. So why did she have that funny feeling in the pit of her stomach when he put his arms around her? It wasn't as if she fancied him. Not one bit. Not even a little. No way. She didn't find him attractive at all . . .

Or did she? Was she just trying to convince herself otherwise? Denying how she really felt because she didn't want to face the truth? Clinging desperately on to her denial, which somehow only made it slip faster through her fingers? *Go on, admit it*, she thought to herself. *Admit how you really feel*.

As the electric guitar twanged lazily through the chorus

one last time, Reilly released his hand from hers and moved it slowly across her back.

Admit that you can't stop thinking about him. Thinking about the way he turns over a cigarette in a new packet for good luck and rubs his chin when he's stressed. Thinking about how much you want to touch the scar above his eyebrow, or trace the wiggly vein that runs down his forearm to the underside of his wrist . . .

Feeling intoxicated with booze and lust, she slid both arms around his neck and, closing her eyes, rested her head on his shoulder.

Admit that you've watched the phone all week. Wishing he'd call, to hear his voice, to see him again . . .

With the last few chords of the song fading away and Reilly holding her tightly, Frankie felt herself finally letting go. Surrendering. Succumbing. Call it whatever. Lifting her head off his shoulder, she looked into his face, his eyes, his mouth, oblivious of the other dancers clearing away from around them. She didn't know whether it was too many margaritas, too much champagne, what the hell it was, but right now, right at this very moment, she didn't care about being the only couple still left clinging to each other in the middle of the whole damn dance floor. She didn't care if people were staring. All she could think about was Reilly. *She fancied him.* She fancied the bollocks off him. She fancied him so much she felt like she was going to go crazy. So crazy that, looking at him right now, at this moment, she wanted nothing more than for him to bend down, pull her towards him, hold her so tightly she could hardly breathe. And then, only then, to kiss the living daylights out of her.

22

Uncorking the bottle of red wine he'd just picked up from Oddbins, Hugh poured a little to taste. He was disappointed. It was OK, but he'd had better for a tenner. Pissed off with his choice – a recommendation from the *Sunday Times* Wine Club – he filled his glass and set about unwrapping a Thai takeaway, his fourth that week. He looked at his watch – eight p.m. – he'd just got back from the office and he was knackered. Too many people looking to buy and not enough flats to sell. Not even when you included all those poky studios with no room to swing a cat, let alone a sofa bed, selling like hot cakes at two hundred and fifty grand.

Emptying the contents of the silver-foil containers on to his plate, he slumped on to the sofa, loosening his tie and kicking off his brogues. Spearing a slimy chunk of lukewarm coconut chicken, he grabbed the remote control and, turning on the telly, flicked idly over the channels. There was nothing even vaguely interesting. BBC1: a documentary on the tsetse fly. BBC2: some wanker of a chef trying to be clever with couscous. ITV: a *Coronation Street* special. Channel 4: another bloody depressing soap. Channel 5: one of those crappy gardening programmes. He stared blankly at the screen, watching a gang of cheery presenters in matching orange T-shirts trying to turn a piece of scrubland into a Japanese garden with only a bit of gravel, a water feature and half an hour.

Hugh turned off the TV in disgust. He was bored. It was a Friday night and he was sitting by himself on the sofa with a cold take-out and a shit bottle of wine. What happened to all the wild nights out he thought he'd be having as a newly single guy? All the parties? All the women? He chewed a mouthful of congealed Pad Thai noodles. There weren't any, that's what. OK, so he'd had a few one-night stands, but they'd petered out pretty quickly. Having a one-night stand wasn't as much of a turn-on as he'd imagined. In fact, it was a bit of a turn-off. And anyway, most of the women he seemed to meet were after something a lot more serious than sex. They wanted a relationship. Which was the last thing he wanted, seeing as he'd only just come out of one. As for the parties, there'd been Adam and Jessica's engagement bash a few weeks ago, but then nothing. November wasn't exactly the best month for parties. It was too cold, too rainy, too dark and too bloody depressing. No wonder everybody seemed to have stopped being single all of a sudden. Everybody had found themselves a mate and had begun hibernating in their living rooms, snuggling up together on the sofa with a DVD and cups of tea. Just like he and Frankie used to.

Still, staying in by himself didn't bother him. In fact, he enjoyed it. Liked the space. Liked being able to do whatever he wanted. Getting up, he flicked on the central heating. The flat was freezing. Not surprising, seeing as it was about minus 20 outside. God knows what had happened to the autumn. London seemed to have bypassed it and plunged straight into an Arctic winter. He caught his reflection on the side of the stainless-steel fridge. Christ, he looked lousy. Pale grey skin with dark circles under his eyes. He could do with a holiday, some sunshine, a bit of a tan. Frankie would probably have a great tan after nearly a month in LA, lapping up all that Californian sunshine. She always went so brown in the sun, not like him. Even with SPF30, his skin was so fair he always burned and went bright red.

Feeling pissed off, he padded into the kitchen and, flicking the pedal bin, scraped his unappetising food into the bin-liner. Not that he missed Frankie. He had done the right thing by finishing with her. She'd become too sensible, too boring, too devoted. All she wanted out of life was to settle down, get married and spend every evening having a quiet night in. That's why it could never have worked between them. He was the complete opposite.

Emptying his wine down the sink, he watched the blood-red liquid swirl down the plughole. And yawned. He looked at his watch. It was only half past eight, but he didn't feel like going out. He was shattered. He was going to stay in and have a long soak in the bath. To be honest, he wouldn't mind getting an early night.

23

'I feel like shit.' Gingerly lifting up her sunglasses in the bright midday sunshine, Rita looked in her rear-view mirror. A pair of bloodshot eyes stared back. 'And I look like shit.' Groaning, she lowered her Persols and sank back behind the wheel of her Thunderbird.

Frankie lay next to her in the passenger seat, which was reclined as far back as it would go, trying – and failing – to ignore her thumping headache. She half opened her eyes, allowing a sliver of UV light to hit her pupils, but it was too glary, even through her sunglasses. 'Ditto,' she croaked, snapping her eyes tightly shut again and pulling down the peak of her baseball cap until it covered her face.

It was the morning after the night before, and they were stuck in the middle of a traffic jam on Sunset, thanks to Rita, who'd had the bright idea of driving to Malibu. Two hours later, it didn't seem so clever. They hadn't reckoned on the all-day rush hour, which meant that instead of recovering on the beach listening to the crashing of the surf, breathing in lungfuls of sea air and topping up their tans, they were stuck at the lights, sweating alcohol in the convertible-turned-sauna, listening to the sound of car horns and breathing in exhaust fumes, their hangovers hanging over them like the Ancient Mariner's albatross.

Frankie watched as the red needle on the pressure gauge dial edged ever higher towards boiling point. Any moment now the car would overheat, and in this 90-degree heat without air conditioning so would she. Opening a five-litre bottle of water meant for the car's radiator, she glugged half of it down, trying to quench her thirst. She felt terrible. Too much alcohol and not enough sleep. God knows what time she got home last night. All she could remember was walking off the dance floor and seeing Rita passed out across the bar next to an ice bucket and an empty magnum of champagne, with half a dozen men circling around her like vultures, and deciding that she'd better take her home in a cab before somebody else did. Well, that wasn't exactly true. She could remember something – somebody – else. *She remembered Reilly.*

Floodgates of panic, guilt, embarrassment and excitement opened as a Polaroid image of them dancing together flashed into her mind. She couldn't really remember what happened. Not properly anyway. All that tequila and champagne had taken its toll, fuzzing her mind, blurring time, blanking out conversations. Part of her was thankful. It was cringe-worthy enough, remembering how she'd been draped across him in the middle of the Cowboy Palace, without knowing the gory details. She'd woken up this morning with a jumble of images and a few snippets of what he'd said. Nothing too hard to handle. And felt relieved. But as the blanket of grogginess began to lift, she realised that last night had left her with two things: a killer of a hangover and some very mixed emotions.

It was all so bloody confusing. She didn't know what the hell to think about last night. Had some unspoken thing happened between them? They hadn't got it together, she could remember that at least, but at the same time she could also remember wanting to. And it was freaking her out. Did that mean she'd suddenly fallen for Reilly? Or was it just a classic case of drinking too much, missing Hugh and wanting affection? After all, it was so long since she'd kissed a bloke, never mind done the full Monty and had sex, who'd blame her for wanting a bit of a song? Even if it was with the wrong man. And Reilly was the wrong man for her. It was Hugh she wanted. Hugh's arms around her. Hugh kissing her. Last night she'd been pissed. Lonely. Mixed up. She fancied Hugh, only Hugh, always Hugh. And she did not, absolutely, definitely, 100 per cent not, fancy Reilly.

The lights changed and the traffic started moving. Seeing a gap in the lane ahead, Rita put her foot down, overtaking a Range Rover with tinted windows – a favourite with the Hollywood celebpack, wanting to be seen but not seen. Leaving the shops and restaurants behind, they were soon cruising past the manicured lawns and colossal houses of Beverly Hills, sweeping through the palm-tree-lined roads, past the young Mexican boys with their familiar blue and yellow signs advertising \$2 STARMAPS – an *A–Z* of out-of-date addresses for nosy tourists wanting to drive around in their rented Mustangs seeing where Julie Andrews had once lived – and the infamous salmon-pink Beverly Hills hotel, home to Elizabeth Taylor and Richard Burton during their first marriage, or was it their second?

Lazily peering through her sunglasses, Frankie lay back in her seat and decided to ignore her hangover and enjoy the view. This was how LA was meant to be seen, through three layers, the first being the dark lenses of her sunglasses (horrified at her lack of eyewear, Dorian had loaned her a pair of last season's tortoiseshell Versaces); the second being the car's windscreen; and the third being, of course, the smog. Smog was the thick brown layer between the horizon and the perfect blue sky, and Frankie had seen it for the first time when she'd stepped off the plane at LAX. The funny thing was, nobody else seemed to notice it. Which was probably because everybody was too busy being obsessed by a different kind of pollution: cigarette smoke. Smoking was lethal, it polluted your lungs and was a danger to society. But smog. What smog?

After five weeks in LA she'd realised that, for Los Angelenos, smog was an optical illusion. It was always 'over there', rather like the end of the rainbow, except in this case it was less pot of gold and more carbon monoxide poisoning. But, as Rita said, in the movie capital of the world, a town built on the manufacture of illusions, being part of it meant believing in perfect, glorious blue, blue, sky . . . because that was the biggest illusion of all.

'I think I'm gonna be sick.' Rita gripped the steering wheel, swaying unsteadily.

'You are joking, aren't you?' Frankie stirred from her semi-conscious state.

'Nope.' She shook her head, inflating her cheeks.

'Maybe you should pull over.'

'What? And throw up on the pavement?'

'Well, it's better than throwing up over me.' Pulling her favourite sarong tightly around her, Frankie edged further away to the side of car.

'I can't, we're in the middle of Bel Air . . .'

'What difference does that make?'

'It makes a lot of difference. This place has more Hollywood film stars, directors and producers per square inch than anywhere else in the world.' Rita leaned over, grabbing what was left of the radiator water and pouring it down her throat without swallowing, as if she was drinking Sangria through one of those 'I've been to Benidorm' bottles with a glass spout and a wicker handle. 'When I said I wanted to make my mark in Hollywood, puking up at the end of Steven Spielberg's driveway wasn't what I had in mind.'

*   *   *

Thankfully, after she had rehydrated, the colour started to return to her cheeks and they carried on without needing to make any emergency stops. They wound along Sunset, endlessly passing through shady suburbs until, finally, they drove over the brow of a hill and into the full glare of the sunlight. The view was glorious picture-postcard stuff, and for the first time in her life Frankie glimpsed the Pacific Ocean, a streak of navy blue on the horizon. It had been a long time coming. And as they headed down towards the coast, she watched it growing wider and wider, stretching back as far as the eye could see, until, like a movie expanding into widescreen, it filled the whole panorama.

Rita parked the car at the side of the Pacific Coast Highway, a busy, dusty stretch of road with six lanes of traffic which continued up towards San Francisco. Frankie felt a stab of disappointment. Where was the famous Malibu beach? Where were all the million-dollar houses? All she could see were ten-foot-high walls and electronic security gates.

'Is this it?' she said, climbing out of the car and following a very shaky Rita through a gate and down a corrugated-iron staircase so steep it made the backs of her legs ache. 'I thought you said Malibu was glamorous.'

'Stop moaning,' puffed Rita, a fag in one hand, the other grasping the handrail for much-needed support. Reaching the bottom, she put her hands on her hips, trying to draw breath. Something told her she needed to do more exercise and stop smoking. Taking a drag of her cigarette, she stood up straight, pushing her sunglasses further up her nose. '*Now* what do you think? Bit better than Brighton, eh?'

Slipping off her knackered old flip-flops, Frankie sank her bare feet into the damp, yellow sand, feeling its soft-ness between her wriggling toes. Stretching out before her was a beach deserted apart from a few joggers and a couple walking their dog. As with everything in America, it was *big*, appearing to go on for miles, past the rocky headlands in the distance, where she could see a group of surfers, probably all the way up to San Francisco. A few feet back from the breaking waves, a string of lavish beach-houses overlooked the ocean, each one completely different from the next. Rising out of the sand like a piece of modern art was a four-storey building made entirely of blue glass; another was a Disneyland castle, complete with turrets and gargoyles; while further along was a whitewashed Mexican-style hacienda, with sun decks on every level, and raspberry-pink bougain-villaea spilling down one side.

'Just a bit,' murmured Frankie, throwing down her beach towel. She flopped on to it, resting on her elbows, and gazed at the view around her. This was the Malibu she'd imagined. The Bo-Derek-running-along-the-beach-with-beads-in-her-hair Malibu. The glamorous-beach-parties-full-of-glamor-ous-women-with-glamorous-figures-in-glamorous-bikinis Malibu that she'd read about as a teenager in all those trashy Jackie Collins novels. For so long this place had been strictly fictional and now it was for real. And here she was, little old Frankie from Fulham. OK, so her bikini wasn't that glam-orous – it was a two-year-old gingham M&S number with underwired cups and total bottom coverage, not itsy bitsy triangles held on by pieces of string – and her figure was more beanpole than Bo Derek. But crikey, what the hell, she was sunbathing on Malibu beach. Taking a deep breath, she arched her back and lifted her face to the sky.

'I love this beach,' sighed Rita, collapsing on to the sand next to her. 'It's so much nicer than the crowded ones down at Venice and Santa Monica. They're packed like sardines, full of Brits abroad . . .' Missing the irony, she rummaged through her bag, pulling out suntan lotion, hair scrunchie, lip-salve, swimming goggles, cigarettes and her latest self-help manual, *Give up Men and Get a Life*. Rita was nothing if not prepared. 'And anyway, the scenery's a lot nicer.' She motioned towards the group of surfers running in and out of the sea in the distance, riding the waves, their wetsuits clinging to their athletic bodies.

'I thought you were off men.'

'I am, but there's no harm in looking.' She smiled. 'Or being looked at.' Unfastening her bikini top, she began smearing herself in SPF 30, tutting at the extra bit of flesh on her stomach. 'Can you do my back?'

Sitting up, Frankie squirted creamy squiggles all over Rita's shoulders and began rubbing them in. Despite a lifetime of sunbeds, fake tan, holidays in Tenerife, and the past four months in California, Rita was still mozzarella white. Being ginger-haired, she never tanned, she freckled, burned and then peeled like a roasted red pepper.

'There you go.' Frankie gave her back the lotion. 'You look as if you're ready to swim the Channel.' Rita was daubed in a thick layer of white gunge.

'Just because you've got bloody olive skin,' she tutted. 'Thin with olive skin. Is there anything I've got that you haven't?'

'Tits.' Frankie smiled, turning to lie on her stomach and wriggling like a fish to unclip her bikini top so she didn't get a tan mark. Unlike Rita, she was too embarrassed to go topless. It wasn't that she had a hang-up about the size of her boobs, 34B was plenty big enough thanks, and it wasn't as if there was anybody around to gawp at them, apart from the surfers, and they had more than an eyeful with Rita's generous pair. But she was too self-conscious. Hugh had always said she had 'lovely breasts . . . a perfect handful', and last year on their fortnight's holiday in the South of France he'd persuaded her to go topless. But she'd only done it the once. She'd felt as if everybody was staring at her nipples. God knows why.

In fact, the beach in Juan les Pins had been nipple city. Hugh had called her inhibited. Which was a bit rich, coming from a man who'd only wear shorts if they went past his knees.

Grabbing Rita's self-help book, she flicked idly to the chapter entitled 'Annoying Male Habits'. It was about sixty pages long.

'How are you feeling?' Rita slathered her ankles in cream.

'Rough,' mumbled Frankie, without looking up.

'Me too. I never normally get hangovers. It must have been those bloody margaritas.'

'And all the champagne,' Frankie reminded her.

Groaning, Rita finished doing her legs and, snapping the lid shut on her suntan lotion, lay back, spread-eagled on her towel, which had 'Club Ibiza Hotel' embroidered in the corner. She giggled to herself. 'I must have been plastered last night. I've just remembered I nearly snogged Dorian.'

'*You didn't.*' Frankie stopped reading about 'men's unacceptable bathroom behavior'. This was far more interesting than Dr Bernstein's professional opinion on the psychological damage inflicted on a female when her male partner did not put the toilet seat down.

'Don't be daft,' Rita tutted indignantly. 'Of course I didn't. I was off my head, not out of it. Well, not completely anyway.' She suddenly got a flashback of herself pulling up her skirt to show off the red devil tattoo on her bum. God, she must have been bollocksed. She didn't have a tattoo – red devil or otherwise. 'Anyway, like I said, I'm off blokes.' Reaching over, she swapped her sunglasses for a pair of sunbed goggles. She didn't want panda eyes. 'You looked as if you were having a good time.'

'What do you mean?' Frankie felt suddenly defensive.

'With Reilly on the dance floor. You looked happy.'

Reilly. She'd decided earlier that she wasn't going to think about him any more. Any feelings she might have had last night had been a mistake. She loved Hugh, remember.

'Do you think so?' she still couldn't resist asking.

'I know so, I saw you both . . . just before I crashed out. If I didn't know better, I'd have thought something was going on between you two.'

'Don't be ridiculous.'

'I'm not saying I did think that . . .' Rita knew she was treading on dodgy ground. Frankie could be so touchy. 'I know you're not interested in him . . .' She flicked an ant off her bellybutton ring. 'Which is just as well.'

'Why?'

Realising she'd opened a can of worms, Rita tried to cover her tracks. 'Well, it'd be awful if you were really into the bloke, wouldn't it?'

'Would it?' Somehow, somewhere, she'd suddenly swapped sides.

'Christ, Frankie, anyone would think you did fancy him the way you're going on.'

'Of course I don't,' she snapped, picking up a shell and scraping off the sand. 'I'm just curious, that's all. Why would it be so awful?'

'Because he's an arsehole.'

'*An arsehole?* Since when?' Frankie felt shocked. And surprisingly defensive. 'You've changed your tune. I thought you really liked him.'

'I did, until last night.'

'Why, what happened last night?' Her mind raced. 'Did I miss something?'

Pushing up her goggles so the elastic hugged her hair like a headband, Rita sat up and began rubbing in zinc whitener stick on her cheekbones. 'Well, I wasn't going to tell you . . .'

Bullshit, Rita could never keep her mouth shut.

'. . . but seeing as you're not bothered about him anyway . . .'

Twisting her body round and holding her bikini top,

Frankie looked up at her. 'Come on, don't keep me in suspense.'

'Look, it's no big deal . . .'

'*Rita.*'

Rita stopped zincing and sighed resignedly. 'Well, apparently he told Dorian that he wasn't interested . . . in you . . .' She added it as an afterthought.

Frankie didn't say anything. She couldn't.

'I mean, what a bighead. As if he'd stand a chance anyway.' Rita tutted, grabbing a mirror and looking at her reflection. 'He's *so* not your type . . .'

Frankie felt as if she'd been hit by a bus. A double-decker. 'When did he say this?' Dazed, she stared at Rita, who was picking off a bit of leftover mascara from an eyelash.

'Last night.'

Last night. Frankie's mind whirled into freefall. Last night he'd wrapped his arms around her on the dance floor . . . Last night he'd looked at her and said he had the most gorgeous woman in his arms . . . Last night . . . She caught hold of herself. Hang on a minute. What had happened last night didn't mean anything to her, so why should it have meant anything to Reilly? And so what if he wasn't interested in her. Why should she care? She wasn't interested in him either. Fastening her top, she sat up cross-legged, feeling the sun hot on her skin, idly watching the waves and listening to them break on the sand, smelling the surf and tasting the salt from the spray. It brought her back to her senses.

Rita lit a cigarette and glanced at her. 'Are you all right? I shouldn't have opened my big gob, should I?'

'Don't be silly, I'm fine. I'm glad Reilly doesn't fancy me.' She fiddled with her watchstrap, unfastening and fastening it. 'Don't get me wrong, it would be flattering if he did.

After all, being dumped doesn't exactly do wonders for your confidence . . .'

'Oh, shit, I knew I shouldn't have said anything.'

Frankie continued, 'But I don't want him to fancy me. It would just complicate things, wouldn't it? Like you and Dorian.'

Rita rolled her eyes. 'Christ, we're not complicated. Dorian wants a shag and I won't give him one. It's pretty simple really.'

Frankie laughed. Her mood lifted. 'You know what I mean. Reilly and I are just friends.' She stopped fiddling with her watch and looked down, running her hands through the sand, watching it trickle between her fingers. 'The only man I want to be interested in me is Hugh.'

'*Frankie.*'

'I know.' Smiling, she held up her hands in surrender. 'Shoot me.'

24

'This is LA County Beach Patrol.'

Frankie must have dozed off, because the next thing she was aware of was a booming voice jolting her awake.

'You are breaking the law.'

The voice again. Where the hell was it coming from? Prising her face off her towel, she looked up, squinting in the glare of the sun – and had the fright of her life. Less than two yards away from her discarded flip-flops was a canary-yellow four-wheel-drive, a life-size Tonka Toy, out of which was leaning a man clutching a megaphone. Seeing her stir, he began climbing down from his seat and strode purpose-fully across the sand towards her. Frankie recoiled. He had the word 'Coastguard' in two-inch letters emblazoned across his zip-up, elasticated bomber jacket. Not that he bore any resemblance to how she imagined a coastguard on Malibu beach would look. With his tobacco-stained sunglasses and suspicious thatch of aubergine-coloured hair, he stood, legs astride, in front of her and breathed in, trying to hitch up his Boy Scout shorts, which were jammed underneath his middle-age spread, and cleared his throat. Twice. 'Excuse me, ma'am, but nude sunbathing is not allowed in the state of California.' He jangled his sprawling bunch of keys, a symbol of both his importance and, no doubt, his big dangly manhood. Not.

'What are you talking about? We're not nude.' Twisting her arms around her back, Frankie grappled with her bikini top, trying to refasten it. Why was it the bloody things were so easy to take off but incredibly fiddly to put back on?

'I'm afraid your . . .' He paused momentarily as he looked across at Rita, who was lolled on her back wearing her goggles, snoring with her mouth open, her naked chest, like two white meringues, on full display. 'Er . . . your friend . . . is breaking the law.'

'You mean topless?' The penny dropped. Is that what all this was about? Surely he wasn't serious. Leaning over, she nudged Rita, who woke, dazed and snuffling.

'Jesus, what's a girl got to do around here to get some shut-eye?' She caught sight of the coastguard, who was scribbling something on his ring-binder notepad, while surreptitiously looking at her chest. 'What the . . .' She sat up, her breasts swinging jauntily in defiance.

Ripping off a piece of paper, he passed it to Rita, who stared at it, trying to focus.

'You're giving me a ticket?'

He nodded. 'You're indecent,' he sounded disapproving, while at the same time having a thorough inspection of her chest.

'Why, thanks.' She smiled, flirtatiously, trying to charm him. He wasn't to be charmed.

Jamming his notepad and pen into the rather snug pocket of his shorts, he cleared his throat – again – and with a podgy, nail-bitten finger shoved his sunglasses on to the sunken bridge of his nose. 'Either replace your top or vacate the beach.' And without waiting for an answer he strutted – as best he could on sand – back to his truck and, winching himself behind the wheel, set off across the beach.

Rita's face fell as she watched him go. 'I can't fucking believe it.' She stared at the ticket in her hand. 'The bastard's given me a sixty-dollar ticket for showing a bit of cleavage.' Grabbing her top, she huffily tied it around her neck.

'Which is a bit rich considering this is where they used to film *Baywatch*.' Screwing it up with disgust, she threw it in her bag. 'C'mon, let's go and get something to eat. I'm ravenous.' Suddenly desperate to feed her hangover, Rita scooped up her towel and threw her bag over her shoulder.

'Are you going to pay it?' Frankie followed her across the beach.

'I've got no choice, have I? I don't want to end up in court.' Pausing at the bottom of the stairs leading up to the road, she turned to Frankie. 'I'd feel like a right tit.'

They looked at each other, her words taking a nanosecond to register, before both cracking up with laughter.

They drove to the Hook, Line and Sinker Inn, a cheap'n'cheerful seafood restaurant along the Pacific Coast Highway that was a favourite with the surfer crowd and the groovier, less glitzy of the Malibu residents. Unlike the other restaurants specialising in seafood, which had white uniformed waiters, a choice of freshly baked rolls and individual pots of butter, a tinkling piano and plenty of hush, this was strictly self-service, with plastic sachets of ketchup and mayo, two-dollar side-orders of onion rings and plenty of noise – from the brawling kitchen staff, as well as the diners.

'They do great fish and chips,' chirped Rita, as they turned into the car park. 'I mean, I know you're a vegetarian and everything, but you can still eat the chips.' Her mouth watered. 'It's a shame you can't taste the king prawns, they're delicious . . . I just wish they'd fry them in breadcrumbs . . .' She sounded wistful. 'There's nothing better than a nice plate of scampi.'

Lazily resting her head on her forearm, which had absorbed all the heat from the sun and was belting it out like a fleshy radiator, Frankie leaned out of the window. Obviously Rita was on the classic seafood diet today. See food and eat it. She smiled at the pun, until she caught sight of something that wiped it from her face and made her stomach take a nose-dive. 'Oh, shit.'

'What?' Rita hit the brakes, causing the car to skid on the gravel, coughing up a veil of dust.

'Straight ahead . . .' Frankie pointed to the mud-splattered truck at the end of the car park, half hidden by some kind of bush. 'It's Reilly's.'

'Are you sure?' Rita squinted, trying to see through the dust.

'Of course I'm sure, I recognise the dent.'

'Crikey, there's no keeping you two apart, is there?' Rita reversed deftly into a space and turned the key in the ignition. The engine died. So did Frankie.

'We're not staying, are we?'

'Yeah, of course we are.' Adjusting her rear-view mirror, Rita applied a coat of fire-engine red lipstick over her zinc-whitened lips. 'Why, don't you want to?' She rubbed them together until they resembled the colour and texture of blancmange.

Frankie didn't say anything. She was too busy battling with herself. What was the big deal about seeing Reilly again? Nothing had happened between them last night. She didn't fancy him, and he'd made it quite clear he didn't fancy her. But if there wasn't a problem, why was she suddenly feeling sick?

'It's because Reilly's here, isn't it?'

Her silence screamed yes.

Rita gasped impatiently. 'What are you bothered about him for? I know he's a bit of a jerk, but it's not as if we have to have lunch with him. Just play it cool. We'll say a few quick "Hi-how-are-you"s and then we'll bugger off and grab some food.' Her stomach rumbled in agreement as she clambered out of the car. 'Anyway, I thought you said you two were friends.'

'We are.'

Frankie forced a smile. She was making a big fuss over nothing. Rita was right, she and Reilly were friends and she just needed to relax and play it cool. *Play it cool?* She'd never been cool in her life. Well, perhaps once at seventeen, when she'd passed her driving test and given Johnny Evans, the most fanciable bloke in the sixth form, a lift home in her mum's Fiat Panda. With her iridescent lilac lipstick, Bros-style ripped jeans and Johnny Evans in her passenger seat, she'd cruised past the other students standing at the bus stop, feeling as if she'd died and gone to heaven. That was about the extent of her coolness.

Flicking down the sun visor, she glanced at her reflection in the hairspray-glazed mirror. Normally it was a very flattering mirror, eradicating bags and shadows, rather like Vaseline over the lens, but not this time. This time, when she needed it the most, it was sharp, in focus and unforgiving. Her reflection blinked back: sandy, sweaty and red-faced, with dry, frazzled hair. Miserably snapping the mirror back against the windscreen, she got out of the car and looked down at what she was wearing – a washed-out, faded bikini, a tie-dye sarong and a pair of blue and white striped flip-flops that had seen better days – i.e. Camden market, summer of '94. It wasn't the kind of outfit she'd have chosen to try and look cool in – a flattering bias-cut dress, a pair of designer jeans, even eyeliner and a bit of mascara would have been nice. She rubbed her face with her towel, trying to remove the last traces of the beach. Right now she would have sold her soul for her make-up bag, nestling where she left it on the bathroom shelf. She didn't like the 'nude look'. She'd leave that to Rita.

★   ★   ★

'Hi there!' They were barely through the front door when Rita, grinning as if she'd won the lottery, locked on to Reilly like a heat-seeking missile and charged straight over to his table.

Frankie could have killed her. What happened to playing it cool? He looked surprised. Shocked even. He was sat with three other people. Opposite him was a man with short blond dreadlocks and a trendy, 'socially aware' type of female with an Annie Lennox haircut and tortoiseshell glasses with spearmint-green lenses. But Frankie's attention honed in on the girl sitting at his elbow.

Blonde, early twenties and pretty, in that rock-chicky dishevelled 'just got out of bed' way – an ironic description for a look that could only be achieved by getting out of bed hideously early in order to do all that time-consuming tousling and smudging – she was wearing a candyfloss-pink vest with a picture of Charlie's Angels on the front, ideal for showing off the kind of arms that can only ever be achieved by thrice-weekly tricep curls and a personal trainer. Leaning over Reilly's plate, she was busy stealing his leftover fries in the way women do when they first meet someone and they're pretending that they actually don't eat fries.

Watching her, it began to dawn on Frankie that there were in fact two men and two women at the table. Which made two couples. Oh-oh, she felt herself wanting to disappear into a hole. *Reilly was on a date.* A double date. Not knowing where to look, she avoided his eyes, pretending to be suddenly very interested in the contents of her beach bag – i.e. a screwed-up towel and *Give Up Men and Get a Life*. A book that only a couple of hours earlier had seemed as boring as hell, was now suddenly riveting. So riveting, in fact, that she had to reread the back cover ten times.

But as if the situation wasn't bad enough, Rita, being her usual perceptive self, hadn't cottoned on to the dating situation and was superglued to the end of their table, twirling strands of hair around her finger and giggling at some invisible joke. She pushed Reilly playfully. 'I can't believe we've bumped into you again. Are you following us?'

No, please, no. It was getting worse. Seeking a better prop, Frankie pretended to rummage for some unseen object in the bottom of her bag, wishing that she had a mobile, that it would ring, that she could talk to someone. Anyone. Directory Enquiries. 911. 69. She didn't care as long as she didn't have to talk to him.

Reilly glanced at Frankie. All he wanted to do was talk to her, but instead he was stuck chatting to her manic friend, Rita. He laughed at something Rita said, but didn't know what. He couldn't concentrate. He was still taken aback from seeing Frankie walk in. She was the last person he'd expected to see at his local hang-out. And she looked gorgeous. Trust him to look like total shit. Even worse, he was with Jed and Sophie, two old friends who, since the divorce, had kept trying to fix him up with their friends. Today it was some blonde chick called Chrissy, a wannabe pop star from Studio City. He watched Frankie. What the hell was she trying to find in that bag? He wished she'd look up and speak to him, talk about last night. But she didn't. Rita was still giggling manically in his ear. He couldn't wait any longer.

'Hi, Frankie.'

His voice. Low. Easy. Friendly. It was like a dart hitting the bull's-eye. She froze and looked up.

'Oh, hi.'

Her voice. High (a bit too high, even squeaky). Surprised (as in, my goodness, fancy seeing you here, I didn't see you there because I was just looking for something terribly important in my bag). Friendly (in a matey, we're such good friends our relationship is like one of brother and sister).

'How are you feeling after last night?' Pushing a strand of wayward hair from his eyes, he leaned back in his chair and away from Chrissy. He didn't want Frankie getting the wrong idea.

Frankie's mind went into overdrive. How should she be feeling after last night? Loved up? Throwing up? Was he referring to *his* effect on her, or the effect of all those margaritas and champagne cocktails? She wasn't sure, but she wanted to get things straight. Seeing as he'd obviously been going around telling Dorian, and anyone who would listen, that he wasn't interested in her, it would be highly embarrassing if he got the wrong idea and thought *she* was interested in him. Which he probably did, considering she'd spent most of the night wrapped around his neck like a pashmina.

'Hungover.' After all that mental activity, only one word sprang to mind. Being pissed was the mother of all excuses.

'Me too.' He smiled. It had a been good night. Well worth the hangover.

Frankie stalled. Was he playing the same game? Or maybe he wasn't getting the message? She decided to make it more obvious. 'God, I was *so* drunk.' She laughed oh-so-casually. 'What do they put in those margaritas? I was so out of my head, I can hardly remember being at the Cowboy Palace.' Surely he couldn't misunderstand that message, it was loud and clear. She was totally unaccountable for her actions and everything she'd done or said was a result of being sloshed. Plastered. Pissed as a fart. Even all that hugging wasn't anything to do with lust, or sex, or raging hormones, she'd only been clinging on to him because she was legless and liable to fall down drunk.

Reilly's mouth went dry. What was she trying to say? That she didn't remember? Surely she must remember. She had to remember.

'You don't remember dancing?'

'Did we dance?' As if she had to ask. She hadn't been able to stop thinking about it all bloody day.

He felt as if he'd been kicked in the guts. *She didn't remember*. How could she forget? Something had happened between them on that dance floor. Something had changed between them. He didn't know why, or how, or what the hell it was, but he did know that it had made him feel fantastic. And he hadn't felt like that in a long time. But maybe he'd got it wrong. Maybe it was one-sided and she hadn't felt anything. That last night had meant nothing. He meant nothing. Picking up his beer from the table, he took a swig. It tasted bitter.

'Yeah, we danced.' He spoke quietly.

They both looked at each other. And the expression on Reilly's face made Frankie suddenly regret her bravado. It wasn't one of cocky confidence and self-assurance. But of hurt and disappointment.

'Hey, aren't you going to introduce us?' Her thoughts were interrupted by the guy with the dreads.

'Oh, yeah, sure.' Snapping out of his daze, Reilly did his social bit. 'This is Jed, Sophie and Chrissy.'

Jed and Sophie exuberantly cheered, 'Hi there, great to meet you,' leaning across each other to shake hands, smiling.

Rock-chick Chrissy didn't seem as chuffed to make their acquaintance. Leaning against Reilly, she smiled without interest and managed a feeble 'hi' while continuing to dip fries in mayonnaise.

And then, for a moment, it felt awkward. Having entered the zone between being introduced and saying hello, and wanting to move on and say goodbye, Frankie didn't know what to do next. She wanted to get the hell out of there, but it was tricky. She didn't want to look rude, but then she didn't want to hang about like a groupie either. Luckily, Rita's stomach took control of the situation by omitting a long, low-bellied rumble.

'God, I'm starving. We haven't eaten.' She giggled.

'We should order.' Frankie motioned to the menu written on huge chalkboards around the restaurant and turned to the table. 'Well, it was nice to meet you.'

'Yeah, you too,' they chorused.

She looked at Reilly. 'Well, see you around.' She made an attempt at sounding cheerful and friendly, but her smile was small and uncomfortable. It gave her away.

'Yeah, sure.' So this was it. The brush-off.

Turning, she followed Rita, who was charging across to the other side of the restaurant. Reilly watched her go.

'Who was that chick?' purred Chrissy, placing her hand on top of his.

He looked away. 'Just a friend.' The words stuck in his throat.

25

Rita was over the moon. After months of 'thanks but no thanks', she'd received a call that morning which had made her dream of being an actress seem closer to becoming a reality. It was her agent, telling her that she'd been asked to reaudition for *Malibu Motel*, not for the original part of Kelly Carter, but as a different character, Tracy Potter, a straight-talking receptionist from England.

'Can you believe it? I was born to play that part,' enthused Rita, standing next to Frankie as they queued for cinema tickets at Mann's Chinese Theatre. Renowned for having the concrete casts of footprints and handprints of numerous Hollywood stars on the forecourt, together with the star-studded sidewalk known as the Walk of Fame directly outside, it was Rita's favourite cinema. 'If anyone can do a brilliant receptionist it's me. Forget method acting and all that crap about having to live the part for six months to get into character. I don't need to. I *was* the part for the past ten years.'

Paying for their tickets, they made their way through the straggling crowds to the entrance.

'Look, it must be a good omen. I've got the same size hands as Marilyn.' Rita could never resist joining the other sightseers who crouched on all fours to place their hands on top of the handprints of Marilyn Monroe. 'The footprints are the same too.' Proudly she showed off the perfect fit of her stiletto heels.

'How many times have you done that?' Frankie smiled, rather tempted herself to have a go.

'A few,' admitted Rita sheepishly. 'But it's still a good sign.'

'You don't need to rely on superstition. You've got talent.'

'Do you mean it?'

Frankie nodded, digging her hands in the pockets of her jacket. 'Not everyone could have played the back end of Daisy the Cow with such pathos.' Unable to keep a straight face, she broke into a smile. 'No, seriously, you're a great actress. You'll definitely get this part.' She was pleased for Rita. Although she never really talked about her career, Frankie knew how important it was to her.

'I hope so,' sighed Rita, crossing her fingers. 'If I don't get it, I don't know what I'm going to do. I've probably got enough money to last another few months, but if I don't get any work it looks as if I might have to come back to London and get a proper job.' She seemed miserable just at the idea. 'Though I don't think I can go back to being a receptionist. I can quite happily handle playing one for ten episodes, but not another ten years of actually being one . . .' Her voice tailed off as she surveyed the Hollywood greats captured for ever in concrete. 'There's more to life than answering phones.'

'Yeah, like learning lines.'

Rita huffily lit a cigarette. 'You obviously can't see the appeal of wanting to be an actress.'

'I can. Five thousand dollars an episode.' Frankie tested her footprint against that of Jane Russell. It was miles too big.

'I'm not in it for the money.' She saw the disbelief on Frankie's face. 'Though of course I'd be lying if I didn't say it would come in handy.' Blowing out a stream of smoke, she flicked her ash all over Humphrey Bogart. 'But I'm not like you. I haven't got a long string of qualifications, I haven't been to university, and until I started acting I thought I was doomed to a life sitting behind a desk, filing my bloody nails and reading *Inside Soap*.'

'I did that with a university degree,' quipped Frankie.

Choosing to ignore her, Rita continued, 'You had opportunities, I didn't. I was trapped. Acting was the only way out.' She caught herself and smiled self-consciously. 'Sorry, I'm going on a bit, aren't I?'

'Not at all, darling,' said Frankie, adopting a theatrical accent.

Rita couldn't help laughing. She knocked off the glowing embers of her cigarette and pinched the end between her fingers. 'Me? A luvvie? With a name like Rita Duffin?' Still laughing, she put the red-lipsticked filter in her pocket for later and, linking arms, they went inside.

'Mmm, I really fancy some of the chilli-cheese tortillas.' Walking into the refreshments foyer, Rita's eyes lit up like a fruit machine. She could smell fried food at fifty paces.

'The camera adds ten pounds,' reminded Frankie, steering Rita away.

'But maybe if you get some, I can have a few,' she said hopefully.

Frankie had known Rita too long not to know that 'a few' meant scoffing the lot. Like a parent with a child, she was about to refuse when she caught sight of her wistful expression. It was difficult to say no, especially when she knew that what Rita liked best about going to the cinema was the opportunity to sit on her bum for two hours, eating sweets and ice cream in the dark. Calories didn't count at the movies.

'What about popcorn?' suggested Frankie, relenting and guiding her over to a line of people queuing to buy family-size bags of M&Ms, pick'n'mix, fizzy drinks and buckets of freshly popped popcorn from the machine blowing out the little cream-coloured balls.

Sticking her hands into her Gucci rip-off leather jacket and through her lining, Rita pulled a face at the low-fat, low-appeal alternative. Until her frown faded and her pupils dilated as she caught sight of something that was a lot more interesting than popped corn. 'Hey, get a load of that,' she hissed, nudging Frankie's with her elbow.

Standing in line, Frankie turned to see exactly what 'that' was. Not surprisingly, it was a man, but not just any man. Frankie groaned. Trust Rita to get the hots for the guy in a short-sleeved red and white striped shirt, colour-coordinated baseball cap and pinafore, standing behind the counter shovelling popcorn into cardboard tubs.

The popcorn seller must have overheard Rita's leching – it would have been difficult not to – and he looked up, taking off his cap to push back his surf-bleached hair. 'Sweet or salt?' he asked, scoop at the ready.

But before either could answer, he suddenly cried, 'Hey, Frankiiiiiiieeeee.' Holding the note, he dropped his plastic scooper and, wiping the sugar from his hands on his pinafore, bounded from behind the counter, flinging out his arms to give her a suffocating hug.

Crushed between a pair of very broad Tropicana tan biceps, Frankie didn't know what the hell was going on. She looked sideways at Rita, who was frozen, her mouth hanging open, unable to hide her disbelief that her friend somehow knew this Adonis.

Releasing her from his grasp, he laughed. 'Hey, don't you remember? It's me, Matt.' He began beating his chest. 'Tarzan.'

Frankie twigged. She hadn't recognised him without his loincloth. She managed a feeble 'Hi', before he drowned her out, jumping around like an over-eager puppy. 'This is soooo cool, man.' His grin stretched wide across his face. 'How are things going?'

'Great.' She tried to look enthusiastic, but it was pretty obvious she'd never make an actress. 'And you?'

'Rockin'.' He nodded, swaying backwards and forwards on his heels, unable to stand still. Noticing her staring at his uniform, he reddened. 'Hey, this is just casual, man, just until I start acting twenty-four-seven.' He continued nodding enthusiastically. 'It won't be long. I've signed with a new agent and I've been offered some really cool jobs. A couple of weeks ago I was a dead guy in *ER*, and this week I had a line in a deodorant commercial.' He stopped smiling and affected a serious face and a dodgy English accent: ' "Keeps odours away, all day." ' His face split back into a grin. 'Cool, hey?'

'You're an actor?' Rita, who'd been dying to interrupt, saw her cue and dived in with perfect timing. 'I'm an actress.' She flashed Matt her headshot smile.

'No way!' Eyes wide with disbelief, Matt looked surprised, as if being an actor was a rare and unusual occupation in LA. Immediately they launched into shop talk. 'Which classes do you attend? What auditions have you been up for? Who's your agent?'

Frankie stood on the sidelines, feeling very green and prickly. She watched their body language – the way they were smiling at each other, how their bodies were moving closer together, how Matt kept rubbing his chest while Rita kept thrusting out hers.

'Hey, how much longer have I gotta wait in line?' interrupted an impatient woman pushing in front of Rita and waggling a ten-dollar bill. 'I wanna large Pepsi with plenny of ice.'

Rita ignored her. 'Let me give you my number.' Making no attempt at subtlety, she dug out one of her cards from her bag and thrust it at him.

'Cool.' Matt gazed at her, hypnotised. 'I'll call you.' He grinned, seemingly oblivious of the growing line of cinema-goers that was beginning to zigzag across the patterned carpet of the foyer. Desperate for confectionery and cola, they were becoming increasingly rowdy.

'Can't wait.' She winked and giggled breathlessly.

Frankie couldn't help but applaud Rita's shameless pulling tactics. There wasn't a stutter, a blush or even a smidgen of self-consciousness. Any minute now and she'd be doing her Marilyn Monroe wiggle.

'Well, bye then.' Rita fluttered her fingers in a wave.

'See ya.' Mesmerised, Matt waved back as a giant of a man strode up behind him and gripped his arm. 'Me an' my wife are gettin' kinda hungry.' He gestured to a colossal woman slumped against the M&Ms. 'I wanna half-dozen Twinkies, two tubs of popcorn – one sweet an' one salt – a pint of Ben and Jerry's Chunky Monkey, *and I wanna have them now.*'

Relieved that they were leaving before it all got ugly, Frankie said goodbye. Matt didn't seem to notice. Despite being pinned against the Snickers promotion by an irate customer, he was too busy staring at Rita as she wiggled across the foyer, transfixed at the way her bottom bobbed up and down, like a surfboard floating on a wave. He couldn't take his eyes off her. Proof that not all gentlemen – surfers included – preferred blondes.

'Where've you been hiding *that*?' Rita stopped wiggling as soon as they turned the corner and began climbing the stairs.

'Nowhere. I met him on that commercial I did.' *The commercial I did with Reilly*, Frankie thought to herself.

'And you never mentioned him?' In disbelief, Rita yanked open the door of Screen One and tottered inside. She looked across at Frankie, a horny grin spread all over her face, and then tutted. 'Bloody hell, you must be in love.'

Frankie flinched. 'I must?' She handed in their tickets to the man who stood at the entrance.

'If you didn't notice Matt, yeah, you really must still be mad about Hugh.' She shook her head, full of awe at her devotion.

'Oh, yeah.' Frankie relaxed. What had made her think Rita was referring to Reilly, not Hugh? Unnerved by her mistake, she changed the subject. 'By your reaction, I take it you liked Matt.' Stuffing the ticket stubs in her pocket, she followed the usher, who was leading them down the aisle, waving his torch from side to side.

'*Liked him?*' Rita rolled her eyes. 'Put it this way, I wouldn't kick him out of bed . . .' She broke off, giggling to herself as she remembered past nocturnal aerobics. 'Well, not if I can help it.'

Finding the correct row number, they squeezed and excused their way past people's knees, trying not to knock over cups of Dr Pepper or send buckets of popcorn scattering like ping-pong balls, before eventually arriving at their seats. Flicking them back, they thankfully sat down.

'But I thought you said you'd gone off men.' It was a feeble attempt, but Frankie had to give it a go. Rita was showing all the signs of sliding down the slippery slope of lust and she knew it was up to her, as Rita's best friend, to try and rescue her with the voice of reason. But it was no good. Rita didn't want to be rescued, ta very much.

'After seeing that, I've been turned on again.' Grabbing a fistful of popcorn, she lay back in her seat and began chewing loudly. 'Who wouldn't be?'

'Sssshhhh,' hissed somebody behind them.

Rita tutted, and continued. Leaning closer to Frankie, she whispered loudly, 'Well, apart from you, of course. But then you'd never even notice another bloke apart from Hugh, would you?'

Frankie hesitated. But she was saved from answering by the title music, which suddenly blared out from the speakers as the film started.

26

Over the next few weeks Rita clocked up six dates with Matt, which in LA was longer than some marriages, and began displaying all the tell-tale signs of a woman smitten: going to bed wearing full make-up and Victoria Secret underwear in case, for some reason known only to those besotted, he should drop by at two in the morning; loss of appetite – even for cheese nachos and Oreos – a phenomenon for Rita; and beginning every sentence with his name, as in Matt's apartment was so funky, Matt was an amazing actor, Matt had the biggest dick she'd ever seen – and Rita had seen a few.

As the loyal best friend, Frankie listened patiently, trying to look interested as Rita played back his voicemail messages, trying to decide whether or not he sounded keen, too keen, over-keen; dug out her relationship bible, *Soulmates in the Stars* and read his'n'hers star signs, working out their compatibility according to Venus rising, full moons and something to do with Mercury; and repeated word for word their conversations, while dissecting, analysing and quizzing every word, phrase and sentence.

For hours at a time she regaled Frankie about every detail of the romance of the century, from the way he'd cooked her spaghetti bolognese, looking steamy and muscular as he leaned over the stove with his Parmesan cheese grater, through their first kiss as they'd walked his dog around Runyan Canyon, to how she'd given him his first blow job in the changing rooms at Urban Outfitters. As yet they hadn't slept together, which in Rita's chequered love life was an achievement in restraint. But it appeared that Matt was the one who'd been less than forthcoming in the bedroom. 'He obviously wants us to get to know each other better,' she'd murmured dreamily, as she'd fingered an old surf sweatshirt he'd put around her shoulders at the movies the night before to keep her warm. 'Isn't that sweet?'

Frankie didn't disagree. After all, if wearing a smelly old sweatshirt and giving fellatio to a man with his Day-Glo O'Neill surfing shorts round his ankles made Rita happy, then Frankie was happy. Except she wasn't. She was fed up. While Rita spent her evenings with Matt enjoying the head rush of coupledom, she was sat on the sofa with Fred and Ginger, sinking into the abyss of singledom, watching *Ally McBeal* reruns and trying not to feel sorry for herself. But she did. Rita's success in both her love life and her career – she'd reauditoned for *Malibu Motel* and was now waiting to hear – only highlighted the glaring failure of her own life. Apart from the small matters of a failed relationship and being of no fixed abode, with a career going nowhere fast.

In the last few weeks she'd gone from feature writer, to photographer's assistant, to her current job – Dorian's cleaner. Not exactly the kind of career ladder she'd been hoping for when she got her 2:1 degree. Knowing she was strapped for cash, Dorian had offered to pay her to clean his flat and water the abundance of plant life on his balcony, which, over the last few weeks, had taken on the appearance of Kew Gardens. She was going to say no, out of pride more than anything else, but the money being offered was too good to refuse.

Not that she didn't like LA. Quite the opposite. She loved the weather, loved going to the beach, loved hanging out with Rita and Dorian. She was living in a fantastic apartment, driving around with her best mate in a Thunderbird convertible, having as much free time as she wanted. Even her cats were enjoying the sunshine. It was the stuff dreams are made of. But not her dreams.

Looking back, she could now see it had been a crazy idea to come to LA, a crazy idea to think running away could change things. To hope that six thousand miles would solve everything. What had she thought would happen? That LA could wave its magic wand and give her life a Hollywood movie ending? Staying in London had meant facing up to a future full of holes where Hugh, their flat in Fulham and her career should be. Exactly, she realised, the same future as she was facing right now. Being in LA hadn't changed anything. The problems were the same, it was just different scenery. So why didn't she admit defeat, pack her bags and take the first plane back to the UK? After all, what was there to keep her in LA?

Reilly. Every time she asked herself that question, his name kept popping into her head. It was ridiculous, she hardly knew the bloke, but ever since that day in Malibu, ever since they'd had that awful, stilted conversation, he'd been on her mind. Things kept reminding her of him – seeing a commercial on TV, hearing a Country and Western track on the radio or going to the Coffee Bean and Tea Leaf for her morning cappuccino. One day when she was grocery shopping at Ralph's Supermarket she thought she saw him near the deli counter, next to the fresh pasta, but when he turned round she discovered it wasn't him at all. In fact, the bloke looked nothing like him – he had a goatee and was wearing black patent-leather slip-ons *with gold chains across the front*. Even driving along Sunset, she'd become aware that, without even realising it, her eyes were unconsciously picking out all the Broncos and taking a second look to see if he was behind the wheel. But he never was. He seemed to have disappeared. Vanished in a puff of cigarette smoke.

It crossed her mind to call him up just to say hi. After all, she could easily get his number from Dorian. But she decided against it. Despite what she'd told Rita, she and Reilly weren't exactly friends – well, not the kind of friends who'd ring each other up just for a chat. What on earth would they chat about? His date with Chrissy? His ex-wife? Her ex-boyfriend? Somehow she couldn't see it. Nope, she wasn't going to ring him, just like she knew he wasn't going to ring her. Which meant that her relationship/friendship/crush/God knows what with Reilly was over before it had even started.

'Guess what?' Rita hobbled into the living room on the heels of her feet, cotton wool wedged firmly between each toe. In one hand she was waving a bottle of VAMP nail varnish – fashion trends seemed to take a while to hit LA, where leggings, big hair and purple lip-liner were still very much in abundance – and in the other the phone's handset.

'What?' Frankie lay flat out on the sofa watching a live police car-chase on TV and working her way through a packet of cheese nachos. Ever since Rita had met Matt they'd lain untouched on the top shelf, gathering dust. Not, Frankie mused, unlike herself.

'That was Dorian on the phone . . . He's invited us to our first Christmas party.'

'*Christmas party?*'

'Well, it is 10 December. Christmas is only two weeks away.'

'Christ,' muttered Frankie, not very religiously. Where had the year gone? She continued watching as the getaway car careered down the 405 with helicopters in pursuit, concentrating on digging the last remaining nachos crumbs from the corner of the bag. She wasn't in Christmas party mood. More of a stuff-her-face-in-front-of-the-telly mood. But, thinking about it, that was pretty Christmassy, wasn't it?

Most people tended to celebrate the big day doing exactly the same thing. She was just getting into the festive spirit a little early this year.

'And guess who's having the party?' Determined to get her friend's interest, Rita hovered in front of the screen, blocking out the climax of the car-chase as the police swooped in to make an arrest.

Realising this was blackmail, Frankie had no choice but to play along. 'Who?'

Taking a deep breath, as if she was about to blow up a balloon, Rita then exploded, *'Carter Mansfield.'*

'Carter Mansfield?' Like an echo, Frankie dropped the crumpled bag of Doritos and sat up, dislodging Ginger, who was curled up in a ball in the folds of her jumper.

Carter Mansfield was a movie legend. In the 1970s he'd been a leading man and housewife's pin-up, famous for his hip-hugging bellbottom Levi's and shirts unbuttoned to reveal his seriously hairy chest and obligatory gold medallion. In the 1980s and early 1990s it all went a bit pear-shaped – along with his waistline – but in the last six or seven years he'd got rid of the love-handles, relaunched his career and made a string of hugely successful movies, starring alongside some of Hollywood's most glamorous leading ladies.

'Is this party tonight?'

'Yeah, Dorian's picking us up at nine,' gabbled Rita excitedly. 'Just think, everyone's going to be there ... film stars, directors, producers, all the big names in Hollywood ...' Her voice tailed off. 'Shit, what am I going to wear? That catsuit I bought last week's still covered in bolognese sauce.' She couldn't resist a faint smile as she remembered how it got there, before snapping back to reality. Dropping the phone and nail varnish on the coffee table, she grabbed Frankie's wrist to look at her watch. 'Five o'clock. Thank God, there's still time.' Without letting go, she attempted to yank her up from the sofa. 'Come on, move your arse.' Unbelievably, this was the same mouth that could recite Shakespeare.

'Where are we going?' Frankie tried to resist. Her hair was a mess, she was wearing a pair of skanky old tracksuit bottoms and she'd just consumed the best part of fifteen hundred calories and seventy-five grams of fat. (If being in LA had taught her one thing, it was the calorie and fat-content value of everything.) The only place she wanted to go was the shower.

'We've been invited to one of the biggest parties in Hollywood and I've got nothing to wear. Where do you think we're going?' Grabbing her wallet and car keys, Rita stuck her feet – complete with cotton-wool inserts – into a pair of Perspex mules. 'Rodeo Drive.'

27

'Hi, and how are you today?'

The grinning assistant swooped on Frankie the moment her mud-splattered Nikes hit the highly polished floor. It must have been a trigger mechanism.

'Erm . . .' she faltered, not sure whether or not to proceed. Being greeted at shop doorways by a member of staff wasn't something that often happened in London. Mumbling a vague reply, she headed blindly to the back of the store and pretended to be really interested in a pair of seen-it-a-million-times-before beige linen trousers.

'I love your jacket.' Not about to give up that easily, the assistant followed her. 'It's so cute.' Blonde, rosy-cheeked and wearing a Santa hat, she spoke in a singsong nursery-rhyme voice.

'Er, thanks.' Was she being sarcastic? Fingering her jacket, a scruffy old suede thing she'd had for years, Frankie didn't know whether to take her seriously or not. In Bond Street, London's equivalent to Rodeo, the shop assistants were the Shop Resistance, eyeing her with suspicion while flicking through the latest issue of *Harpers and Queen*, or experiencing a sudden loss of hearing when she asked for something in a different size. She wasn't used to being complimented. On the contrary, she was used to feeling like something the cat had dragged in.

'I'd love to buy one. Where did you get it?'

Her cosy friendliness (or was it fake enthusiasm?) was beginning to grate. 'Portobello market,' replied Frankie, trying to move away to another part of the store. But there was to be no escape. Everywhere she turned, the assistant was there behind her, like Banquo's ghost.

'Is that a store in Beverly Hills?'

'No, London.'

'Oh, you're from London. I have relatives in London.'

She was about to start reciting her family tree when, luckily for Frankie, she was distracted by the sight of Rita, who'd discovered a table stacked with piles of neatly folded tops and was pulling them out one by one, flinging them all over the place and spinning around like a whirling-dervish.

'Would you like me to find your size?' Falling over herself with eagerness, the shop assistant forgot all about Frankie and rushed to Rita's aid. Rummaging through the jumble, she piled herself up like a mule with the stack of clothes Rita had already selected and cheerily steered her towards the changing room, gushing, 'If you need anything, I'll be right outside.'

'Do these trousers make me look fat?'

Twenty minutes and as many outfits later, Rita stood in front of the full-length mirror, which had been annoyingly positioned *outside* the changing rooms. She was wearing a flared white suit which the cooing shop assistant had tried to persuade her made her look like Bianca Jagger on her wedding day. She wasn't convinced. In fact, she had a sneaking suspicion she looked more like Elvis on a rhinestone, fried-banana-sandwich day. Needing the honest opinion that only a best friend could give, she turned to Frankie, who was flicking idly through a pile of glossies while flaked out on the leather sofa thoughtfully provided by the management to prevent bored husbands and boyfriends from wandering off – and taking their credit cards with them.

Rita pulled a face. 'Elvis?'

Glancing up from *AmericanVogue,* Frankie nodded sympathetically. 'Live in Las Vegas.'

Swearing, Rita barged past the still-smiling assistant and dived back inside the changing room. Pulling off the offending suit, she threw it on the heap of rejected items that was beginning to take on the proportions of the millennium dome. Everything she'd tried on was either the wrong colour, the wrong size, the wrong fit or the wrong style. It was a bloody nightmare. Whoever described shopping as retail therapy must have been in therapy. And after this shopping trip, so would she be.

'What about the Gap?' After leaving behind the store, and its members of staff folding and replumping every item of clothing Rita could fit into, they stood on the pavement waiting for the lights to change. Being unusually law-abiding, Rita was refusing to jaywalk in case she got another ticket, and instead was trying to see if there was anyone famous driving the shocking-pink Corvette which had pulled up alongside a red Ferrari Testarossa being revved by a man old and bald enough to know better.

'Fruit-coloured twin sets and Capri pants?' Rita pulled a face at Frankie's suggestion. 'We're going to a party in Beverly Hills, not a knees-up down the local.'

For the first time in her life, she was willing to sacrifice her fondness for high-street fashion in favour of something a bit more upmarket. She had a feeling that this party was going to be an opportunity to 'network', a word she kept hearing being whispered on people's lips as the secret of success in Hollywood. As yet, the only people she'd had the opportunity to network with were Matt's surfing mates, valet parkers and the Mexican blokes who packed her groceries at Ralph's, which probably explained why her only LA part to date was as a life-size furry chicken in a KFC commercial.

The lights changed and they crossed, swerving to avoid a crowd of Japanese tourists, weighed down with zoom-lens Nikons and billboard-size shopping bags bursting with Christmas presents, having their picture taken in front of the Regent Beverly Wilshire, home to Richard Gere's penthouse in *Pretty Woman*.

'The idea's to walk in and knock 'em dead,' she continued, watching a leopard-skin and diamond-clad blonde who'd had so many facelifts she looked as if she were permanently in a wind tunnel popping out of the pink Corvette with her Pekinese and into Cartier for yet more baubles. 'What about that shop over there?' She pointed further up the street to a huge, three-floor, glass-fronted monolith.

'Versace?' Frankie was amazed. What the hell had got into Rita? Since when had she worn designer clothes? She favoured Top Shop and New Look and anything skimpy for under twenty quid. 'Isn't that a bit out of our price range? Liz Hurley might be able to afford a wardrobe full of their dresses, but I don't think she's on the same budget as us.'

'Speak for yourself,' huffed Rita. At the mention of Liz Hurley, her mind was made up. 'If it's good enough for her, then it's good enough for us.' Unaware that she'd somehow managed to get that the wrong way round, she clattered determinedly ahead down the pavement, her ankles wobbling precariously on her needle-thin heels.

As the highly polished smoked-glass door was opened by an unsmiling Lurch character in a puce-coloured suit, Frankie knew she'd been lulled into a false sense of security about shopping in Beverly Hills. There was no meet and greet policy here. No hiyas, beaming smiles, candy-coloured uniforms and swinging jazz on the shop stereo, as in the Land of the Gap. Instead there was a deathly silence, broken only by the solemn chant of Benedictine monks on CD, and sour-faced Italian assistants dotted around like statues.

Oblivious of the drop in temperature, which hadn't been caused by the airconditioning, Rita barged inside and began bustling around the store, unfolding sequined tops from their protective layers of tissue paper and yanking mirrored scraps of material masquerading as dresses off their hangers with wild abandon. 'What about this?' Pulling a slashed-to-the-thigh embroidered number from the rail, she held it up against herself. About four feet and a bit of it trailed on the ceramic tiled floor – obviously Donatella didn't design for five-foot-nothings.

Frankie didn't answer. This was not the place to dash around, mussing up neatly folded jumpers, picking up skirts and yelling, 'Hey, look, this would be great with that new halter-neck from Zara.' No. No. No. It was like being in a museum. A place to walk around whispering and pointing. Where customers were meant to look but not touch, unless of course they were loaded – or Liz Hurley herself. And she was neither.

'Hmm, maybe not. It looks a bit common.' Rita was about to shove the dress back on the rail when an assistant materialised by her side and eased it from her grasp, as if removing something precious from a sticky-fingered toddler. 'I'm afraid we're closing,' she hissed in a thick Mafia accent.

'You're joking? Already?' She turned to Frankie in surprise. 'What time is it?'

Frankie caught a look from the assistant that came straight out of *GoodFellas*. 'Time to go.'

'I never did like all that safety-pinned stuff anyway,' huffed Rita after being ushered to the door, which Lurch had closed firmly behind them. Ruffled, she lit a cigarette and, standing with her hands on her hips, glared down Rodeo Drive, smoke billowing out of her nostrils like a dragon. 'At that price you'd think they'd at least be able to afford bloody zips.'

'Hurry up. It's nearly seven o'clock.' Knackered, Frankie sat cross-legged on the changing-room floor. She'd lost count of how many shops they'd been in, but Rita had promised her this would be the last. 'At this rate we're never going to get to the party.' She leaned back against the floor-length mirror.

'Won't be a sec.' Rita's voice wafted out from behind a curtain. After all that walking, her feet had swollen up inside her Perspex mules like loaves in the oven and, being lazy, she'd attempted to take off her trousers without taking off her shoes first. As a result, her trousers were now firmly wedged, inside out, around the stiletto heels. 'I just want to find something special for tonight. You know, something with a bit of oomph.' Her head reappeared from the side of the curtain. 'Matt's been invited to this party as well, and I've got a feeling that tonight's going to be the night that we finally do it . . . You know . . . sleep together.' Making a final effort, she pulled the bottom of her trousers. 'I can't wait. The suspense is killing me . . . *And so are these fucking trousers,*' she muttered, giving them a final tug. Like the pop of a cork, her feet appeared and she fell backwards, grabbing the curtain for balance and tearing it partly from its hooks. 'Fuck,' she swore, managing to stand upright. Catching her breath, she looked at Frankie. 'I've already bought some great underwear, especially for the occasion. It's black satin trimmed with red lace. Real hooker stuff.' She let out a Sid James cackle.

Frankie smiled. Rita didn't have to tell her. She'd already spotted the bulging Trashy Lingerie carrier bags stuffed behind the laundry basket in the bathroom. 'So is it serious between you and Matt?'

'Definitely.' Rita nodded. 'You know what it's like when you meet someone. It only takes a few minutes, sometimes less, to suss out if the relationship's going to work or not.'

'A bit like drying your hair.' Smiling wryly, Frankie pulled a ringlet and let it spring back. 'Sometimes you know it's going to look great before you've even picked up the hair-dryer, and other times you spend ages faffing around, trying all kinds of things. But even after all that effort it still ends up going wrong and looking terrible.'

'Exactly.' Rita grinned. 'Well, this is one time I know it's going to work. I can tell it's going to be great. He's the one . . . I just know it.' Grabbing a pair of leather trousers, she started pulling them on.

'You said that about Barry,' Frankie reminded her, picking up some of Rita's discarded clothes from the floor and putting them back on their hangers. Barry was a Scotsman who'd said he was a millionaire and worked in transportation, and with whom Rita had had a fling a couple of years ago. 'In fact, didn't you say you were going to marry him?'

Rita blushed. 'That was before I ordered a take-out one night and found him on our doorstep with a twelve-inch Meat Feast.'

Frankie started laughing at the memory.

'Well, how was I to know "working in transportation" meant zipping around London on a fifty-cc moped deliv-ering Domino's pizzas?' Rita couldn't help but laugh too. 'There was I, imagining a lifetime of luxury – holidays in Florida twice a year, big detached house with a double garage, fancy sports cars, the works – and instead I was faced with a future of extra garlic bread and doughballs. I think I had a lucky escape.' She stopped yanking the trousers. Wedged across her calves, the leather stretched tightly like the skin of a drum, they refused to go any higher. 'God, I give up. I'm never going to fit into these. I must have picked up the wrong size.' Tugging them off, she tossed them across to Frankie. 'Why don't you try them?'

'Me? In leather trousers? You've got to be joking.'

'Why? You've got the figure for them.'

Tempted, Frankie looked at them, before dismissing the idea. 'I couldn't afford them anyway.'

'I'll lend you the money.' Rita wasn't going to let her get off that lightly.

'Thanks, but they're just not me.'

'What is you? For God's sake, you're twenty-nine, not eighty-nine. Be bold. Wear something different for once.' Rita stood in her G-string, hands adamantly on hips.

Frankie deliberated. Perhaps Rita was right, perhaps she did need a change of image. Deciding there was no harm in trying, she peeled off her trainers and jeans and tried on the leather trousers, together with a little shoestring strap top Rita had discarded earlier. Both fitted perfectly.

Rita let out a long, low whistle. 'Bloody hell, you look amazing.'

Frankie looked at her reflection, and surprised herself. She looked completely different. 'Do you think so?' She wasn't used to wearing clothes like these. Hugh always used to like her in dresses or trousersuits, something smart-casual. This outfit was neither. The trousers were like a second skin and the top was definitely on the skimpy side. 'Are you sure it doesn't make me look . . . well . . . *tarty*?'

Rita pulled a face. 'C'mon, would I ever choose something that's tarty?'

Frankie was afraid to answer. Luckily she didn't have to.

'Now, what about this?' asked Rita, wriggling into a red silk dress. Breathing in, she twirled in front of the mirror.

'You look great.'

Frankie wasn't just saying that. After a fortnight's diet of raging hormones and a racing pulse, the pounds had dropped off, leaving Rita with the perfect hour-glass figure – boobs, bum and waist – a body shape hated by the fashion world, but loved by men in the real world.

'Do you think it makes my boobs look too big?'

'We're in LA, remember. Since when could boobs be too big?'

Sticking out her chest, she tweaked the material. 'You've got a point.'

'Judging by all those before and after photos I've seen in *LA Weekly*, you've got about five thousand dollars' worth there. You should be proud of them, they're a valuable asset.' Frankie peered down at her own silhouette. 'I'll be lucky if I've got ten bucks.'

Laughing, Rita yanked the straining bra straps that were beginning to dig deep grooves into her shoulders. 'Let's just hope Matt's a boob man.'

'Well, you'll certainly find out tonight in that outfit.'

Rita's expression became serious. 'I never thought I'd say this, but I'm glad we haven't slept together. This way it feels as if we've been able to have a proper courtship without the whole sex thing taking over.'

'A courtship? It's only been a few weeks.'

Rita pouted sulkily. 'Don't get all prudey with me, you slept with Hugh after three days . . .' She broke off, regretting what she'd just said. Her and her big mouth.

Frankie pushed a curl of hair behind her ear and didn't say anything. Instead she stood looking at herself in the mirror, remembering. After a moment she spoke. 'I know, New Year's Eve. God, it seems so long ago.' Her voice was quiet.

'Well, it was nearly two years ago. Things have changed, we've all changed.' Rubbing her friend's arm affectionately, Rita gave her a smile of reassurance. 'Even you.' Raising an eyebrow she stood back and looked Frankie up and down. 'Just look at you! Hugh would hardly recognise you.'

Frankie hardly recognised herself. It was as if she was looking at a different person.

'Well? Are you getting those or what?' Pulling on her leggings and halter-neck top, Rita picked up the dress, ready to pay for it at the cash register. 'Come on, you only live once. *And* it's Christmas.' The classic excuse for everything.

Staring at her reflection, something inside Frankie kick-started. For the first time in ages she liked what she saw, and it wasn't just the clothes. For weeks she'd thought of herself as a failure, the helpless victim that things kept happening to. It had taken something as simple as a new outfit to make her see a different Frankie, a new Frankie, one who was going to start taking control again. Rita was right. And what better way to celebrate her one and only life than by buying a pair of three-hundred-dollar leather trousers? She smiled. 'Yeah, why the hell not?'

28

The party was already in full swing by the time they arrived. Uniformed waiters were busy serving drinks and sushi to the hundreds of guests mingling outside on the stadium-sized terrace, while around the edges of the pink, heart-shaped swimming pool coked-up leggy blondes with silicone tits and gravity-defying bikinis were dancing to the live band's blasting rendition of '*Play That Funky Music, White Boy*'. It was like walking into an MTV video.

'I feel a bit overdressed,' hissed Rita, pausing at the top of the mosaic-tiled steps leading down to the terrace. 'Nobody said bring a bikini.' She looked disappointed.

Frankie felt relieved. One look at the gyrating Barbie dolls and she shuddered at the thought of getting into her M&S two-piece, underwired cups or not. 'I don't know about you, but I need a drink,' she said, trying to attract the attention of one of the waiters. The wine she'd brought suddenly seemed a mistake. This wasn't the kind of house party where you bring a bottle, even if, at ten bucks, it was better than the plonk she usually bought from Oddbins. Catching the waiter's eye she quickly hid the Chardonnay behind a marble statue and grabbed a couple of cocktails.

From the moment they'd been whisked through the huge electronic gates by security men with walkie-talkies and Frankie had caught her first glimpse of the huge White

House-style mansion, she knew that, despite a face plastered with Clarins Beauty Flash Balm and Estée Lauder cosmetics, forty minutes spent with her curls clamped between Rita's hair straighteners and a pair of leather trousers from Rodeo Drive, she was completely out of her depth. To date, her experience of house parties had been the ones she'd been to with Hugh in one-bedroom flats in west London where there'd been *Chillout Ibiza* wafting out of the stereo, a fold-out dining-room table full of M&S nibbles and Tesco's readymade 95 per cent fat-free dips, and a choice of Penfolds white or red to drink in Habitat wine glasses, or chipped mugs for those arriving late from the pub. None of them had put on horse-drawn carriages to ferry the celebrity guests to the entrance, live bands together with a couple of famous pop stars as entertainment, or men in white uniforms bearing a striking resemblance to Richard Gere in *An Officer and a Gentleman* and serving Bellinis and oysters on silver trays. It was intimidating stuff, but at least there was one consolation. She wasn't there by herself. She had Rita.

'Christ, have you seen all the free booze?' whooped Rita, taking a swig from her crystal glass. 'Makes a bit of a change from some of the parties I've been to. At most of them you'd be lucky to scrounge a warm can of Fosters.' She licked the bubbles from her top lip. Still, it's a bit of a shame I can't take full advantage.'

'Why not?' Frankie had never known Rita pass up alcohol, especially when she wasn't paying for it.

'I don't want to be drunk when Matt gets here, do I?' Trying to fluff her hair, which she'd earlier sprayed rock solid with hairspray, she tutted. 'I want to seduce him, and falling all over the place with my dress up to my armpits and mascara down to my chin isn't exactly attractive.'

'What time's he arriving?' Frankie fiddled self-consciously with the lace-trim on her top. She wasn't used to showing so much cleavage. Even if most of it was Wonderbra.

'In about half an hour. He's coming straight from an audition.' As she squinted down at the party below, a smile curled up the corners of Rita's mouth. 'Bloody hell, I wondered where Dorian had disappeared to.'

'I thought he said he had some business to attend to.' Frankie stopped fiddling and tried to see what was so amusing.

'Well, he's certainly attending to something.' Rita pointed towards the swimming pool, where Dorian was rubbing himself up and down one of the pneumatic blondes in a zebra-print thong, bikini. 'Isn't that Pamela whatshername?'

'Looks like her,' agreed Frankie, 'but then most of the women do.' Sipping her drink, she watched him. He obviously didn't feel out of his depth.

'I'll tell you who I haven't seen, yet . . .' Noticing that the plasters which she'd put on her toes to stop her new sling-backs from hurting were peeling off, Rita crouched down to restick them. 'I haven't seen Reilly.'

'Reilly?' Frankie attempted indifference. 'You didn't mention he was invited.' Taking a large sip of her drink, she felt her hand tremble.

'Sorry, I completely forgot. You know me, memory like a sieve.' Satisfied that her plasters were now firmly in place, she stood back up and switched her attention to nicotine. 'Dorian invited him and that blonde, I can't remember her name, the one he was with in Malibu.' She began hunting around in her handbag for her American Spirit.

'Chrissy?' Frankie hadn't forgotten her name. It was stamped, like a cattle-brand, on her memory.

'Yeah, that's her.' Finding her crumpled packet of fags, she offered it to Frankie.

There was only one left, and normally Frankie would have refused, but this time need overcame her manners. Taking it, she accepted a light and inhaled sharply. So Reilly was going out with Chrissy? She didn't know why it should bother her so much, but it did.

Swallowing a mouthful of Cosmopolitan, she savoured the sharp taste of vodka, cranberry and sting of lime. The cigarettes and alcohol made her head spin and she took another drag. She'd promised herself that tonight she was going to forget about everything and enjoy herself, have a laugh, *live a little*. But what was stopping her? So what if Reilly was turning up with his new girlfriend? It didn't have to spoil her evening. It didn't have to stop her from having a good time. Did it? Draining the last mouthful of alcohol, she waved her empty glass. She felt like getting drunk. 'Fancy another?'

'Bloody hell, you're certainly getting into the party spirit.' Rita grinned approvingly.

'Why not? After all, you're the one who keeps telling me I'm young, free and single,' responded Frankie, rescuing two more drinks from one of the attractive waiters and thrusting one on Rita. 'Come on, we can't stand here all night.' Taking a gulp of her drink, which threatened to slosh over the side of the cocktail glass, she knew there was nothing else for it but to dive in at the deep end. And so without waiting for Rita, who was lingering behind to swipe a couple of cucumber rolls – well, OK, three, but sushi was practically fat-free – Frankie summoned up every last scrap of courage she had, and set off down the steps to the party below.

A trayful of Kir Royals later, Frankie was feeling brave enough to circulate without Rita, who, now that Matt had arrived, was sitting astride him next to the seafood buffet, determinedly feeding him oysters and rubbing his crotch as if she was polishing her mother's silver candlesticks.

For years Rita had been lecturing her on how confidence makes a person more attractive to the opposite sex, and finally Frankie was discovering she'd been right all along. Never before had she had so much male attention. And it wasn't just the leather trousers, even though they definitely helped. What was it with men and leather trousers? Like bees round a honeypot, they couldn't keep away. One after another, they came up to her, asking if they could run their hands up and down her thighs to check if they were 'real' (she presumed they were talking about her trousers, not her thighs). No wonder Hugh had been so dead set against her getting a pair.

Instead of blushing hotly with embarrassment and not knowing what to say, she laughed flirtily and, feeling wittier than Stephen Fry, happily engaged in conversation, eagerly telling stories that not long ago had seemed dull and rather boring, but now had suddenly turned into hilariously amusing and entertaining anecdotes. Tanned, confident and laughing, Frankie felt like a different person from the snivelling wreck who'd sat at Heathrow with holes in her forty-denier tights. And she loved it.

29

'Frankie, darling, Frankie.' Pink and perspiring in a ruffled Liberace shirt which he'd unbuttoned down to his hairy navel, Dorian emerged from the dance floor and, spotting her by herself – the first time that evening – breathlessly slid his arms around her waist. 'Fuck, are you looking sexy tonight. Let me introduce you to one of the most charming men in LA.' Pressing his hot, sticky cheek against hers, he swept her past a display of ice sculptures, towards a group of film people playing roulette at a table specially flown in from Las Vegas.

As they approached, one of the men, an oldish guy wearing a plain black T-shirt and jeans, stood up. 'Dorian, good to see you've still got an eye for the ladies.' Holding out his arms in a Godfather embrace, he slapped him on the back and let loose a tobacco-rich laugh.

Like a dutiful son, Dorian smiled respectfully. 'This is Frankie, my wonderful new English neighbour.' He squeezed her tightly. 'And Frankie, I'd like you to meet Carter, your more than generous host.'

Carter? This was Carter Mansfield? Frankie couldn't believe it. He looked nothing like he did in the movies. On celluloid he'd always seemed larger than life, an enigmatic leading man all the ladies, on and off screen, fell for. But here he was, barely five foot five, with thinning comb-over hair and a Palm Springs suntan. Not that he was unattractive. To be honest, for a fifty-six-year-old he didn't look too bad. But then who hadn't heard the rumours about a facelift a few years ago, and several operations to remove the fat that had collected under his chin, like water from a leaky tap?

'Enchanted.' Keeping one coloured-contact-lensed eye on Dorian, Carter Mansfield allowed the other to roam freely up and down Frankie, who evidently passed some sort of test. He held out his still-half-full glass towards Dorian. 'I don't suppose you could get me a refill?' There was no suppose about it. This was Dorian's cue to make himself scarce, and, having just had his attention caught by a miniskirted croupier, he was more than willing. Winking at Frankie, he took the glass and, blotting his forehead with his chiffon cuff, beat a hasty retreat, via the blackjack table.

'So, Frankie, what do you think of the party?' Speaking in a thick Dallas accent, he took her hand in his soft, manicured one and pressed it to his thin lips.

'It's great.' She didn't know what else to say. Carter Mansfield was kissing her hand. It was unreal. And very unnerving. She felt as if she'd just been offered up as some kind of human sacrifice.

He smiled, revealing a perfect set of porcelain veneers, oddly white against his orange, leathery skin. 'Cute trousers.'

'Thanks.'

'Are you a model?'

She couldn't help but smile. So even film stars resorted to using the oldest chat-up lines in the book. But instead of greeting his question with a snort of laughter and an incredulous, 'Me? A model?' she gave a flattered laugh. 'No, I'm a writer . . .' Something caught her eye, causing her to falter. Across the lawn, leaning against the railings at the top of the steps, was a figure. *Reilly.* Her legs suddenly went all shaky, like the time she'd once attempted the running machine at the gym.

'A writer?' Unaware, Carter continued. 'You should give me your number. My production company is always on the lookout for talented writers.'

'Erm, yeah, that sounds fantastic.' Dragging her eyes away from the steps, she looked back at him. 'Would I know anything you've produced?' She was grappling around for conversation, but finding it almost impossible to concentrate.

Carter mistook her agitation for nervousness. It was understandable – after all, he was a movie star. He put his hand on her arm to reassure her. 'I'm sure you will. I produce for both film and TV and currently one of the projects in production is a groundbreaking new daytime show . . .'

Not really listening, she glanced over his shoulder towards the steps. Reilly was still there. She watched as he turned his face towards her, his profile silhouetted against the light. He was smoking a cigarette. And he was by himself. Where was Chrissy?

'. . . *Malibu Motel.*'

'Did you say *Malibu Motel*?' Recognising the name, she switched her attention back to Carter Mansfield. And noticed he had his hand around the top of her arm. 'My flatmate auditioned for that. Twice.' Feeling awkward, she moved sideways and, unable to resist, glanced back towards the staircase. Reilly was walking down it and he appeared to be looking for someone. Probably Chrissy, she thought, watching as he scanned the party until his gaze came to rest in her direction. She could tell, by the expression on his face, that he'd recognised her.

'Well, if she's anything as beautiful as you, get her to give me a call.'

She suddenly gave Carter Mansfield a full-on smile. But it was for Reilly's benefit, not his. Aware that he was watching her, she wanted him to believe she was having a wonderful time with one of Hollywood's most famous film stars, not being bored to death by an ageing cinema has-been's attempts at flirtation.

Carter was rather surprised by her sudden warm reaction to his suggestion, and delighted. For a moment then, he thought he'd been losing his charm. 'Here, take my number.' He squeezed her arm, his tightening fingers reminiscent of one of those Velcro bandages her doctor used to take her blood pressure.

'Thanks.' Flicking her hair around for good measure, she took one of his cards – complete with autographed head-shot – and squashed it into her snug backpocket. Feeling very pleased with herself, she sneaked a quick look at Reilly. The smile slid from her lips. He wasn't there any more.

What the hell was Frankie doing flirting with that slimeball? Carter Mansfield was the biggest tart in town. Still, if that's what made her happy, some rich old dude, what did he care? Reilly smarted as he saw her smiling at Carter, remembering how she'd looked when she'd smiled at him after they'd danced together at the Cowboy Palace. But there was no point thinking about that. Reilly bitterly took a drag of his cigarette. It was going to be awkward interrupting Frankie and her geriatric playboy, but he had no choice. And anyway, being brutally honest about it, he wanted nothing more than to break up the cosy scene.

'Have you seen Dorian?' Frankie swung round to see Reilly standing behind her. His face cold and hard.

'I don't know.' If he was going to be unfriendly, then so was she.

'I need to talk to him.'

'Hey, is this guy bothering you?' Carter Mansfield pushed out his grey hairy chest, thankfully hidden underneath his T-shirt, and tried to form a barrier between Reilly and Frankie. 'You wanna watch it, pal, or else I'll get security.'

Reilly ignored him. On screen Carter Mansfield had been a convincing bad guy. In real life he was comical. Reilly looked straight at Frankie. 'It's urgent.' At that moment, a juddering sound above them made everyone look. A helicopter was swooping into view over the tops of the palm trees, its powerful beam of light starkly illuminating the party in a harsh white glare.

'What the hell is that?' Shielding his eyes, while trying to make sure his ten-thousand-dollar hairweave remained stuck to his scalp, Carter Mansfield stumbled slightly backwards, as panic began to spread through the party.

A megaphoned voice suddenly boomed above the noise, 'This is the police,' triggering off an outbreak of pandemonium among the partygoers, most of whom were high on drugs and alcohol after spending half the night playing pass-the-parcel in the toilets. An innocent enough game, except the parcel was no longer made of newspaper and sweets, but cellophane and white powder.

The deafening noise of the whirring blades and thudding engines, and the shrieking wail of police sirens intermingled with the DJ mix-master. The spiralling blasts of wind ripped through the lawns, causing people to scatter like marbles as they tried to run from the party. A couple of bigshot film directors and the twenty-something actresses they were having affairs with missed their footing and lost their balance, plunging into the swimming pool in their designer outfits. A few more, pissed out of their heads and flying high as kites, thought it was part of the entertainment and joined them, stripping off their clothes and jumping in stark naked. The party had turned into a a riot.

Grabbing Frankie by the arm, Reilly pulled her towards the bushes, away from the upturned seafood buffet, which had spilled its catch around the edges of the swimming pool, hurling the live lobsters into a chlorine sea. 'Wait for me here, I'll be back in a moment.'

'Where are you going?'

'I've got to find Dorian.'

'Why? *What the hell's going on?*'

At that moment she caught sight of Rita, who'd been engaging in a spot of foreplay with Matt, emerging semi-clad from the bushes. She was hurriedly pulling up her dress, while Matt seemed to have lost his trousers.

'Frankie, what's going on?' Rita yelled, waving at her frantically. Grasping Matt, she began trying to make her way towards Frankie, across the lawn that was now strewn with broken glasses and champagne bottles, staggering blindly in her stilettos, which kept sinking like irrigation spikes into the lawn.

Watching her, Frankie shook her head and murmured quietly, 'I don't know.'

She was soon to find out. Watching a swarm of armed police gatecrashing the party, she saw officers from the LAPD handcuffing Carter Mansfield, who was shaking his head in disbelief, what remained of his hair waving like wispy fronds, and shouting, 'This is just plain outrageous. Do you know who I am, son? Do you? I'm real friendly with the commissioner and he'll see you fired, you understand? He'll see they kick your ass.'

But the burly policeman ignored him. 'Mr Clive Carter, alias Donald Algernon Marglethwite, you are under arrest for being in possession of Class A drugs.'

Frankie turned to Reilly, who had returned alone from his search. 'They've arrested Carter Mansfield for drugs?'

Reilly nodded, looking vexed. 'He's not the only one,' he muttered, nodding over to where the police were rounding up groups of people and leading them out of the party.

It was over a hundred yards away and at first she couldn't see anyone she recognised in the throng. Until she spotted a flash of pink chiffon.

'Dorian?'

His name escaped from her lips just as Rita arrived with Matt, muddied and breathless. She cast a startled look at Frankie and then back at Dorian. Nobody spoke. Instead they stood huddled together, Matt and Rita with their arms twined around each other, Reilly and Frankie awkwardly apart, staring as Dorian was suddenly lit up in a pool of light from the helicopter beam. With his wrists handcuffed behind his back, he was being pushed roughly up the stairs, like a prisoner to the gallows. Flailing, he turned round, desperately searching for help, and looked directly at them. His expression was one of sheer terror. But he couldn't see his friends, blinded as he was by the searchlights. And turning away he stumbled forward, disappearing from view through the trellised archway to the waiting cop cars beyond.

30

They drove back from Beverly Hills Police Headquarters in silence. Reilly hunched grimly behind the wheel, Frankie slumped next to him, eyes closed, face tilted towards an opened window, while squeezed in the back, among a dismantled barbecue, camera equipment and piles of old newspapers, cuddled Rita and Matt.

The party spirit had long gone. They'd just spent over two hours with the LAPD trying to find out what was happening to Dorian. It had been a waste of time, one of those red tape, jobsworth situations, being passed from officer to sergeant and then back to the clerk at the front desk. Not being blood relatives they were treated suspiciously, as if they were guilty accomplices, and curtly informed that although as yet no charges had been made against Mr Dorian Wildes, he was being held in the cells overnight. Which, reading between the lines, was the same place they were going to end up if they didn't stop asking questions.

'Poor Dorian,' murmured Rita. 'Having to spend the night in there.' She knew he was used to his super-sprung, extra-soft mattress, goose-down duvet and faux-fur eiderdown. A glass of mineral water by his bedside and aromatherapy candles to gently ease him to sleep. A concrete cell would kill him. 'What do you think's going to happen to him?' She leaned forward, speaking louder to make herself heard above the noise of the truck.

'I don't know.' Reilly shook his head, his eyes never leaving the road. 'I really don't know.' He repeated it quietly, as if he were speaking to himself, his face creased with worry.

A few minutes later they turned into Rita's drive. Pulling up behind her Thunderbird, Reilly kept the engine running while Frankie climbed out first. As the Bronco was only a two-door, she needed to pull the front seat forward for the two lovebirds in the back.

'Thanks for the lift,' Rita said, clambering out, still managing to hold tightly on to Matt. Without waiting for Frankie, they began sauntering up the driveway together, arms around waists, wrapped up in a blanket of lust and anticipation.

Frankie let them go. Her hangover was beginning to kick in and she felt like shit. Tonight she could do without having to sleep on the sofa with a pillow over her head, trying to block out the sounds that would no doubt be coming from Rita's bedroom. After sharing a flat with her for over five years, she'd been privy to Rita's vociferous dirty talk and ear-splitting orgasmic howls more times than she cared to remember.

Glad of the cool night breeze, she leaned against the opened passenger door and glanced at Reilly. Apart from a few words at the party, they hadn't spoken all evening and she groped around for something to say, aware of the seconds trickling like coloured sand through an egg timer.

'So, what's with your roommate and the surfer?' Reilly spoke first.

'She met him a couple of weeks ago,' Frankie relaxed, relieved the ice was broken. 'She's in love.'

'Yeah?'

Frankie nodded. Why were they making small talk about Rita and Matt? It was two in the morning and their relationship was the last thing she wanted to talk about. But then again, it was much easier and a lot less awkward than talking about themselves. 'It's great for Rita, but not so great for me, seeing as I get to spend another night on the sofa.' As soon as she'd said that, she wished she hadn't. Sad, lonely and desperate wasn't the kind of image she wanted to convey.

'Are you telling me you guys share a bed?'

Frankie smiled self-consciously, realising she'd just provided him with every man's fantasy.

'It's a one-bedroom apartment,' she explained. 'We don't have much choice.'

Resting his arms on the steering wheel, Reilly turned away and stared ahead out of the windscreen. After a moment he spoke. 'Look, I don't know if you're interested, but there's always a spare bed at my place ...' His voice tailed off uncertainly.

Surprised by his offer, Frankie hesitated. 'Won't Chrissy mind?' Her name was the first thing that sprang to mind. Immediately she regretted mentioning it.

Reilly's face wrinkled into a frown. 'Chrissy?' He ran the flat of his palm across his stubble. 'Who's Chrissy?'

Frankie felt a creeping embarrassment. 'The girl I saw you with at Malibu. Dorian said he'd invited you and her to the party and I just assumed ...' She faltered, realising that nobody had actually said Chrissy was Reilly's girlfriend. As usual she'd just put two and two together and come to about a hundred and fifty.

Noticing his cigarette had burned down to the filter, Reilly tossed it out of the window and, flicking open the lid of an old Zippo, lit up another one. Inhaling, he leaned back against his seat, shaking his head. 'Dorian is one helluva matchmaker,' he muttered, a faint smile on his lips. Turning sideways, he looked straight at Frankie. 'I've met her once, the day I saw you. To be honest I didn't even remember her name.'

'Oh.' His gaze was unnerving and she stared down at her hand, still grasping the door handle, and began fiddling with the bracelet on her wrist. She felt a mixture of relief, satisfaction, excitement. And embarrassment that she now looked like the jealous female.

'But then, it's not as memorable a name as Carter Mansfield, is it?' added Reilly after a pause. 'That's one you'll never forget.'

His sarcasm wasn't lost on Frankie, who looked up. 'No, but it's not one you want to remember either, is it?'

'Isn't it? You both looked pretty close before I interrupted.' Now Reilly was the one sounding jealous.

Frankie was surprised. But even more so by her reaction. She was flattered that he was jealous. Pleased. 'Thank God you did interrupt. If you hadn't I might have been arrested with the creep.'

'I doubt it.'

'Why not? Dorian was.'

Taking a long drag from his cigarette, Reilly stubbed it out in the overflowing ashtray, grinding the embers against the blackened filters of dried-out stubs. 'Dorian was arrested because the cops had a tip-off someone was dealing drugs at the party.' He spoke quietly, his voice barely audible over the engine. 'They were waiting outside the gates when I arrived. I overheard a couple of them talking about it.'

'It was probably Carter Mansfield.'

'C'mon, Frankie. A multi-millionaire film star?' Agitated, he ran his fingers through his dishevelled hair. 'I'm sure the guy's not impartial to a few lines of coke, but the only drug dealing he's ever done has been in those God awful movies of his.'

'Well, if it wasn't him, who was it?'

He ran his teeth over his bottom lip and didn't say anything. Frankie translated his silence as an admission of guilt.

'*You?*'

'Hell, no, what do you take me for?'

'Well, who then?' She was confused, and beginning to get exasperated. It was too late to start playing Guess Who's the Drug Dealer.

Reilly released a deep sigh. 'I think they were looking for Dorian.'

'*Dorian?*' she gasped, looking around in the darkness as if worried somebody might be listening in the shrubbery. She lowered her voice to a whisper. 'You're saying it was Dorian?' Frankie couldn't believe it. This was like a storyline straight out of one of Carter Mansfield's films. It would never have happened in Fulham. 'You're telling me he's a drug dealer?' Suddenly it all fell into place. Mobile phones constantly ringing, endlessly driving around meeting people 'for a coffee', his bulging wallet full of cash, the silver attaché case which never parted company from his wrist. No wonder he was Mr Popular at parties, and invited to every celebrity bash in town.

'It's not like it sounds. He's not into the hard stuff, it's mainly pot.'

Frankie looked blank.

'You know, marijuana.'

'I know what pot is,' snapped Frankie. 'I have been a student.'

Reilly looked out of the window, the muscle in his jaw twitching.

Regretting her irritability, Frankie tried to appear casual. 'Where does he get it all from?'

'He grows it.'

There was a pause. 'Don't tell me. On his balcony.' Frankie suddenly experienced a flashback. One of her, taken from over the last fortnight, lovingly watering his plants. *His marijuana plants*. Christ, she was an accomplice . . .

Eventually, Reilly sighed. 'It's been a long day. I better be heading back as I've got an early start tomorrow. I'm flying down to Mexico for a couple of weeks. Work, not a holiday.' He caught her expression. 'I would have asked you along to assist, but it's a big advertising shoot and I needed someone with experience.'

'Don't worry about it.' But she couldn't hide her disappointment.

Fiddling with the frayed ends of the woven bracelet on his wrist, Reilly debated whether or not to repeat his offer of a place to sleep. If he did she'd probably think he was coming on to her and tell him to get lost. But if he didn't this could be the last time he saw her. What had he got to lose? 'The offer's still open about the spare room.'

Frankie hesitated. It reminded her of that old Clash song, 'Should I stay or should I go?' Normally she would have said no, but she wasn't feeling normal. Not after the kind of night she'd had. As she deliberated, a gust of wind blew across the bonnet of the Bronco, wafting echoes of laughter and over-enthusiastic shrieks from the apartment. Frankie glanced at Reilly and they both couldn't help smiling. As always, Rita was right on cue.

Without needing to say anything, she jumped back inside the Bronco, slamming the door as Reilly revved the engine. Leaning back over his seat, one hand on the wheel, he began reversing out of the drive. Frankie watched him, letting her eyes navigate the familiar contours of his face: the fine lines criss-crossed underneath his eyes, a sharp crease etched down the middle of his forehead – a result of frowning too much, dappled freckles on the bridge of his nose which were almost indiscernible underneath his tan. It reminded her of the first time she'd ever looked at him, on the flight to LA. Back then he'd been a stranger, someone who'd annoyed the hell out of her, someone she'd hoped she'd never see again. It was ironic to think that after everything that had happened, she was sitting next to him, looking at his face once more. Except this time she was seeing a completely different person.

'It's nice to see you again, Reilly.' She couldn't help herself.

For a moment she thought he hadn't heard her, as he didn't say anything.

Because he couldn't.

Frankie's words might have been softly spoken, but each one was ringing loudly in his ears. On paper it didn't sound like any big deal; after all, it wasn't as if she'd just declared her undying love. But he knew there was a lot more significance attached to those words than just a casual 'Nice to see ya'. It was the first time she'd admitted he meant anything to her. The first time he felt she cared about him.

Putting the car into gear, he turned back to face her, looking straight into her eyes. 'It's nice to see you too, Frankie.'

They stared at each other. Neither said anything. Neither had to. Finally Reilly looked away and, putting his foot down, accelerated towards Laurel Canyon and into the headlight-flecked darkness ahead.

31

Reilly's house was perched at the top of a narrow winding street and could be reached only by a steep climb, along a path splattered with ripe figs from the overhanging trees and through an overgrown garden with a bleached-out hammock strung across the veranda. Judging by his truck, Frankie had been expecting an untidy bachelor pad – a poky apartment littered with dirty washing, a week's worth of take-out cartons, a sink full of encrusted coffee cups – but it wasn't anything like that. For a start it was tidy.

'The cleaner's just been,' he admitted sheepishly, turning on a lamp as she followed him into the vaulted living room.

Frankie looked around. There were two large old velvet sofas, worn almost bald in patches and faded from the sun, a sprawling bookcase stuffed full of books and CDs, none of which seemed to be in their cases, and a low wooden table that bore the marks of a thousand cups of coffee, red wine, olive oil. The place had a good feel to it. A real fireplace stood in the centre of the far wall, with its blackened brickwork and mantelshelf cluttered with knick-knacks picked up from travels abroad – a piece of driftwood, a carved African statue with a broken spear, a toy propeller plane made from a Budweiser can, a silver photograph frame from Mexico laid on its side.

Frankie picked it up. The glass had fallen out, or broken, but there was still a photograph inside. She held it up to the lamp to get a better look. It was a picture of Reilly and a woman, the same woman she'd seen in his wallet. They were standing on the beach with their arms round each other. She was laughing into the camera and holding her hair back from blowing across her face, and he was looking down at her, smiling. He looked different. His hair was much shorter and he was thinner, younger, happier.

'Is this your ex-wife?'

He nodded, striking a match and bending down to light the candles in a candlebrum that stood in the grate, dripping with years of melted wax. 'Yeah, Kelly and I. Before we got married.'

'What happened to the glass?'

'Smashed.' He smiled shame-facedly. 'I can't remember if she threw it or I did.' Disappearing into the kitchen, he returned with a bottle of Jack Daniel's and two glasses. 'Do you want a drink?'

'Yeah, why not.' Alcohol would probably put the brakes on her hangover, and anyway, she rather liked the idea of drinking whiskey wearing a pair of leather trousers in a man's house – Reilly's house – at three in the morning. Taking the glass, she sipped the brown liquid, enjoying the sensation as it scorched her tongue. She smiled to herself. If Hugh could see her now. She looked down at the picture again, rubbing the dust away with her thumb. 'How long were you married for?' Studying the image of Kelly, Frankie was surprised at the feelings of jealousy that stirred within her.

Pouring himself a glass, Reilly put the bottle on the table and flopped down on the sofa, putting his feet up on the table.

'Less than two years. I've been divorced longer than I was married.'

'Do you miss her?' As soon as she said it, Frankie knew she shouldn't. 'Sorry, it's none of my business.' She stood the photograph back on the shelf, then changed her mind and lay it on its side.

Reilly watched her for a moment, not saying anything, before leaning forwards and pulling open a drawer underneath the table. Searching through the junk, he eventually found what he was looking for and grabbed a packet of Rizlas and a clear plastic wallet full of pot. 'Do you miss your ex?' He licked the sticky side of the Rizla papers and began building a joint.

Frankie hesitated. Her knee-jerk reaction was to scream yes, but something stopped her. 'I think about him.' Running her fingers over the rough plaster walls, she walked over to the French windows that had been left open and, with her back to Reilly, looked out into the darkness of the garden, listening to the distant howls of coyotes. 'I wonder what he's doing, who he's with. If he's missing me.' She spoke quietly, almost to herself.

'When did you guys break up?'

'Oh, about seven weeks, five days and –' twirling round, she looked down at her watch – 'coming up for ten hours.' She smiled and took a gulp of whiskey, watching for Reilly's reaction. 'That was supposed to be a joke.'

'I know.' Reilly smiled. 'I'm not that much of a dumb-ass American.' Grinning sardonically, he twisted the end of the joint and lit it, watching the paper curl and burn into ashes. Putting it to his lips he took a long, satisfied drag. Blowing out the smoke, he held it out towards her. 'Here, try some of Dorian's finest.'

It had been years since Frankie had smoked a joint, and she'd forgotten how much she used to enjoy it. Reilly put on a couple of CDs, American bands she'd never heard of before, and they lay around on the sofa, drinking whiskey, smoking, laughing, talking. Time played that sneaky game of pretending to stand still but, while their backs were turned, racing along at breakneck speed. Hour-long CDs started and finished in what felt like five minutes, joints were put out seconds after being lit up, and all the time she and Reilly never stopped talking. Never paused to think of something to say, or suffered the dreaded awkward silence. Frankie couldn't remember the last time she had felt so comfortable with someone who wasn't Hugh.

'So, what do you think of my new trousers?' Feeling stoned, she couldn't resist flirting a little. Lifting up one of her legs from the sofa, she turned it from side to side to show them off.

'You look great.' He smiled, watching her waving her legs in the air. Frankie was very funny when she was stoned. 'You always look great . . . Well, maybe not the day we met at the airport.' He ducked as she threw a cushion at him.

Laughing, she hugged her knees up to her chest, feeling the leather waistband digging into her stomach. 'They were Rita's idea,' she explained, taking a puff of the joint that he passed her. 'She said I needed to change my image, but I'm still not sure if it's really me.' Suddenly aware that she was beginning to gabble, she passed him back the joint. Now she knew why she'd missed so many lectures at university. Her head was beginning to spin.

'What is you?'

Frankie's laughter petered out and she looked thoughtful. 'God, I don't know any more. For a long time I thought it was having a career, a nice flat, getting married to Hugh . . .' Sighing, she leaned back on the sofa. Her head felt suddenly very heavy and she let it sink down into the cushion.

'So why didn't you?' Hot ash fell on his T-shirt and he flicked it on to the floor before it burned a hole.

'Hugh didn't want to get married, not to me anyway.' Curling a piece of hair around her finger, she let it slowly unravel. 'He said he wanted space.' She giggled. '*Space.* What a stupid thing to say.' She paused, remembering the scene at her birthday, the way she'd felt that night, emotions that she'd thought would never, ever go away. Without warning, tears began to prickle her eyelashes. 'Why didn't he just tell me he didn't love me any more?' she murmured quietly.

'Hey.' Leaning over, Reilly stroked her hair away from her face as a tear fell down her cheek.

Frankie sniffed, feeling embarrassed. 'Sorry, just ignore me. I didn't mean to get upset.' She wiped her face, smearing her mascara down her cheeks. 'It's just the alcohol . . . and Dorian and the police and everything.' A barely black tear trickled off the end of her nose. 'God, you must think I'm an idiot . . .'

Reilly looked at her small face, pinched and blotchy, and had a sudden urge to put his arms around her. She looked so fragile, so vulnerable. 'C'mon, you're gonna get upset sometimes. Breaking up is a shitty business. Someone always gets hurt. This time it happens to be you.' He squeezed her hand, his fingers lacing between hers. 'If it's any consolation, I thought about Kelly for six months, maybe a year. Until one day I woke up and realised I was over her. In fact I'd been over her for a while, I just hadn't noticed.'

'But how do you know you're over someone?' She rubbed her bloodshot eyes.

'You just do.' Leaning forward, he filled their glasses. 'One day you'll hear that song you both liked on the radio and it won't make you cry. You'll wake up one morning and they won't be the first thing you think about, or the last thing you think about when you're falling asleep at night. Their face won't be the one you see any more when you close your eyes, or in a crowd when you're walking down a street. And when something makes you laugh, or cry, they won't be the person you want to share it with.' Taking the joint from her, he put it between his lips and sucked hard. But it had gone out. 'You'll forget their telephone number, maybe even their birthday and your anniversary, but you'll never forget them.' Lighting the joint, he inhaled, blowing out a spiral of bluish smoke. 'Sorry, it's the dope, it makes me do the whole therapist bit.' He smiled self-consciously.

Feeling tired, Frankie stretched out on the sofa. 'So why did you and Kelly finish?'

He shrugged. 'It just didn't work out. She wanted someone with a big career, ambition. I used to drive her crazy, messing around in my truck, hanging out, taking a few photos. I was just starting out back then.' He broke off to squash the roach into the ashtray. 'She said I needed to grow up, but her idea of growing up meant wearing a suit and working in an office.' Smiling ruefully, he looked at Frankie. 'In the end she left me for a guy at work. Some rich lawyer who drove a hundred-thousand-dollar Mercedes and played golf at the Bel Air golf club.'

'Hugh plays golf.' Frankie couldn't resist interrupting.

'Is he a lawyer?'

'No, an estate agent.' The thought suddenly seemed amusing and she smiled. 'But he does wear a suit . . . and a tie.'

Her mood swung from sadness to amusement, and she started giggling. Reilly watched her, her face creased with laughter, her hair fanned out across the cushion. Stretching out his hand, he pushed the dark curls away from her eyes, letting his fingers brush across her forehead. Her giggles wound down, like a mechanical toy, and, catching her breath, she lay still for a moment. Looking at him. Anticipating. Wondering what was going to happen next.

'I need some water.' Something inside made her break away and sit up. As if there was part of her still loyal to Hugh. Standing up unsteadily from the sofa, she padded towards the kitchen. But an object caught her eye, tucked away in the far corner near the window. It was a small upright piano.

'Do you play?' She walked over to it and, lifting up the lid, ran her fingers over the keys. They made a tinkling noise, reminding her of when she was a kid and her dad used to play for her.

'A little. When I was a teenager I used to fancy myself as a bit of a songwriter.'

'Will you play something?'

'Oh, c'mon. It's late.' He stretched out across the cushions and lit up a cigarette.

'Please.' She stuck her bottom lip out, beseechingly.

How could he refuse? Hauling himself up from the sofa, Reilly walked over to her, easing himself on to the small bench. Running his fingers through his hair, he placed them on the keys and started messing around, intros of old Beatles tracks, a few bars of a Bob Dylan number, a bit of Cat Stevens. She leaned against the piano, watching his hands. Listening.

'No, come on, seriously.' Leaning towards him, she removed the cigarette hanging from the corner of his mouth. 'Play one of your songs.'

He smiled, shaking his head.

'For me.'

He hesitated. 'Are you sure about this?' Despite being stoned, he felt nervous. He hadn't played his own stuff in years. Not since the divorce.

Frankie nodded, smiling. 'I'm sure.'

Pausing, he let his hands wander over the black and white keys. For a brief moment Frankie thought he was going to bottle out, before he leaned forward and pressed them down, letting them linger for a moment before his fingers found the next notes. And the next. The opening chords of the song, slowly and gently filled the room and then she heard his voice, low and soft, almost speaking the words.

> *'There's someplace far inside of me,*
> *Only you find,*
> *Feelings far inside of me,*
> *You left behind.'*

With each chord, any embarrassment or awkwardness melted away. She watched him in the glow of the lamplight, his broad shoulders hunched over the piano, his hair flopping over his face, and knew she couldn't fight her feelings for him any longer. Denying them wasn't going to make them go away. And looking at him right at this moment, she didn't want them to. Putting her empty glass on the top of the piano, she sat down next to him.

> *'Just close my eyes and you take me there,*
> *I just close my eyes and you take me there.'*

The last note faded. He raised his eyes to look at her. Her at him. Each blink, every breath, was loaded with What Happens Now? Frankie waited. She knew she was at the edge of some great chasm, balancing precariously, feeling her grip loosening, slipping through her fingers. But she didn't try to fight it. She wanted to fall.

Unable to stop herself, she moved forward and touched the side of his face. A light brush with her fingertips that was more intimate and thrilling than anything she'd experienced with Hugh during their two years together. She could hardly breathe as she touched the scar above his eyebrow, down the side of his face, over his stubble, which wasn't prickly but soft, and down towards the corners of his mouth. And then, leaning slowly towards him, she did something she realised she'd been wanting to do for such a long time. She kissed him.

For a second he hesitated, before letting himself fall with her, and, pulling her close, he wrapped his arms around her, pressing her to him. Breathing her in. His lips against hers. Tongue against tongue. Eyes closed. Hearts thudding. Deep, long, hungry kisses born out of the lack of any feelings of self-consciousness or embarrassment. Just two people wanting each other. Holding each other. Kissing the life out of each other.

It had been a long time coming.

32

At exactly eleven minutes past six in the morning, Frankie felt the earth move. But this time it didn't have anything to do with Reilly. Looking at him, lying asleep next to her under the duvet, his naked body wrapped tightly around hers, she still couldn't believe what had happened between them. *What was happening between them.*

Hers was a jumbled blur of memories – his head nuzzling into her neck, running her hands over the soft skin of his bare shoulders, the clash of notes as he'd pushed her up against the piano, discovering the blue ink of a dragon tattoo partly hidden underneath the hair on his chest, feeling his tongue snaking a line across her stomach, down past her bellybutton. The journey to the bedroom upstairs was a blank, but she remembered tumbling on to the king-size bed, pulling at each other's clothes – God knows how he'd ever managed to get her leather trousers off, but they'd sure as hell come off, along with his jeans and fiddly, awkward bits of underwear that had got tangled around limbs and ankles. And then they'd been naked. *She'd been naked.* In bed with a man who wasn't Hugh.

But instead of being racked with insecurities, feeling self-conscious and worrying about cellulite, wobbly bits, boobs that weren't big enough, firm enough, *up there enough*, and a stomach that hadn't come within an exercise mat of an abdominal crunch in God knows how long, she'd listened to Reilly telling her how gorgeous she was, how beautiful she was, how sexy she was. And believed him. She might not have shaved her legs in a fortnight, or found the courage to face hot wax and tackle a bikini line that had become more than a little fuzzy around the edges, but Reilly had made her feel all those things and a lot, lot more.

Wonderful, horny, can't-keep-my-hands-off-him Reilly. Everything about him gave her that toothpaste tingly feeling. She'd always promised herself she'd never sleep with a guy on the first date – not that you could even call this a first date – but some promises were meant to be broken. And this was one of them. Resisting Reilly would have been like resisting a cigarette when she was drunk, a four-finger KitKat the day before her period, Karen Millen when she'd just been paid. Even though being with Reilly felt strange – after all, she had shared a bed with Hugh for nearly two years – it was also bloody exciting. To put it bluntly: the sex had been fucking unbelievable. In fact she'd never known sex like that existed, except in carefully choreographed bedroom scenes in movies, or on the pages of bonkbusters written by middle-aged women with vivid imaginations. But this was the real thing. What she'd had with Hugh was good, but compared to what she'd experienced with Reilly, it seemed like a shoddy imitation. As if she'd suddenly been given a taste of Dom Perignon, after a lifetime of M&S Cava.

There it was again. She was suddenly jolted out of her daydreams. No mistaking it. *The earth was actually moving.*

Lifting her head from the pillow, she peered into the unfamiliar darkness of the bedroom. But she couldn't see anything. Only feel it. A shuddering sensation similar to when she'd lived in a basement flat in Earls Court and the tube trains used to pass nearby, rattling the cups on the draining board and making the picture on the telly go squiggly. Except of course the District Line didn't go as far as LA. Which could only mean one thing. *An earthquake.*

Oh my God. Panic grabbed her by the throat as she felt the floor beginning to shake beneath her and out of the corner of her eye saw the 1930s-style wardrobe trembling on its walnut legs. She'd seen pictures of earthquakes on the news, houses being reduced to rubble, motorways collapsing, people being buried alive.

'Reilly.' She gasped his name.

He didn't stir.

She daren't move. Terror made her illogical and she was scared that the slightest movement would cause the room to shake even more.

'Reilly.' Louder this time.

A glass fell off the trunk, smashing into splinters on the wooden floor and waking Reilly. He lazily opened his eyes, blinking like a cat basking in the sun. 'What's wrong?'

His croaky whisper waved a magic wand. No sooner had he uttered those words than the earthquake rumbled to a halt, stopping just as quickly as it had started. The only evidence it left behind was the shards of glass scattered on the floorboards and the distant sound of car alarms and neighbours' dogs barking in the street below.

Stretching out his broad arm, Reilly scooped her towards him. 'It was just a tremor, nothing to worry about,' he whispered, smiling at her naïvety and the frightened expression on her face.

'But I was so scared. I thought . . .'

'Ssshhhh, you're OK. Nothing's gonna happen to you.' He started softly kissing her face, moving his lips across her eyelids. 'Well, maybe not nothing.' His hand ran stealthily along her inner thigh.

Her body trembled, but this time she wasn't scared. Closing her eyes, she let out a deep sigh of satisfaction. It was starting all over again. Repeats had never seemed so good.

*   *   *

'Guess what . . .'

The front door slammed and Frankie's footsteps thudded down the hallway into the darkened living room. She stopped short when she caught sight of Rita, slumped sullenly on the sofa, picking her chipped nailpolish and watching *E* with the curtains drawn. It was three in the afternoon and she was still in her dressing gown.

'What?' muttered Rita, not even bothering to look up.

Something told Frankie that now might not be the best time to share her news about Reilly. Doing a complete U-turn, she did what only a sensible British girl could do when caught in a tricky situation: she talked about the weather. Luckily, as with everything in LA, the weather was bigger, better and more outrageous than anywhere else, which meant there was a lot more to talk about than the UK's uninspiring drizzle, drizzle or more drizzle. For a start, there were earthquakes.

'Did you feel the earth move last night?'

'Move? It didn't even twitch,' spat Rita bitterly. 'Matt wasn't interested.'

Frankie was confused. 'Matt? I'm talking about the earthquake. *Didn't you feel it?*'

'What earthquake? What are you going on about?'

Frankie gasped in exasperation. Rita was a heavy sleeper, but surely even she hadn't managed to snore her way through a tremor measuring 3.5 on the Richter scale. Grabbing the remote from her, she flicked the TV on to CNN News and a big-haired, lip-glossed reporter who was doing an outside broadcast concerning structural damage to the freeways caused by the earthquake.

'Oh.' Showing about as much interest as if Frankie had just switched on the baseball results, Rita continued concentrating on her thumbnail, taking her bad mood out on her non-chip topcoat. 'That earthquake.'

*   *   *

Realising there was no point pushing Rita when she was in one of her moods, Frankie lay back against the cushions and, kicking off her slingbacks, closed her eyes. Her mind was still whirling from the events of the last twelve hours. First the party, then the drugs bust and Dorian being arrested, and finally *Reilly*. She smiled as she thought about him. Remembering how she'd woken to find he'd left for Mexico, and lain in his bed for hours, not wanting to move, as if leaving it would break the spell. Breathing in the pillow where he'd slept, she'd shifted on to his side of the bed, soaking up the warmth of his body that was still on the mattress, smiling to herself like a lovesick teenager. She'd just discovered something that she never thought existed. Life after Hugh.

'Do you want an Oreo?' Rita waved the packet in front of her like an olive branch. It was a sign that she wanted to talk.

'No, thanks.' Dragging herself away from her thoughts, Frankie shook her head. 'So come on, what's the matter? I thought you'd be all loved up.'

'You mean fucked up.' The muscle in the side of Rita's jaw twitched angrily as she snatched an Oreo from the packet and snapped it in two. Something told Frankie the biscuit had taken on symbolic properties and represented something, or, more likely, *someone*.

'Last night I tried everything. Champagne, oysters, an essential oil massage, new underwear, aromatherapy candles . . .'

'And?'

'It was the most expensive non-event of my whole life.' Angrily she shoved both halves of the Oreo into her mouth and chewed determinedly. Her diet of lust and raging hormones was definitely over. 'We did all the usual foreplay stuff. I mean, I must have spent about twenty minutes with his dick in my mouth. But then, when it came to the crunch, nothing happened. Zilch. Fuck all.'

'You mean you didn't sleep together?'

'Sleep's about the only bloody thing we did do.'

'But I thought . . .'

'So did I,' muttered Rita miserably. 'How wrong can you be?'

'Maybe he'd had a bit too much to drink?' Frankie was trying to think of helpful suggestions.

'Brewer's droop?' Rita huffed bitterly at the idea. 'You must be joking. The bastard waved it around like Luke Skywalker with his light sabre.' She finished picking at her fingernails and turned her attention to her toenails. 'That's why I couldn't believe it when he said he didn't want to. Talk about dangling the carrot.'

Frankie was feeling confused. She'd had about two hours' sleep and now Rita was making *Star Wars*-slash-vegetable analogies.

'Maybe he's got a problem.'

'I'm the one with the problem,' sulked Rita miserably. 'I'm the one with a boyfriend who refuses to have sex.'

'Maybe he has a low sex drive.' Frankie was getting desperate.

'You mean frigid?'

'Well, he could be.'

'Are you telling me I've managed to find the only straight guy in LA without a sex drive?' Rita shook her head in disbelief. 'That would be just my luck, wouldn't it? I finally manage to find a good-looking bloke in LA who isn't either gay or married, in a twelve-step programme or a scientologist and bingo, he's bloody frigid.'

Frankie looked sympathetic. 'It's like that episode of *Sex and the City*. You know the one, where Sarah Jessica Parker met that good-looking bloke and it was perfect on paper . . .'

'. . . bad in bed,' finished Rita gloomily. 'I saw it.' Lighting a cigarette, she stared at the glowing tip. 'Maybe it's not that at all. Maybe he just doesn't fancy me.' She took a deep drag. 'It's not exactly beyond the realms of possibility, is it?' She looked down at herself in her terry-towelling bathrobe. She was still wearing her Trashy Lingerie knicker and bra set. A painful reminder of what might have been. 'Maybe I just don't turn him on.' Picking up her compact mirror, which lay among the make-up strewn across the coffee table, she opened it and peered at her reflection. 'And who would blame him? I look terrible. Look at me.' She grabbed the skin on her face as if she was kneading dough.

'Rubbish. You look fine,' insisted Frankie.

Rita huffed. 'It's all right for you to say, you've got cheekbones.'

'So have you.'

'No, I haven't. Cheekbones are like coat hangers for the face . . .' She prodded her face with her finger. 'And you know what happens when you don't hang up your clothes – they get all creased and crumpled.' She looked in the mirror. 'Like me.'

Rita's tragic soliloquy was interrupted by the sound of screeching tyres outside. Looking out of the window, Frankie saw one of Dorian's cars reverse out of his drive and take off at sixty miles an hour towards Laurel Canyon.

'Was that Dorian?' She hadn't been able to see the driver through the BMW's tinted windows.

Rita nodded. 'Yep. He got home a couple of hours ago, while you were still out. Apparently they didn't charge him. No evidence.' Deciding that cigarettes and Oreos didn't go together, she stubbed out her American Spirit. 'Which isn't surprising. I mean, Dorian's the last person to be involved with drugs.'

Frankie didn't say anything. She felt an attack of guilt. After everything that had happened between her and Reilly, she'd completely forgotten about Dorian's arrest. 'How is he?'

'Sore.' Rita pulled a face. 'Apparently they didn't hold back during the strip search.'

Frankie winced.

'When I saw him this morning he looked awful. The poor bloke's had all the stuffing knocked out of him. He could hardly speak. I made him a cup of liquorice tea with brandy in it and he could barely hold the cup his hand was trembling so much.' Snapping the mirror shut, she looked at Frankie, and for the first time suddenly noticed she was still wearing clothes from the night before. Plunged into her pit of depression, she hadn't been able to see anything else but her own disastrous situation. 'Where've you been?' Her forehead creased as her eyes narrowed.

Frankie smiled sheepishly, delightedly, barely able to contain her excitement. Her voice was practically a whisper. 'Reilly's.'

Rita gasped. Even in her state of angst, she couldn't miss the glint in Frankie's eye. 'Bloody hell, you didn't?' She couldn't believe it. Surely not. Not devoted-to-Hugh Frankie, there'll-never-be-anyone-but-Hugh Frankie, I-can't-even-look-at-another-man-if-it's-not-Hugh Frankie.

Frankie nodded.

Dumbfounded, Rita fell back against the sofa, her mouth hanging open. 'Fuck.'

'Yep,' grinned Frankie. 'Three times.'

33

For the next few days, the grin never left Frankie's face. Any initial doubts she may have had about sleeping with Reilly evaporated with his first phone call. Not a cool couple of days later, but just a few hours after he'd left her asleep in his bed. A scratchy, echoing line all the way from baggage reclaim at Cancun Airport in Mexico, and his low, lazy voice telling her what a great time he'd had last night and how he couldn't wait to get back to LA to 'take up where we left off'.

Pressing the receiver tightly against the side of her face, her lips touching the mouthpiece, she'd drank in his words. She knew when she repeated them back to Rita they'd probably sound silly, even a bit sleazy, but they hadn't been spoken in a blokish nudge-nudge, wink-wink kind of way. If anything, he'd sounded nervous, unsure, hesitant. As if he couldn't quite believe what had happened between them.

He wasn't the only one.

'Well, I think it's great,' declared Rita as they trudged around Firs for the Stars, a Christmas tree plot in Beverly Hills, trying to find the perfect Norwegian spruce for their apartment. 'A fling is just what you need. Especially at this time of year. Just think about all that smooching under the mistletoe.' Grabbing a clump from a display basket, she stood on tiptoes, teetering on her cork platforms as she tried to waggle it above Frankie's head.

Laughing, Frankie pushed her away, but she couldn't help thinking twice about Rita's choice of words. *A fling*. Is that all it was going to be? A few whirlwind weeks of being drunk and flirty in Italian restaurants, with melted candles in wine bottles on the table and his hand groping her thigh underneath, snogging on dance floors and having more sex than she knew what to do with?

After a week of long-distance phone calls from the far-flung beaches of Tulum and the Mayan ruins of Chichen Itzá – brief snatches of conversation across crackly lines from Mexican coin-boxes – Frankie couldn't help feeling that underneath their casual chitchat there lay unspoken feelings. That it was going to be more than an affair that just fizzled out as quickly as it ignited, with a thanks-see-you-around-sometime farewell. A bit of fun that would leave her with nothing but hazy drunken memories of nights out, a massive credit card bill, and if she was unlucky or lucky, depending which way she looked at it, a bout of cystitis from all that energetic shagging.

This felt different.

Absent-mindedly running her fingers over the spiky needles of a tree, she turned to Rita. 'I think this one's perfect.'

'Do you?' Pouncing on the branches, Rita shook the fir tree vigorously, holding it away from her to get a better look. 'Yep, you're right. I think it's perfect too.' Grinning jubilantly at her discovery, she tottered off in search of the good-looking dude in charge, fluffing up her hair and undoing her top button in preparation.

Frankie watched her weaving her way between dark glasses and baseball-capped celebrities and inflatable Santas and smiled to herself. She hadn't been talking about the Christmas tree.

Over the past week Frankie had accepted that she was no longer just Hugh's ex but Reilly's lover. *Reilly's lover*. It sounded illicit and exciting, a damn sight more exciting than *Hugh's ex*. But it was also going to take more than a little getting used to. Even now, a whole seven days later, she still couldn't quite believe it. For the first few days after Reilly had left for Mexico, she'd been nagged by pangs of guilt. As if somehow she was cheating on Hugh. She knew hers was a crazy, warped sense of loyalty, but it wasn't easy to break the habit of what she'd once hoped would be for a life-time. Only two months ago she'd been hearing wedding bells, day-dreaming about Tiffany's diamond solitaires, practising her signature as Mrs Hugh Hamilton, and now, out of the blue, this had happened. Without any warning she'd fallen for a beer-swilling, meat-eating, untidy, arrogant . . . *bloody gorgeous American she couldn't stop thinking about.*

Except as the days had passed, the more she'd thought about it, the more she'd had to admit that what had happened between her and Reilly wasn't a surprise at all. The signs had been there for weeks, she'd just failed to see them. It was as if she'd been staring at one of those pictures made up of a thousand tiny meaningless dots, and suddenly she was able to make sense of it and see the real picture underneath. She'd been so immersed in Hugh, so wrapped up in Hugh and what she didn't have, that she'd been unable to see what she did have. What she *could* have if she reached out and grabbed it with both hands. And now she had, she was going to enjoy it. Whatever happened.

'Crikey, it's massive. Do you think you're going to be able to squeeze it in?'

Rita stared not so innocently at the assistant, a gum-chew-ing, six-footer called Michael, who was wearing Ray-Bans and a baseball cap on back to front. He was trying to fit the Christmas tree on the back seat of the Thunderbird, which was already crammed with multicoloured tinsel, several boxes of baubles and six cans of fake snow. Rita didn't like the designer festive look – a minimalist display of silver twigs and a few tastefully arranged tealights – she preferred flashing rainbow fairy lights, canned snow sprayed around the windows (complete with stencils of holly and snowmen) and Christmas cards strung like banners across the ceiling.

Wiping a trickle of sweat from his forehead with one of his suede gardening gloves, Michael smiled knowingly at both Rita and Frankie. 'I've never had a problem before.' His delivery was as slick as his gelled ponytail, which hung like a black shiny slug out of the back of his baseball cap.

Frankie kept a stony face. What a creep. Surely he didn't think he was being sexy?

Rita obviously did. Giggling provocatively, she leaned over the bonnet of the car, squeezing her boobs together to make sure that if Michael hadn't noticed her cleavage before, he sure as hell would now. She knew she was being an outrageous flirt, but she didn't care. Playing imaginary footsie with the twenty-year-old assistant at the Christmas tree plot was the only kind of sexual kicks she was going to be getting.

Despite the disappointing night of Carter Mansfield's party, she and Matt were still seeing each other, but she was beginning to have serious doubts about how long she could last with a surfer who liked riding the waves and not redheads from Lancashire. It had been a month and they still hadn't had sex, and it was becoming more and more frustrating. She'd heard of taking things slowly, but this was crazy. If she didn't get a shag soon her hymen would have grown back and she'd turn into a born-again virgin.

Not that it wasn't for want of trying. After the embarrassing failure of the Trashy Lingerie and massage oil, she'd taken Frankie's advice, which had been to sit down and talk calmly about what was causing his celibacy. Unfortunately, Rita's interpretation of 'sitting down and talking calmly' had been to stand in the middle of the bedroom clutching the cellulite on her buttocks and yelling, 'It's because of this, isn't it?' Not surprisingly, this softly-softly approach didn't provide any answers. She still didn't know why Matt didn't want to have sex. In fact, the only thing she *did* know was that she wasn't getting it. And it was getting to her. Big time.

'Be careful you don't prick yourself on all those needles. They can be pretty sharp.' Michael finished tying the tree across the back seat. It was the only way it would fit, despite his earlier testosterone-charged boasts.

'Don't worry, I could do with a decent prick.' Rita winked at Frankie, who was trying not to cringe.

She felt relieved when their verbal shagging was interrupted by the strains of 'Mission: Impossible' coming from Rita's leopard-skin handbag. It was Rita's new mobile phone. She'd bought it only last week on the advice of her agent, who said she needed to be able to contact her at any time. Unfortunately, for some reason her number kept getting mixed up with that of a twenty-four-hour Thai takeaway on Ventura Boulevard, and instead of being flooded with offers of auditions and film roles, she was being inundated night and day with orders for sweet and sour pork, Pad Thai noodles and boiled rice.

'If it's another bloody order for green chicken curry I'm going to tell them to sod off,' she hissed, scrabbling around in the bottom of her bag. She pulled the phone out just as it was about to ring off.

'Yes?' she snapped, ready to launch into a tirade of verbal abuse. Except she didn't. Wrinkling her forehead, she pressed the phone to her ear. It was difficult to hear, what with Michael Bolton's unplugged version of 'Jingle Bells' being piped out of the overhead speakers.

'Yeah, speaking . . .' There was a pause.

Frankie watched Rita's face drain of colour.

'Oh ... OK ... yeah ... I mean, of course ... Yeah ... OK ... bye.' She stared blankly at the phone in her hand as if she'd never seen a Nokia before.

'Well?' Frankie was worried something was up. She'd never seen Rita so pale. 'What's happened?'

For the first time ever, Rita had been rendered speechless. She seemed to be in a daze, a state of shock.

'Rita, for Christ's sake will you tell me what's going on?'

With a shaking hand, Rita pulled out her packet of cigarettes and lit one. She took a deep drag as the colour came flooding back into her face and her shock gave way to excitement. And a smile plastered itself across her face, so she looked like one of those lottery winners you see in the papers clutching a cardboard cheque. Blowing out a cloud of smoke, she bit her lip and spoke slowly, deliberately, as if she was having trouble getting her mind around the words she was speaking. 'I got it ...' She paused, blowing two chimneys of smoke down her nostrils. 'I got the part in *Malibu Motel*. Of Tracy Potter, the receptionist ...' Her voice broke off as the reality of what she was saying sank in. Gripping Frankie, she stared at her. '*Can you fucking believe it? I got the fucking part ...*'

The incognito celebrity customers at Firs for the Stars stopped loading up their sports utility vehicles with Trafalgar Square-size Norwegian spruces and turned to see where all the shrieking was coming from. Trying to crease their botoxed foreheads, they stared through their designer sunglasses at a pint-size redhead in a leopard-skin top and a miniskirt, whooping with joy and jigging up and down in crazed exhilaration. Grabbing her friend, she'd wrapped strands of tinsel around herself and the sales assistant like silver feather boas and was squirting fake snow into the air, so that it fluttered down over them as if they were plastic figures in one of those snow shakers.

Rita knew everybody was staring, and she didn't care. She was going to be on the receiving end of a lot more attention in the future, so she might as well start getting used to it. *She was going to be famous.* It was hard to believe, but she'd finally done it.

Rita Duffin was set to become a star. A Hollywood fucking soap star.

34

'Happy Christmas, darlings.' Waving a branch of mistletoe and wearing a butcher's pinny over the top of a snake-skin-print suit, Dorian greeted Rita and Frankie at the door and kissed them both hungrily. 'Looking totally fabulous as ever.' He grinned, licking his lips and wrapping his arms snugly around their waists. Ushering them over the threshold and on to his balcony, which he'd decorated with fairy lights and a deluxe, top-of-the-range gold tinsel tree from Barneys, he picked up a cut-glass decanter that was glinting in the sun. 'Fancy a sherry?'

It was Christmas Day and they'd gone next door to spend it with Dorian, who, after his drugs scare, had turned his Versace back on his sex-drugs-and-party lifestyle. Not that he wasn't still dealing, but instead of illegal substances, he was now making his fortune trading stocks and shares on the Internet. As well as his new career, he'd also begun some kind of health kick. Instead of lying in bed all day with a hangover and a fully paid-up member of the LA ChildWoman species, he was now up at six a.m., jogging around the Hollywood reservoir with Elvis on a retractable lead, and after working at his laptop all day he spent his evenings cooking low-fat smoked salmon risotto for one, watching films on his state-of-the-art DVD player and going to bed early.

'I thought you might be missing home and so I made a special trip to the English store in Santa Monica. The old dear that runs the place told me to buy a Harrods Christmas pudding, some of that Bird's custard, Paxo stuffing and a couple of bottles of Bristol Cream.' Looking delighted with himself, Dorian took a swig from a glass and pulled a face. 'Jesus Christ, how can you drink this stuff?' Coughing, he tipped it into one of his many now-empty plant pots and reached for a bottle of Sky vodka. 'What about a Bloody Mary instead?' His new health regime obviously hadn't vetoed alcohol.

'Yeah, why not?' Frankie smiled, trying to look cheerful, when inside she felt anything but.

The day before Reilly had called her from God knows where in Mexico. The line was appalling, but just as the pips ran out she managed to hear what he was saying: 'There's been a pretty bad storm . . . a few days to get to Mexico City . . . I'm really sorry . . .' She didn't need to fill in the gaps to realise he wasn't going to be back in LA for Christmas. She'd pretended it was no big deal, but the disappointment was crushing her.

For the past two weeks, she'd been like the space shuttle on countdown. A mixture of nerves, anticipation and excitement at the thought of seeing him again. Looking forward to being able to hold him and unwrap him as if he were her very own Christmas present. Ever since he'd left for Mexico she'd been mentally ticking off the days, hours, minutes until he got back. And now she had no idea how long that would be.

'Frankie's fed up,' announced Rita bluntly, blowing her friend's brave face. 'Reilly's marooned God knows where in Mexico.' Plonking herself down on the hammock, she swung towards the pile of luxury mince pies that were stacked, in an ice-sugary mountain, in the middle of the rattan coffee table. 'I've told her to cheer up, but you know what it's like . . .' Her voice was muffled as she licked her fingers between mouthfuls of pastry . . . 'You can't help it when you're young and in love.'

Frankie cringed. She didn't want everybody to know how she felt about Reilly. Especially not Dorian. But it was too late.

'Yes, a little birdie did tell me you two were more than just good friends,' Dorian exchanged looks with Rita that revealed they'd obviously been gossiping. 'Silly boy. Fancy leaving you home alone.' Tutting, he finished adding the Angostura bitters and tomato juice to his silver cocktail shaker and began rattling it around his head as if he was about to break into *Aaa-gaaa-do-do-do*. After a couple of seconds he poured out the spicy contents into three glasses. 'If you ever get too lonely, remember I'm only next door.' Passing Frankie her drink, he winked roguishly.

'How could I forget?' she deadpanned, shaking her head. But she couldn't help smiling. It was impossible to remain annoyed with Dorian.

'I propose a toast. Here's to absent friends.' He raised his Bloody Mary.

Frankie knew he was referring to Reilly, but she was suddenly reminded of Hugh back in England. Six thousand miles away. She banished the thought as quickly as it had appeared. He was a ghost of Christmas past. She needed to concentrate on the present. Standing here, in the Californian sunshine with her friends on Christmas Day. Feeling happier and luckier than she could ever have imagined just a few months ago.

Smiling, she took a deep breath and clinked her glass. 'To absent friends.'

Hugh pulled up outside his parents' house in Tunbridge Wells and turned the key in the ignition. The engine died and he sat motionless in his Golf for a moment, watching the snow-flakes fall on his windscreen. Thick, floury lumps that piled up in the corners and coated the glass like white confetti.

For some reason he was suddenly reminded of Frankie, of last year when they'd driven to his parents, both nursing the after-effects of a Christmas Eve party. How she'd huddled next to him in the passenger seat as they'd raced down the M25 wearing a fluffy hat with flaps that pulled down over her ears and a bloody awful jumper that his mum had bought her as a birthday present. Even now, he could still remember taking his eyes off the road for a moment to look at her. And thinking that, despite her hangover, she looked beautiful.

Glancing at the empty seat next to him, he caught himself. Christmas was turning him into a sentimental idiot. Opening the door, he climbed out of the car and its snug warmth, and into the bitter December weather. Icy blasts of wind whirled around his ankles, up underneath the layers of his cashmere jumper and Ralph Lauren shirt. Tightly wrapping his overcoat around him, he leaned into the car, gathering together the presents that lay sprawled on the back seat, trying not to drop them into a snowdrift as he fiddled with his keys. Finally, after pressing his alarm several times, the car responded by beeping and flashing its side lights. 'Bloody weather,' he swore, as he slipped, almost falling on the pavement, before steadying himself and walking up the path to his parents' front door.

He wasn't looking forward to spending the day with his relatives. Last year he'd been with Frankie and together they'd laughed at his dad's attempts at charades, made polite conversation with his boring brother-in-law, Jerry, played with his sister's brattish four-year-twins, and endured twelve hours of boring telly. But today it was just him, by himself. Sighing, he put his key in the latch. He would have to face *The Sound of Music* alone.

'. . . and then I told him, "If you're not going to fuck me, you can fuck off." ' Rita helped herself to another slice of spicy salami pizza.

Frankie sipped her glass of champagne and smiled absent-mindedly. She wasn't really listening to Rita's explanation of how she'd let Matt down lightly. Instead she was thinking about how surreal it was to be sitting on Dorian's balcony on Christmas Day, eating take-out pizza, getting a bit of a tan and gazing at the view of LA's skyline. It sure as hell beat being back in London.

'I mean, for God's sake, I'm not the Virgin Mary, am I?' Rita waved her pizza slice at Frankie, strings of melted cheese trailing from her lips.

'Hardly,' quipped Dorian, who was playing waiter and ladling out dollops of stuffing. He was determined they could still eat it as a side dish, despite having had to abort his valiant attempt at roast turkey a few hours before.

It had been all that weight-to-cooking-time ratio stuff that had done it. Dorian had never been much of a mathematician and he'd got mixed up and divided when he should have multiplied. Which, at Frankie's rough estimate, meant that even with the gas full on, his prize-winning bird wouldn't be ready until Boxing Day. So, after deciding to let it rest in peace in its oven grave, spread-eagled on the middle shelf among the shrivelled-up carrots and raw potatoes, Dorian had got out his hoard of hundreds of take-away pamphlets – he'd always known they would come in useful one day – and dialled Domino's Pizza. It was the first time Frankie's Christmas dinner had come with two extra toppings and a free litre of diet Coke. But hey, this was LA. What did she expect? Something conventional?

'But I'm not going to get upset about it. To be honest, I knew from the beginning that we weren't right for each other anyway,' continued Rita, ignoring Dorian and lying through her teeth and a forkful of Paxo's sage and onion. 'It wasn't as if I was in love with him, like you were with Hugh.'

Frankie flinched at the mention of Hugh's name. Over the past couple of weeks she hadn't thought about him, but for some reason today she kept being reminded of him. Even her parents, who were spending the holidays on a cruiseliner, ballroom-dancing round the Grand Canaries, had asked her if she'd spoken to Hugh when they'd called to wish her happy Christmas. Her mum had always had a soft spot for Hugh and his perfectly ironed shirts, and she hadn't been able to hide her disappointment when Frankie had said no.

'Anyone for a glass of bubbly?' interrupted Dorian, reappearing from the kitchen with another bottle of champagne and a bag of fortune cookies.

Whooping tipsily, Rita held out her glass for a refill. 'I tell you what. I bet he's having a crap Christmas without you.'

Frankie didn't say anything. Instead she glanced at her watch – it would be evening in London. 'I'm sure Hugh's fine,' she murmured, waiting for Dorian to finish pouring before taking a large gulp of champagne. 'He's probably watching *The Sound of Music* as we speak.'

She looked at Rita for a second before they both burst out laughing, clutching their stomachs in drunken giggles and leaving a bemused Dorian wondering what the hell could be so funny about a film starring Julie Andrews?

> *Doe a deer, a female deer,*
> *Ray, a drop of golden sun.*

Wedged in between his grandmother and Great-aunt Prudence on the button-back leather sofa, Hugh sighed frustratedly. He didn't think he could stand any more. He'd just sat through a two-hour Christmas special of *Only Fools and Horses* and now this. He fidgeted uncomfortably. The telly was blaring out, as was the central heating, and he felt too hot and too full. Grumpily he ran his eye around the room.

His dad had nodded off in the armchair and his party hat, which had slipped down across his face, was fluttering like a purple paper flag with each snore; despite second helpings of trifle, his heavily pregnant sister, Belinda, was concentrating on working her way through a Terry's Chocolate Orange, while his brother-in-law, Jerry, who voted Green and wore corduroy jackets with patches on the sleeves, was on his hands and knees on the floor playing trains with the twins from hell.

'Anyone for more tea?' trilled his mother, popping her head round the side of the sliding panelled doors.

'What?' boomed Great-aunt Prudence, who was as deaf as a post but refused to admit it. Jolting upright on the sofa, she cupped her hand to her ear. 'What did you say?'

'Tea,' bellowed his mother, waggling a teacup for added emphasis.

'Well, why didn't you say so?' she tutted impatiently. 'But I want it brewed properly. In a teapot.'

'Do we have any of that super Christmas cake left that Granny made?' cooed Belinda, finishing off the last chocolate segment. She wasn't eating for two, she was eating for the Third World. Her request for cake went unanswered as a piercing scream arose from Crispin, who'd just had a piece of plastic rail track jammed up his nose by his sister, Jemima.

'Any chance of putting the *Thomas the Tank Engine* video on?' asked Jerry brightly. It was a rhetorical question. 'Crispin loves Thomas the tank engine, don't you, Crispy-wispy.'

Crispy-wispy suddenly stopped crying and, clutching his bleeding nose, nodded vigorously.

Hugh scowled. He couldn't bear it any longer. As if this wasn't bad enough, there was the family New Year get-together to get through next week. His heart sank. It was too awful to even contemplate.

*   *   *

'Whatever happened to that nice young woman of yours?' asked his gran, suddenly coming to life as Julie Andrews disappeared over the hills and Thomas the tank engine puffed on to the screen. 'She bought me a lovely pair of sheepskin slippers last year.'

Hugh sighed. He'd deliberately not told his older relatives about the split with Frankie as they were constantly nagging him to get married and 'provide us with more grandchildren'.

'She's in America.'

'America,' barked Prudence, showing a miraculous flash of hearing. 'What on earth is she doing there?'

'Having a good time, I suppose,' sighed Hugh enviously.

'But America's an awfully long way away,' continued his grandmother, peering at him through the inch-thick magnifying lenses of her reading glasses. 'I simply can't understand young people today. During the war we had to be apart from our loved ones . . . I didn't see your grandfather for nearly eighteen months.' At the mention of her long-dead husband her voice wavered and she gently touched her wedding ring, a worn band of gold that nestled against her paper-thin skin, before continuing, 'but now there's simply no need for it. And especially not at this time of year. Don't you love her?'

The question silenced Hugh. Frankie had been on his mind a lot lately, but he'd just assumed that was because of the time of year. A time to look back over what had happened during the last twelve months and make resolutions for the next. But now, staring his grandmother's question in the face, he realised he was fooling himself. It had got nothing to do with the time of year. He was thinking about Frankie because he missed her. The grass hadn't been greener being single. It had been a desert. A lonely, miserable few months of meaningless one-night stands, eating take-outs, waking up alone on Sunday mornings. There'd been no one to cuddle up to on the sofa and watch DVDs with, no one to cook dinner for

– OK, so he'd only cooked dinner twice in two years, but still – no one to eat croissants and drink coffee with on Sunday morning in that little French café around the corner where they read all the papers – him the sport section in *The Times*, her the *Mail on Sunday*'s YOU magazine. Finally he had to admit to himself that he'd got it wrong. He didn't want all this space. He wanted Frankie to fill it. He wanted her back.

Looking up into the watery-blue eyes of his grandmother, he nodded. 'I suppose I must do.'

'Well, then, go to her. Otherwise you'll lose her.' She poked him with a bony finger.

'I think I already have,' he muttered, suddenly feeling a chink in his confidence.

'What? What did he say?' boomed Prudence, leaning forwards. 'Speak up.'

'I said I've lost her . . . I've lost Frankie.' Used to having it all, he found this difficult to admit.

'Utter rot,' she spat, shaking her head and making her dentures rattle. 'Call yourself a man? If you love her, go out there and get her.' Clenching her fist, she suddenly felt rather empowered. 'Because if you don't, somebody else will.'

It was later and the fairy lights twinkled in the chilly darkness. Rita, Frankie and Dorian had managed to work their way through four king-size pizzas and most of the drinks cabinet and were lying on the balcony – three beached whales wrapped in Mexican blankets, smoking cigarettes, eating chocolates and playing strip poker while Sister Sledge wafted out from the foot-high speakers.

'I'm bored of this,' moaned Dorian, who'd only suggested the game so he could see Rita naked. Unfortunately for him, he hadn't known that her six older brothers were all gamblers and that Rita had spent her childhood playing with cards instead of with dolls. As a result, she remained fully clothed, he was now starkers under his scratchy Mexican blanket. 'Why don't we do fortune cookies instead?'

'OK,' smirked Rita, collecting up the cards. 'I'll go first.' Grabbing the bag, she stuck in her hand as if it was a lucky dip and, pulling out a cookie, bit it in half, revealing a white ribbon of paper. ' "Listen and heed signs, and you will find success." ' She smiled jubilantly as she read out her fortune. 'Yep, that's me. A successful actress.' She threw the bag across to Dorian. 'What does yours say?'

'Erm . . .' Lying on the hammock, he tried unpeeling the piece of paper while clinging on to the blanket covering his bare chest. It was times like these that he wished he'd actually worked out at the gym, and not just hung out by the swimming pool chatting up Lycra-clad women. ' "Sex is on the cards with a redhead from across the Atlantic." '

Rita chucked a strawberry cream at him, as they all burst out laughing.

'And what about yours, Frankie?'

Taking the bag from Dorian, Frankie delved inside. 'Well, here goes.' She smiled wryly, breaking open the cookie. 'It says, "A surprise is just around the corner." ' She rolled her eyes. 'Yeah right. What surprise?'

'If you knew that, it wouldn't be one.'

Frankie jumped. It was a voice. A man's voice. A familiar voice.

She turned round to see where it was coming from. And there in the shadows, standing at the entrance of the balcony, was Reilly.

'You didn't hear me knocking the music was so loud, so I let myself in.' Running his fingers through his hair, he smiled nervously. 'I managed to get a flight back from Veracruz. Better late than never, hey?' His voice was apologetic and he looked nervously at Frankie, who'd stood up and was staring at him in disbelief. Smears of dirt and mud coated his jeans and T-shirt and his skin was scorched a deep tan. Chunks of sun-bleached hair fell on to his face, while his stubble had grown into a thick, dark beard coating his chin and throat. He looked more dishevelled and messier than ever, but it didn't stop her stomach flipping over like an Olympic gymnast.

She hesitated, not knowing what to say or do. Her heart was telling her one thing, but her head was telling her another. It was Reilly who made the first move. Bending down, he scooped her up and, holding her tight, buried his head in her hair. 'Boy, did I miss you.' It was the Christmas present Frankie had been waiting for.

Hugh knew he couldn't wait any longer. His gran and Great-aunt Prudence were absolutely right. Why hadn't he realised it before? It was as if he'd spent the last couple of months struggling through a difficult exam and now two old-age pensioners had just shown him all the answers. Shown him what he had to do.

'Thanks,' he whispered, kissing his gran and Great-aunt Pru on their powdery, lavender-scented cheeks before jumping up from the sofa, stepping over Belinda and Jerry, who were singing along to Thomas with a twin in each lap.

'Mum, I'm going.' Grabbing his mother as she reappeared from the kitchen with half a Christmas cake and her antique bone-china cups, he gave her a quick hug.

'What?' Her pearls bobbed up and down round her neck as she watched him disappearing down the hallway. 'But I've just made more tea and Daddy wanted us to play *Who Wants to be a Millionaire?* later. Why have you got to leave so early? Where are you going?'

Without missing a beat, Hugh opened the front door, letting in a blast of icy wind. 'Los Angeles.'

35

Frankie couldn't remember whose idea it had been to go to Las Vegas for the millennium. It was probably Dorian's. But then it could have been Rita's. To be honest, after Reilly's appearance, the rest of Christmas Day had become a bit of a blur.

Nevertheless, here she was at three p.m. on New Year's Eve, cuddled up next to Reilly on the back seat of Dorian's brand-new Ford Expedition – a Christmas present to himself – gazing out of the tinted windows as they pulled off Highway 15. Rising before her out of the dusty desert was a neon-flashing strip of glittering hotels and their larger-than-life casinos. Huge self-contained fantasy lands where the religion was gambling, the language was money and time was measured by the revolutions of a roulette wheel. Frankie felt a flutter of excitement. So this was Las Vegas.

'Bloody hell, it's a bit better than Blackpool illuminations,' gasped Rita, as Dorian pulled up outside Caesar's Palace and they emerged from the coolness of the airconditioning and into the baking heat of the Nevada desert.

'Are we staying here?' whispered Frankie, taken aback as the shiny-shoed, waistcoated porters swept down upon them and began loading up their luggage. She'd been expecting to stay at some cheap twenty-bucks-a-night motel with fag burns in the carpet, quilted headboards and cellulite-enhancing aquarium lighting in the bathroom. Despite its neon tackiness, this place didn't look cheap.

'Absolutely,' chirped Dorian, doing his hamstring stretches, as if he was limbering up for a marathon. Catching her worried expression, he let out a snort of laughter. 'Don't look so worried. It's on me.'

'Dorian's a high roller,' yawned Reilly, who'd been asleep since Death Valley. Blinking in the bright sunlight, he rubbed the sleep from his eyes. 'In Vegas that's the name they give to the big gamblers.' Grabbing his dusty Stetson, he put his arm around Frankie's shoulder, pulling her towards him as they followed the porters scurrying across the forecourt. 'The casinos love him,' he whispered, sleepily nuzzling into her neck.

Dorian overheard as he marched ahead towards the entrance. 'You won't have to pay for anything. Hotels, room service, food, drink . . . it's all free,' he declared, waving his arms enthusiastically around in the air as if he was conducting his own symphony.

'*Free?*' parroted Rita, trying to keep up in her skyscraper heels as they were ushered on to the moving walkway that swept them past a full-size replica of Michelangelo's *David*. She made a mental note to buy herself a pair of shoes she could actually walk in – after being in LA for six months she'd got out of the habit. '*Everything?*'

'Only if you play your cards right,' smirked Dorian, suggestively slipping his arm around her waist as they entered a vast labyrinth of slot machines, mirrors, multicoloured lights and green baize.

Rita pulled a face. Something told her he wasn't talking poker.

As Dorian steered Rita deftly through the sliding doors and into the smoked-glass VIP reception area, Frankie loitered behind, gazing at the rows of shorts'n'vest brigade with buckets of dimes, feeding the slot machines like animals at the zoo. 'Do you gamble?' She looked up at Reilly.

'Sometimes. It depends if I'm feeling lucky.'

'And are you?' Her voice was quiet against the jingly, jangly soundtrack of the amusement arcade which sprawled out before them in all directions, as far as the eye could see.

Reilly couldn't help smiling. Ever since that night at his house, he hadn't been able to believe how lucky he was. That someone like Frankie would be interested in someone like him. Putting both arms around her waist, he pulled her closer. 'What do you think?'

Over the last week, Frankie had broken every rule of the dating game:·1) leaving seventy-two hours between each phone call, 2) inventing a hectic social life when arranging a date and 3) playing it cool and *not* inviting him in for coffee even if you're gagging for it – and instead had spent every moment, waking and sleeping, with Reilly. For the first time in her adult life, she'd ignored what all those women's magazines, her best mate Rita and years of experience had taught her about how to keep a bloke guessing with all those complicated bluffs and double bluffs. She didn't want to play games. She just wanted to be with Reilly. It was as simple as that.

And so throwing the rulebook out of the window, they'd spent every day together. Days walking barefoot along Malibu beach watching the dolphins turning somersaults over the surf, driving to Santa Barbara in his beaten-up Bronco and drinking beer as the sun set in orange and pink marbled streaks over the eighteenth-century Mission high on the hill. Evenings spent having barbecues in his garden – her with her veggie burgers and Chardonnay, him with his sixteen-ounce steaks and Jack Daniel's – and afterwards curling up like cats in his hammock, swapping childhood stories, looking at old photographs and talking about their lives until their words turned into drunken kisses and they couldn't keep their hands off each other any longer.

Frankie was completely unprepared for any of it. After Hugh she'd never expected to find someone who could make her laugh one minute and feel horny as hell the next. Everything was too good to be true, even the sex was amazing. Not in a gymnastic, throwing-your-head-back-and-wailing-to-the-moon kind of way, but in a deliciously intimate, unhurried, Barry White feel-like-we're-making-love kind of way.

But wasn't it always supposed to be great in the beginning? Lying naked next to Reilly one afternoon, bathed in the afterglow of orgasm and stubble burn, Frankie pondered the question. The beginning of what? She stopped herself right there before she got carried away by the lust and thrust of it all. If splitting up with Hugh had taught her one thing, it was that relationships couldn't be predicted. There were no guarantees. Who knew what would happen in the future?

After all, it wasn't as if she and Reilly had talked about how they felt about each other. They hadn't had any of those awkward 'what happens now?' chats, where each person is afraid to say how they feel, in case they've completely misjudged the situation and the other person feels exactly the opposite. Maybe Rita was right, maybe it was just a fling and she was reading too much into it. Maybe Reilly was only interested in a fling. A few weeks of sex, with no strings attached. Looking at it from his point of view, he probably assumed it was just a holiday romance, something short and intense, and that it would be over as soon as she left LA.

The thought saddened her and she stared up at the ceiling. So much had happened over the past couple of weeks, it was difficult to know what to think. But one thing was for certain, she couldn't stay in LA for ever. Very soon she was going to have to face the grim reality of going back to London and trying to pick up the pieces of her life. Finding a room to rent, paying off her debts, probably signing up with a temp agency until she sorted out what to do about her career. She sighed. Just thinking about it depressed her. Turning her head against the pillow, she looked across at Reilly, his bare torso half covered by a sheet, and she couldn't help smiling. For the moment reality could wait.

'I think I'm going to burst,' mumbled Dorian, abandoning a king prawn and pushing away a plate piled high with translucent pink carcasses. 'I can't eat another thing.'

'Me neither,' groaned Reilly, eating the last mouthful of steak and leaning back against his chair. He would have loosened his belt if he'd had one.

Lunch had been Dorian's idea, even though it was after four o'clock, and so after checking in to their lavish penthouse suites they'd gone downstairs to find something to eat. Less than an hour later they'd become victims of the Las Vegas buffet. A huge, winding zigzag of tables groaning with mounds of seafood which jostled alongside gigantic platters of cold meats, cheeses, breads, salads, fruits, which in turn led into avenues of chiller cabinets of shiny desserts glistening under the lights – cheesecake, gâteaux, Mississippi mud pies, chocolate chip cookies . . . The calories just went on and on and on.

Faced with more food than Sainsbury's, Frankie had been taken aback. So this was where people from LA went to pig out when they'd had enough of the Zone. Forget less is more. This was gimme more, and more and more, until I simply can't eat any more. And all for $6.99.

'Anyone for pudding?' yelled Rita, from the dessert counter. For the first time since puberty, she wasn't on a diet, and it was all thanks to the director of *Malibu Motel*, who, after being struck with the 'totally awesome' idea of making Tracy Potter a *plump* British receptionist, had instructed her to put on ten pounds. Ironically, in a cruel twist of fate, now that she'd been given free rein to eat anything she wanted without feeling guilty, Rita had discovered she didn't want to and had lost three pounds in a week.

Ignoring the Mississippi mud pie, she reappeared with a bowl of fruit salad. 'You didn't answer so I've got four spoons and we can all dig in,' she breezed, plonking the bowl down on the table. Forget Del Monte and a few diced-up bits of pear with a fluorescent pink cocktail cherry thrown in for colour, this was a delicious combination of exotic fruits.

'Thanks, but I'm going to have to pass.' Holding up his hands in defeat, Dorian stood up. Catching sight of his silhouette in the wall-to-wall mirrors, he tried adjusting the waistband of velvet trousers that had suddenly become more than a little snug. And then gave up and put his jacket back on. 'Anyone fancy a game of blackjack?'

'Yeah, why not?' said Reilly, scraping back his chair. It was a couple of years since he'd been to Vegas and he was in the mood for gambling. Especially seeing as they were with Dorian, whose reputation preceded him like a red carpet. Since they'd arrived they'd been getting lots of nodding, smiling and any-friends-of-Mr-Wilde-are-always-welcome-type handshakes.

'Come on, guys, it's time to watch the professional at work.'

'Only on one condition,' said Rita, chewing thoughtfully on a mouthful of kumquat.

Dorian paused in anticipation. Perhaps his persistence had paid off. 'What?'

'This time you've got to keep your clothes on.' Rita let out a snort of laughter that boomeranged around the restaurant, causing the rest of the diners to pause mid-mouthful and stare across at Dorian, who'd blushed the colour of his rasp-berry velvet suit.

Trying to hide his acute embarrassment at being reminded of his humiliating defeat at strip poker, Dorian gave a tight-lipped smile. He had a delicate ego and he bruised easily. Something which Rita seemed to delight in. Turning on his Gucci loafers, he set off towards the bright lights of the casino. Something told him she was never going to let him live that down.

36

Walking into the casino was like entering another world. A completely sealed environment where plastic chips replaced money, natural daylight was replaced by multicoloured neon, and the absence of any clocks meant that time had no meaning and the outside world ceased to exist. Lost in a maze of bottle-green baize, roulette wheels and crystal chandeliers, everyone was suddenly equal. From the dinner-jacketed multi-millionaires on their red velvet thrones gambling with hundred-thousand-dollar chips to the peroxide OAPs on metals buffets betting dimes, everybody was pursuing the same goal. Everybody was hoping that on the next turn of the card or yank of a slot-machine handle they'd strike it lucky, hit the jackpot, win a million. And if it didn't happen this time, it could be the next, or the next, or the next. No wonder Vegas was addictive.

'I'm Valeen and this is my husband, Bunt.' Across the craps table, a heavily made-up woman wearing a strapless, low-cut dress and too much gold jewellery grinned broadly at Frankie. 'We're celebrating our ruby wedding anniversary, aren't we, honey?' Putting down her lipstick-smeared martini glass, she affectionately patted her cigar-smoking husband's paunch. 'Forty years, can you believe it?'

Frankie smiled politely and shook her head. Valeen only looked about forty-five. Perhaps she'd been a child bride. In fact, thinking about it, hadn't she once read a special report about Middle America and under-age brides in *Marie Claire*? But watching closely, Frankie suddenly noticed the crêpe-papery cleavage and dappled age spots on her hands and realised that Valeen wasn't a child bride from Oklahoma, but a high-maintenance sixty-something from Texas who'd had a couple of facelifts, eyebag removal, a chin tuck and one of those ski-slope-type nose jobs that had been popular back in the 1970s.

'Did you get married here in Vegas?' Aware that she was staring, Frankie made an attempt at conversation.

'We sure did,' beamed Valeen, delighted at finding someone to tell her life story to. 'At the little white chapel of the Lord. It was the happiest day of our lives, wasn't it, honey?' She looked adoringly at Bunt, who puffed gruffly on his cigar and continued gambling. Bunt, it seemed, was a man of few words. 'We'd only known each other two weeks, but I knew he was the one. I knew I'd love him for the rest of my life.'

Frankie nodded as Valeen gushed on. It was like the lyrics of a Country and Western song.

'Is that your husband?' Valeen winked, taking a swig of martini and raising her plucked-out-and-then-painted-back-on eyebrows towards Reilly, who was sat further along the table drinking beer and discussing gambling techniques with Dorian and Rita, who were getting drunk on free champagne.

'Oh, no.' Frankie smiled, suddenly feeling self-conscious. 'We're . . .' She groped around for the right word. What could she say? That they were lovers? That he was her boyfriend? That they were having a fling? She felt herself blush with embarrassment. 'We're just seeing each other. It's nothing serious.' She glanced at Reilly, who caught her eye and smiled back, reaching out a hand to squeeze her thigh.

'Not from where I'm sitting honey,' drawled Valeen. 'No, sir-ee.'

*   *   *

It was seven thirty and they'd been gambling in the casino for nearly two hours. Not that anyone was aware of the time. Fuelled by the never-ending rounds of free drinks, Marlboro Lights and exhilaration, Frankie had never imagined losing money could be so enjoyable. Being a complete novice, she'd blown the fifty bucks that Reilly had given her in less than five minutes at the blackjack table, followed shortly by Reilly, and then Rita, who won two hundred at poker and then promptly lost it at roulette. Only Dorian was on a winning streak.

'Come on, Mr Chips,' yelled Rita, creasing up with laughter and drunkenly clinging on to the gambling table as Dorian counted up his winnings. 'Put your money where your mouth is.' Mr Chips was Rita's new nickname for Dorian, who, after a successful flutter at the poker table, was up ten thousand dollars.

Stacking his multicoloured chips into towering piles, he rose to the challenge. Dorian always loved being a showman. 'OK, I'll bet the lot on one roll of the dice.'

Rita whooped excitedly.

'Can I be Demi Moore and kiss the dice?' Frankie laughed, taking a sip of her margarita as Dorian accepted the two small red cubes from the croupier.

'Only if I can be Robert Redford.'

'Don't even think about it,' murmured Reilly, wrapping his arms protectively around Frankie. 'This woman is worth more than a million dollars of anyone's money.'

'Hey, are you folks from England?' hollered Valeen, who was feeling left out at the other side of the table. Draining her martini she plucked the olive from the toothpick and waved her empty glass at a passing waitress.

'Of course,' laughed Rita, and then immediately regretted it.

Valeen shrieked and clasped her crêpe-paper cleavage with her diamond-encrusted hands. 'Oh, my lord, I just adore your royal family,' she whooped, eyes bright, emotion quivering in her voice. 'Your queen is such an amazing lady. But, and I say this with no disrespect to dear Liz, I've always thought she could do with a little help with her style, don't you think?' Valeen broke off to accept a fresh martini, spilling it on her dress. 'Bunt always says I could give her a few tips. You know, show a little leg, some cleavage, maybe try more blusher and a few highlights.' She patted her Ivana Trump-style thatch of yellow hair. 'I mean, it doesn't do no harm to help yourself a little, does it? It can still be subtle. Why, look at me.' And laughing loudly, she threw back her head, revealing her cosmetic surgery scars and rattling the clip-on diamanté earrings that made her ear lobes droop like a King Charles spaniel's.

'Would everyone place their bets?' The croupier finished moving things around on the table, as a few people began gathering around to watch. With any game, if the stakes were high, it created interest. People love to watch gambling.

A few players round the table placed ten or twenty bucks. There was a hundred from the small guy in glasses and a herring-bone blazer. Bunt chewed pensively on his cigar before eventually putting down five hundred, while Dorian took a deep breath and moved his chips across the green baize. 'I'll bet everything on seven.'

There was a collective intake of breath from around the table. It was double or nothing. If he threw a seven he'd win another ten thousand dollars. Any other number, he'd lose everything.

'OK, here goes,' he whispered, shaking the dice.

'Give it some welly,' shrieked Rita, high on champagne and adrenalin.

With a flick of his wrist, he threw the dice. It was one of those moments when, if it had been in a movie, everything would have been slowed down, frame by frame, allowing the audience to watch the small scarlet rocks breaking free from the palm of his hand, escaping through his fingers and soaring through the air. Passing the excited, anxious, mesmerised faces of the crowds gathered around the table and then descending, falling, until they landed on the table.

Frankie held her breath as they hit the table, bounced once against the sides, twice more on the green, rolled and then came to a halt. There was a second's pause – as long as it took to register. A five and a two. A total of seven.

'Fucking hell, I can't believe it,' whooped Rita, breaking the suspense and bringing the film up to speed. Leaping from her stool, she knocked over her glass, splashing Valeen's cleavage. Not that Rita noticed. She was too busy shrieking, 'I can't believe it, I can't believe it,' like a police siren and elbowing out of the way a couple of shaggy perms in marblewash jeans who were nuzzling up close to Dorian, dollar signs flashing in their eyes like fruit machines. Finally grabbing him by his lapels, Rita panted breathlessly, 'You were bloody amazing,' before kissing him full on the lips.

Frankie wasn't sure what was more thrilling for Dorian, his twenty-thousand-dollar winnings or being kissed by Rita. She watched as he resurfaced. He looked stunned. As did Rita, who'd just realised what she'd done. And for a moment they both stared at each other, neither of them saying anything.

'You're one lucky son of a bitch,' congratulated Reilly, clapping him on the back and shaking his head. 'I've got to hand it to you, that was something.'

'Yeah, well done,' said Frankie, her cheeks flushed with excitement, her arms around Reilly's waist.

Dorian grinned. He couldn't believe his luck. His head stopped spinning and, remembering who he was and where he was, his vanity took over and he wiped his mouth with a napkin and smoothed down his hair, which had become fluffy and tousled in all the excitement. Rubbing his hands together, he watched as a waitress dressed in a skimpy gladiator's costume, revealing a Roman bust that was definitely not made of marble, wiggled towards him carrying a magnum of Dom Perignon. 'The management offers you their warmest congratulations,' she beamed as she recited the oft-repeated patter. 'How many glasses do you need, sir?'

Dorian looked at Reilly, who shook his head. 'No, thanks.'

'You're not going to celebrate with me?' Dorian looked disappointed.

'We're going to pop back to the room to freshen up,' explained Frankie, resting her head against Reilly's shoulder.

Rita rolled her eyes and grinned. She knew exactly what freshen up meant. And it didn't involve cold water and flannels. 'OK,' she said, winking conspiratorially and nudging Dorian. 'But don't be too long. The band's on soon.' She nodded towards the dance floor, decorated with hundreds of helium balloons and silver and gold streamers, where, in the middle of the raised stage, a drum kit, keyboards and a microphone had been set up. A troupe of sequined dancing girls and the perma-tanned crooner himself – Tom Jones – were all set to pelvis-thrust Vegas into the twenty-first century.

Watching Frankie and Reilly weave through the floor, all love-birdy and wrapped around each other like elastic bands, Rita felt a pang. It was New Year's Eve and she didn't have a fella. Even Valeen and Bunt had each other.

'Are you OK?' Dorian caught her expression.

'Yeah,' she breezed, trying to hitch herself on to her barstool. Wearing a miniskirt while under the influence of half a dozen Long Island Ice Teas, two Tequila Sunrises and a couple of glasses of champagne made it slightly tricky. Like trying to get into the saddle. At the third attempt she gave up pretending to be modest and, hitching her skirt up past her G-string, finally got her leg over. 'I'm all right, you know me.' Lighting a cigarette, she tried to cheer herself up with a reassuring lungful. 'It's just this time of year, counting down to a new century, singing "Auld Lang Syne" and all that.' Finishing off her drink, she fished around in the bottom of her glass for an ice cube and attempted to suck it dry of alcohol. 'It just makes me wish I had someone to share it with.'

'You've got me,' said Dorian quietly, passing her a champagne flute. They clinked glasses and he took a sip. Now that his adrenalin had stopped pumping, he realised he was suddenly feeling rather slushy. And rather pissed.

Rita looked at Dorian through the blurry veil of alcohol. His two faces came back into focus.

'Thanks,' she said, and then began giggling as a thought struck her.

'What's so funny?'

Rita smiled. 'If neither of us pulls tonight, at least we can snog each other at midnight.'

Dorian leaned drunkenly towards her, steadying himself on her bare legs as his stool tipped dangerously. 'You don't have to wait until midnight.'

Rita looked at his hand, the fingers still wrapped around her thigh. She realised she rather liked his hand being there. In fact, to be honest, she was actually beginning to feel quite turned on. 'Do you ever give up?' she murmured, conscious that her words were beginning to slur.

Dorian leaned closer. 'Do you want me to?'

Rita deliberated. What with Randy, and then Matt, it felt like for ever since she'd had a shag, and looking at Dorian, pissed and horny, he had shag written all over his perspiring forehead. 'No,' she whispered, shaking her head.

And, like athletes springing from their starting blocks, they lunged at each other, grappling like two horny teenagers at two a.m. in a nightclub, probing tongues, wandering hands, fiddly bra straps, straining hard-on. Rita hadn't enjoyed herself so much in ages.

Reilly looked at Frankie lying next to him in the mammoth bed. Her long limbs sprawled lazily across the mattress, half covered by the sheets, hair over her face, eyes closed. Champagne glasses lay next to the bed, together with an empty bottle of Moët and a bowl of half-eaten strawberries. Sleepily he traced his finger across Frankie's shoulder blade, before moving his hand slowly down her spine.

It was hard to believe they'd only been seeing each other for a week. It felt as if he'd known her for ever. Watching her now, half sleeping, he couldn't imagine being without her. Neither of them had talked about what was happening between them. To be honest, at first he'd thought that she was probably on the rebound from her ex-boyfriend. That this was just going to be a holiday romance and he was the bloke to make her feel better, to boost her confidence and help her lick her wounds until she'd recovered enough to get back on her feet again. But even after that first night together, he'd hoped that just maybe it was going to be something more. That night had been electric. Mind-blowing. He couldn't think of any other words to describe it. And it wasn't just the sex, although, yeah, that had been great. It was just being together. Talking, laughing, looking at each other, the way she smiled, smelled, *was*. Everything about her just clicked. As if she'd flicked a switch inside him that had been turned off for a long, long time.

At first he'd tried to persuade himself he was getting carried away, that he'd been so long without a woman he was confusing love with lust. That Frankie was only interested in a fling, nothing heavy. He'd tried to play it down on the phone from Mexico, but he couldn't stop thinking about her the whole time he was working, couldn't stop counting the days until he flew back to LA. He knew it was too much to hope for that she'd feel the same way about him when he got back. For God's sake, they'd slept together once and then he'd fucked off to Central America. But that was the most amazing thing about all of this, because when he saw her again, on Dorian's balcony, wrapped up in that moth-eaten old blanket, she'd looked at him and he'd known, right there and then, that he'd got nothing to worry about. She felt the same way.

Now, just a week later, he was still letting it sink in. After Kelly, he'd never thought he'd meet anyone who made him feel like this again, but Frankie had changed all that. *This stubborn, argumentative, headstrong, amazing, gorgeous woman had changed everything*. And now, lying next to her, he was suddenly overwhelmed by the desire to tell her how he felt. Maybe it was because he was pissed and feeling emotional, or maybe it wasn't. But whatever the hell it was, one thing was for sure, it didn't mean what he was going to say wasn't true. He just finally had the balls to say it.

'Hi.' She opened her eyes and smiled a deep smile of satisfaction that turned into a yawn. Rolling over on to her side, she propped herself up on one elbow and, choosing a strawberry, bit into it.

Reilly smiled, and ran his hand over her knotted hair. 'What do you want to do now?'

'Gamble I suppose.' She shrugged, offering him the rest of her strawberry. 'What else is there to do in Vegas?'

Reilly hesitated. It was now or never. 'We could get married.'

His words took a moment to register. A split second, where everything seemed to freeze for a moment before – *Wham!* – they hit Frankie full force. *Married?* Her mind whirled like a roulette wheel. Where the hell did that come from? She didn't know what to say. Surely Reilly wasn't being serious. One minute she'd been trying not to get too carried away, telling herself that all Reilly wanted was a brief fling. And now here he was telling her he wanted to spend the rest of his life with her. *She couldn't believe it.* They'd spent less than a week together, they'd never even met each other's parents, she didn't even know his surname . . .

Breathless with confused emotion and unanswered questions, she looked into the dark blue flecks of his eyes.

Then again, she felt as if she'd known him for ever, her parents would love him and . . .

'What's your surname?'

He frowned, creasing up his forehead. 'McKenzie, why?'

The dice suddenly fell into place. Francesca McKenzie. It went together. They went together. She stopped herself. Why was she even thinking about it? They were both drunk, it was New Year's Eve, they weren't thinking straight. Getting married to Reilly would be a crazy thing to do.

'Give me one good reason why I should say yes.'

'Because I love you.'

Four words. That's all it took. And suddenly it didn't seem so crazy any more.

37

'*You're doing what?*' screeched Rita. After coming up for air after a marathon snogging session, she was trying to gain some kind of composure. It didn't appear to be working. Wobbling precariously on her barstool, she grabbed hold of Dorian, who, covered in lip gloss, was hurriedly tucking in his shirt, while at the same time trying to hide his enormous erection.

'Getting married.' Frankie smiled excitedly, waggling her finger and showing off the ring Reilly had made out of a gold tinfoil champagne wrapper.

'When?'

'Tonight.' Reilly grinned.

There was a gasp, a pause, and then Rita suddenly burst into wailing sobs. Frankie was taken aback. She'd expected Rita to swear, laugh, scream. Anything but this.

'Fuck, I'm sorry,' sniffled Rita, trying to stifle her bawling.

Dorian was silent, still reeling from the shock of being manhandled by a redhead from Lancashire.

'I can't help it,' Rita hiccuped, dabbing her eyes with a Bacardi-soaked coaster. 'Weddings always make me cry.' And letting out a howl, she threw her arms round the happy couple and clung to them both in a soggy bear hug.

So this was it. She was getting married. Frankie still couldn't believe it. It was all happening so fast. As soon as she'd said yes, Reilly had scooped her against his bare chest, hugging and kissing her, telling her how happy he was, picking her up and whirling her round the room until they'd both collapsed back on to the bed, laughing at how stupid they looked, how happy they were. And unable to contain their elation, they'd thrown on their clothes and taken a cab to the City Hall to fill out the forms so they could get their wedding licence. The whole procedure had taken less than an hour and it seemed no time before they were back in the casino, breaking the news to Dorian and Rita.

Breathless with excitement, Frankie hadn't stopped to think. She didn't want to. Nearly all her life had been spent being rational and sensible. As a child she went to bed early, always did her homework and grew up to be a school prefect. Even as a teenager she'd never rebelled, never dyed her hair with one of those Wash-in-Wash-outs that came free with *Jackie Magazine*, had her ears pierced or hung out at the smokers' corner. Always so careful and considerate, she'd done as everyone expected – passed her A-levels, gone to university, got a good job. OK, so she'd smoked a bit of dope and got hideously drunk a few times, but even now, at twenty-nine, she'd never had a one-night stand, never taken E and still only crossed the road when the little green man was lit up. Until Frankie had jumped on the plane to LA, she'd never made a rash decision, never taken a risk. And what had she got to show for it? A P45, an ex-boyfriend who'd dumped her on her birthday and an empty bank account.

But now all that had changed. She wanted to be impulsive and reckless. She was enjoying being carried away on a wave of champagne cocktails and romance. And why not? It was bloody fantastic. So outrageously romantic, it felt as if it couldn't be true. As if it was a storyline from one of those Hollywood movies, with Julia Roberts in the lead role. Except this time she wasn't sat on the sofa, watching things unfold on a rented video. Wistfully imaging it could really happen, but knowing it was just make-believe. Because it wasn't.

This was real life. *Her life.*

'What about the beige trousersuit?'

'Too boring.'

'My little black dress?'

'Too Friday night.'

Groaning with frustration, Frankie flung both outfits on top of the other rejected clothes already strewn over mono-grammed carpet and delved back into her suitcase. This was bloody impossible. For the last half an hour she'd been with Rita in her hotel suite, trying to choose something to wear, and she was beginning to panic. Time was running out. Deciding what to wear to go to the pub was hard enough, but her own wedding? It didn't help that her suitcase didn't hold anything vaguely wedding dressy. Hardly surprising seeing as when she'd packed last night she'd been thinking more along the lines of shorts and a bikini, not full-length satin meringue and matching veil.

'What about this?' Lounging on the bed, cigarette hang-ing out of the corner of her mouth, Rita held up a crocheted dress and a matching velvet-trimmed cardi. It was the Karen Millen birthday outfit.

Shaking her head, Frankie pulled a face. 'Bad memo-ries,' she muttered, abandoning the now-empty suitcase and rifling through the heap of clothes on the floor as if she was in Hennes on the first day of the sales. It was like looking for a needle in a haystack. She caught her reflection in the mirror. Talking of which, she needed to do something with her hair, which had that post-shag look about it – i.e. a complete mess. How come she never managed the just-got-out-of-bed look? Even when she had just got out of bed.

'Are you sure about the trousersuit?' Feeling desperate, she held up the beige two-piece again. Perhaps Rita would take pity on a bride-to-be in her underwear and reconsider.

She should have known better. Looking aghast, Rita broke off from making vodka and champagne cocktails and waved the bottle menacingly at Frankie. 'For fuck's sake, you can't get married in a bloody suit from Next. It's a wedding, not a job interview.' She topped up her alcohol levels with a glug of her StollyBolly. 'If Reilly sees you in that thing he won't ask you to marry him, he'll ask you to do some bloody photocopying.'

'Well, that's it, I give up,' said Frankie sulkily, sitting down on the bed next to Rita, who, in true best-friend spirit, passed her an extra-strength cocktail and a cigarette. Begrudgingly accepting them both, Frankie smiled ruefully. 'Sorry, I'm being ratty, aren't I?'

'Don't be daft, it's just wedding nerves.' Rita grinned, struggling to get off the bed and swaying dangerously towards the bathroom. 'Every bride gets them.' With all six brothers married, she was a dab hand at soothing tearful brides.

A bride. Frankie repeated the words in her head. It still hadn't sunk in. She'd always imagined being a bride meant standing in WH Smith at lunchtime surreptitiously flicking through all those wedding magazines. Devoting twelve months of her life to choosing flower arrangements and organising hot and cold finger buffets. Fitting in visits to Hatton Garden to buy his'n'her wedding rings and trips to Harvey Nicks to try on all the dresses, knowing full well she could never afford one. But she'd never imagined it would be like this. Getting pissed with her best mate in a Las Vegas hotel suite, wearing a tinfoil ring and, by the looks of it, something that wasn't even ironed.

Watching her bridesmaid stagger into the bathroom, Frankie took a sip of her drink and continued the conversation. After years of going to the loos in pairs she was used to chatting through toilet doors. 'Ever since I was little I've fantasised about what my wedding day would be like.' She sighed, savouring the sensation of the champagne and vodka fizzing on her tongue. 'I remember when I was little and I used to dream about having a Princess Di dress, lots of pearls and satin and a big long train.' She smiled ironically. 'Don't worry, I soon went off that idea. But I've always thought I'd wear a dress. Not one of those satin marquees, but something simple, with a veil.' She lay back and rested her head against the pillows. 'And that I'd have bridesmaids and a three-tiered cake with those little miniature people on the top. And I'd ride in a vintage Rolls-Royce with my dad to the church, and walk up the aisle and everyone would watch me and think how lovely I looked.' She laughed, slightly embarrassed, and took a gulp from her glass. 'And when I got to the top of the aisle, waiting for me in one of those morning suits with a carnation buttonhole would be the man I was going to marry . . .' She faltered as her memory suddenly flashed up a snapshot of herself a couple of months ago, sitting on the pedal bin in the kitchen of her flat in Fulham, holding the receipt for a Tiffany's engagement ring. 'I always thought it would be Hugh.'

She fell silent and, lighting up her cigarette, took a throat-scorching drag. Her head whirled. And it wasn't just the mixture of champagne and nicotine. Being suddenly reminded of Hugh had knocked her off balance and caused a flood of memories to come rushing in. 'Tonight would have been our two-year-anniversary,' she murmured, remembering New Year's Eve a couple of years ago, being drunk under the duvet, spending their first night together. She caught herself. What was she thinking about Hugh for? A few moments ago she'd been delirious with happiness and excitement and now she was overcome with feelings of sadness and regret.

'Do you think I'm mad?'

There came a yell from the bathroom. 'What? For going out with that dickhead for two years or for tying the knot with the sexiest bloke since George Clooney?'

Frankie couldn't help smiling. She could always rely on Rita for a blunt answer. 'So you're not surprised Reilly and I are getting married?'

'Well, it is a bit quick. But the only thing I think's a shame is that you didn't have a hen night. You could have gone in fancy dress to the Cloudsbar. It would have been a right laugh.'

Frankie shuddered at the thought of the most exclusive bar in Los Angeles, full of supermodels and film stars. Where appearance was everything. And then tried to imagine herself in a veil and L-plates. She couldn't. Thank God.

The bathroom door swung open to reveal Rita sat on the loo. 'Look, it doesn't matter what anyone else thinks, it's your life, it's your decision.' For some reason Rita always took on the role of a philosopher when she'd had a few too many, and loved nothing better than spending hours sharing her pearls of wisdom. 'Look at me, coming out to LA to try and be an actress. *Me, a Hollywood actress.*' She smiled excitedly, envisaging herself in the role of Tracy Potter that she was to start filming in a few days. 'Everybody thought I was barmy, but I didn't give a shit. OK, it was a risk. But what had I got to lose if it all went wrong anyway? A temping job? A knackered old Mini with a leaky radiator. That poky rented flat of ours.' She pulled a face. 'But I was lucky. I made the right decision. Look at me now.'

Frankie looked. Pissed as a fart, with her knickers round her ankles, Rita had kohl eyeliner smudged halfway down her face and a roll of loo paper in her hand. Catherine Zeta Jones eat your heart out.

'Life's just one big casino. Everything's a risk. There's no guarantees. But if you want something badly enough you have to go for it. If your happiness depends on it you've got no choice but to take the gamble and follow your heart. Live for the moment. If you don't you'll always wonder what might have been.' Yanking up her G-string, Rita stood up, a little too quickly, and grabbed hold of the marble washbasin for support. 'And anyway, if it goes wrong you can always call 1–800-DIVORCE. It's dead easy, I've seen the adverts. You just listen to the automated message and then press 1 if you've got kids, 2 if you've got a mortgage together, 3 if . . .'

'OK, OK, I get the idea.' Frankie smiled, shaking her head. She'd heard of dial-a-pizza, but dial-a-divorce? Perhaps they even put leaflets through your letter box with 'get a divorce and get a second one half-price' special offers. Dismissing the thought, she hauled herself off the bed and opened a small bottle of Evian from the minibar. She drank it down in one go, diluting the evening's intake of alcohol. Maybe getting drunk wasn't such a good idea. All the champagne was making her feel confused, maudlin, over-emotional, nostalgic. Hugh was part of her past. It was Reilly she was getting married to. Reilly who was her future.

'I think you should wear these.'

Frankie turned round to see Rita, who'd emerged from the bathroom and was holding up an item of clothing.

'Are you joking? *Leather trousers!*' exclaimed Frankie. 'To my own wedding . . . Isn't that a bit unconventional?'

Rita gave her one of her 'I know best' looks. 'You're getting married in the Elvis Chapel, your engagement ring's made out of a champagne top, we'll be singing "Suspicious Minds" instead of "All Things Bright and Beautiful" and the vicar's going to be wearing a white rhinestone jumpsuit.' She waggled the trousers. 'Need I say more?'

Unable to keep a straight face at the prospect, Frankie started laughing, and, grabbing them from Rita, disappeared into the bathroom to get ready.

38

'It's here; it's here.' Jumping up and down outside Caesar's Palace in a hastily assembled bridesmaid's outfit of crushed-velvet hipsters and a Lycra halter-neck, Rita waved frantically at the white stretch limo that had been hired to drive them to the chapel.

Reilly and Dorian had gone ahead five minutes earlier thanks to Rita, who, taking her role as bridesmaid very seriously, had told them in no uncertain terms that it was bad luck to see the bride before the wedding, and that no, they couldn't all share a minicab.

Standing next to her, Frankie felt a rush of exhilaration and excitement as she watched the white ribbon fluttering on the bonnet of the limousine as it swept into the forecourt. So this was it. It was happening. *She was getting married.* Her stomach began jigging up and down in time with Rita, and she felt a lump come into her throat. Even anaesthetised with champagne she still felt nervous.

'Are you sure I look OK?' Anxiously she turned to Rita. She was having serious doubts about the leather trousers. They'd gone down a treat at the Beverly Hills party, but her own wedding? She'd probably end up looking like one of those people who want to be 'wacky and alternative' and dress up like the cast from *Grease* and get married on a big dipper. 'Maybe you were right. Maybe I should have worn the Karen Millen.'

'Stop worrying, you look fucking gorgeous,' reassured Rita, giving her lippy a quick touch-up. 'Reilly's a lucky fella.'

She clicked her compact shut and shoved it back in her hand-bag. 'Most brides look like bloody lampshades. At least you'll look sexy in all the wedding photies.'

Frankie suddenly clutched Rita's arm. 'Oh, shit.'

'What?'

'The camera. Have you got it?'

Rita looked blank.

'Don't you remember? Reilly asked you to bring his camera to the chapel,' jabbered Frankie, beginning to panic as she realised that Rita was so pissed she'd be lucky to remember her own name, let alone the camera equipment. 'We're not going to have any pictures.' She felt suddenly tearful.

'Oh, c'mon, Frankie, there's no need to get your knickers in a twist,' soothed Rita. 'It's probably still in the room. I'll go back and get it.'

For a moment Frankie was relieved by Rita's offer. Until she saw her stumble drunkenly in her stilettos and had second thoughts. 'No, you stay here. I'll be back in five minutes,' she instructed, shoving her bouquet into Rita's hands.

Cobbled together from the fresh flower arrangement in the hotel room, Rita had been chuffed to bits that her night-school course in floristry had finally come in useful.

'Don't worry, it's traditional for the bride to be late,' she yelled reassuringly as Frankie ran back inside the hotel. Watching her disappear into the foyer, she was left to be greeted by the rather tasty-looking chauffeur, who, thinking she was the bride, offered his congratulations and opened the door. She tried to look demure and suitably bridal as she clambered on to the back seat. All this wedding malarky was rather enjoyable, she thought, nestling into the leather uphol-stery and helping herself to the complimentary minibar.

Caesar's Palace was jam-packed with gamblers and New Year's Eve revellers, and with less than twenty minutes to go until midnight, spirits were high and the casino buzzed with anticipation and celebration. Trying to make her way towards the lifts, Frankie pushed through the hordes of boisterous tourists, scantily clad waitresses and die-hard gamblers, before finally reaching the lobby. The lift doors opened and she squeezed in between partygoers laughing hysterically and blowing party trumpets, and pushed the button for the twelfth floor. And then waited.

Squashed next to a couple trying to break the record for French-kissing and a dull-looking, big-boned girl in a flowery dress who'd draped herself in silly string in a vain attempt to make herself look as if she was a party animal, Frankie watched the Roman numerals, denoting floors, light up with agonising slowness. 'Come on, come on,' she hissed, as the lift stopped at every floor, emptying out people trailing streamers as they rushed to various parties being held in different hotel rooms, and filling up again with yet more partygoers – everybody going somewhere in time for the countdown. Until finally it reached the twelfth floor and the doors sprang open, releasing Frankie from its claustrophobic confines.

Hurrying down the corridor, she looked at her watch. Shit, less than ten minutes to go. She scanned the numbers on the doors, looking for her room. Before it had been so easy to find, but now, feeling pissed and panicky, it was a lot more difficult. Eventually she spotted it – 1204 – and began fumbling drunkenly in her handbag for the credit-card key. As she did, she was hit by the thought of how comical this moment would seem in the months and years ahead, when she was an old married woman. Smiling to herself, she found her key and began humming the Wedding March as she tried to find the slot in the lock.

'Frankie?'

A voice. It startled her. The key slid out of her fingers, landing silently on the carpet. Turning, she saw a figure across the hallway, almost hidden in the shadows. And stopped humming as the notes froze inside her body. *It couldn't be.* She peered harder, trying to focus. *It wasn't.* The figure stepped forward into the light . . . *It was.*

Hugh.

Her stomach flipped as her knees buckled beneath her. She steadied herself against the door handle. For a split second she had the stomach-churning sensation of being catapulted backwards through time, across the Atlantic, back to Fulham, to October, to Hugh. Taking a few deep breaths, she tried to get her head straight, but it was impossible. *Hugh? In Las Vegas?* She felt as if she was having some kind of weird champagne-induced hallucination. Surely it couldn't be happening. Could it?

But it was. Unable to move, she stared at him, transfixed. He looked exactly the same. Wearing exactly the same clothes as he always did – a pale blue Ralph Lauren shirt, jeans that he always ironed a crease down the front of, his JP Tod brogues. Smart and clean-shaven, he'd gelled his blond hair into that quiff, just like he always used to, and had that instantly recognisable smell of deodorant, mouthwash and Hugo Boss aftershave. It seemed so familiar. And at the same time so unfamiliar.

For a few minutes all she could do was stand there, staring, reeling, her heart fluttering like a deck of cards. She tried to speak but her voice seemed to have disappeared into the back of her throat. As if all her senses had shut down with the shock of seeing Hugh, in front of her, only a few feet away. She suddenly felt horribly sober.

Hugh stared at Frankie. Thank God he'd finally found her. He thought he was never going to in this bloody awful town, full of tacky Americans and even tackier hotels. It had taken hours and, what with his jet lag, he didn't think he was ever going to track her down before midnight. But finally, twenty minutes ago, he'd struck lucky. The receptionist at Caesar's Palace had said she'd checked into one of the penthouse suites – God knows how she'd been able to afford that – and putting the phone down he'd raced straight over from his motel. He had his speech planned, he'd even rehearsed it a few times in front of the mirror, but now bumping into her like this had thrown him. To be honest, he was as shocked as she was. She looked so different. Almost unrecognisable. Since when did she buy leather trousers? And that little top, there was practically nothing to it. No doubt it was the idea of that daft friend of hers, Rita. He stared at her, leaning against the door of her suite, not saying anything. And suddenly a thought struck him. Was she drunk?

'What are you doing here?' Frankie eventually managed to whisper.

'Looking for you.' He walked towards her and then, thinking better of it, stopped a couple of feet away. 'I flew to LA, but when I finally found your apartment your neighbours said you'd come to Las Vegas. I managed to hire a car and drive out here and I've been in every hotel in this town, all day, trying to find you.' He paused and ran his fingers through his hair, like he always used to. 'I needed to see you, to tell you that I made a stupid mistake. I was such an idiot, Frankie. A stupid bloody idiot.'

Frankie couldn't believe what she was hearing, what she was seeing. Dumbstruck she watched him, fiddling self-consciously with cufflinks. He always was so uncomfortable when he talked about his feelings, what he always used to call PDA – Public Display of Affection.

Standing up straight, he threw his shoulders back, as if he was bracing himself. 'Being on my own these last few months . . .' he swallowed a few times as he remembered the one-night stands '. . . has made me realise that I don't want to be without you.' He took a deep breath. 'I've missed you, Frankie. I want you to give me a second chance.'

His speech was drowned out by the sound of the band starting up from downstairs and the sound of the countdown beginning: *Ten, Nine, Eight, Seven* . . .

They both stared at each other. Neither of them speaking. And then suddenly, right in front of her, he bent down and, balancing awkwardly on one knee, cleared his throat. 'What I'm trying to say is this . . .' Pulling a small velvet box from out of his breast pocket, he tried to open it.

Six, Five, Four . . .

He fumbled with the catch for a few seconds, his fingers hot and sweaty . . .

Three . . .

Finally it sprang open.

Two . . .

It was a Tiffany's diamond ring.

One . . .

A huge cheer went up. The deafening roar of the whole of Las Vegas celebrating the New Year swept around the building, the sound of fireworks exploding in the sky above, balloons bursting, people screaming. The sound of the band downstairs starting up with 'Auld Lang Syne'.

But amidst the noise, all Frankie heard was Hugh's voice.

'Will you marry me?'

39

The scenery sped past the car window, barren scrubland, a ramshackle general store, a gas station. Frankie buzzed down the electric window. Her head throbbed with the mother of all hangovers. Closing her eyes, she lay back against the headrest and breathed in deep lungfuls of hot dusty air. So this was it, 1 January. The new year. There hadn't been an apocalypse, the world hadn't ended in a ball of fire. It was still here, still exactly the same. Except of course it wasn't. Things would never be the same again.

Last night Hugh had walked back into her life and everything had turned upside down. In just a few seconds – the time it had taken for him to propose – everything had changed, everything had been thrown into confusion and doubt. Her emotions, beliefs, desires – *her future*. Hugh was asking her to marry him. He was asking her to make the biggest decision of her life. But what he didn't know was that he was asking her to choose. To decide between a lover of just one week and an ex-boyfriend of two years. Between taking a gamble on a new life and playing it safe by going back to her old one.

Frankie hadn't known what to think. Looking at Hugh in the dimly lit corridor, balancing awkwardly on one knee, she'd felt a mixture of joy and horror. Out of the blue Hugh wanted her back, wanted to marry her, wanted them to spend the rest of their lives together and live happily ever after. Wasn't that everything she'd ever dreamed of? A Tiffany ring, a white wedding and Hugh, all dressed up in a top hat and tails with a carnation in his button hole. *To be Mr and Mrs Hugh Hamilton.* Isn't that what she'd longed for? All those nights when she'd lain awake next to Rita, her pillow soggy with tears, feeling as if her heart was breaking.

But what about Reilly? He'd be waiting for her at the chapel. Laughing and joking with Dorian, blissfully unaware of what was happening. Expecting her to arrive at any moment. Her heart had lurched. She'd felt sick. Normally she didn't believe in such things, but maybe this was fate. Maybe Hugh's appearance was a sign. A sign that marrying Reilly would be a mistake. That Rita had been right all along and she and Reilly were just a fling. She'd been on the rebound and high on hormones and too many margaritas, she'd got carried away by the euphoria of New Year's Eve and the millennium and confused lust with love.

Feeling shaky, she'd clung on to the door for support. Maybe this was for the best. Maybe Reilly was having second thoughts and would be grateful if she called it off. Maybe he'd changed his mind and wasn't even at the chapel. The idea had saddened but consoled her, even though it jarred with the memory of Reilly lying next to her in bed, telling her that he loved her, asking her to marry him. She'd tried to blot out the image. He hadn't meant what he'd said. It had just been the booze talking. By leaving now she'd be doing him a favour. At least this way tomorrow he'd only wake up with a hangover. Waking up with a wife he didn't want would have been a lot more of a headache.

She'd tried focusing on Hugh. His sudden appearance had sobered her up and brought her to her senses. He made the last few months feel like a dream. Being in LA, living with Rita, falling for Reilly. None of it had been real life, none of it could have lasted for ever – but hadn't she known that all along? Hadn't she run away to LA until she was able to face things again, get her life back on track, go back to London?

And now she could.

Within the last few seconds her wish had been granted. Hugh had come back. Was she going to risk losing him a second time?

With the sounds of partygoers echoing from every room and a jumble of thoughts whirling around in her head, Frankie had known the answer to the question. Looking at the man with whom she'd shared memories, a home, holidays abroad, family gatherings, *a history*, she'd known she couldn't take a gamble. This might be Vegas but the stakes were too high. And so in those few brief seconds she'd made her choice. She'd said yes.

Frankie broke away from her thoughts as she saw a sign for the Grand Canyon up ahead. They were going to stay there for a few days. 'Regroup', as Hugh called it, before driving back to LA so that she could pack up her things and catch the next plane back to Heathrow. Back to his flat in Fulham and their old life together. She glanced across at Hugh, wearing his driving glasses and furrowing his brow in concentration as he tried to get to grips with the etiquette of freeway driving. It still felt weird, being back together. A couple again. She had to keep checking it was really him sitting next to her, and not her alcohol-addled brain playing tricks.

'Shouldn't we have turned off there?' An exit sign flashed past.

'Shit.' He braked, causing the truck behind him to screech its tyres and honk loudly. 'Christ, what's wrong with the bloody Yanks? Can't they drive or something?' Without indicating, he swerved across two lanes, nearly causing a pile-up as the rented car ploughed off the freeway at a 90-degree angle.

Frankie gripped her seat belt. She was used to relaxing

with her feet up on the dash of Reilly's Bronco, chatting as he drove and laughing at Howard Stern on the radio. She'd forgotten Hugh's short temper behind the wheel and how tense she used to get when they drove to visit his parents in Kent. Once his road rage had nearly got him punched by a London cabbie.

'Sorry, darling, it's the ridiculous signs they have here.' He smiled sheepishly, reaching across and clasping her hand. 'Are you OK?'

'Yeah, fine.' Frankie nodded, taking a deep breath and closing her eyes.

They'd spent the rest of last night in a haze – leaving Vegas in the early hours, driving through the dawn, drinking weak coffee in Seven-11s, snatching a few hours' kip in the car – and now, in the glare of the midday sun, they were both feeling knackered. And they still had another hundred miles to go. With any luck they'd get there before dark. And still in one piece.

After spending a further four hours getting lost, doing U-turns, asking in gas stations, drugstores and yet more Seven-11s, they eventually began driving up the winding path that led to the rim of the Grand Canyon. By the time they arrived at the Southside Lodge, it was almost four o'clock and getting dark. While Hugh checked in, Frankie made a couple of phone calls from the coin-box in the lobby.

Last night she'd packed her things and left a note at reception. She couldn't go and find Rita, pissed as a fart in the back of the stretch limo that was wrapped up in a white satin ribbon. How would she have explained that to Hugh? What would she have said? 'Sorry, could you wait for a few minutes while I just have a quick word with my bridesmaid?' That would have meant confessing to him that she was about to marry another man. She flinched at the thought. Sometimes honesty was not the best policy.

Dialling the number, she listened to the ringing tone, waiting for Rita to pick up. Except she didn't, it was the answering machine. 'Happy Fucking New Year. We've gone to win millions in Vegas. Leave us a message,' Rita's voice singsonged.

The beep sounded and Frankie left a brief message, saying she was safe and well with Hugh, but that she'd explain everything when she came back to LA. She knew Rita would understand. Best friends always did when it came to men.

Replacing the receiver, she stared out of the window, watching the last streak of sunset disappear into dusk. For a moment she thought about calling Reilly and then changed her mind. What the hell would she say? Sorry? Elton John was right when he said it was the hardest word. She caught herself. Christ, she must be knackered. She was quoting Elton John.

'A bottle of the Chardonnay. And could you make sure it's chilled?' Closing the wine list, Hugh waved it at the waiter. He looked at Frankie and smiled. 'Oh, sorry, darling, would you have preferred champagne? To celebrate?'

'Oh, God, no. Wine's fine . . . honestly,' Frankie reassured him hastily. After last night she never wanted to drink champagne again. Her stomach still hadn't recovered from having its lining dissolved by half a dozen bottles of the stuff.

They were having dinner at the Lodge's rather upmarket restaurant, a snug dining room with an open fire and wood-panelled walls. It was one of those restaurants where the waiters hovered at your elbow and everyone – even Americans – talked in hushed voices. Frankie sat opposite Hugh, who seemed miles away across a large linen tablecloth with lots of different-sized spotlessly clean glasses and a whole trayful of cutlery.

Leaning across the table, Hugh reached out and held her hand. 'You look beautiful tonight.' At his suggestion she was wearing one of his favourite outfits, the beige trousersuit, and had clipped up her hair. 'Just like the old you again.'

Frankie smiled at the compliment. Being together at the restaurant, it was as if the last few months had never happened. Hugh hadn't changed at all. He still looked as handsome as ever. And her memory hadn't exaggerated how long he took to get ready – he still took ages. Tonight she'd waited for half an hour, listening to the squirts of various aerosols, until eventually he'd emerged from the bathroom in a cloud of steam, as if he was an *X Factor* contestant appearing from the swirling fog of dry ice.

'What do you think about Valentine's Day?'

'What?' She broke away from her thoughts, dropping the bread roll she'd been absent-mindedly demolishing into a pile of crumbs.

Hugh paused as the waiter reappeared with the wine. Watching him put his arm behind his back and pour a little in Hugh's glass, Frankie couldn't help feeling rankled. Why did waiters always do that? Why was it always the man who tasted the wine? Hugh sniffed it before taking a sip and made a point of rolling it around on his tongue for a while – well, he was a member of the *Sunday Times* Wine Club. Except he didn't spit, he swallowed and nodded his approval.

'For the wedding.' Having answered Frankie's question, Hugh laughed at her surprised expression. 'I know what you're thinking, it's cheesy – I thought so too at first. But thinking about it, it's actually rather kitsch. Love hearts and all that. It could be rather fun.' He fiddled with one of his silver cufflinks shaped like golf clubs. 'OK, I confess. Adam and Jessica suggested it.'

'*Adam and Jessica?*'

'Well, I told them I was coming here to propose. They gave me a lift to the airport. Did I tell you Adam's bought himself one of those new Jags?'

Frankie wasn't listening. It had suddenly dawned on her that Hugh had never doubted she'd accept his proposal. Always knew that she'd forgive him and take him back. Even before he'd apologised or said he'd made a mistake, he'd known she'd say yes. And he was right, wasn't he? She had forgiven him, she had said yes.

So why did it bother her? She didn't know. But what bothered her even more was the thought that her wedding was being planned by some dickhead in a Hawaiian shirt and his stick-thin girlfriend who thought cool was celebrating a birthday in a bloody bowling alley.

She bit her lip. All those times she'd missed Hugh and her life back in London, she'd forgotten about people like Adam and Jessica. It was strange how selective the memory could be, remembering the good bits but conveniently editing out all the others.

'Well, what do you think?'

'Yeah, it's a good idea.' She nodded, trying to look enthusiastic. After all, it didn't matter about Adam and Jessica. What mattered was that Hugh was finally talking about their relationship. After two years, he wasn't discussing interest rates, the housing market or how Tiger Woods was doing in the American Open. He was talking about weddings. Their wedding.

'And afterwards I think Adam can swing it for us to have the reception at Soho House.'

'*Sounds great.*' Sounds bloody awful, she cringed, trying to smile and at the same time not think about all the pretentious wankers who were members – such as Adam.

★ ★ ★

Eventually the food arrived. Salmon en croûte for Hugh, pasta for Frankie. Not that she ate much, she wasn't hungry. Instead she picked at her food and drank more than a little too much wine as they chatted their way through the courses. Both of them had decided not to speak about the last few months. Hugh had said it was probably best they kept that to themselves. A clean start. Why talk about the past when they had their whole future to talk about? She'd agreed. Talking about the past would have meant talking about Reilly.

Instead they continued their conversation about their forthcoming nuptials, or rather Hugh talked and Frankie listened. To his views on wedding guests: 'I can't stand my boss, Graeme, or Sandra, his wife, but I don't want to jeopardise my chances of promotion. What do you think about just inviting them to the evening do?' The church: 'Do you really want a church wedding? I was actually thinking Chelsea Register Office.' The honeymoon: 'I know you like lying on the beach, darling, but I rather fancied Nepal.'

How ironic, thought Frankie. For so long she'd wanted to talk about weddings but now, after just one evening, she realised how dull planning a wedding actually was. As Hugh moved on to the subject of his stag party – Adam had suggested he and a few chaps spent a weekend away paintballing – she gazed distractedly at her engagement ring, shiny and sparkling, sitting upright on her finger like the new kid in class. A solitaire diamond thrust upwards in 22-carat gold clasps. Touching it, she was suddenly reminded of the ring Reilly had made for her, a twisted piece of gold tinfoil from the champagne bottle. She didn't know where it was, probably lost in the rush to leave Las Vegas. Remembering it gave her a twinge of sadness. She was being silly. Hugh's engagement ring was beautiful, why was she thinking about Reilly's?

*   *   *

Finishing off their coffees and those orange circles of chocolate that came with them, they made their way back to the room. After a couple of glasses of wine she was dying for a cigarette but remembering how much Hugh hated her smoking, she waited until he went into the bathroom. No doubt he'd be in there for ages brushing, flossing, mouthwashing – plenty of time to have a quick fag.

Wrapping her old fleece around her shoulders, she slid open the doors leading on to the small decked terrace and, sitting on one of the wrought-iron patio chairs, lit up one of Rita's American Spirits. She took a drag, watching the embers glow orange against the chilly darkness, and feeling the cold metal of the chair seep through her trousers. It was so quiet and still out here. No faint roar of traffic, noise from the television, hum of people talking. The lodge was perched right on the edge of the canyon. When it was light there was a wonderful view from here, according to the hotel's colour brochure, but tonight all she could see was velvety blackness dotted with the faint glow of lights from neighbouring inns.

After a few minutes she began to notice the cold. Shivering, she wriggled her arms into the sleeves of her fleece, sticking up the collar and pulling it tighter. As she did she saw something fall out of one of the pockets. A flash of something, before it disappeared between the cracks in the wooden decking. For a moment she ignored it, finishing off her cigarette, until her curiosity overcame her and she bent down, running her fingers along the edge of the planks until she felt something. Small and fragile. She picked it up. It was Reilly's ring. All bent out of shape from being squashed in a pocket. She must have put it there last night when she was packing in a rush and forgotten all about it. Resting it in the palm of her hand, she stared at it. Seeing it again conjured up so many memories. So many mixed emotions.

'What are you doing out there?' Hugh appeared.

'Oh, nothing,' she answered breezily, her fingers snapping shut around the ring like a Venus Flycatcher. 'Just getting some fresh air.'

Hugh smiled affectionately and, putting his arms around her, leaned towards her to kiss her. Not a passionate tongues'n'saliva snog, but a firm kiss on the lips. It was their first kiss since he'd proposed and Frankie was surprised to realise how awkward she felt. Where were the fireworks? The racing pulse? The breathlessness? She dismissed the thought. She was a stupid romantic. Fireworks were for the movies.

'Have you been smoking?' Hugh wrinkled up his nose.

'No,' said Frankie guiltily. She felt like a kid caught nicking sweets.

'Mmmm.' Sounding disbelieving, he hugged her closer. 'Are you coming to bed?'

This was Hugh's way of saying he wanted to make love. Ten years as a boarder at an all-boys public school hadn't made it easy for him to talk about sex, and instead he'd say things such as 'Are you tired?' or 'Shall we have an early night?'

She hesitated. This was the moment they were supposed to melt into each other's arms, tumble into bed and shag each other's brains out. The moment she'd dreamed about for months, imagining what she'd say, how she'd react. But in all that time she'd never imagined she'd feel like this. Nervous, awkward, unsure, *guilty*. It hit her without warning. The real-isation that sleeping with Hugh would make her feel she was being unfaithful to Reilly. It was the weirdest notion. What was she thinking about? This was crazy. She was being ridic-ulous. She was marrying Hugh. She loved Hugh. Didn't she?

Smiling, she squeezed his hand affectionately. 'In a minute.'

Watching Hugh disappear inside the room, she leaned against the iron railings, trying to clear her head. Everything that had happened over the last forty-eight hours was making her totally confused. She'd probably feel a whole lot better after she'd had a proper night's sleep. Give herself time to let things sink in. Unclasping her hand, she took another brief look at the ring, before stuffing it firmly back into her pocket. She wished she had lost it. The bloody thing was nothing but trouble.

The bedside lamps cast a dim light across the room, throwing shadows over a vase that was now full of flowers Hugh had bought for her in one of the gas stations. She glanced at Hugh. He was already in bed, his body turned away from her. She noticed his clothes folded neatly on a chair, not strewn all over the floor like Reilly's would have been.

'Hugh.' He didn't answer. Unzipping her fleece, she dropped it on to the floor. Well, there had to be some mess for the cleaners. 'Hugh?' She stretched out her hand to touch his shoulder and then she heard his breathing. Deep and heavy. He was asleep. A mixture of jet lag and two bottles of Chilean Chardonnay. She smiled to herself and then stopped. Why did she feel so relieved?

40

'Bloody hell, it's the runaway bride.' As Frankie tentatively opened the door of the apartment, she was greeted by Rita, who appeared from the bedroom, hastily tying her satin dressing gown around her waist.

Dropping her suitcase on to the floor, Frankie smiled guiltily. 'I can explain everything.'

'Fine,' breezed Rita. Padding into the kitchen she calmly clicked on the kettle, before leaning against the fridge, arms folded, and fixing Frankie with an accusing stare. 'But this better be good.'

They sat outside on the balcony, mopping up the warmth from the weak January sun, and over three cups of Tetley's tea and half a pack of cigarettes Frankie told Rita everything – about Hugh's sudden appearance on New Year's Eve, his proposal and her reaction, and how, in those few seconds, she'd been forced to choose. It was a relief to talk to someone finally, to unburden the weight of all the thoughts and emotions that had been whirling around in her head over the last forty-eight hours. And as best friend and confidante, Rita listened patiently, stewing tea bags, finding matches, nodding sympathetically.

'But I know I made the right decision to marry Hugh,' Frankie murmured, stroking Fred, who was sprawled across her lap like a sheepskin rug. 'You know how devastated I was when we broke up, don't you?' She glanced across at Rita. 'I never thought we'd get back together. I thought our relationship was over for good. That's why, when I met Reilly ...' Her voice trailed off as she played with Fred's velvety ears. 'Well, anyway, I'm really happy.'

Rita wasn't entirely convinced. For someone who was supposed to be happy and in love, Frankie looked completely miserable. But for once she was going to keep her opinions to herself. She'd never liked Hugh, but now wasn't the time to start slagging him off. Frankie needed her to do the supportive friend bit. And that meant keeping her gob well and truly shut.

Forcing a smile, she shoved her thoughts to one side and squeezed Frankie's hand reassuringly. 'What time's your flight?' She made an attempt at chirpiness.

'Five-thirty tonight.'

'And what about these two?' Rita shifted Ginger, who was taking up most of the sun-lounger, to one side.

'That's the hardest bit,' sighed Frankie, rubbing her finger underneath Fred's chin, initiating a rasping purr as he stretched out his chin indulgently. 'They're both getting on, Fred's got arthritis in his paws and Ginger's prone to chest infections. I hate to think of them both having to spend six months in quarantine ... being stuck in a cage ...' Her voice tailed off. She didn't want to admit that Hugh had actually suggested putting them to sleep, saying it was 'for the best and nothing whatsoever to do with his allergies'.

'Of course they can stay here with me.' Rita pre-empted Frankie's question. 'I think the LA lifestyle suits them a lot more than being stuck in that cramped flat in Fulham anyway.' She looked at them both, stretched out and purring in the sun. 'This can be their retirement home,' she said, laughing and running a chipped fingernail across Ginger's paws. 'Which isn't bad, considering my gran ended up in a prefab bungalow in Scarborough.'

Frankie knew she was right, but she couldn't help feeling gutted. Leaving Fred and Ginger behind would be a wrench. 'Thanks . . .' She smiled gratefully. 'For everything.' Brushing her T-shirt free of tortoiseshell hairs, she looked at her watch. 'Shit, is that the time already? I better get a move on and start packing my stuff.' Standing up, she went back inside the apartment.

'Hang on a minute.'

Rita sprang up from her sun-lounger, but it was too late. Frankie had already pushed open the bedroom door, and got the shock of her life. So had Dorian, who'd been left gagged and handcuffed to the futon wearing nothing but Rita's Victoria's Secret underwear for over half an hour. Not knowing whether to laugh or scream, Frankie clamped her hand over her mouth as, only seconds later, Rita appeared and made up a threesome. Blushing the colour of her roots, she took one look at Frankie's expression and gasped, 'I can explain everything.'

It didn't take long to pack. It was strange how in just a few months most of her clothes had begun to look old and frumpy. Christ, did I really wear this? she thought, digging out a hideous A-line skirt with side pleats. It might have been in last year's *Vogue*, but it was going to be in this year's charity shop. Chucking it into a binliner, she consoled herself with the thought that cleaning out her wardrobe would give her a good excuse to go shopping when she got back to London – although she didn't know what with. Her credit cards had long since been maxed-up to the limit and she still owed Rita a thousand dollars.

Trying not to think about the appalling state of her finances, she emptied two drawers of toiletries and stuffed the rest of her clothes and her books into two suitcases. She'd pay Rita back just as soon as she got a job. She looked at her luggage. It bulged uncomfortably and she had to sit on the suitcases to make them close, stretching the tattered beige vinyl until she could fasten the zips. She felt a lump in her throat. Now it was coming to the crunch, it was hard to go. Looking around the bedroom and out into the rest of the apartment, she realised how attached she had become. How, without even realising it, she'd come to think of the place as home.

'Well, that's about it.' Trying to sound all bright and breezy, she dragged her luggage into the hallway. Why was it that clothes became three times as heavy as soon as you packed them? Shoving them in the corner, she caught her breath.

'You're not going already, are you? I've just made you some liquorice tea.' After being rumbled in the bedroom, Dorian, dressed rather aptly in a 'Never Mind the Bollocks' T-shirt, was in the kitchen, fussing over refreshments in an attempt to hide his embarrassment. Proud of his reputation of being good in bed, and of his flirting and sexual innuendo, being caught by a flatmate in a push-up bra and lace suspenders was a blow to his manhood. Of which Frankie had got a good eyeful.

'What have I told you about making that stuff in here? It stinks the bloody place out,' grumbled Rita, swiping him good-naturedly with a teatowel.

Frankie smiled. Rita had told her it was just sex – she'd been gagging for it and Dorian was better than a vibrator – but watching them together, laughing and joking around, she could tell there was a lot more between them than simultaneous orgasms. They were like an old married couple.

'I better go. Hugh's been waiting for me outside in the car all this time. We're going to drive straight to the airport.' She glanced at Rita. 'He said it was probably best if he didn't come in.'

'Fucking hell, woman, ask him in. I'd like to meet your husband-to be.' Dorian grinned, trying to show there were no hard feelings about what had happened in Vegas. Until he caught Rita's expression and changed his mind. 'Though maybe you're right. The traffic can be a bitch on the 405.' Grabbing Frankie by the waist, he squeezed her tightly and gave her a lingering kiss. 'Goodbye, gorgeous. Remember to look after yourself.' He suddenly felt rather emotional.

Frankie smiled weakly. She was going to miss Dorian. There was no one quite like him in Fulham.

'Well, I suppose this is it.' Standing on the driveway in her dressing gown, Rita bit her lip. She was trying to put a brave face on things, but she'd never been one for saying goodbyes. Any minute now she was going to start bawling her eyes out.

Frankie nodded and forced a smile. There was just one more thing. She hadn't spoken about Reilly. She'd been too frightened of what Rita might say. But now she knew she couldn't leave without asking.

Except she didn't have to. Rita read her mind. 'I told him you were coming over today to get your things. That you were leaving this afternoon.' She glanced up at Frankie, almost afraid to meet her eye. 'He didn't want to see you.' She gave a small apologetic smile. 'But he wanted me to give you this. He said to wait until you'd packed everything. I think he wanted it to be your last reminder of LA.' She pulled a photograph out of her pocket and handed it to Frankie. It was a black and white picture he'd taken of her on Malibu beach. A wave had soaked her jeans and she was running out of the surf, laughing. Normally she hated having her picture taken, she always felt so stiff and awkward, but that day Reilly had made her feel at ease in front of the camera, relaxed and natural. Remembering, Frankie gazed at the image. She'd never seen herself look so happy.

'I was wrong,' Rita broke her thoughts.

'What?' She glanced up from the photograph.

'It wasn't just a fling . . . not for him anyway.'

They both looked at each other, neither of them speaking.

'Frankie, can you hurry it up? We're going to be late,' Hugh bellowed from the car, honking on his horn.

'Yeah . . . coming.'

Trying to swallow the huge lump in her throat, Frankie hugged Rita, who'd put on her sunglasses ready to hide her tears, and with a small wave walked towards Hugh, who was now waiting to load her luggage into the boot. She didn't look back.

41

'Qantas, Virgin, Delta, Air Malaysia . . .' Hugh recited the list as he scoured the check-in desks for the familiar red, white and blue motif of British Airways. At LAX it was business as usual and the airport bustled with people milling around with luggage and badly wrapped souvenirs, relatives and friends saying their farewells, uniformed security guards with their walkie-talkies and the Vietnam War veterans rattling buckets of coins for charity. Following Hugh, who'd commandeered a trolley, Frankie walked through the terminal, air-conditioned cool after the humidity outside, weaving in and out of queues of passengers, clutching passports and tickets, waiting to check in.

'Aaah, here it is,' announced Hugh brightly, and then groaned. 'Bloody typical. It's always got to be the longest one.' A line of people and their belongings zigzagged backwards and forwards between white barrier tapes. Begrudgingly he joined the back of the queue. 'Are you OK, darling? You've been very quiet.'

'Yeah, fine.' Frankie half-heartedly forced a smile. But she wasn't fine. All the way on the drive to the airport she hadn't been able to stop thinking about Rita's last words. '*It wasn't just a fling . . . not for him anyway.*' They threw her judgement into doubt. For so long she'd been trying to convince herself that Reilly had been just a holiday romance – and she nearly had – but now she felt as if she'd been hiding from the truth.

That first night she'd spent with Reilly, after the party, he'd said something to her that she'd never forgotten. That she'd know when she was over someone when she didn't think about them before she fell asleep at night or when she woke up in the morning. Their face wouldn't be the one she saw when she closed her eyes. And last night when she'd lain in bed next to Hugh, trying to fall asleep to the steady rhythm of his breathing, it hadn't been Hugh her mind had wandered to in that drowsy state between awake and sleeping, and it hadn't been his face she'd seen when she turned out the light. It had been Reilly's.

The queue moved forward. In front of them was a couple in their late twenties. He had his arm around her, she was leaning her head on his shoulder. They seemed so comfortable together. Frankie couldn't help watching as they kissed tenderly. And at the way he looked at her. It was exactly how Reilly used to look at her. Trying to ignore the tug of sadness she felt, she turned away and glanced across at Hugh.

Busy filling in baggage tags, he was paying no attention to her. He was always like this at airports, always intent on taking control. She watched as he painstakingly attached them with their elastic fasteners to her suitcases, which were fraying at the edges from years of going on package holidays. A stark contrast to his expensive matching set of ergonomically shaped luggage on wheels from Samsonite.

'Next please.' The British Airways attendant behind the desk waved them forward.

'Blimey, that's us,' hissed Hugh, dropping his biro as he rushed to manoeuvre their trolley forwards. Always competitive, he raced towards the desk as if he was crossing the finishing line.

Frankie wasn't in such a hurry. In fact she felt rooted to the spot.

'How many pieces of luggage?'

'Six, I'm afraid. My fiancée doesn't like to travel light.' Hugh gave a false laugh in an attempt to charm the stewardess into letting them off a charge for excess baggage, and maybe even upgrading them into business. 'Do you, darling?' He put his arm round her waist, but it felt awkward and stiff. A Public Display of Affection for the benefit of the uniform behind the counter.

Frankie didn't answer. She couldn't say anything, but inside she was being deafened by a voice yelling, 'Stop, I've made a mistake.' Because she had. She'd made one hell of a mistake. Hugh might not have changed but she had. She was a different person from the girl who'd propped up the bar at Heathrow, knocking back vodkas in an attempt to block out the pain, and who'd arrived in LA nursing a hangover and a broken heart.

And by finally admitting it to herself, she knew there was no way she could go back to her life with Hugh. Their relationship was past its sell-by date. Hugh had asked her to marry him, but never once had he told her he loved her. And she hadn't told him. Because she wasn't in love with Hugh any more. Her heart started beating like a jackhammer as she finally admitted it. *She was in love with Reilly.*

'Would you prefer a window seat or an aisle?'

'Neither.'

'What?' The stewardess and Hugh spoke in unison.

'I'm not going with you.' Her pulse was racing so fast she could hardly get the words out. But as she did she felt a huge wave of release. There was no doubt in her mind that she was doing the right thing. In fact, for the first time in weeks she felt sure. She loved Reilly. OK, so she'd probably blown it for ever, but maybe, just maybe, there was a chance, and if she didn't try she'd never know. Rita was right. She had to follow her heart. It wasn't a gamble. She'd got nothing to lose.

She looked at Hugh. For the first time ever he seemed flustered.

'Have you forgotten something? If you've left something behind we can always ship it over,' he jabbered, his voice rising higher. He pulled at his collar, which was beginning to feel tight and uncomfortable.

Frankie shook her head. 'I haven't forgotten anything.' She was unshakeable. Now she'd started she couldn't stop. 'It's not the same between us any more, Hugh. When you finished the relationship I was devastated, I never thought I was going to get over it. You broke my heart, you know . . .' She looked at him for a moment. Suddenly she felt rather sorry for him. 'I suppose a lot of it's my fault. I shouldn't have said yes when you asked me to marry you. But when you turned up in Vegas, all those old feelings came flooding back. Except now I know that's exactly what they are. Old feelings.' She swallowed and took a deep breath. 'I'm not in love with you any more.'

It was a slap in the face. Hugh looked incredulous. He couldn't believe what he was hearing.

'Look, I know it's going to take a bit of time to get used to each other again,' he said, clearing his throat self-consciously. 'And if you're trying to tell me you've slept with someone else that's fine. Obviously I don't want to know the details, but I'd be a hypocrite if I didn't admit to a couple of liaisons.' He blushed. 'I mean, I haven't exactly been celibate these past few months either.'

Despite his confession, Frankie remained steadfast. 'It's got nothing to do with me sleeping with someone else.'

'*You mean you have?*' He was aghast.

Becoming impatient, passengers were beginning to stare, craning their necks to see what was holding them up at the front of the queue. Feeling their eyes upon him, Hugh began to shuffle uncomfortably. He didn't like being the centre of attention, unless he was on the golf course. What were all the bloody Americans staring at? What did they think he was? An animal in a zoo?

Clearing his throat again, he ran his fingers through his hair exasperatedly and, leaning closer, hissed, 'Look, is this some kind of way of paying me back? I know you were upset about us breaking up on your birthday, but I've said I'm sorry.' He glared at a woman eating popcorn who was straying over the painted line so that she could hear better and relay information back along the line to the other passengers.

'I'm not trying to pay you back.'

'If you want me to grovel, I'm not going to.' Irritated by his unwelcome audience, Hugh threw the crowd his filthiest look. At this rate he might as well start selling tickets.

But they ignored him and continued watching. This was better than the movies.

'I don't want you to.' Frankie sighed and, wriggling her finger, she took off the ring and held it out to him. 'I'm sorry, Hugh.'

The buzz of anticipation quietened as the passengers strained to hear the cliffhanger. As did the stewardesses, who'd been watching the scenario unfold with bated breath.

In disbelief, Hugh stared at the ring. 'What are you saying?'

She couldn't resist using his line. 'I'm saying it's over.'

There was the sound of a few handclaps as, gathering together her luggage, Frankie turned and left Hugh stunned at the check-in. She knew he wouldn't follow her, his pride wouldn't let him. And she was glad. She didn't want him to. Feeling as if a huge weight had been lifted from her shoulders, she dragged her luggage through the crowds of passengers, who stared at her as if she was some kind of minor celebrity, across the airport towards the sliding doors. God knows what happened now. What she was going to do in LA with no money or job. She hadn't thought that far ahead. But one thing was certain – this time she'd made the right decision.

She didn't stop walking until she was outside. Until the handles of her suitcases were cutting into her fingers and, unable to carry them any further, she had to drop them on the pavement. Taking a deep breath of hot, dusty, polluted Californian air, she leaned wearily against the wall, idly watching the stream of cars dropping off at departures, coming and going.

Wasn't this the part in the movie when the guy the heroine's in love with turns up out of the blue and tells her he loves her? She smiled to herself glumly. This might be LA, but she was under no illusion. Her earlier optimism was just wishful thinking. She'd blown it with Reilly. Well and truly fucked up. He was never going to forgive her, and who could blame him? She'd left him standing at the altar on New Year's Eve.

Crouching down on the floor, she fumbled in her bag and pulled out a crumpled packet of cigarettes. Rita had given them to her 'in case of emergencies'. She smiled to herself. She should really call Rita, but she couldn't face it just yet. She needed a few minutes by herself, to try and get her head straight. She'd phone her after she'd had this cigarette. Now, if she could just find a light . . . Bloody typical, she had everything but matches – Tampax, chewing gum, a couple of leaky biros.

Her fingers brushed against her wallet and underneath, half hidden, she saw Reilly's ring. She'd been going to throw it away but something had stopped her – sentimentality, stupidness, hope . . . call it what you want but she hadn't been able to. She slipped it on her finger. She was being stupid. She and Reilly were over, and the sooner she accepted that and got on with the rest of her life the better. She sniffed. Now where were those bloody matches?

'Do you need a light?'

Hearing a voice behind her, she looked up.

Reilly.

For a moment she didn't say anything. She couldn't. She'd rehearsed what to say if she ever saw him again, she'd got it all worked out. But now, staring at him as he stood in front of her, wearing his knackered old jeans and a scruffy T-shirt he refused to throw away, unshaven, with his hair all over the place and those bloody big blue eyes she could drown in, her prepared speech went out the window.

'What are you doing here?'

He held her gaze, his face breaking into a long, lazy smile. 'Did you really think I was going to let a pain-in-the-ass English chick get away that easily?'

It wasn't exactly the romantic answer she'd been hoping for. 'Are you saying I'm a pain in the arse?'

'Well, you did jilt me.'

'I wouldn't call it that exactly . . .'

She broke off as Reilly pulled her towards him. 'Shut up, Frankie.'

And before she could argue, he leaned down and kissed her.

Who said it only ever happened in the movies?

ALEXANDRA POTTER

You're the One That I Don't Want

How do you know he's The One?
Are you getting butterflies just thinking about him?
Have you dreamt of marrying him?
Do you just *know*?

When Lucy meets Nate in Venice, aged 18, she knows
instantly he's The One. And, caught up in the whirlwind
of first love, they kiss under the Bridge of Sighs at sunset.
Which – according to legend – will tie them together
forever.

But ten years later, they've completely lost contact. That is,
until Lucy moves to New York and the legend brings them
back together. Again. And again. And again.

But what if Nate isn't The One? How is she going to get rid
of him? Because forever could be a very long time . . .

*A funny, magical romantic comedy about how finding The One
doesn't always have to mean happily ever after.*

HODDER

ALEXANDRA POTTER

What's New, Pussycat?

What would you do if your boyfriend proposed?

– Say yes and throw your arms around him
– Text everyone with your good news
– Take out a subscription to Brides magazine

Delilah does none of the above. Instead she packs her bags
and heads to London in search of a new life, and a new
man. Only she meets two. Charlie, the sexy media mogul
and Sam, best friend and confidante.

Everything seems perfect. Thrown into a whirlwind of
glamorous parties, five-star restaurants and designer pent-
houses, Delilah couldn't be happier. After all, it's a million
miles away from her old life. And her old self. Which is
exactly what she wanted.

Isn't it?

HODDER

ALEXANDRA POTTER

Me and Mr Darcy

He's every woman's fantasy . . .

After a string of nightmare relationships, Emily Albright has
decided she's had it with modern-day men. She'd rather pour
herself a glass of wine, curl up with *Pride and Prejudice* and
step into a time where men were dashing, devoted and honour-
able, strode across fields in breeches, their damp shirts clinging
to their chests, and *weren't* into internet porn.

So when her best friend invites her to Mexico for a week of
margaritas and men, Emily decides to book a guided tour of
Jane Austen country instead.

She quickly realises she won't find her dream man here. The coach
tour is full of pensioners, apart from one Mr Spike Hargreaves, a
foul-tempered journalist sent to write a piece on why Mr Darcy's
been voted the man most women would love to date.

Until she walks into a room and finds herself face-to-face with
Darcy himself. And every woman's fantasy suddenly becomes
one woman's reality.

HODDER

ALEXANDRA POTTER

Calling Romeo

What is the worst thing that could happen to you on
Valentine's Day?

Getting stood up by your boyfriend?
Having to spend the evening alone?
Being drenched by an idiot driving a sportscar?

When all three happen to Juliet on the same night, she reck-
ons her love life can't get any worse. But it's actually about
to get a lot more complicated . . .

Because the identity of the driver of the sportscar is
revealed to be her arch business rival. She knows she should
stay away. Except it's not that easy.
Handsome, sexy and utterly glamorous, Sykes is determined
to sweep her off her feet and away from her boyfriend Will.

But is it worth risking everything for? Are they really
destined to be star-crossed lovers? Or is Romeo actually a
little closer to home?

Juliet is about to find out in Alexandra Potter's delightful
romantic comedy about passion, truth and how the path to
true love never did run smooth . . .

HODDER